THE GOLDEN DREAM

THE R.M. BALLANTYNE ADVENTURE LIBRARY

THE GOLDEN DREAM

R.M. Ballantyne

WILDSIDE PRESS

THE GOLDEN DREAM

CHAPTER I.

Adventures in the Far West.
The Cause of the Whole Affair.

Ned Sinton gazed at the scene before him with indescribable amazement! He had often witnessed strange things in the course of his short though chequered life, but he had never seen anything like this. Many a dream of the most extravagant nature had surrounded his pillow with creatures of curious form and scenes of magic beauty, but never before, either by actual observation or in nightly vision, had Ned Sinton beheld a scene so wonderful as that which now lay spread out before him.

Ned stood in the centre of a cavern of vast dimensions — so vast, and so full of intense light, that instead of looking on it as a huge cave, he felt disposed to regard it as a small world. The sides of this cavern were made of pure gold, and the roof — far above his head — was spangled all over with glittering points, like a starry sky. The ground, too, and, in short, everything within the cave, was made of the same precious metal. Thousands of stalactites hung from the roof like golden icicles. Millions of delicate threads of the same material also depended from the star-spangled vault, each thread having a golden ball at the end of it, which, strange to say, was transparent, and permitted a bright flame within to shine through, and shed a yellow lustre over surrounding objects. All the edges, and angles, and points of the irregularly-formed walls were of burnished gold, which reflected the rays of these pendant lamps with dazzling brilliancy, while the broad masses of the frosted walls shone with a subdued light. Magnificent curtains of golden filigree fell in rich voluminous folds on the pavement, half concealing several archways which led into smaller caverns, similar to the large one. Altogether it was a scene of luxurious richness and splendour that is utterly indescribable.

But the thing that amazed Ned Sinton most was, that the company of well-dressed ladies and gentlemen who moved about in these splendid halls, and ate golden ices, or listened to the exquisite strains of music that floated on the atmosphere, were all as yellow as guineas! Ned could by no means understand this. In order to convince himself that there was no deception in the matter, he shook hands with several of the people nearest to him, and found that they were cold and hard as iron; although, to all appearance, they were soft and pliable, and could evidently move about with perfect freedom.

Ned was very much puzzled indeed. One would have thought he must have believed himself to be dreaming. Not a bit of it. He knew perfectly well that he was wide-awake. In fact, a doubt upon that point never crossed his mind for a moment. At length he resolved to ask the meaning of it all, and, observing a stout old gentleman, with a bland smile on his yellow countenance, in the act of taking a pinch of golden snuff from a gold snuff-box, he advanced and accosted him.

"Pray, sir," began Ned, modestly, "may I take the liberty of asking you what is the meaning of all this?"

"All what, sir?" inquired the old gentleman, in a deep metallic voice.

"This golden cave, with its wonderful lamps, and especially these golden people; and — excuse me, sir, for remarking on the circumstance — you seem to be *made of gold* yourself. I have often heard the term applied to extremely rich persons, but I really never expected to see a man who was literally 'worth his weight in gold.'"

The old gentleman laughed sarcastically at this sally, and took an enormous pinch of gold-dust.

As he did not seem inclined to be communicative, however, Ned said again, "What is the meaning of it all? can you explain what has done it?"

Smiling blandly at his interrogator, this gentleman of precious metal placed his head a little on one side, and tapped the lid of his snuff-box, but said nothing. Then he suddenly exclaimed, at the full pitch of his voice, "California, my boy! That's what's done it, Edward! *California for ever!* Ned, hurrah!"

As the deep tones of his voice rang through the star-spangled vault, the company took up the shout, and with "California for ever!" made the cavern ring again. In the excess of their glee the gentlemen took off their hats, and the ladies their wreaths and turbans, and threw them in the air. As many of them failed to catch these portions of costume in their descent, the clatter caused by their fall on the golden pavement was very striking indeed.

"Come here, my lad," said the old gentleman, seizing Ned Sinton by the arm, and laughing heartily as he dragged him towards an immense mirror of burnished gold; "look at yourself there."

Ned looked, and started back with horror on observing that he himself had been converted into gold. There could be no mistake whatever about it. There he stood, staring at himself like a yellow statue. His shooting-jacket was richly chased with alternate stripes of burnished and frosted work; the buttons on his vest shone like stars; his pantaloons were striped like the coat; his hair was a mass of dishevelled filigree; and his hands, when, in the height of his horror, he clasped them together, rang like a brass-founder's anvil.

For a few moments he stood before the mirror speechless. Then a feeling of intense indignation unaccountably took possession of him, and he turned fiercely on the old gentleman, exclaiming —

"*You* have done this, sir! What do you mean by it? eh!"

"You're quite mistaken, Ned. I didn't do it. California has done it. Ha! ha! my boy, you're done for! Smitten with the yellow fever, Neddy? California for ever! See here —"

As he spoke, the old gentleman threw out one leg and both arms, and began to twirl round, after the fashion of a peg-top, on one toe. At first he revolved slowly, but gradually increased his speed, until no part of him could be distinctly observed. Ned Sinton stood aghast. Suddenly the old gentleman shot upwards like a rocket, but he did not quit the ground; he merely elongated his body until his head stuck against the roof of the cave. Then he ceased to revolve, and remained in the form of a golden stalactite — his head surrounded by stars and his toe resting on the ground!

While Ned stood rooted to the spot, turning the subject over in his mind, and trying to find out by what process of chemical or mechanical action so remarkable a transformation could have been accomplished, he became aware that his uncle, old Mr. Shirley, was standing in the middle of the cave regarding him with a look of mingled sarcasm and pity. He observed, too, that his uncle was not made of gold, like the people around him, but was habited in a yeomanry uniform. Mr. Shirley had been a yeoman twenty years before his nephew was born. Since that time his proportions had steadily increased, and he was now a man of very considerable rotundity — so much so, that his old uniform fitted him with excessive tightness; the coat would by no means button across his capacious chest, and, being much too short, shewed a very undignified amount of braces below it.

"Uncle!" exclaimed Ned Sinton, rushing up to his relative, "what *can* be the meaning of all this? Everybody seems to be mad. I think you must be mad yourself, to come here such a figure as that; and I'm quite sure *I* shall go mad if you don't explain it to me. What *does* it all mean?"

"California," replied Mr. Shirley, becoming more sarcastic in expression and less pitiful.

"Why, that's what everybody cries," exclaimed Ned, who was now driven almost to desperation. "My dear uncle, do look like yourself and exercise some of your wonted sagacity. Just glance round at the cave and the company, all made of gold, and look at me — gold too, if not pinchbeck, but I'm not a good-enough judge of metals to tell which. What *has* done it, uncle? *Do* look in a better humour, and tell me how it has happened."

"California," replied Mr. Shirley.

"Yes, yes; I know that. California seems to be everything here. But how has it come about? Why are *you* here, and what has brought me here?"

"California," repeated Mr. Shirley.

"Uncle, I'll go deranged if you don't answer me. What do you mean?"

"California," reiterated Mr. Shirley.

At the same moment a stout golden lady with a filigree turban shouted, "for ever!" at the top of a very shrill voice, and immediately the company took up the cry again, filling the cave with deafening sounds.

Ned Sinton gave one look of despair at his relative — then turned and fled.

"Put him out," shouted the company. "Down with the intruder!"

Ned cast a single glance backward, and beheld the people pushing and buffeting his uncle in a most unceremonious manner. His helmet was knocked down over his eyes, and the coat — so much too small for him — was rendered an easy fit by being ripped up behind to the neck. Ned could not stand this. He was stout of limb and bold as a lion, although not naturally addicted to fighting, so he turned suddenly round and flew to the rescue. Plunging into the midst of the struggling mass of golden creatures, Ned hit out right and left like a young Hercules, and his blows rang upon their metal chests and noses like the sound of sledge-hammers, but without any other effect.

Suddenly he experienced an acute sensation of pain, and — awoke to find himself hammering the bed-post with bleeding knuckles, and his uncle standing beside his bed chuckling immensely.

"O uncle," cried Ned, sitting up in his bed, and regarding his knuckles with a perplexed expression of countenance, "I've had *such* an extraordinary dream!"

"Ay, Ned," interrupted his uncle, "and all about California, I'll be bound."

"Why, how did you guess that?"

"It needs not a wizard to guess that, lad. I've observed that you have read nothing in the newspapers for the last three months but the news from the gold-diggings of California. Your mind has of late been constantly running on that subject, and it is well-known that day-dreams are often reproduced at night. Besides, I heard you shouting the word in your sleep as I entered your room. Were you fighting with gold-diggers, eh! or Indians?"

"Neither, uncle; but I was fighting with very strange beings, I assure you, and —"

"Well, well," interrupted Mr. Shirley, "never mind the dream just now; we shall have it at some other time. I have important matters to talk over with you, my boy. Morton has written to me. Get up and come down as quickly as you can, and we'll discuss the matter over our breakfast."

As the door closed after the retreating form of his uncle, Edward Sinton leaped out of bed and into his trousers. During his toilet he wondered what matters of importance Mr. Shirley could intend to discuss with him, and felt half inclined to fear, from the grave expression of his uncle's face when he spoke of it, that something of a disagreeable nature awaited him. But these thoughts were intermingled with reminiscences of the past night. His knuckles, too, kept constantly reminding him of his strange encounter, and, do what he would, he could not banish from his mind the curious incidents of that remarkable golden dream.

CHAPTER II.

Our Hero.

We have entered thus minutely into the details of our hero's dream, because it was the climax to a long series of day-dreams in which he had indulged ever since the discovery of gold in California.

Edward Sinton was a youth of eighteen at the time of which we write, and an orphan. He was tall, strong, broad-shouldered, fair-haired, blue-eyed, Roman-nosed, and gentle as a lamb. This last statement may perhaps appear inconsistent with the fact that, during the whole course of his school-life, he had a pitched battle every week — sometimes two or three in the week. Ned never began a fight, and, indeed, did not like fighting. But some big boys *will* domineer over little ones, and Ned would not be domineered over; consequently he had to be thrashed. He was possessed, even in boyhood, of an amount of physical courage that would have sufficed for any two ordinary men. He did not boast. He did not quarrel. He never struck the first blow, but, if twenty boys had attacked him, he would have tried to fight them all. He never tyrannised over small boys. It was not his nature to do so; but he was not perfect, any more than you are, dear reader. He sometimes punched small boys' heads when they worried him, though he never did so without repenting of it, and doing them a kindness afterwards in order to make up. He was very thoughtless, too, and very careless; nevertheless he was fond of books — specially of books of adventure — and studied these like a hero — as he was.

Boys of his own size, or even a good deal bigger, never fought with Ned Sinton. They knew better than that; but they adored him, in some cases envied him, and in all cases trusted and followed him. It was only *very* big boys who fought with him, and all they got by it was a good deal of hard pummelling before they floored their little adversary, and a good deal of jeering from their comrades for fighting a small boy. From one cause or another, Ned's visage was generally scratched, often cut, frequently swelled, and almost always black and blue.

But as Ned grew older, the occasions for fighting became less frequent; his naturally amiable disposition improved, (partly owing, no doubt, to the care of his uncle, who was, in every sense of the term, a good old man,) and when he attained the age of fifteen and went to college, and was called "Sinton," instead of "Ned," his fighting days were over. No man in his senses would have ventured to attack that strapping youth with the soft blue eyes, the fair hair, the prominent nose, and the firm but smiling lips, or, if he had, he would have had to count on an hour's extremely hard work, whether the fortune of war went for or against him.

When Ned had been three years at college, his uncle hinted that it was time to think of a profession, and suggested that as he was a first-rate mathematician, and had been fond of mechanics from his childhood, he should turn an engineer. Ned would probably have agreed to this cheerfully, had not a thirst for adventure been created by the stirring accounts which had begun to arrive at this time from the recently-discovered gold-fields of California. His enthusiastic spirit was stirred, not so much by the prospect of making a large fortune suddenly by the finding of a huge nugget — although that was a very pleasant idea — as by the hope of meeting with wild adventures in that imperfectly-known and distant land. And the effect of such dreams was to render the idea of sitting down to an engineer's desk, or in a mercantile counting-room, extremely distasteful.

Thus it came to pass that Edward Sinton felt indisposed to business, and disposed to indulge in golden visions.

When he entered the breakfast-parlour, his mind was still full of his curious dream.

"Come along, my lad," cried Mr. Shirley, laying down the Bible, and removing his spectacles from a pair of eyes that usually twinkled with a sort of grave humour, but in which there was now an expression of perplexity; "set to work and get the edge off your appetite, and then I'll read Moxton's letter."

When Mr. Shirley had finished breakfast, Ned was about half done, having just commenced his third slice of toast. So the old gentleman complimented his nephew on the strength of his appetite, put on his spectacles, drew a letter from his pocket, and leaned back in his chair.

"Now, lad, open your ears and consider what I am about to read."

"Go on, uncle, I'm all attention," said Ned, attacking slice number four.

"This is Moxton's letter. It runs thus —

"'Dear Sir, — I beg to acknowledge receipt of yours of the 5th inst. I shall be happy to take your nephew on trial, and, if I find him steady, shall enter into an engagement with him, I need not add that unremitting application to business is the only road to distinction in the profession he is desirous of adopting. Let him call at my office tomorrow between ten and twelve. — Yours very truly, Daniel Moxton.'"

"Is that all?" inquired Ned, drawing his chair towards the fire, into which he gazed contemplatively.

Mr. Shirley looked at his nephew over the top of his spectacles, and said —

"That's all."

"It's very short," remarked Ned.

"But to the point," rejoined his uncle. "Now, boy, I see that you don't relish the idea, and I must say that I would rather that you became an engineer than a lawyer; but then, lad, situations are difficult to get now-a-days, and, after all, you might do worse than become a lawyer. To be sure, I have no great love for the cloth, Ned; but the ladder reaches very high. The foot is crowded with a struggling mass of aspirants, many of whom are of very questionable character, but the top reaches to one of the highest positions in the empire. You might become the Lord High Chancellor at last, who knows! But seriously, I think you should accept this offer. Moxton is a grave, stern man, but a sterling fellow for all that, and in good practice. Now, what do you think!"

"Well, uncle," replied Ned, "I've never concealed my thoughts from you since the day you took me by the hand, eleven years ago, and brought me to live under your roof; and I'll not begin to dissemble now. The plain truth is, that I don't like it at all."

"Stop, now," cried Mr. Shirley, with a grieved expression of countenance; "don't be hasty in forming your opinion. Besides, my boy, you ought to be more ready to take my advice, even although it be not altogether palatable."

"My dear uncle, you quite misunderstand me. I only tell you what I *think* about the proposal. As to taking your advice, I fully intend to do that whether I like it or not; but I think, if you will listen to me for a few minutes, you will change your mind in regard to this matter. You know that I am very fond of travelling, and that I dislike the idea of taking up my abode on the top of a three-legged stool, either as a lawyer's or a merchant's clerk. Well, unless a man likes his profession, and goes at it with a will, he cannot hope to succeed, so that I have no prospect of getting on, I fear, in the line you wish me to adopt. Besides, there are plenty of poor fellows out of work, who love sitting still from nine a.m. to ten p.m., and whose bread I would be taking out of their mouths by devoting myself to the legal profession, and —"

At this point Ned hesitated for a moment, and his uncle broke in with —

"Tell me, now, if every one thought about business as you do, how would the world get on, think you?"

"Badly, I fear," replied the youth, with a smile; "but everybody doesn't think of it as I do; and, tell me, uncle, if everybody thought of business as you would wish me to do, what would come of the soldiers and sailors who defend our empire, and extend our foreign trade, and achieve the grand geographical discoveries that have of late added so much lustre to the British name?"

Ned flushed and became quite eloquent at this point. "Now, look at California," he continued; "there's a magnificent region, full of gold; not a mere myth, or an exaggeration, but a veritable fact, attested by the arrival of letters and gold-dust every month. Surely that land was made to be peopled; and the poor savages who dwell there need to be converted to Christianity, and delivered from their degraded condition; and the country must be worked, and its resources be developed; and who's to do it, if enterprising clergymen, and schoolmasters, and miners do not go to live there, and push their fortunes?"

"And which of the three callings do you propose adopting?" inquired Mr. Shirley, with a peculiar smile.

"Well uncle, I — a — the fact is, I have not thought much about that as yet. Of course, I never thought of the first. I do not forget your own remark, that the calling of a minister of the gospel of Christ is not, like other professions, to be adopted merely as a means of livelihood. Then, as to the second, I might perhaps manage that; but I don't think it would suit me."

"Do you think, then, that you would make a good digger?"

"Well, perhaps I would," replied Ned, modestly.

Mr. Shirley gravely regarded the powerful frame that reclined in the easy-chair before him, and was compelled to admit that the supposition was by no means outrageous.

"Besides," continued the youth, "I might turn my hand to many things in a new country. You know I have studied surveying, and I can sketch a little, and know something of architecture. I suppose that Latin and Greek would not be of much use, but the little I have picked up of medicine and surgery among the medical students would be useful. Then I could take notes, and sketch the scenery, and bring back a mass of material that might interest the public, and do good to the country."

"Oh," said the old gentleman, shortly; "come back and turn author, in fact, and write a book that nobody would publish, or which, in the event of its being published, nobody would read!"

"Come, now, my dear uncle, don't laugh at me. I assure you it seems very reasonable to me to think that what others have done, and are doing every day, I am able to do."

"Well, I won't laugh at you; but, to be serious, you are wise enough to know that an old man's experience is worth more than a youth's fancies. Much of what you have said is true, I admit, but I assure you that the bright prospects you have cut out for yourself are very delusive. They will never be realised, at least in the shape in which you have depicted them on your imagination. They will dissolve, my boy, on a nearer approach, and, as Shakespeare has it, 'like the baseless fabric of a vision, leave not a wrack behind,' or, at least, not much more than a wrack."

Ned reverted to the golden dream, and felt uneasy under his uncle's kind but earnest gaze.

"Most men," continued Mr. Shirley, "enjoy themselves at first, when they go to wild countries in search of adventure, but they generally regret the loss of their best years afterwards. In my opinion men should never emigrate unless they purpose making the foreign land they go to their *home*. But I won't oppose you, if you are determined to go; I will do all I can to help you, and give you my blessing; but before you make up your mind, I would recommend you to call on Mr. Moxton, and hear what prospects he holds out to you. Then take a week to think seriously over it; and if at the end of that time, you are as anxious to go as ever, I'll not stand in your way."

"You are kind to me, uncle; more so than I deserve," said Ned earnestly. "I'll do as you desire, and you may depend upon it that the generous way in which you have left me to make my own choice will influence me against going abroad more than anything else."

Ned sighed as he rose to quit the room, for he felt that his hopes at that moment were sinking.

"And before you take a step in the matter, my boy," said old Mr. Shirley, "go to your room and ask counsel of Him who alone has the power to direct your steps in this life."

Ned replied briefly, "I will, uncle," and hastily left the room. Mr. Shirley poked the fire, put on his spectacles, smoothed out the wrinkles on his bald forehead with his hand, took up the *Times*, and settled himself down in his easy-chair to read; but his nephew's prospects could not be banished from his mind. He went over the whole argument again, mentally, with copious additions, ere he became aware of the fact, that for three-quarters of an hour he had been, (apparently), reading the newspaper upside down.

CHAPTER III.

Hopes and Fears — Mr. Shirley receives a Visit and a Wild Proposal.

When Edward Sinton left his chamber, an hour after the conversation related in the last chapter, his brow was unruffled and his step light. He had made up his mind that, come what might, he would not resist the wishes of his only near relative and his best friend.

There was a day in the period of early boyhood that remained as fresh on the memory of young Sinton as if it had been yesterday — the day on which his mother died. The desolation of his early home on that day was like the rising of a dark thunder-cloud on a bright sky. His young heart was crushed, his mind stunned, and the first ray of light that broke upon him — the first gush of relief — was when his uncle arrived and took him on his knee, and, seated beside the bed where that cold, still form lay, wept upon the child's neck as if his heart would break. Mr. Shirley buried the sister whom he had been too late to see alive. Then he and his little nephew left the quiet country village and went to dwell in the great city of London. From that time forward Mr. Shirley was a father to Ned, who loved him more than any one else on earth, and through his influence he was early led to love and reverence his heavenly Father and his blessed Redeemer.

The subject of going abroad was the first in regard to which Ned and his uncle had seriously disagreed, and the effect on the feelings of both was very strong.

Ned's mind wandered as he put on his hat, and buttoned his great-coat up to the chin, and drew on his gloves slowly. He was not vain of his personal appearance; neither was he reckless of it. He always struck you as being a particularly well-dressed man, and he had naturally a dashing look about him. Poor fellow! he felt anything but dashing or reckless as he hurried through the crowded streets in the direction of the city that day.

Moxton's door was a green one, with a brass knocker and a brass plate, both of which ornaments, owing to verdigris, were anything but ornamental. The plate was almost useless, being nearly illegible, but the knocker was still fit for duty. The street was narrow — as Ned observed with a feeling of deep depression — and the house to which the green door belonged, besides being dirty, retreated a little, as if it were ashamed of itself.

On the knocker being applied, the green door was opened by a dis-agreeable-looking old woman, who answered to the question, "Is Mr. Moxton in?" with a short "Yes," and, without farther remark, ushered our hero into a very dingy and particularly small office, which, owing to the insufficient quantity of daylight that struggled through the dirty little windows, required to be lighted with gas. Ned felt, so to speak, like a thermometer which was falling rapidly.

"Can I see Mr. Moxton?" he inquired of a small dishevelled clerk, who sat on a tall stool behind a high desk, engaged in writing his name in every imaginable form on a sheet of note paper.

The dishevelled clerk pointed to a door which opened into an inner apartment, and resumed his occupation.

Ned tapped at the door indicated.

"Come in," cried a stern voice.

Ned, (as a thermometer), fell considerably lower. On entering, he beheld a tall, gaunt man, with a sour cast of countenance, standing with his back to the fire.

Ned advanced with a cheerful expression of face. Thermometrically speaking, he fell to the freezing-point.

"You are young Sinton, I suppose. You've come later than I expected."

Ned apologised, and explained that he had had some difficulty in finding the house.

"Umph! Your uncle tells me that you're a sharp fellow, and write a good hand. Have you ever been in an office before?"

"No, sir. Up till now I have been at college. My uncle is rather partial, I fear, and may have spoken too highly of me. I think, however, that my hand is not a bad one. At least it is legible."

"At least!" said Mr. Moxton, with a sarcastic expression that was meant for smile, perhaps for a grin. "Why, that's the *most* you could say of it. No hand is good, sir, if it is not legible, and no hand can possibly be bad that *is* legible. Have you studied law?"

"No, sir, I have not."

"Umph! you're too old to begin. Have you been used to sit at the desk?"

"Yes; I have been accustomed to study the greater part of the day."

"Well, you may come here on Monday, and I'll speak to you again, and see what you can do. I'm too busy just now. Good-morning."

Ned turned to go, but paused on the threshold, and stood holding the door-handle.

"Excuse me, sir," he said, hesitatingly, "may I ask what room I shall occupy, if — if — I come to work here?"

Mr. Moxton looked a little surprised at the question, but pointed to the outer office where the dishevelled clerk sat, and said, "There." Ned fell to twenty below the freezing-point.

"And pray, sir," he continued, "may I ask what are office-hours?"

"From nine a.m. till nine p.m., with an interval for meals," said Mr. Moxton, sharply; "but we usually continue at work till eleven at night, sometimes later. Good-morning."

Ned fell to zero, and found himself in the street, with an indistinct impression of having heard the dishevelled clerk chuckling vociferously as he passed through the office.

It was a hard struggle, a very hard struggle, but he recalled to mind all that his uncle had ever done for him, and the love he bore him, and manfully resolved to cast California behind his back for ever, and become a lawyer.

Meanwhile Mr. Shirley received a visit from a very peculiar personage. He was still seated in his arm-chair pondering his nephew's prospects when this personage entered the room, hat in hand — the hat was a round straw one — and cried heartily, "Good day, kinsman."

"Ha! Captain Bunting, how are ye? Glad to see you, old fellow," exclaimed Mr. Shirley, rising and seizing the sailor by the hand. "Sit down, sit down, and let's hear your news. Why, I believe it's six months since I saw you."

"Longer, Shirley, longer than that," replied the captain, seating himself in the chair which Ned Sinton had vacated a short time before. "I hope your memory is not giving way. I have been half round the world, and it's a year and six months today since I sat here last."

"Is it?" cried Mr. Shirley, in surprise. "Now, that is very remarkable. But do you know, captain, I have often thought upon that subject, and wondered why it is that, as we get older, time seems to fly faster, and events which happened a month ago seem as if they only occurred yesterday. But let me hear all about it. Where have you been, and where are you going next?"

"I've been," replied the captain, who was a big, broad man with a rough over-all coat, rough pilot-cloth trousers, rough red whiskers, a shaggy head of hair, and a rough-skinned face; the only part of him, in fact, which wasn't rough was his heart; that was soft and warm —

"I've been, as I remarked before, half round the world, and I'm goin' next to America. That's a short but comprehensive answer to your question. If you have time and patience, kinsman, I'll open the log-book of my memory and give you some details of my doings since we last met. But first tell me, how is my young friend, Ned?"

"Oh, he's well — excellently well — besides being tall and strong. You would hardly know him, captain. He's full six feet high, I believe, and the scamp has something like a white wreath of smoke over his upper lip already! I wish him to become an engineer or a lawyer, but the boy is in love with California just now, and dreams about nothing but wild adventures and gold-dust."

The captain gave a grunt, and a peculiar smile crossed his rugged visage as he gazed earnestly and contemplatively into the fire.

Captain Bunting was a philosopher, and was deeply impressed with the belief that the smallest possible hint upon any subject whatever was sufficient to enable him to dive into the marrow of it, and prognosticate the probable issue of it, with much greater certainty than any one else. On the present occasion, however, the grunt above referred to was all he said.

It is not necessary to trouble the reader with the lengthened discourse that the captain delivered to his kinsman. When he concluded,

Mr. Shirley pushed his spectacles up on his bald head, gazed at the fire, and said, "Odd, very odd; and interesting too — very interesting." After a short pause, he pulled his spectacles down on his nose, and looking over them at the captain, said, "And what part of America are you bound for now?"

"California," answered the captain, slowly.

Mr. Shirley started, as if some prophetic vision had been called up by the word and the tone in which it was uttered.

"And that," continued the captain, "brings me to the point. I came here chiefly for the purpose of asking you to let your nephew go with me, as I am in want of a youth to assist me, as a sort of supercargo and Jack-of-all-trades. In fact, I like your nephew much, and have long had my eye on him. I think him the very man for my purpose. I want a companion, too, in my business — one who is good at the pen and can turn his hand to anything. In short, it would be difficult to explain all the outs and ins of why I want him. But he's a tight, clever fellow, as I know, and I *do* want him, and if you'll let him go, I promise to bring him safe back again in the course of two years — if we are all spared. From what you've told me, I've no doubt the lad will be delighted to go. And, believe me, his golden dreams will be all washed out by the time he comes back. Now, what say you!"

For the space of five minutes Mr. Shirley gazed at the captain over his spectacles in amazement, and said nothing. Then he threw himself back on his chair, pushed his spectacles up on his forehead, and gazed at him from underneath these assistants to vision. The alteration did not seem to improve matters, for he still continued to gaze in silent surprise. At last his lips moved, and he said, slowly but emphatically —

"Now, that is the most remarkable coincidence I ever heard of."

"How so?" inquired the captain.

"Why, that my nephew should be raving about going to California, and that you should be raving about getting him to go, and that these things should suddenly come to a climax on the same forenoon. It's absolutely incredible. If I had read it in a tale, now, or a romance, I would not have been surprised, for authors are such blockheads, generally, that they always make things of this kind fit in with the exactness of a dove-tail; but that it should *really* come to pass in my own experience, is quite incomprehensible. And so suddenly, too!"

"As to that," remarked the captain, with a serious, philosophical expression of countenance, "most things come to a climax suddenly, and coincidences invariably happen together; but, after all, it doesn't seem so strange to me, for vessels are setting sail for California every other day, and —"

"Well," interrupted Mr. Shirley, starting up with energy, as if he had suddenly formed a great resolve, "I *will* let the boy go. Perhaps it will do him good. Besides, I have my own reasons for not caring much about his losing a year or two in regard to business. Come with me to the city, captain, and we'll talk over it as we go along." So saying, Mr. Shirley took his kinsman by the arm, and they left the house together.

CHAPTER IV.

The End of the Beginning — Farewell to Old England.

As Captain Bunting sagaciously remarked, "most things come to a climax suddenly."

On the evening of the day in which our tale begins, Edward Sinton — still standing at zero — walked into his uncle's parlour. The old gentleman was looking earnestly, though unintentionally, at the cat, which sat on the rug; and the cat was looking attentively at the kettle, which sat on the fire, hissing furiously, as if it were disgusted at being kept so long from tea.

Ned's face was very long and sad as he entered the room.

"Dear uncle," said he, taking Mr. Shirley by the hand, "I'm not going to take a week to think over it. I have made up my mind to remain at home, and become a lawyer."

"Ned," replied Mr. Shirley, returning his nephew's grasp, "I'm not going to take a week to think over it either. I have made up my mind that you are to go to California, and become a — a — whatever you like, my dear boy; so sit down to tea, and I'll tell you all about it."

Ned was incredulous at first, but as his uncle went on to explain how matters stood, and gradually diverged from that subject to the details of his outfit, he recovered from his surprise, and sprang suddenly up to 100° of Fahrenheit, even in the shade of the prospect of parting for a time from old Mr. Shirley.

Need we be surprised, reader, that our hero on that night dreamed the golden dream over again, with many wonderful additions, and sundry remarkable variations.

Thus it came to pass that, two weeks afterwards, Ned and his uncle found themselves steaming down the Thames to Gravesend, where the good ship *Roving Bess* lay riding at anchor, with a short cable, and top-sails loose, ready for sea.

"Ned," said Mr. Shirley, as they watched the receding banks of the noble river, "you may never see *home* again, my boy. Will you be sure not to forget me! will you write often, Ned!"

"Forget you, uncle!" exclaimed Ned, in a reproachful voice, while a tear sprang to his eye. "How can you suggest such a —"

"Well, well, my boy, I know it — I know it; but I like to hear the assurance repeated by your own lips. I'm an old man now, and if I should not live to see you again, I would like to have some earnest, loving words to think upon while you are away." The old man paused a few moments, and then resumed —

"Ned, remember when far from home, that there is another home — eternal in the heavens — to which, if you be the Lord's child, you are hastening. You will think of that home, Ned, won't you! If I do not meet you again here at any rate I shall hope to meet you *there*."

Ned would have spoken, but his heart was too full. He merely pressed old Mr. Shirley's arm.

"Perhaps," continued his uncle, "it is not necessary to make you promise to read God's blessed Word. You'll be surrounded by temptations of no ordinary kind in the gold-regions; and depend upon it that the Bible, read with prayer, will be the best chart and compass to guide you safely through them all."

"My dear uncle," replied Ned, with emotion, "perhaps the best promise I can make is to assure you that I will endeavour to do, in all things and at all times, as you have taught me, ever since I was a little boy. If I succeed, I feel assured that I shall do well."

A long and earnest conversation ensued between the uncle and nephew, which was interrupted at last, by the arrival of the boat at Gravesend. Jumping into a wherry, they pushed off, and were soon alongside of the *Roving Bess*, a barque of about eight hundred tons burden, and, according to Captain Bunting, "an excellent sea-boat."

"Catch hold o' the man-ropes," cried the last-named worthy, looking over the side; "that's it; now jump! all right! How are ye, kinsman? Glad to see you, Ned. I was afraid you were goin' to give me the slip."

"I have not kept you waiting, have I?" inquired Ned.

"Yes, you have, youngster," replied the captain, with a facetious wink, as he ushered his friends into the cabin, and set a tray of broken biscuit and a decanter of wine before them. "The wind has been blowin' off shore the whole morning, and the good ship has been straining at a short cable like a hound chained up. But we'll be off now in another half-hour."

"So soon?" said Mr. Shirley, with an anxious expression on his kind old face.

"All ready to heave up the anchor, sir," shouted the first mate down the companion.

The captain sprang on deck, and soon after the metallic clatter of the windlass rang a cheerful accompaniment to the chorus of the sailors. One by one the white sails spread out to the breeze, and the noble ship began to glide through the water.

In a few minutes more the last words were spoken, the last farewell uttered, and Mr. Shirley stood alone in the stern-sheet of the little boat, watching the departing vessel as she gathered way before the freshening breeze. As long as the boat was visible Ned Sinton stood on the ship's bulwarks, holding on to the mizzen shrouds, and waving his handkerchief from time to time. The old man stood with his head uncovered, and his thin locks waving in the wind.

Soon the boat was lost to view. Our hero brushed away a tear, and leaped upon the deck, where the little world, of which for many days to come he was to form a part, busied itself in making preparation for a long, long voyage. The British Channel was passed; the Atlantic Ocean was entered; England sank beneath the horizon; and, for the first time in his life, Ned Sinton found himself — at sea.

CHAPTER V.

The Sea — Dangers of the Deep, and Uncertainty of Human Affairs — A Disastrous Night and a Bright Morning — California at last.

Only those who have dwelt upon the ocean for many months together can comprehend the feelings of delight with which the long-imprisoned voyager draws near to his desired haven. For six long months did the *Roving Bess* do battle with the surging billows of the great deep. During that time she steered towards the Gulf of Mexico — carefully avoiding that huge reservoir of sea-weed, termed the Saragossa sea, in which the unscientific but enterprising mariners of old used to get becalmed oftentimes for days and weeks together — she coasted down the eastern shores of South America; fired at, and "shewed her heels" to, a pirate; doubled Cape Horn; fought with the tempests that take special delight in revelling there; and, finally, spreading her sails to the genial breezes of the Pacific Ocean, drew near to her voyage-end.

All this the good ship *Roving Bess* did with credit to herself and comfort to her crew; but a few weeks after she entered the Pacific, she was met, contrary to all expectation, by the bitterest gale that had ever compelled her to scud under bare poles.

It was a beautiful afternoon when the first symptoms of the coming storm were observed. Captain Bunting had just gone down below, and our hero was standing at the weather gangway, observing the sudden dart of a shoal of flying-fish, which sprang out of the sea, whizzed through the air a few hundred feet, and fell with a splash into the water, in their frantic efforts to escape from their bitter enemy, the dolphin.

While Ned gazed contemplatively at the spot where the winged fish had disappeared, the captain sprang on deck.

"We're goin' to catch it," he said, hurriedly, as he passed forward; "tumble up, there; tumble up; all hands to shorten sails. Hand down the royals, and furl the t'gallant sails, Mr. Williams, (to the first mate,) and look alive."

"Ay, ay, sir," was answered in that prompt tone of voice which indicates thorough discipline and unquestioning obedience, while the men scrambled up the fore-hatch, and sprang up the ratlines hand over hand. A moment before, the vessel had lain quietly on the bosom of the unruffled deep, as if she were asleep, now she was all uproar and apparent confusion; sails slewed round, ropes rattled, and blocks creaked, while the sonorous voice of the first mate sounded commands like a trumpet from the quarter-deck.

"I see no indication of a storm," remarked young Sinton, as the captain walked aft.

"Possibly not, lad; but *I* do. The barometer has fallen lower, all of a sadden, than I ever saw it fall before. You may depend upon it, we shall have to look out for squalls before long. Just cast your eyes on the horizon over the weather bows there; it's not much of a cloud, and, to say truth, I would not have thought much of it had the glass remained steady, but that faithful servant never —"

"Better close-reef the top-sails, sir," said the mate, touching his cap, and pointing to the cloud just referred to.

"Do so, Mr. Williams, and let the watch below remain on deck, and stand by to man the halyards."

In less than an hour the *Roving Bess* was running at the rate of twelve knots, under close-reefed top-sails, before a steady gale, which in half-an-hour later increased to a hurricane, compelling them to take in all sail and "lay to." The sun set in a blaze of mingled black and lurid clouds, as if the heavens were on fire; the billows rose to their utmost height as the shrieking winds heaved them upwards, and then, cutting off their crests, hurled the spray along like driving clouds of snow, and dashed it against the labouring ship, as if impatient to engulf her in that ravening maw which has already swallowed up so many human victims.

But the little vessel faced the tempest nobly, and rose like a sea-mew on the white crest of each wave, while the steersmen — for there were two lashed to the wheel — kept her to the wind. Suddenly the sheet of the fore trysail parted, the ship came up to the wind, and a billow at that moment broke over her, pouring tons of water on her deck, and carrying away the foremast, main-top-masts, and the jib-boom.

"Clear the wreck — down the helm, and let her scud," shouted the captain, who stood by the mizzen-mast, holding on to a belaying-pin. But the captain's voice was drowned by the whistling winds, and, seeing that the men were uncertain what to do, he seized one of the axes which were lashed to the foot of the mast, and began to cut away the ropes which dragged the wreck of the foremast under the lee of the ship. Williams, the mate, and the second mate, followed his example, while Ned sprang to the wheel to see the orders to the steersmen obeyed. In half-an-hour all was clear, and the ship was scudding before the gale under bare poles.

"We've not seen the worst of it," remarked the captain, as he resumed his post on the quarter-deck, and brushed the brine from his whiskers; "I fear, too, that she has received some bad thumps from the wreck of the foremast. You'd better go below, Sinton, and put on a top-coat; its no use gettin' wetter than you can help."

"I'm as wet as I can be, captain; besides, I can work better as I am, if there's anything for me to do."

"Well, there ain't much: you'll have enough to do to keep yourself from being washed overboard. How's her head, Larry?"

"Nor' east an' by east," replied one of the men at the wheel, Larry O'Neil by name — a genuine son of Erin, whose jovial smile of rollicking good humour was modified, but by no means quenched, by the serious circumstances in which he found himself placed. His comrade, William Jones, who stood on the larboard side of the wheel, was a short, thick-set, stern seaman, whose facial muscles were scarcely capable of breaking into a smile, and certainly failed to betray any of the owner's thoughts or feelings, excepting astonishment. Such passions as anger, pity, disgust, fear, and the like, whatever place they might have in Jones's breast, had no visible index on his visage. Both men were sailor-like and powerful, but they were striking contrasts to each other, as they stood — the one sternly, the other smilingly — steering the *Roving Bess* before that howling storm.

"Is not 'nor' east and by east' our direct course for the harbour of San Francisco?" inquired Ned Sinton.

"It is," replied the captain, "as near as I can guess; but we've been blown about so much that I can't tell exactly. Moreover, it's my opinion we can't be far off the coast now; and if this gale holds on I'll have to bring to, at the risk of bein' capsized. Them plaguey coral-reefs, too, are always springin' up in these seas where you least expect 'em. if we go bump against one as we are goin' now, its all up with us."

"Not a pleasant idea," remarked Ned, somewhat gravely. "Do these storms usually last long?"

Before the captain could reply, the first mate came up and whispered in his ear.

"Eh! how much d'ye say?" he asked quickly.

"Five feet, sir; she surged heavily once or twice on the foremast, and I think must have started a plank."

"Call all hands to work the pumps; and don't let the men know how much water there is in the hold. Come below, Ned. I want you. Keep her head steady as she goes."

"Ay, ay, sir," sang out O'Neil, as the captain descended the companion-hatch to the cabin, followed by his young friend.

The dim light in the swinging lamp flickered fitfully when the ship plunged into the troughs of the seas, and rose again with a violent surge, as each wave passed under her, while every plank and spar on board seemed to groan under the strain. Darkness now added to the terrors of the wild storm.

Sitting down on a locker, Captain Bunting placed his elbows on the table, and covering his face with his hands, remained silent for several minutes, while Ned sat down beside him, but forbore to interrupt his thoughts.

"Boy," he said, at length, looking up anxiously, "we've sprung a leak, and a few minutes will shew what our fate is to be. Five feet of water in the hold in so short a time implies a bad one."

"Five feet two, sir," said the mate, looking in at the cabin door; "and the carpenter can't get at the leak."

"I feared as much," muttered the captain. "Keep the men hard at the pumps, Mr. Williams, and let me hear how it stands again in ten minutes."

"Captain," said Ned, "it does not become a landsman to suggest, perhaps, but I can't help reminding you, that leaks of this kind have been stopped by putting a sail below the ship's bottom."

"I know it, boy, I know it; but we could never get a sail down in such a night."

"Can nothing be done, then?"

"Yes, lad; it's hard to do it, but it must be done; life is more precious than gold — we must heave the cargo overboard. I have invested every farthing I have in the world in this venture," continued Captain Bunting, sadly, "but there's no help for it. Now, you were at the shifting of the cargo when we opened the hatches during the calms off the Brazilian coast, and as you know the position of the bales and boxes, I want you to direct the men so as to get it hove out quickly. Luckily, bein' a general cargo, most o' the bales are small and easily handled. Here comes the mate again — well, Mr. Williams?"

"Up another inch, sir."

"Go, Ned, over with it. I'll superintend above; so good-bye to our golden dreams."

There was a slight tone of bitterness in the captain's voice as he spoke, but it passed away quickly, and the next instant he was on deck encouraging his men to throw the valuable cargo over the side. Bale after bale and box after box were tossed ruthlessly out upon the raging sea until little was left in the ship, save the bulky and less valuable portion of the cargo. Then a cry arose that the leak was discovered! The carpenter had succeeded in partially stopping it with part of a sail, and soon the pumps began to reduce the quantity of water in the hold. At last the leak was gained and effectually stopped, and before daybreak the storm began to subside. While part of the crew, being relieved from the harassing work at the pumps, busied themselves in repairing damages, Ned went to his cabin to put on dry clothes and take a little rest, of which he stood much in need.

Next day the bright sun rose in a cloudless sky, and a gentle breeze now wafted the *Roving Bess* over the Pacific, whose bosom still heaved deeply from the effects of the recent storm. A sense of fervent thankfulness to God for deliverance filled the heart of our hero as he awoke and beheld the warm sunbeams streaming in at the little window of his cabin. Suddenly he was roused from a deep reverie by the shout of "Land, ho!" on deck.

Words cannot convey an adequate idea of the effect of such a shout upon all on board. "Land, ho!" was repeated by every one, as he sprang in dishabille up the hatchway.

"Where away?" inquired Captain Bunting.

"Right ahead, sir," answered the look-out.

"Ay, there it is," said the captain, as Ned, without coat or vest, rushed to his side, and gazed eagerly over the bow, "there it is, Ned, — California, at last! Yonder rise the golden mountains that have so suddenly become the world's magnet; and yonder, too, is the 'Golden Gate' of the harbour of San Francisco. Humph! much good it'll do us."

Again there was a slight tone of bitterness in the captain's voice.

"Don't let down your spirits, captain," said Ned, in a cheering tone; "there is still enough of the cargo left to enable us to make a start for the gold-fields. Perhaps we may make more money there than we would have made had we sold the cargo at a large profit by trafficking on the coast."

Captain Bunting hooked his thumbs into the armholes of his waistcoat, and shook his head. It was evident that he had no faith in gold-digging. Meanwhile the crew had assembled on the forecastle, and were looking out ahead with wistful and excited glances; for the fame of the golden land to which they were approaching had spread far and wide, and they longed to see the gold-dust and nuggets with their own eyes.

"It's a beautiful land, intirely," exclaimed Larry O'Neil, with an irrepressible shout of enthusiasm, which called forth a general cheer from the men.

"Arrah, now," remarked another Patlander, "don't ye wish ye wos up to the knees and elbows in the goolden sands already? Faix I'd give a month's pay to have wan day at the diggin's."

"I don't believe a word about it — I don't," remarked Jones, with the dogged air of a man who shouldn't, wouldn't, and didn't believe, and yet felt, somehow, that he couldn't help it.

"Nother do I," said another, "It's all a sham; come, now, ain't it, Bill?" he added, turning to a bronzed veteran who had visited California two years before.

"A sham!" exclaimed Bill. "I tell 'e wot it is, messmate, when you comes for to see the miners in San Francisco drinkin' *sham*pain like water, an' payin' a dollar for a glass o' six-water grog, you'll —"

"How much is a dollar?" inquired a soft-looking youth, interrupting him.

Bill said it was "'bout four shillin's," and turned away with a look of contempt at such a display of ignorance.

"*Four shillin's!*" exclaimed the soft youth, in amazement.

"Clear the anchor, and clew up the main-topsail," shouted the mate.

In another moment the crew were scattered, some aloft to "lay out" on the topsail yard, some to the clew-lines, and some to clear the anchor, which latter had not been disturbed since the *Roving Bess* left the shores of Old England.

CHAPTER VI.

San Francisco — An Unexpected Desertion — Captain Bunting takes a Gloomy View of Things in General — New Friends and New Plans — Singular Facts and Curious Fancies.

The "Golden Gates," as they are called, of San Francisco, are two rocky headlands, about a mile apart, which form the entrance to one of the finest harbours, or rather land-locked seas, in the world. This harbour is upwards of forty miles long, by about twelve miles broad at its widest point, and receives at its northern end the waters of the noble Sacramento river, into which all the other rivers in California flow.

Nearly opposite to the mouth of the Sacramento, on the southern shores of the bay, stands the famous city of San Francisco, close to which the *Roving Bess* let go her anchor and clasped the golden strand.

The old adage that, "truth is strange, stranger than fiction," was never more forcibly verified than in the growth and career of this wonderful city. No dreams of Arabian romance ever surpassed the inconceivable wonders that were matters of every-day occurrence there during the first years of the gold-fever; and many of the results - attributed to Aladdin's wonderful lamp were almost literally - accomplished — in some cases actually surpassed — in and around the cities of California.

Before the discovery of gold, San Francisco was a mere hamlet. It consisted of a few rude cottages, built of sun-dried bricks, which were tenanted by native Californians; there were also a few merchants who trafficked in hides and horns. Cruisers and whalers occasionally put into the harbour to obtain fresh supplies of water, but beyond these and the vessels engaged in the hide-trade few ships ever visited the port, and the name of San Francisco was almost unknown.

But the instant the rumour got abroad that gold had been discovered there, the eyes of the world were turned towards it. In a few months men and ships began to pour into the capacious harbour; a city of tents overspread the sand-hills on which the hamlet stood; thousands upon thousands of gold-hunters rushed to the mines; the golden treasures of the land were laid bare, and immense fortunes were made literally in the course of a few weeks. In many cases these were squandered or gambled away almost as soon as made; but hundreds of men retired from the gold-fields after a few months' labour, and returned home possessed of ample fortunes. Thousands, too, failed — some from physical inability to stand the fatiguing labour of the mines, and some from what they termed "want of luck," though want of perseverance was, in nine cases out of ten, the real cause;

while many hundreds perished from exposure and from the diseases that were prevalent in the country.

Well would it have been for these last had they remembered God's word, "Make not haste to be rich;" but the thirst for gold, and the prospect of the sudden acquisition of enormous wealth, had blinded them to the fact that their frames were not equal to the rough life at the mines.

The excitement was at its height when the *Roving Bess* anchored off the shores of this land of gold.

The sun was just setting as the anchor dropped, and the crippled ship swung round towards the shore, for the tide had just begun to rise.

"Faix, it's a quare town," said Larry O'Neil to Ned, who was gazing in wrapt, astonishment and admiration ever the stern.

It was indeed "quare." The entire city was made up of the most flimsy and make-shift materials that can be conceived. Many of the shops were mere tents with an open framework of wood in front; some were made of sheet-iron nailed to wooden posts; some were made of zinc; others, (imported from the States), of wood, painted white, and edged with green; a few were built of sun-dried bricks, still fewer of corrugated iron, and many of all these materials pieced together in a sort of fancy patchwork. Even boats were used as dwellings, turned keel up, with a hole cut in their sides for the egress of a tin smoke-pipe, and two others of larger size to serve as door and window.

Finding space scarce, owing to the abrupt rise of the hills from the shore, many enterprising individuals had encroached upon the sea, and built houses on piles driven into the sand nearly half-a-mile below the original high water mark.

Almost every nation under the sun had representatives there, and the consequent confusion of tongues was equal to that of Babel.

The hills overhanging the lower part of the town were also well covered with tents, temporary houses, and cottages that had some appearance of comfort about them.

Such was the city on which the sun went down that night, and many were the quaint, sagacious, and comic remarks made by the men as they sat round their various mess-tables in the forecastle of the *Roving Bess*, speculating noisily and half-seriously on the possibility of getting a run into the interior for a day or two.

But there was a party of men in the ship whose conversation that night was neither so light-hearted nor so loud. They sat in a dark corner of the forecastle talking earnestly in subdued tones after the watch for the night was set. Their chief spokesman was a rough, ill-looking fellow, named Elliot.

"Ye see, lads," said this man to the half-dozen comrades around him, "we must do it tonight, if we're to do it at all. There's the captain's small boat layin' out astern, which comes quite handy, an', as we lose all our pay by the dodge, I don't see why we shouldn't take it."

The man struck his fist into his left palm, and looked round the circle for opinions.

"I don't half like it," said one; "it seems to me a sneaking way of doin' it."

"Bah!" ejaculated another, "wot gammon you do talk. If *he* lose the boat, don't *we* lose the tin? Besides, are we agoin' to let sich a trifle stand in the way o' us an' our fortins?"

"Have ye spoken to the other men, Elliot?" inquired one of the group.

"Ay, in coorse I have; an' they're all agreeable. Young Spense stood out pretty stiff at first; but I talked him over. Only I said nothing to Larry O'Neil or Bill Jones. I know it's of no use. They'll never agree; and if we wos to speak of it to either on 'em, he'd go right away aft an' tell the captain. Their watch below 'll come on in an hour, an' then the watch on deck'll be on our side. So, lads, go and git ready — an' sharp's the word."

The party broke up, and went quietly below to prepare for flight, leaving no one on deck except O'Neil and Jones, and two of their comrades, who formed part of the watch. As Elliot had said, the watch was changed in about an hour. The mate and captain came on deck, looked round to see that all was right, and then returned to the cabin, to consult about the preliminary arrangements for disposing of the remnant of the cargo. Ned Sinton had turned in to have a good sleep before the expected toil and bustle of the following day; O'Neil and Jones, being relieved from duty, were glad to jump into their hammocks; and the deck was left in charge of the conspirators.

It was a clear, lovely night. Not a zephyr stirred the surface of the sea, in whose depths the starry host and the images of a hundred ships of all shapes and tonnage were faithfully mirrored. Bright lights illumined the city, those in the tents giving to them the appearance of cones and cubes of solid fire. The subdued din of thousands of human voices floated over the water, and mingled with the occasional shout or song that rose from the fleet and the splash of oars, as boats passed to and from the shore. Over all, the young moon shed a pale, soft light, threw into deep shadow the hills towards the north, which rose abruptly to a height of 3000 feet, and tipped with a silver edge the peak of Monte Diavolo, whose lofty summit overlooks all the golden land between the great range of the Sierra Nevada and the ocean. It was a scene of peaceful beauty, well fitted to call forth the adoration of man to the great and good Creator. Doubtless there were some whose hearts rose that night above the sordid thoughts of gain and gold; but few such were recognisable by their fellow-men, compared with the numerous votaries of sin and so-called pleasure.

Towards midnight, Captain Bunting turned in, ordering the steward to call him at daybreak; and shortly afterwards the mate retired, having previously looked round the deck and spoken the watch. A few minutes after, Elliot and his comrades appeared on deck, with their boots and small bundles in their hands.

"Is all right?" whispered Elliot.

"All right!" replied one of the watch.

Nothing more was said; the boat was hauled softly alongside, and held firmly there while two men descended and muffled the oars; then one by one the men slid down the side, and a bag of biscuit and a junk of beef were lowered into it by the second mate, who was one of the conspirators.

At that moment the first mate came on deck, and went forward to inquire what was wrong.

"It's something in the boat, sir," replied the second mate.

The mate looked over the side, and the sailors felt that they must be discovered, and that their plans were about to be frustrated. But the second mate was a man of decision. He suddenly seized Williams round the neck, and, covering his mouth with his hand, held him as if in a vice until he was secured and gagged.

"Shall we leave him!" whisperingly inquired one of the men.

"No, he'd manage to kick up a row; take him with us."

The helpless mate was immediately passed over the side, the rope was cast off; and the boat floated softly away. At first, the oars were dipped so lightly that no sound was heard, even by those on board, except the drops of brine that trickled from the blades as they rose from the water; then, as the distance increased, the strokes were given more vigorously, and, at last, the men bent to it "with a will;" and they were soon shooting over the vast bay in the direction of the Sacramento river, up which they meant to proceed to the "diggings."

With the exception of O'Neil and Jones, who had already reached the diggings in their dreams, the whole crew, sixteen in all, levanted, leaving Captain Bunting to navigate the ship back to Old England as he best might.

It is easier to conceive than to describe the feelings of the captain, when, on the following morning, he discovered that his crew had fled. He stamped, and danced, and tugged his hair, and pursed up his lips so tight that nothing but an occasional splutter escaped them! Then he sat down on the cabin skylight, looked steadily at Ned, who came hurriedly on deck in his shirt and drawers to see what was wrong, and burst into a prolonged fit of laughter.

"Hallo, captain! what's up!"

"Nothin', lad, ha! ha! Oh yes, human flesh is up, Ned; sailors is riz, an' we've been sold; — we have — uncommon!"

Hereupon the captain roared again; but there was a slight peculiarity in the tone, that indicated a strong infusion of rage with the seeming merriment.

"They're all gone — every man, Jack," said Jones, with a face of deep solemnity, as he stood looking at the captain.

"So they are, the blackguards; an' that without biddin' us good mornin', bad luck to them," added O'Neil.

At first, Ned Sinton felt little disposed to take a comic view of the affair, and urged the captain strongly to take the lightest boat and set off in pursuit; but the latter objected to this.

"It's of no use," he said, "the ship can't be repaired here without heavy expense; so, as I don't mean to go to sea again for some time, the desertion of the men matters little after all."

"Not go to sea again!" exclaimed Ned, in surprise. "What, then, do you mean to do?"

"That's more than I can tell. I must see first how the cargo is to be disposed of; after that, it will be time enough to concoct plans for the future. It is quite clear that the tide of luck is out about as far as it can go just now; perhaps it may turn soon."

"No doubt of it, captain," cried his young *protégé* with a degree of energy that shewed he had made up his mind as to what *his* course should be, in the event of things coming to the worst. "I'll go down and put on a few more articles of clothing, and then we'll have a talk over matters."

The "talk," which was held over the breakfast-table in the cabin, resulted in the captain resolving to go ashore, and call on a Scotch merchant, named Thompson, to whom he had a letter of introduction. Half-an-hour later this resolve was carried out. Jones rowed them ashore in the smallest boat they had, and sculled back to the ship, leaving O'Neil with them to assist in carrying up two boxes which were consigned to Mr. Thompson.

The quay on which they stood was crowded with men of all nations, whose excited looks, and tones, and "go-ahead" movements, testified to the high-pressure speed with which business in San Francisco was transacted.

"It's more nor I can do to carry them two boxes at wance," said Larry O'Neil, regarding them with a puzzled look, "an' sorra a porter do I see nowhere."

As he spoke, a tall, gentlemanly-looking young man, in a red-flannel shirt, round-crowned wide-awake, long boots, and corduroys, stepped forward, and said, "I'll help you, if you like."

"D'ye think ye can lift it!" inquired Larry, with a dubious look.

The youth replied by seizing one of the boxes, and lifting it with ease on his shoulder, shewing that, though destitute of fat, he had more than the average allowance of bone and sinew.

"I doubt if you could do it better than that yourself, Larry," said Ned, laughing. "Come along, now, close at our heels, lest we get separated in the crowd."

The young porter knew the residence of Mr. Thompson well, and guided them swiftly through the crowded thoroughfares towards it. Passing completely through the town, he led them over the brow of one of the sand-hills beyond it, and descended into a little valley, where several neat villas were scattered along the sides of a pleasant green slope, that descended towards another part of the bay. Turning into the little garden in front of one of these villas, he placed the box on the wooden platform before the door, and said, "This is Mr. Thompson's house."

There was something striking in the appearance of this young porter; he seemed much above his station in life; and Ned Sinton regarded his bronzed and handsome, but somewhat haggard and dissipated countenance, with interest, as he drew out his purse, and asked what was to pay.

"Two dollars," answered the man.

Ned looked up in surprise. The idea of paying eight shillings for so slight a service had never entered his imagination. At that moment the door opened, and Mr. Thompson appeared, and invited them to enter. He was a shrewd, business-like man, with stern, but kind expression of countenance.

"Come in, come in, and welcome to California," he said, on perusing the captain's letter of introduction. "Glad to see you, gentlemen. You've not had breakfast, of course; we are just about to sit down. This way," he added, throwing open the door of a comfortable and elegantly-furnished parlour. "Bring the boxes into the passage — that will do. Here, Lizette, pay the men, dear; two dollars a-piece, I fancy —"

"Excuse me," interrupted Captain Bunting, "only one bas to be paid, the other is one of my sailors."

"Ah! very good; which is he?"

Larry O'Neil stepped forward, hat in hand.

"Go in there, my man, and cook will attend to you."

Larry passed through the doorway pointed out with a pleasant, fluttering sensation at the heart, which was quickly changed to a feeling of considerable disappointment on discovering that "cook" was a negro.

Meanwhile Lizette took two dollars from her purse, and bowing modestly to the strangers as she passed out of the room, advanced with them towards the young porter.

Now, Lizette was *not* beautiful — few women are, in the highest sense of the term, and the few who are, are seldom interesting; but she was pretty, and sweet, and innocent, and just turned sixteen. Fortunately for the male part of the world, there are many such. She had light-brown hair, which hung in dishevelled curls all round, a soft fair complexion, blue eyes, and a turned-up nose — a pert little nose that said plainly, "I *will* have my own way; now see if I don't." But the heart that animated the body to which that nose belonged, was a good, kind, earnest one; therefore, the nose having its own way was rather a blessing than otherwise to those happy individuals who dwelt habitually in the sunshine of Lizette's presence.

At this particular time, ladies were scarce in California. The immense rush of men from all parts of the earth to the diggings had not been accompanied as yet by a corresponding rush of women, consequently the sight of a female face was, as it always ought to be, a source of comfort to mankind. We say "comfort" advisedly, because life at the gold-mines was a hard, riotous, mammon-seeking, rugged, and, we regret to say it, ungodly life; and men, in whom the soft memories of "other days" were not entirely quenched, had need, sometimes, of the comforting reflection that there still existed beings on the earth who didn't rant, and roar, and drink, and swear, and wear beards, and boots, and bowie-knives.

There was double cause, then, for the gaze of respectful admiration with which the young porter regarded Lizette, as she said, "Here is your fare, porter," and put the money into his hand, which he did not even thank her for, but continued to hold extended as if he wished her to take it back again.

Lizette did not observe the gaze, for she turned away immediately after giving him the money, and re-entered the parlour, whereupon the youth thrust both hands into his breeches-pockets, left the house, and returned slowly to the city, with the expression on his countenance of one who had seen a ghost.

Meanwhile Captain Bunting and Ned Sinton sat down with their host and hostess to a second breakfast, over which the former related the circumstances of the double loss of his crew and cargo.

"You are unfortunate," said Mr. Thompson, when the captain paused; "but there are hundreds in nearly the same predicament. Many of the fine-looking vessels you see in the harbour have lain helplessly there for months, the crews having taken French leave, and gone off to the diggings."

"It's awkward," said the captain, with a troubled expression, as he slowly raised a square lump of pork to his mouth; "what would you advise me to do?"

"Sell off the remnant of the cargo, and set up a floating boarding-house."

The square lump of pork disappeared, as the captain thrust it into his cheek in order to say, "What?" with a look of intense amazement.

Lizette laughed inadvertently, and, feeling that this was somewhat rude, she, in her effort to escape, plunged deeper into misfortune by turning to Sinton, with a blushing countenance, and asking him to take another cup of tea — a proposal that was obviously absurd, seeing that she had a moment before filled up his second cup.

Thus suddenly appealed to, Ned stammered, "Thank you — if you — ah! — no, thank you, not any more."

"Set up a floating boarding establishment," reiterated the merchant, in a tone of decision that caused them all to laugh heartily.

"It may sound strange," he continued, "but I assure you it's not a bad speculation. The captain of an American schooner, whose crew deserted the very day she arrived, turned his vessel into a floating boarding-house, about two months ago, and I believe he's making a fortune."

"Indeed," ejaculated the captain, helping himself to another mass of pork, and accepting Lizette's proffer of a third cup of tea.

"You have no idea," continued the merchant, as he handed the bread to Ned, and pressed him to eat — "you have no idea of the strange state of things here just now, and the odd ways in which men make money. Owing to the rush of immigrants everything is enormously dear, and house-room is not to be had for love or money, so that if you were to fit up your ship for the purpose you could fill it at once. At the various hotels in the city an ordinary meal at the *table d'hôte* costs from two to three dollars — eight and twelve shillings of our money — and there are some articles that bear fabulous prices. It's a fact that eggs at this moment sell at a shilling each, and onions and potatoes at the same price; but then wages are enormously high. How long this state of things will last no one can tell; in the meantime, hundreds of men are making fortunes. Only the other day a ship arrived from New York, and one of the passengers, a "cute' fellow, had brought out fifteen hundred copies of several newspapers, which he sold for a dollar each in less than two hours! Then, rents are tremendous. You will scarcely believe me when I tell you that the rent paid by the landlord of one of the hotels here is 110,000 dollars — about £22,000 — a year, and it is but a poor building too. My own warehouse, which is a building of only one storey, with a front of twenty feet, is rented to me at 40,000 dollars — £8000 a year — and rents are rising."

Ned and the captain leaned back in their chairs aghast at such statements, and began to entertain some doubts as to the sanity of their host; but the worthy merchant was a grave, quiet man, without a particle of romance in his composition, and he went on coolly telling them facts which Ned afterwards said made his hair almost stand on end, when he thought of how little money he possessed, and how much he would have to pay for the bare necessaries of life.

After some further converse on men and things in general, and on prospects at the mines, Mr. Thompson said, "And now, Captain Bunting, I'll tell you what I'll do. I will go down to your ship, overhaul the cargo, and make you an offer for the whole in the lump, taking the saleable with the unsaleable. This will, at any rate, put you in funds at once, and enable you to follow what course seems best. Will that suit you?"

"It will," said the captain, "and thank 'ee. As for turning a boardin'-house keeper, I don't think I'm cut out for it. Neither is my friend Sinton, eh?"

"Certainly not," answered Ned, laughing: "we might as well become washerwomen."

"You'd make a pretty good thing of it if you did," retorted Mr. Thompson; "would they not, Lizette? you know more about these things than I do."

"Indeed, I cannot tell, papa, as I do not know the capabilities of our friends in that way; but I think the few washerwomen in the city must be making fortunes, for they charge two shillings a-piece for everything, large and small."

"Now, then, gentlemen," said the merchant, rising, "if you have quite finished, we will walk down to the harbour and inspect the goods."

An arch smile played round Lizette's lips as she shook hands with Ned at parting, and she seemed on the point of speaking, but checked herself.

"I beg pardon," said Ned, pausing, "did you —"

"Oh, it was nothing!" said Lizette; "I was only going to remark that — that if you set up in the washing line, I shall be happy to give you all the work I can."

"Ahem!" coughed Ned gravely, "and if we should set up in the *other* line, will you kindly come and board with us?"

"Hallo, Ned, what's keeping you?" roared the captain.

"Coming," shouted Ned, as he ran after him. "Where has Larry O'Neil gone?"

"He's away down before us to have a look at the town. We shall find him, I doubt not, cruising about the quay."

In a few minutes the three friends were wending their way through the crowded streets back to the shore.

CHAPTER VII.

The Fate of the Roving Bess — Gambling Scenes —
Mr. Sinton makes a New Friend —
Larry O'Neil makes Money in Strange Ways —
A Murder, and a Beggar's Death —
Ned becomes a Poor Man's Heir.

The remnant of the cargo of the *Roving Bess* proved to be worth comparatively little — less even than had been anticipated. After a careful inspection, Mr. Thompson offered to purchase it "in the slump" for 1000 dollars — about £200 sterling. This was a heavy blow to poor Captain Bunting, who had invested his all — the savings of many years — in the present unfortunate venture. However, his was not a nature to brood over misfortunes that could not be avoided, so he accepted the sum with the best grace he might, and busied himself during the next few days in assisting the merchant to remove the bales.

During this period he did not converse much with any one, but meditated seriously on the steps he ought to take. From all that he heard, it seemed impossible to procure hands to man the ship at that time, so he began to entertain serious thoughts of "taking his chance" at the diggings after all. He was by nature averse to this, however; and had nearly made up his mind to try to beat up recruits for the ship, when an event occurred that settled the matter for him rather unexpectedly. This event was the bursting out of a hurricane, or brief but violent squall, which, before assistance could be procured, dragged the *Roving Bess* from her moorings, and stranded her upon the beach, just below the town. Here was an end to sea-faring prospects. The whole of his limited capital would not have paid for a tenth part of the labour necessary to refloat the ship, so he resolved to leave her on the beach, and go to the diggings.

Mr. Thompson advised him to sell the hull, as it would fetch a good price for the sake of the timber, which at that time was much wanted in the town, but the captain had still a lurking hope that he might get his old ship afloat at some future period, and would not hear of it.

"What," said he, "sell the *Roving Bess*, which stands *A1* at Lloyd's, to be broken up to build gold-diggers houses? I trow not. No, no; let her lie where she is in peace."

On the day after the squall, as Ned and the captain were standing on the shore regarding their late floating, and now grounded, home in sad silence, a long-legged, lantern-jawed man, in dirty canvas trousers, long boots, a rough coat, and broad straw hat, with an enormous cigar in his mouth, and both hands in his trousers-pockets, walked up and accosted them. It did not require a second glance to know that he was a Yankee.

"Guess that 'ere's pretty wall fixed up, stranger," he said, addressing the captain, and pointing with his nose to the stranded vessel.

"It is," answered the captain, shortly.

"Fit for nothin' but firewood, I calculate."

To this the captain made no reply.

"I say, stranger," continued the Yankee, "I wouldn't mind to give 'e 1000 dollars for her slick off."

"I don't wish to sell her," replied the captain.

"Say 1500," replied the man.

"I tell you, I *won't* sell her."

"No! Now that *is* kurous. Will 'e loan her, then!"

Here Ned whispered a few words to the captain, who nodded his head, and, turning to the Yankee, said —

"How much will you give?"

"Wall, I reckon, she's too far out to drive a screamin' trade, but I don't mind sayin' 100 dollars a month."

After some consultation with Ned, and a little more talk with the Yankee, Captain Bunting agreed to this proposal, only stipulating that the bargain should hold good for a year, that the hull should not be cut or damaged in any way, and that the rent should be paid in advance into the hands of Mr. Thompson, as he himself was about to proceed to the gold-fields. Having sealed and settled this piece of business at a neighbouring tavern, where the Yankee — Major Whitlaw — ordered a "brandy-smash" for himself and two "gin-slings" for his companions, (which they civilly declined, to his intense amazement,) the contracting parties separated.

"That's rather a sudden transfer of our good ship," said Ned, laughing, as they walked towards the Plaza, or principal square of the town, where some of the chief hotels and gambling-houses were situated.

"I feel half sorry for havin' done it," replied the captain; "however, it can't be helped now, so I'll away to our friend Thompson's office, and tell him about it."

"Then I shall wander about here until you return. It will be dinner time at the hotels two hours hence. Suppose we meet at the Parker House, and talk over our future plans while we discuss a chop?"

To this the captain agreed, and then hurried off to his friend's office, while Ned entered the hotel. A large portion of this building was rented by gamblers, who paid the enormous sum of 60,000 dollars a year for it, and carried on their villainous and degrading occupation in it night and day. The chief games played were monte and faro, but no interest attached to the games *as such*, the winning or losing of money was that which lent fascination to the play.

Ned had intended to stroll through the hotel and observe the various visitors who thronged the bar, but the crash of a brass band in the gambling-saloons awakened his curiosity, and induced him to enter.

The scene that met his eyes was, perhaps, the strangest and the saddest he had ever looked upon. The large saloon was crowded with representatives of almost every civilised nation under the sun. English, Scotch, Irish, Yankees, French, Russians, Turks, Chinese, Mexicans, Indians, Malays, Jews, and negroes — all were there in their national costumes, and all were, more or less, under the fascinating influence of the reigning vice of California, and especially of San Francisco. The jargon of excited voices can neither be conceived nor described. Crowds surrounded the monte tables, on which glittering piles of gold and silver coin were passing from hand to hand according to varying fortune. The characteristics — and we may add the worst passions — of the various nations were ever and anon brought strongly out. The German and Spaniard laid down their money, and lost or won without a symptom of emotion; the Turk stroked his beard as if with the view of keeping himself cool; the Russian looked stolid and indifferent; the Frenchman started, frowned, swore, and occasionally clutched his concealed pistol or bowie-knife; while the Yankee stamped and swore. But, indeed, the men of all nations cursed and swore in that terrible place.

Those who dwelt in the city staked gold and silver coin, while the men just returned from the mines staked gold-dust and nuggets. These last were conspicuous from their rough clothing, rugged, bronzed, and weather-worn countenances. Many of them played most recklessly. Several successful diggers staked immense sums, and either doubled or lost, in two or three throws, the hard earnings of many months of toil, and left the rooms penniless.

At one end of the saloon there was a counter, with a plentiful supply of stimulants to feed the excitement of the wretched gamblers; and the waiter here was kept in constant employment. Ned had never been within the unhallowed precincts of a gambling-house before, and it was with a feeling of almost superstitious dread that he approached the table, and looked on. A tall, burly, bearded miner stepped forward at the moment and placed a huge purse of gold-dust on the table —

"Now, then," he cried, with a reckless air, "here goes — neck or nothin'."

"Nothin'!" he muttered with a fearful oath, as the president raked the purse into his coffers.

The man rose and strode sullenly from the room, his fingers twitching nervously about the hilt of his bowie-knife; an action which the president observed, but heeded not, being prepared with a concealed revolver for whatever might occur. Immediately another victim stepped forward, staked five hundred dollars — and won. He staked again a thousand dollars — and won; then he rose, apparently resolved to tempt fickle fortune no more, and left the saloon. As he retired his place was filled by a young man who laid down the small sum of two dollars. Fortune favoured this man for a long time, and his pile of dollars gradually increased until he became over-confident and staked fully half of his gains — and lost.

Ned's attention was drawn particularly to this player, whom he thought he had seen before. On looking more fixedly at him, he recognised the young porter who had carried up the box to the merchant's house. His next stake was again made recklessly. He laid down all he possessed — and lost. Then he rose suddenly, and drawing a pistol from his breast, rushed towards the door. None of the players who crowded the saloon paid him more than momentary attention. It mattered not to them whether he meditated suicide or murder. They made way for him to pass, and then, closing in, were deep again in the all-absorbing game.

But our hero was not thus callous. A strong feeling of sympathy filled his breast, prompting him to spring through the doorway, and catch the youth by the shoulder just as he gained the street. He turned round instantly, and presented the revolver at Ned's breast, but the latter caught his right arm in his powerful grasp and held it in the air.

"Be calm, my poor fellow," he said, "I mean you no harm; I only wish to have a word of conversation with you. You are an Englishman, I perceive."

The young man's head fell on his breast, and he groaned aloud.

"Come, come," said Ned, releasing his arm, "don't give way like that."

"I'm lost," said the youth, bitterly. "I have struggled against this passion for gaming, but it has overcome me again and again. It is vain to fight against it any longer."

"Not a bit of it, man," said Ned, in a cheering tone, as he drew the arm of the young man within his own, and led him slowly along the street. "You are excited just now by your disappointments. Let us walk together a while, for I have something to say to you. I am quite a stranger here, and it's a comfort to have a countryman to talk with."

The kind words, and earnest, hearty manner of our hero, had the effect of soothing the agitated feelings of his new friend, and of winning his confidence. In the course of half-an-hour, he drew from him a brief account of his past history.

His name, he said, was Collins; he was the son of a clergyman, and had received a good education. Five years before the period of which we now write, he had left his home in England, and gone to sea, being at that time sixteen years of age. For three years he served before the mast in a South-Sea whale-ship, and then returned home to find his father and mother dead. Having no near relations alive, and not a sixpence in the world, he turned once more towards the sea, with a heavy heart and an empty pocket, obtained a situation as second mate in a trading vessel which was about to proceed to the Sandwich Islands. Encountering a heavy gale on the western coast of South America, his vessel was so much disabled as to be compelled to put into the harbour of San Francisco for repairs. Here the first violent attack of the gold-fever had set in. The rush of immigrants was so great, that goods of all kinds were selling at fabulous prices, and the few bales that happened to be on board the ship were disposed off for twenty times their value. The captain was in ecstasies, and purposed sailing immediately to the nearest civilised port for a cargo of miscellaneous goods; but the same fate befell him which afterwards befell Captain Bunting, and many hundreds of others — the crew deserted to the mines. Thereupon the captain and young Collins also betook themselves to the gold-fields, leaving the ship to swing idly at her anchor. Like most of the first arrivals at the mines, Collins was very successful, and would soon — in diggers' parlance — have "made his pile," — i.e., his fortune, had not scurvy attacked and almost killed him; compelling him to return to San Francisco in search of fresh vegetables and medicine, neither of which, at that time, could be obtained at the mines for love or money. He recovered slowly; but living in San Francisco was so expensive that, ere his health was sufficiently recruited to enable him to return to the gold-fields, his funds were well-nigh exhausted. In order to recruit them he went, in an evil hour, to the gaming-saloons, and soon became an inveterate gambler.

In the providence of God he had been led, some years before, to become an abstainer from all intoxicating drinks, and, remaining firm to his pledge throughout the course of his downward career, was thus saved from the rapid destruction which too frequently overtook those who to the exciting influences of gambling added the maddening stimulus of alcohol. But the constant mental fever under which he laboured was beginning to undermine a naturally-robust constitution, and to unstring the nerves of a well-made, powerful frame. Sometimes, when fortune favoured him, he became suddenly possessor of a large sum of money, which he squandered in reckless gaiety, often, however, following the dictates of an amiable, sympathetic disposition, he gave the most of it away to companions and acquaintances in distress. At other times he had not wherewith to pay for his dinner, in which case he took the first job that offered in order to procure a few dollars. Being strong and active, he frequently went down to the quays and offered his services as a porter to any of the gold-hunters who were arriving in shoals from all parts of the world. It was thus, as we have seen, that he first met with Ned Sinton and his friends.

All this, and a great deal more, did Ned worm out of his companion in the course of half-an-hour's stroll in the Plaza.

"Now," said he, when Collins had finished, "I'm going to make a proposal to you. I feel very much interested in all that you have told me; to be candid with you, I like your looks, and I like your voice — in fact, I like *yourself*, and — but what's your Christian name?"

"Tom," replied the other.

"Very well; then I'll call you Tom in future, and you'll call me Ned. Now, Tom, you must come with me and Captain Bunting to the gold-fields, and try your fortune over again — nay, don't shake your head, I know what you would say, you have no money to equip yourself, and you won't be indebted to strangers, and all that sort of stuff; but that won't do, my boy. I'm not a stranger; don't I know all your history from first to last?"

Tom Collins sighed.

"Well, perhaps I don't know it all, but I know the most of it, and besides, I feel as if I had known you all my life —"

"Ned," interrupted the other, in an earnest tone of voice, "I feel your kindness very much — no one has spoken to me as you have done since I came to the diggings — but I cannot agree to your proposal today. Meet me at the Parker House tomorrow, at this time, and I shall give you a final answer."

"But why not give it now?"

"Because — because, I want to — to get paid for a job I expect to get —"

"Tom," said Ned, stopping and laying his hand on the shoulder of his companion, while he looked earnestly into his face, "let us begin our friendship with mutual candour. Do you not intend to make a few dollars, and then try to increase them by another throw at the gaming-table!"

The youth's brow flushed slightly as he answered, "You are right, I had half an intention of trying my fortune for the last time —"

"Then," said Ned firmly and emphatically, "you shall do nothing of the sort. Gambling for money is a mean, pitiful, contemptible thing — don't frown, my dear fellow, I do not apply these terms to *you*, I apply them to the principle of gambling — a principle which you do not hold, as I know from your admission, made to me not many minutes ago, that you have often striven against the temptation. Many men don't realise the full extent of the sinfulness of many of their practices, but although that renders them less culpable, it does not render them innocent, much less does it justify the evil practices. Gambling is all that I have styled it, and a great deal worse; and you *must* give it up — I insist on it. Moreover, Tom, I insist on your coming to dine with me at the Parker House. I shall introduce you to my friend Captain Bunting, whom you already know by sight — so come along."

"Well, I will," said Tom, smiling at his friend's energy, but still hanging back; "but you must permit me to go to my lodgings first. I shall be back immediately."

"Very good. Remember, we dine in the course of an hour, so be punctual."

While Tom Collins hurried away to his lodgings, Ned Sinton proceeded towards the shores of the bay in a remarkably happy frame of mind, intending to pass his leisure hour in watching the thousands of interesting and amusing incidents that were perpetually taking place on the crowded quays, where the passengers from a newly-arrived brig were looking in bewildered anxiety after their luggage, and calling for porters; where traffic, by means of boats, between the fleet and the land created constant confusion and hubbub; where men of all nations bargained for the goods of all climes in every known tongue.

While he gazed in silence at the exciting and almost bewildering scene, his attention was attracted to a group of men, among whose vociferating tones he thought he distinguished familiar voices.

"That's it; here's your man, sir," cried one, bursting from the crowd with a huge portmanteau on his shoulder. "Now, then, where'll I steer to?"

"Right ahead to the best hotel," answered a slim Yankee, whose black coat, patent-leather boots, and white kids, in such a place, told plainly enough that a superfine dandy had mistaken his calling.

"Ay, ay, sir!" shouted Bill Jones, as he brushed past Ned, in his new capacity of porter.

"Faix, ye've cotched a live Yankee!" exclaimed a voice there was no mistaking, as the owner slapped Bill on the shoulder. "He'll make yer fortin', av ye only stick by him. He's just cut out for the diggin's, av his mother wos here to take care of him."

Larry O'Neil gave a chuckle, slapped his pockets, and cut an elephantine caper, as he turned from contemplating the retreating figure of his shipmate's employer, and advanced towards the end of the quay.

"Now, thin, who's nixt?" cried he, holding out both arms, and looking excited, as if he were ready to carry off any individual bodily in his arms to any place, for mere love, without reference to money. "Don't all spake at wance. Tshoo dollars a mile for anythin' onder a ton, an' yerself on the top of it for four! Horoo, Mister Sinton, darlint, is it yerself? Och, but this is the place intirely — goold and silver for the axin' a'most! Ah, ye needn't grin. Look here!"

Larry plunged both hands into the pockets of his trousers, and pulled them forth full of half and quarter dollars, with a few shining little nuggets of gold interspersed among them.

Ned opened his eyes in amazement, and, taking his excited comrade apart from the crowd, asked how he had come by so much money.

"Come by it!" he exclaimed; "ye could come by twice the sum, av ye liked. Sure, didn't I find that they wos chargin' tshoo dollars — aiqual to eight shillin's, I'm towld — for carryin' a box or portmanter the length o' me fut; so I turns porter all at wance, an' faix I made six dollars in less nor an hour. But as I was comin' back, I says to myself, says I, 'Larry, ye'll be the better of a small glass o' somethin' — eh!' So in I goes to a grog-shop, and faix I had to pay half-a-dollar for a thimbleful o' brandy, bad luck to them, as would turn the stomik o' a pig. I almost had a round wi' the landlord; but they towld me it wos the same iverywhere. So I wint and had another in the nixt shop I sees, jist to try; and it was thrue. Then a Yankee spies my knife, — the great pig-sticker that Bob Short swopped wi' me for my junk o' plumduff off the Cape. It seems they've run out o' sich articles just at this time, and would give handfuls o' goold for wan. So says I, 'Wot'll ye give?'

"'Three dollars, I guess,' says wan.

"'Four,' says another; 'he's chaitin' ye.'

"'Four's bid,' says I, mountin' on a keg o' baccy, and howldin up the knife; 'who says more? It's the rale steel, straight from Manchester or Connaught, I misremimber which. Warranted to cut both ways, av ye only turn the idge round, and shove with a will.'

"I begood in joke; but faix they took me up in arnest, an' run up the price to twenty dollars — four pounds, as sure as me name's Larry — before I know'd where I wos. I belave I could ha' got forty for it, but I hadn't the heart to ax more, for it wasn't worth a brass button."

"You've made a most successful beginning, Larry. Have you any more knives like that one?"

"Sorrow a wan — more's the pity. But that's only a small bit o' me speckilations. I found six owld newspapers in the bottom o' me chist, and, would ye belave it, I sowld 'em, ivery wan, for half-a-dollar the pace; and I don't rightly know how much clear goold I've got by standin' all mornin' at the post-office."

"Standing at the post-office! What do you mean?"

"Nother more or less nor what I say. I suppose ye know the mail's comed in yisterday mornin'; so says I to myself this mornin', 'Ye've got no livin' sowl in the owld country that's likely to write to ye, but ye better go, for all that, an' ax if there's letters. Maybe there is; who knows?' So away I wint, and sure enough I found a row o' men waitin' for their letters; so I crushes for'ard — och! but I thought they'd ha' hung me on the spot, — and I found it was a rule that 'first come first sarved — fair play and no favour.' They wos all standin' wan behind another in a line half-a-mile long av it wos a fut, as patient as could be; some readin' the noosepapers, and some drinkin' coffee and tay and grog, that wos sowld by men as went up an' down the line the whole mornin'. So away I goes to the end o' the line, an' took my place, determined to stand it out; and, in three minutes, I had a tail of a dozen men behind me. 'Faix, Larry,' says I, 'it's the first time ye iver comminced at the end of a thing in order to git to the beginnin'.'

"Well, when I wos gittin' pretty near the post-office windy, I hears the chap behind me a-sayin' to the fellow behind him that he expected no letters, but only took up his place in the line to sell it to them what did. An' sure enough I found that lots o' them were there on the same errand. Just then up comes a miner, in big boots and a wide-awake.

"'Och,' says he, 'who'll sell me a place?' and with that he offered a lot o' pure goold lumps.

"'Guess it's too little,' says the man next me.

"'Ah, ye thievin' blackguard!' says I. 'Here, yer honer, I'll sell ye my place for half the lot. I can wait for me letter, more be token I'm not sure there is wan.' For, ye see, I wos riled at the Yankee's greed. So out I steps, and in steps the miner, and hands me the whole he'd offered at first.

"'Take them, my man,' says he; 'you're an honest fellow, and it's a trate to meet wan here.'"

"Capital," cried Ned, laughing heartily; "and you didn't try for a letter after all?"

"Porter there?" shouted a voice from the quay.

"That's me, yer honer. Here ye are," replied the Irishman, bounding away with a yell, and shouldering a huge leathern trunk, with which he vanished from the scene, leaving Ned to pursue the train of thought evoked by his account of his remarkable experiences.

We deem it necessary here to assure the reader that the account given by Larry O'Neil of his doings was by no means exaggerated. The state of society, and the eccentricities of traffic displayed in San Francisco and other Californian cities during the first years of the gold-fever, beggars all description. Writers on that place and period find difficulty in selecting words and inventing similes in order to convey anything like an adequate idea of their meaning. Even eye-witnesses found it almost impossible to believe the truth of what they heard and saw; and some have described the whole circle of life and manners there to have been more like to the wild, incongruous whirl of a pantomime than to the facts of real life.

Even in the close and abrupt juxtaposition of the ludicrous and the horrible this held good. Ned Sinton had scarcely parted from his hilarious shipmate, when he was attracted by shouts, as if of men quarrelling, in a gaming-house; and, a few moments later, the report of a pistol was heard, followed by a sharp cry of agony. Rushing into the house, and forcing his way through the crowd, he reached the table in time to see the bloody corpse of a man carried out. This unfortunate had repeatedly lost large sums of money, and, growing desperate, staked his all on a final chance. He lost; and, drawing his bowie-knife, in the heat of despair, rushed at the president of the table. A dozen arms arrested him, and rendered his intended assault abortive; nevertheless, the president coolly drew a revolver from under the cloth, and shot him dead. For a few minutes there was some attempt at disturbance, and some condemned, while others justified the act. But the body was removed, and soon the game went on again as if nothing had occurred.

Sickened with the sight, Ned hurried from the house, and walked rapidly towards the shores of the bay, beyond the limits of the canvas town, where he could breathe the free ocean air, and wander on the sands in comparative solitude.

The last straggling tent in that quarter was soon behind bun, and he stopped by the side of an old upturned boat, against which he leaned, and gazed out upon the crowded bay with saddened feelings. As he stood in contemplation, he became aware of a sound, as if of heaving, plethoric breathing under the boat. Starting up, he listened intently, and heard a faint groan. He now observed, what had escaped his notice before, that the boat against which he leaned was a human habitation. A small hole near the keel admitted light, and possibly, at times, emitted smoke. Hastening round to the other side, he discovered a small aperture, which served as a doorway. It was covered with a rag of coarse canvas, which he lifted, and looked in.

"Who's there?" inquired a voice, as sharply as extreme weakness would allow. "Have a care! There's a revolver pointing at your head. If you come in without leave, I'll blow out your brains."

"I am a friend," said Ned, looking towards the further end of the boat, where, on a couch of straw, lay the emaciated form of a middle-aged man. "Put down your pistol, friend; my presence here is simply owing to the fact that I heard you groan, and I would relieve your distress, if it is in my power."

"You are the first that has said so since I lay down here," sighed the man, falling back heavily.

Ned entered, and, advancing as well as he could in a stooping posture, sat down beside the sick man's pallet, and felt his pulse. Then he looked anxiously in his face, on which the hand of death was visibly placed.

"My poor fellow!" said Ned, in a soothing tone, "you are very ill, I fear. Have you no one to look after you?"

"Ill!" replied the sick man, almost fiercely, "I am dying. I have seen death too often, and know it too well, to be mistaken." His voice sank to a whisper as he added, "It is not far off now."

For a few seconds Ned could not make up his mind what to say. He felt unwilling to disturb the last moments of the man. At last he leaned forward, and repeated from memory several of the most consoling passages of Scripture. Twice over he said, "Though thy sins be as scarlet, they shall be white as wool," and, "Him that cometh unto Me, (Christ), I will in no wise cast out."

The man appeared to listen, but made no reply. Suddenly he started up, and, leaning on his elbow, looked with an awfully earnest stare into Ned's face.

"Young man, gold is good — gold is good — remember that, *if you don't make it your god.*"

After a pause, he continued, "*I* made it my god. I toiled for it night and day, in heat and cold, wet and dry. I gave up everything for it; I spent all my time in search of it — and I got it — and what good can it do me *now*? I have spent night and day here for weeks, threatening to shoot any one who should come near my gold — Ha!" he added, sharply, observing that his visitor glanced round the apartment, "you'll not find it *here*. No, look, look round, peer into every corner, tear up every plank of my boat, and you'll find nothing but rotten wood, and dust, and rusty nails."

"Be calm, my friend," said Ned, who now believed that the poor man's mind was wandering, "I don't want your gold; I wish to comfort you, if I can. Would you like me to do anything for you after —"

"After I'm dead," said the man, abruptly. "No, nothing. I have no relations — no friends — no enemies, even, *now*. Yes," he added, quickly, "I have one friend. *You* are my friend. You have spoken kindly to me — a beggar. You deserve the name of friend. Listen, I want you to be my heir. See here, I have had my will drawn up long ago, with the place for the name left blank I had intended — but no matter — what is your name?"

"Edward Sinton."

"Here, hand me that ink-horn, and the pen. There," continued the man, pushing the paper towards him, "I have made over to you the old boat, and the ground it lies on. Both are mine. The piece of ground is marked off by four posts. Take care of the —"

The man's voice sank to a mere whisper; then it ceased suddenly. When Ned looked at him again, he started, for the cold hand of death had sealed his lips for ever.

A feeling of deep, intense pity filled the youth's heart, as he gazed on the emaciated form of this friendless man — yet he experienced a sensation approaching almost to gladness, when he remembered that the last words he had spoken to him were those of our blessed Saviour to the chief of sinners.

Spreading the ragged piece of canvas that formed a quilt over the dead man's face, he rose, and left the strange dwelling, the entrance to which he secured, and then hastened to give information of the death to the proper authorities.

Ned was an hour too late for dinner when he arrived at the hotel, where he found Captain Bunting and his new friend awaiting him in some anxiety. Hastily informing them of the cause of his detention, he introduced them to each other, and forgot for a time the scene of death he had just witnessed, in talking over plans for the future, and in making arrangements for a trip to the diggings.

CHAPTER VIII.

Our Hero and his Friends start for the Diggings —
The Captain's Portrait — Costumes, and Scenery, and
Surprises — The Ranche by the Road-Side — Strange
Travellers — They meet with a New Friend,
and adopt him — The Hunter's Story — Larry offers
to fight a Yankee — High Prices and Empty Purses.

Ovid never accomplished a metamorphosis more striking or complete than that effected by Captain Bunting upon his own proper person. We have said, elsewhere, that the worthy captain was a big, broad man, with a shaggy head of hair, and red whiskers. Moreover, when he landed in San Francisco, he wore a blue coat, with clear brass buttons, blue vest, blue trousers, and a glazed straw hat; but in the course of a week he effected such a change in his outward man, that his most intimate friend would have failed to recognise him.

No brigand of the Pyrenees ever looked more savage — no robber of the stage ever appeared more outrageously fierce. We do not mean to say that Captain Bunting "got himself up" for the purpose of making himself conspicuous. He merely donned the usual habiliments of a miner; but these habiliments were curious, and the captain's figure in them was unusually remarkable.

In order that the reader may have a satisfactory view of the captain, we will change the scene, and proceed at once to that part of the road to the gold-fields which has now been reached by our adventurers.

It is a wide plain, or prairie, on which the grass waves like the waters of the sea. On one side it meets the horizon, on another it is bounded by the faint and far-distant range of the Sierra Nevada. Thousands of millions of beautiful wild-flowers spangle and beautify the soft green carpet, over which spreads a cloudless sky, not a whit less blue and soft than the vaunted sky of Italy. Herds of deer are grazing over the vast plain, like tame cattle. Wild geese and other water-fowl wing their way through the soft atmosphere, and little birds twitter joyously among the flowers. Everything is bright, and green, and beautiful; for it is spring, and the sun has not yet scorched the grass to a russet-brown, and parched and cracked the thirsty ground, and banished animal and vegetable life away, as it will yet do, ere the hot summer of those regions is past and gone.

There is but one tree in all that vast plain. It is a sturdy oak, and near it bubbles a cool, refreshing spring, over which, one could fancy, it had been appointed guardian. The spot is hundreds of miles from San Francisco, on the road to the gold-mines of California. Beneath that solitary oak a party of weary travellers have halted, to rest and refresh themselves and their animals; or, as the diggers have it, to take their "nooning." In the midst of that party sits our captain, on the back of a long-legged mule.

On his head is, or, rather, was — for he has just removed it, in order to wipe the perspiration from his forehead — a brown felt wide-awake, very much battered in appearance, suggesting the idea that the captain had used it constantly as a night-cap, which, indeed, is the fact. Nothing but a flannel shirt, of the brightest possible scarlet, clothes the upper portion of his burly frame, while brown corduroys adorn the lower. Boots of the most ponderous dimensions engulf, not only his feet, but his entire legs, leaving only a small part of the corduroys visible. On his heels, or, rather, just above his heels, are strapped a pair of enormous Mexican spurs, with the frightful prongs of which he so lacerated the sides of his unfortunate mule, during the first part of the journey, as to drive that animal frantic, and cause it to throw him off at least six times a day. Dire necessity has now, however, taught the captain that most difficult and rarely-accomplished feat of horsemanship, to ride with the toes well in, and the heels well out.

Round Captain Bunting's waist is a belt, which is of itself quite a study. It is made of tough cow-hide, full two and a half inches broad, and is fastened by a brass buckle that would cause the mouth of a robber-chief to water. Attached to it in various ways and places are the following articles: — A bowie-knife of the largest size — not far short of a small cutlass; a pair of revolving pistols, also large, and having six barrels each; a stout leathern purse; and a leathern bag of larger dimensions for miscellaneous articles. As the captain has given up shaving for many weeks past, little of his face is visible, except the nose, eyes, and forehead. All besides is a rugged mass of red hair, which rough travel has rendered an indescribable and irreclaimable waste. But the captain cares not: as long as he can clear a passage through the brushwood to his mouth, he says, his mind is easy.

Such is Captain Bunting, and such, with but trifling modifications, is every member of his party. On Ned Sinton and his almost equally stalwart and handsome friend, Tom Collins, the picturesque costume of the miner sits well; and it gives a truly wild, dashing look to the whole party, as they stand beneath the shade of that lovely oak, preparing to refresh themselves with biscuit and jerked beef, and pipes of esteemed tobacco.

Besides those we have mentioned, Larry O'Neil is there, — busy carrying water in a bucket to the horses, and as proud of his Mexican spurs as if they were the golden spurs of the days of chivalry. Bill Jones is there, with a blue instead of a red-flannel shirt, and coarse canvas ducks in place of corduroys. Bill affects the sailor in other respects, for he scorns heavy boots, and wears shoes and a straw hat; but he is compelled to wear the spurs, for reasons best known to his intensely obstinate mule. There is also among them a native Californian, — a *vaquero*, or herd, — who has been hired to accompany the party to the diggings, to look after the pack-mules, of which there are two, and to assist them generally with advice and otherwise. He is a fine athletic fellow — Spanish-like, both in appearance and costume; and, in addition to bad Spanish, gives utterance to a few sounds, which *he* calls "Encleesh." The upper part of his person is covered by the *serape*, or Mexican cloak, which is simply a blanket, with a hole in its centre, through which the head of the wearer is thrust, the rest being left to fall over the shoulders.

Our travellers had reached the spot on which we now find them by means of a boat voyage of more than a hundred miles, partly over the great bay of San Francisco, and partly up the Sacramento River, until they reached the city of Sacramento. Here they purchased mules and provisions for the overland journey to the mines — a further distance of about a hundred and fifty miles, — and also the picks, shovels, axes, pewter plates, spoons, pans, and pannikins, and other implements and utensils that were necessary for a campaign among the golden mountains of the Sierra Nevada. For these the prices demanded were so enormous, that when all was ready for a start they had only a few dollars left amongst them. But being on their way to dig for gold, they felt little concern on this head.

As the Indians of the interior had committed several murders a short time before, and had come at various times into collision with the gold-diggers, it was deemed prudent to expend a considerable sum on arms and ammunition. Each man, therefore, was armed with a rifle or carbine, a pistol of some sort, and a large knife or short sword. Captain Bunting selected a huge old bell-mouthed blunderbuss, having, as he said, a strong partiality for the weapons of his forefathers. Among other things, Ned, by advice of Tom Collins, purchased a few simple medicines; he also laid in a stock of drawing-paper, pencils, and water-colours, for his own special use, for which he paid so large a sum that he was ashamed to tell it to his comrades; but he was resolved not to lose the opportunity of representing life and scenery at the diggings, for the sake of old Mr. Shirley, as well as for his own satisfaction. Thus equipped they set forth.

Before leaving San Francisco, the captain, and Ned, and Tom Collins had paid a final visit to their friend the merchant, Mr. Thompson, and committed their property to his care — i.e., the hull of the good ship *Roving Bess* — the rent of which he promised to collect monthly — and Ned's curious property, the old boat and the little patch of barren sand on which it stood. The boat itself he made over, temporarily, to a poor Irishman who had brought out his wife with him, and was unable to proceed to the diggings in consequence of the said wife having fallen into a delicate state of health. He gave the man a written paper empowering him to keep possession until his return, and refused to accept of any rent whereat the poor woman thanked him earnestly, with the tears running down her pale cheeks.

It was the hottest part of an exceedingly hot day when the travellers found themselves, as we have described, under the grateful shade of what Larry termed the "lone oak."

"Now our course of proceeding is as follows," said Ned, at the conclusion of their meal — "We shall travel all this afternoon, and as far into the night as the mules can be made to go. By that time we shall be pretty well off the level ground, and be almost within hail of the diggings —"

"I don't belave it," said Larry O'Neil, knocking the ashes out of his pipe in an emphatic manner; "sure av there *was* goold in the country we might have seed it by this time."

Larry's feelings were a verification of the words, "hope deferred maketh the heart sick." He had started enthusiastically many days before on this journey to the gold regions, under the full conviction that on the first or second day he would be, as he expressed it, "riding through fields of goold dust;" instead of which, day after day passed, and night after night, during which he endured all the agonies inseparable from a *first* journey on horseback, and still not a symptom of gold was to be seen, "no more nor in owld Ireland itself." But Larry bore his disappointments like an Irishman, and defied "fortin' to put him out of timper by any manes wotiver."

"Patience," said Bill Jones, removing his pipe to make room for the remark, "is a wirtue — that's wot I says. If ye can't make things better, wot then? why, let 'em alone. W'en there's no wind, crowd all canvas and ketch wot there is. W'en there *is* wind, why then, steer yer course; or, if ye can't, steer as near it as ye can. Anyhow, never back yer fore-topsail without a cause — them's my sentiments."

"And very good sentiments they are, Bill," said Tom Collins, jumping up and examining the girth of his horse; "I strongly advise you to adopt them, Larry."

"Wot a bottle o' wisdom it is," said O'Neil, with a look of affected contempt at his messmate. "Wos it yer grandmother, now, or yer great wan, that edicated ye? — Arrah, there ye go! Oh, morther, ye'll break me heart!"

The latter part of this remark was addressed to his mule, which at that moment broke its laryat, and gambolled gaily away over the flowering plain. Its owner followed, yelling like a madman. He might as well have chased the wind; and it is probable that he would never have mounted his steed again had not the vaquero come to his aid. This man, leaping on his own horse, which was a very fine one, dashed after the runaway, with which he came up in a few minutes; then grasping the long coil of line that hung at his saddle-bow, he swung it round once or twice, and threw the lasso, or noose, adroitly over the mule's head, and brought it up.

"Yer a cliver fellow," said Larry, as he came up, panting; "sure ye did it be chance?"

The man smiled, and without deigning a reply, rode back to the camp, where the party were already in the saddle. In a few minutes they were trotting rapidly over the prairie.

Before evening closed, the travellers arrived at one of the road-side inns, or, as they were named, ranches, which were beginning at this time to spring up in various parts of the country, for the accommodation of gold-hunters on their way to the mines. This ranche belonged to a man of the name of Dawson, who had made a few hundred dollars by digging, and then set up a grog-shop and house of entertainment, being wise enough to perceive that he could gain twice as much gold by supplying the diggers with the necessaries of life than he could hope to procure by digging. His ranche was a mere hovel, built of sun-dried bricks, and he dealt more in drinks than in edibles. The accommodation and provisions were of the poorest description, but, as there was no other house of entertainment near, mine host charged the highest possible prices. There was but one apartment in this establishment, and little or no furniture. Several kegs and barrels supported two long pine planks which constituted at different periods of the day the counter, the gaming-table, and the *table d'hôte*. A large cooking stove stood in the centre of the house, but there were no chairs; guests were expected to sit on boxes and empty casks, or stand. Beds there were none. When the hour for rest arrived, each guest chose the portion of the earthen floor that suited him best, and, spreading out his blankets, with his saddle for a pillow, lay down to dream of golden nuggets, or, perchance, of home, while innumerable rats — the bane of California — gambolled round and over him.

The ranchero, as the owner of such an establishment is named, was said to be an escaped felon. Certainly he might have been, as far as his looks went. He was surly and morose, but men minded this little, so long as he supplied their wants. There were five or six travellers in the ranche when our party arrived, all of whom were awaiting the preparation of supper.

"Here we are," cried the captain, as they trotted into the yard, "ready for supper, I trow; and, if my nose don't deceive me, supper's about ready for us."

"I hope they've got enough for us all," said Ned, glancing at the party inside, as he leaped from the saddle, and threw the bridle to his vaquero. "Halloo, Boniface! have ye room for a large party in there?"

"Come in an' see," growled Dawson, whose duties at the cooking stove rendered him indifferent as to other matters.

"Ah, thin, ye've got a swate voice," said Larry O'Neil, sarcastically, as he led his mule towards a post, to which Bill Jones was already fastening his steed. "I say, Bill," he added, pointing to a little tin bowl which stood on an inverted cask outside the door of the ranche, "wot can that be for?"

"Dunno," answered Bill; "s'pose it's to wash in."

At that moment a long, cadaverous miner came out of the hut, and rendered further speculation unnecessary, by turning up his shirt sleeves to the elbow, and commencing his ablutions in the little tin bowl, which was just large enough to admit both his hands at once.

"Faix, yer mouth and nose ought to be grateful," said Larry, in an undertone, as he and Jones stood with their arms crossed, admiring the proceedings of the man.

This remark had reference to the fact that the washer applied the water to the favoured regions around his nose and mouth, but carefully avoided trespassing on any part of the territory lying beyond.

"Oh! morther, wot nixt?" exclaimed Larry.

Well might he inquire, for this man, having combed his hair with a public comb, which was attached to the door-post by a string, and examined himself carefully in a bit of glass, about two inches in diameter, proceeded to cleanse his teeth with a *public tooth-brush* which hung beside the comb. All these articles had been similarly used by a miner ten minutes previously; and while this one was engaged with his toilet, another man stood beside him awaiting his turn!

"W'en yer in difficulties," remarked Bill Jones, slowly, as he entered the ranche, and proceeded to fill his pipe, "git out of 'em, if ye can. If ye can't, why wot then? circumstances is adverse, an' it's o' no use a-tryin' to mend 'em. Only my sentiments is, that I'll delay washin' till I comes to a river."

"You've come from San Francisco, stranger?" said a rough-looking man, in heavy boots, and a Guernsey shirt, addressing Captain Bunting.

"Maybe I have," replied the captain, regarding his interrogator through the smoke of his pipe, which he was in the act of lighting.

"Goin' to the diggin's, I s'pose?"

"Yes."

"Bin there before?"

"No."

"Nor none o' your party, I expect?"

"None, except one."

"You'll be goin' up to the bar at the American Forks now, I calc'late?"

"Don't know that I am."

"Perhaps you'll try the northern diggin's?"

"Perhaps."

How long this pertinacious questioner might have continued his attack on the captain is uncertain, had he not been suddenly interrupted by the announcement that supper was ready, so he swaggered off to the corner of the hut where an imposing row of bottles stood, demanded a "brandy-smash," which he drank, and then, seating himself at the table along with the rest of the party, proceeded to help himself largely to all that was within his reach.

The fare was substantial, but not attractive. It consisted of a large junk of boiled salt beef, a mass of rancid pork, and a tray of broken ship-biscuit. But hungry men are not particular, so the viands were demolished in a remarkably short space of time.

"I'm a'most out o' supplies," said the host, in a sort of apologetic tone, "an' the cart I sent down to Sacramento some weeks ago for more's not come back."

"Better than nothin'," remarked a bronzed, weatherbeaten hunter, as he helped himself to another junk of pork. "If ye would send out yer boy into the hills with a rifle now an' again, ye'd git lots o' grizzly bars."

"Are grizzly-bears eaten here?" inquired Ned Sinton, pausing in the act of mastication, to ask the question.

"Eaten!" exclaimed the hunter, in surprise, "in coorse they is. They're uncommon good eatin' too, I guess. Many a one I've killed an' eaten myself; an' I like 'em better than beef — I do. I shot one up in the hills there two days agone, an' supped off him; but bein' in a hurry, I left the carcase to the coyotes." (Coyotes are small wolves.)

The men assembled round the rude *table d'hôte* were fifteen in number, including our adventurers, and represented at least six different nations — English, Scotch, Irish, German, Yankee, and Chinese. Most of them, however, were Yankees, and all were gold-diggers; even the hunter just referred to, although he had not altogether forsaken his former calling, devoted much of his time to searching for gold. Some, like our friends, were on their way to the diggings for the first time; others were returning with provisions, which they had travelled to Sacramento city to purchase; and one or two were successful diggers who had made their "piles," — in other words, their fortunes — and were returning home with heavy purses of gold-dust and nuggets.

Good humour was the prevailing characteristic of the party, for each man was either successful or sanguinely hopeful, and all seemed to be affected by a sort of undercurrent of excitement, as they listened to, or related, their adventures at the mines. There was only one serious drawback to the scene, and that was, the perpetual and terrible swearing that mingled with the conversation. The Americans excelled in this wicked practice. They seemed to labour to invent oaths, not for the purpose of venting angry feelings, but apparently with the view of giving emphasis to their statements and assertions. The others swore from *habit*. They had evidently ceased to be aware that they were using oaths — so terribly had familiarity with sinful practices blunted the consciences of men who, in early life, would probably have trembled in this way to break the law of God.

Yes, by the way, there was one other drawback to the otherwise picturesque and interesting group, and this was the spitting propensity of the Yankees. All over the floor — that floor, too, on which other men besides themselves were to repose — they discharged tobacco-juice and spittle. The *nation* cannot be too severely blamed and pitied for this disgusting practice, yet we feel a tendency, not to excuse, but to deal gently with *individuals*, most of whom, having been trained to spitting from their infancy, cannot be expected even to understand the abhorrence with which the practice is regarded by men of other nations.

Nevertheless, brother Jonathan, it is not too much to expect that you ought to respect the universal condemnation of your spitting propensities — by travellers from all lands — and endeavour to *believe* that ejecting saliva promiscuously is a dirty practice, even although you cannot *feel* it. We think that if you had the moral courage to pass a law in Congress to render spitting on floors and carpets a capital offence, you would fill the world with admiration and your own bosoms with self-respect, not to mention the benefit that would accrue to your digestive powers in consequence thereof!

All of the supper party were clad and armed in the rough-and-ready style already referred to, and most of them were men of the lower ranks, but there were one or two who, like Ned Sinton, had left a more polished class of mortals to mingle in the promiscuous crowd. These, in some cases, carried their manners with them, and exerted a modifying influence on all around. One young American, in particular, named Maxton, soon attracted general attention by the immense fund of information he possessed, and the urbane, gentlemanly manner in which he conveyed it to those around him. He possessed in an eminent degree those qualities which attract men at once, and irresistibly good nature, frankness, manliness, considerable knowledge of almost every subject that can be broached in general conversation, united with genuine modesty. When he sat down to table he did not grasp everything within his reach; he began by offering to carve and help others, and when at length he did begin to eat, he did not gobble. He "guessed" a little, it is true, and "calculated" occasionally, but when he did so, it was in a tone that fell almost as pleasantly on the ear as the brogue of old Ireland.

Ned happened to be seated beside Maxton, and held a good deal of conversation with him.

"Forgive me, if I appear inquisitive," said the former, helping himself to a handful of broken biscuit, "but I cannot help expressing a hope that our routes may lie in the same direction — are you travelling towards Sacramento city or the mines?"

"Towards the mines; and, as I observed that your party came from the southward, I suppose you are going in the same direction. If so, I shall be delighted to join you."

"That's capital," replied Ned, "we shall be the better of having our party strengthened, and I am quite certain we could not have a more agreeable addition to it."

"Thank you for the compliment. As to the advantage of a strong party, I feel it a safeguard as well as a privilege to join yours, for, to say truth, the roads are not safe just now. Several lawless scoundrels have been roving about in this part of the country committing robberies and even murder. The Indians, too, are not so friendly as one could wish. They have been treated badly by some of the unprincipled miners; and their custom is to kill two whites for every red-man that falls. They are not particular as to whom they kill, consequently the innocent are frequently punished for the guilty."

"This is sad," replied Ned. "Are, then, all the Indian tribes at enmity with the white men?"

"By no means. Many tribes are friendly, but some have been so severely handled, that they have vowed revenge, and take it whenever they can with safety. Their only weapons, however, are bows and arrows, so that a few resolute white men, with rifles, can stand against a hundred of them, and they know this well. I spent the whole of last winter on the Yuba River; and, although large bands were in my neighbourhood, they never ventured to attack us openly, but they succeeded in murdering one or two miners who strayed into the woods alone."

"And are these murders passed over without any attempt to bring the murderers to justice?"

"I guess they are not," replied Maxton, smiling; "but justice is strangely administered in these parts. Judge Lynch usually presides, and he is a stern fellow to deal with. If you listen to what the hunter, there, is saying just now, you will hear a case in point, if I mistake not."

As Maxton spoke, a loud laugh burst from the men at the other end of the table.

"How did it happen?" cried several.

"Out wi' the yarn, old boy."

"Ay, an' don't spin it too tight, or, faix, ye'll burst the strands," cried Larry O'Neil, who, during the last half-hour, had been listening, open-mouthed, to the marvellous anecdotes of grizzlies and red-skins, with which the hunter entertained his audience.

"Wall, boys, it happened this ways," began the man, tossing off a gin-sling, and setting down the glass with a violence that nearly smashed it. "Ye see I wos up in the mountains, near the head waters o' the Sacramento, lookin' out for deer, and gittin' a bit o' gold now an' again, when, one day, as I was a-comin' down a gully in the hills, I comes all of a suddint on two men. One wos an Injun, as ugly a sinner as iver I seed; t'other wos a Yankee lad, in a hole diggin' gold. Before my two eyes were well on them, the red villain lets fly an arrow, and the man fell down with a loud yell into the hole. Up goes my rifle like wink, and the red-skin would ha' gone onder in another second, but my piece snapped — cause why? the primin' had got damp; an' afore I could prime agin, he was gone.

"I went up to the poor critter, and sure enough it wos all up with him. The arrow went in at the back o' his neck. He niver spoke again. So I laid him in the grave he had dug for himself, and sot off to tell the camp. An' a most tremendous row the news made. They got fifty volunteers in no time, and went off, hot-fut, to scalp the whole nation. As I had other business to look after, and there seemed more than enough o' fightin' men, I left them, and went my way. Two days after, I had occasion to go back to the same place, an' when I comed in sight o' the camp, I guess there was a mighty stir.

"'Wot's to do?' says I to a miner in a hole, who wos diggin' away for gold, and carin' nothin' about it.

"'Only scraggin' an Injun,' he said, lookin' up.

"'Oh,' says I, 'I'll go and see.'

"So off I sot, and there wos a crowd o' about two hundred miners round a tree; and, jest as I come up, they wos puttin' the rope round the neck of a poor wretch of an old grey-haired red-skin, whose limbs trembled so that they wos scarce able to hold him up.

"'Heave away now, Bill,' cried the man as tied the noose.

"But somethin' was wrong with the hitch o' the rope round the branch o' the tree, an' it wouldn't draw, and some time wos spent in puttin' it right. I felt sorter sorry for the old man, for his grave face was bold enough, and age more than fear had to do with the tremblin' o' his legs. Before they got it right again, my eye fell on a small band o' red-skins, who were lookin' quietly on; and foremost among them the very blackguard as shot the man in the galley. I knew him at once by his ugly face. Without sayin' a word, I steps for'ard to the old Injun, and takes the noose off his neck.

"'Halloo!' cried a dozen men, jumpin' at me. 'Wot's that for?' 'Scrag the hunter,' cries one. 'Howld yer long tongues, an' hear what he's got to say,' shouts an Irishman.

"'Keep your minds easy,' says I, mountin' a stump, 'an' seize that Injun, or I'll have to put a ball into him before he gits off' — for, ye see, I observed the black villain took fright, and was sneakin' away through the crowd. They had no doubt who I meant, for I pinted straight at him; and, before ye could wink, he was gripped, and led under the tree, with a face paler than ever I saw the face o' a red-skin before.

"'Now,' says I, 'wot for are ye scraggin' this old man?' So they told me how the party that went off to git the murderer met a band o' injuns comin' to deliver him up to be killed, they said, for murderin' the white man. An' they gave up this old Injun, sayin' he wos the murderer. The diggers believed it, and returned with the old boy and two or three others that came to see him fixed off.

"'Very good,' says I, 'ye don't seem to remimber that I'm the man what saw the murder, and told ye of it. By good luck, I've come in time to point him out — an' *this is him.*' An' with that I put the noose round the villain's neck and drawed it tight. At that he made a great start to shake it off, and clear away; but before you could wink, he was swingin' at the branch o' the tree, twinty feet in the air.

"Sarved him right," cried several of the men, emphatically, as the hunter concluded his anecdote.

"Ay," he continued, "an' they strung up his six friends beside him."

"Sarved 'em right too," remarked the tall man, whose partiality for the tin wash-hand basin and the tooth-brush we have already noticed. "If I had my way, I'd shoot 'em all off the face o' the 'arth, I would, right away."

"I'm sorry to hear they did that," remarked Larry O'Neil looking pointedly at the last speaker, "for it only shewed they was greater mortherers nor the Injuns — the red-skins morthered wan man, but the diggers morthered six.

"An' who are *you* that finds fault wi' the diggers?" inquired the tall man, turning full round upon the Irishman, with a tremendous oath.

"Be the mortial," cried the Irishman, starting up like a Jack-in-the-box, and throwing off his coat, "I'm Larry O'Neil, at yer sarvice. Hooroo! come on, av' ye want to be purtily worked off."

Instantly the man's hand was on the hilt of his revolver; but, before he could draw it, the rest of the company started up and over-powered the belligerents.

"Come, gentlemen," said the host of the ranche, stepping forward, "it's not worth while quarrelling about a miserable red-skin."

"Put on your coat, Larry, and come, let's get ready for a start," said Ned; "you can't afford to fight till you've made your fortune at the dig-gings. How far is it to the next ranche, landlord?"

This cool attempt to turn the conversation was happily successful. The next ranche, he was told, was about ten miles distant, and the road comparatively easy; so, as it was a fine moonlight night, and he was desirous of reaching the first diggings on the following day as early as possible, the horses and mules were saddled, and the bill called for.

When the said bill was presented, or rather, announced to them, our travellers opened their eyes pretty wide; they had to open their purses pretty wide too, and empty them to such an extent that there was not more than a dollar left among them all!

The supper, which we have described, cost them two and a half dollars — about ten shillings and sixpence a head, including a glass of bad brandy; but not including a bottle of stout which Larry, in the ignorance and innocence of his heart, had asked for, and which cost him *three dollars* extra! An egg, also, which Ned had obtained, cost him a shilling.

"Oh, morther!" exclaimed Larry, "why didn't ye tell us the price before we tuck them?"

"Why didn't ye ax?" retorted the landlord.

"It's all right," remarked Maxton. "Prices vary at the diggings, as you shall find ere long. When provisions run short, the prices become exorbitant; when plentiful, they are more moderate, but they are never *low*. However, men don't mind much, for most diggers have plenty of gold."

Captain Bunting and Bill Jones were unable to do more than sigh out their amazement and shake their heads, as they left the ranche and mounted their steeds; in doing which the captain accidentally, as usual, drove both spurs into the sides of his mule, which caused it to execute a series of manoeuvres and pirouettes that entertained the company for a quarter of an hour, after which they rode away over the plain.

It was a beautiful country through which they now ambled pleasantly. Undulating and partially wooded, with fine stretches of meadow land between, from which the scent of myriads of wild-flowers rose on the cool night air. The moon sailed low in a perfectly cloudless sky, casting the shadows of the horsemen far before them as they rode, and clothing hill and dale, bush and tree, with a soft light, as if a cloud of silver gauze had settled down upon the scene. The incident in the ranche was quickly banished, and each traveller committed himself silently to the full enjoyment of the beauties around him — beauties which appeared less like reality than a vision of the night.

CHAPTER IX.

A Night Ride in the Woods — The Encampment —
Larry's First Attempt to dig for Gold — An Alarm —
A Suspicious Stranger — Queer Creatures.

In less than two hours the travellers reached the second ranche, which was little better, in appearance or accommodation, than the one they had left. Having no funds, they merely halted to water their cattle, and then pushed forward.

The country became more and more undulating and broken as they advanced, and beyond the second ranche assumed the appearance of a hill country. The valleys were free from trees, though here and there occurred dense thickets of underwood, in which Maxton told them that grizzly-bears loved to dwell — a piece of information that induced most of the party to carry their rifles in a handy position, and glance suspiciously at every shadow. Large oaks and bay-trees covered the lower slopes of the hills, while higher up the white oak and fir predominated.

About an hour after midnight the moon began to descend towards the horizon, and Ned Sinton, who had been unanimously elected commander of the little band, called a halt in the neighbourhood of a rivulet, which flowed round the base of an abrupt cliff whose sides were partially clothed with scrubby bushes.

"We shall encamp here for the night, comrades," said he, dismounting; "here is water and food for our nags, a fine piece of greensward to spread our blankets on, and a thick-leaved oak to keep the dew off us. Now, Maxton, you are an old campaigner, let us see how soon you'll have a fire blazing."

"I'll have it ready before you get the camp kettles and pans out," answered Maxton, fastening his horse to a tree, seizing an axe, and springing into the woods on the margin of the stream.

"And, Captain Bunting," continued Ned, "do you water the horses and mules: our vaquero will help you. Jones will unpack the provender. Tom Collins and I will see to getting supper ready."

"An', may I ax, commodore," said Larry O'Neil, touching his hat, "wot *I'm* to do?"

"Keep out of everybody's way, and do what you pleases, Larry."

"Which manes, I'm to make myself ginerally useful; so here goes." And Larry, springing through the bushes, proceeded to fulfil his duties, by seizing a massive log, which Maxton had just cut, and, heaving it on his powerful shoulder, carried it to the camp.

Each was immediately busied with his respective duties. Bustling activity prevailed for the space of a quarter of an hour, the result of which was that, before the moon left them in total darkness, the ruddy glare of a magnificent fire lighted up the scene brilliantly, glanced across the sun-burnt faces and vivid red shirts of our adventurers, as they clustered round it, and threw clouds of sparks in among the leaves of the stout old oak that overspread the camp.

"Now, this is what I call uncommon jolly," said Captain Bunting, sitting down on his saddle before the cheerful blaze, rubbing his hands, and gazing round, with a smile of the utmost benignity on his broad, hairy countenance.

"It is," replied Maxton, with an approving nod. "Do you know, I have often thought, captain, that an Indian life must be a very pleasant one —"

"Av coorse it must," interrupted Larry, who at that moment was luxuriating in the first rich, voluminous puffs of a newly-filled pipe — "av coorse it must, *if* it's always like this."

"Ay," continued Maxton, "but that's what I was just going to remark upon — it's *not* always like this. As a general rule, I have observed, men who are new to backwoods life, live *at first* in a species of terrestrial paradise. The novelty and the excitement cause them to revel in all that is enjoyable, and to endure with indifference all that is disagreeable; sometimes, even, to take pleasure in shewing how stoically they can put up with discomfort. But after a time the novelty and excitement wear away, and then it is usual to hear the praises of Indian life spoken of immediately before and immediately after supper. Towards midnight — particularly if it should rain, or mosquitoes be numerous — men change their minds, and begin to dream of home, if they can sleep, or to wish they were there, if they can't."

"Get out! you horrid philosopher," cried Tom Collin as he gazed wistfully into the iron pot, whose savoury contents, (i.e., pork, flour, and beans), he was engaged in stirring. "Don't try to dash the cup of romance from our lips ere we have tasted it. Believe me, comrades, our friend Maxton is a humbug. I am an old stager myself; have lived the life of an Indian for months and months together, and I declare to you, I'm as jolly and enthusiastic *now* as ever I was."

"That may be quite true," observed Maxton, "seeing that it is possible you may have never been jolly or enthusiastic at all; but even taking your words as you mean them to be understood, they only tend to enforce what I have said, for, you know, the exception proves the rule."

"Bah! you sophisticator," ejaculated Tom, again inspecting the contents of the pot.

"Och, let him spake, an' be aisy," remarked Larry, with a look of extreme satisfaction on his countenance; "we're in the navelty an' excitement stage o' life just now, an faix we'll kape it up as long as we can. Hand me a cinder, Bill Jones, an' don't look as if ye wos meditatin' wot to say, for ye know that ye can't say nothin'."

Bill took no further notice of this remark than to lift a glowing piece of charcoal from the fire with his fingers, as deliberately as if they were made of iron, and hand it to O'Neil, who received it in the same cool manner, and relighted his pipe therewith.

"It strikes me we shall require all our jollity and enthusiasm to keep up our spirits, if we don't reach the diggings tomorrow," said Ned Sinton, as he busied himself in polishing the blade of a superb hunting-knife, which had been presented to him by a few college friends at parting; "you all know that our funds are exhausted, and it's awkward to arrive at a ranche without a dollar to pay for a meal — still more awkward to be compelled to encamp beside a ranche and unpack our own provisions, especially if it should chance to be a wet night. Do you think we shall manage to reach the diggings tomorrow, Maxton?"

"I am certain of it. Twelve miles will bring us to Little Creek, as it is called, where we can begin to take initiative lessons in gold-washing. In fact, the ground we stand on, I have not a doubt, has much gold in it. But we have not the means of washing it yet."

Larry O'Neil caught his breath on hearing this statement. "D'ye mane to tell me," he said, slowly and with emphasis, "that I'm maybe sittin' at this minute on the top o' rale goold?"

"You may be," answered Maxton, laughing.

"W'en ye don't know," remarked Bill Jones, sententiously, removing the pipe from his lips, and looking fixedly at his messmate, "W'en ye don't know *wot's* under ye, nor the coorse o' nature, w'ich is always more or less a-doin' things oncommon an' out o' the way, ye shouldn't ought to speckilate on wot ye know nothin' about, until ye find out how's her head, an' w'ich way the land lies. Them's my sentiments."

"Halloo! Larry," cried the captain and Tom Collins simultaneously, "look out for the kettle. It'll boil over."

Larry's feelings had been deeply stirred at that moment, so that the union of the sudden shout, with the profundity of Bill's remark, had the effect of causing him to clutch at the tea-kettle with such haste that he upset it into the fire.

"Oh! bad luck to ye!"

"Clumsy fellow!" ejaculated Ned. "Off with you to the creek, and refill it."

Larry obeyed promptly, but the mischance, after all, was trifling, for the fire was fierce enough to have boiled a twenty-gallon caldron in a quarter of an hour. Besides, the contents of the iron pot had to be discussed before the tea was wanted. In a few minutes supper was ready, and all were about to begin, when it was discovered that O'Neil was missing.

"Ho! Larry, come to supper!" shouted one.

"Hi! where are you?" cried another.

But there was no reply, until the captain put both hands to his mouth, and gave utterance to the nautical halloo with which, in days gone by, he was wont to hail the look-out at the main-top.

"Ay, ay, comin' sir—r—r," floated back on the night wind; and, shortly afterwards, the Irishman stumbled into camp with his hands, his face, and his clothes plentifully bedaubed with mud.

"Why, what have you been about?" inquired Ned.

"Diggin' for goold, sure. I've made a hole in the banks o' the creek with me two hands that ye might bury a young buffalo in, an' sorrow a bit o' goold have I got for me pains."

A general laugh greeted the enthusiastic digger, as he wiped his hands and sat down to supper.

"Musha! av I didn't git goold, I've dug up a mortial big appetite, anyhow. Hand me the wooden spoon, Mister Collins; it's more the gauge o' me pratie-trap than the pewter wans. D'ye know, comrades, I'm a'most sure I seed an Injun in the bush. Av it wasn't, it was a ghost."

"What like was he?"

"Look there, and judge for yourselves," cried O'Neil, jumping suddenly to his feet, and pointing towards the wood, where a solitary figure was seen dimly against the dark background.

Every man leaped up and seized his weapons.

"Who goes there?" shouted Ned, advancing towards the edge of the circle of light.

"A friend," was the reply, in English.

Relieved to find that he was not the advance-guard of a band of savages, Ned invited the stranger to approach, and immediately he stepped within the sacred circle of the camp-fire's light. This unexpected addition to the party was by no means a pleasant one. His complexion was exceedingly dark, and he wore a jet-black beard. In manners he was coarse and repulsive — one of those forbidding men who seem to be born for the purpose of doing evil in whatever position of life or part of the world they happen to be placed. The rude garments of the miner harmonised with the rugged expression of his bearded and bronzed face, and the harsh voice in which he addressed the party corresponded therewith.

"I s'pose ye'll not object to let me rest by yer fire, strangers?" he said, advancing and seating himself without waiting for a reply.

"You're welcome," answered Ned, curtly, for he neither liked the manners nor the aspect of the man.

"Ye might ha' wished us the top o' the mornin', I think," suggested Larry. "Here, try an' soften yer sperrits with a sup," he added, pushing a pewter plate of soup and a spoon towards him.

The man made no reply, but ate ravenously, as if he had been starving. When he had finished, he lighted his pipe, and drew his knees up to his chin as he warmed his hands before the blaze. Little information of any kind could be drawn out of this taciturn wanderer. To Ned's questions, he replied that he had been at the diggings on the Yuba River, which he described as being rich; that he had made enough gold to satisfy all his wants, and was on his way to San Francisco, where he intended to ship for England. His name, he said, was Smith.

He carried a short rifle, with a peculiarly large bore, and a heavy hunting-knife, the point of which was broken off. This last Bill Jones observed, as the man laid it down, after cutting up some tobacco, preparatory to refilling his pipe.

"A good knife! How did ye break it?" inquired Bill, taking up the weapon and examining it.

"Never you mind," answered the man, snatching it rudely from him, and sheathing it.

At this O'Neil regarded him with an angry expression.

"Faix, av ye wasn't livin', so to spake, in me own house, I'd make ye change yer tone."

"I don't mean no offence," said Smith, endeavouring to speak a little less gruffly. "The fact is, gents, I'm out o' sorts, 'cos I lost a grizzly bar in the hills an hour or two agone. I shot him dead, as I thought, and went up and drove my knife into his side, but it struck a rib and broke the pint, as ye see; and a'most afore I could get up a tree, he wos close up behind me. He went away after a while, and so I got clear off."

To the immense satisfaction of every one, this disagreeable guest arose after finishing his pipe, knocked the ashes out, shouldered his rifle, and, bidding his entertainers good-night, re-entered the forest, and disappeared.

"You're well away," remarked Tom Collins, looking after him; "I couldn't have slept comfortably with such a fellow in camp. Now, then, I'm going to turn in."

"So am I," said Maxton, rolling himself in a blanket, and pillowing his head on a saddle, without more ado.

In a few minutes the camp was as silent as it had previously been noisy. Captain Bunting's plethoric breathing alone told that human beings rested on that wild spot; and this, somewhat incongruously united with the tinkling of the rivulet hard by, and the howling of coyotes, constituted their lullaby. During the night the most of the travellers were awakened once or twice by a strange and very peculiar sensation, which led them to fancy the earth on which they reposed was possessed of life. The lazy members of the party lay still, and dreamily wondered until they fell asleep; those who were more active leaped up, and, lifting their blankets, gazed intently at the sward, which darkness prevented them from seeing, and felt it over with their hands, but no cause for the unwonted motion could be discovered, until the light of dawn revealed the fact that they had made their beds directly above the holes of a colony, of ground-squirrels, which little creatures, poking upwards with their noses in vain attempts to gain the upper world, had produced the curious sensations referred to.

Rough travelling, however, defies almost all disadvantages in the way of rest. Tired and healthy men will sleep in nearly any position, and at any hour, despite all interruptions, so that when our friends rose at daybreak to resume their journey, they were well refreshed and eager to push on.

CHAPTER X.

Game and Cookery — Arrival at the Diggings — Little
Creek — Law and Order in the Mines — Nooning at
Little Creek — Hard-up — Our Adventurers get Credit
and begin Work — A Yankee Outwitted.

Deer, hares, crows, blackbirds, magpies, and quails, were the creatures that bounded, scampered, hopped, and flew before the eyes of
the travellers at every step, as they wended their way pleasantly,
beneath a bright morning sun, over the hills and through the lesser
valleys of the great vale of the Sacramento. And all of these creatures,
excepting the crows and magpies, fell before the unerring and unexpectedly useful blunderbuss of Captain Bunting, passed a temporary
existence in the maw of the big iron pot, and eventually vanished into
the carnivorous jaws of Ned Sinton and his friends.

Crows were excluded from their bill of fare, because the whole
party had an unconquerable antipathy to them; and Larry said he had
"aiten many pies in his lifetime, but he had niver aiten magpies, and
he'd be shot av he wos goin' to begin now."

The duties of chief hunter devolved upon the captain, — first,
because he was intensely fond of shooting; and, secondly, because
game was so plentiful and tame, that it was difficult to avoid hitting
something, if one only fired straight before one. For the same reasons
the blunderbuss proved to be more effectual than the rifle. The captain used to load it with an enormous charge of powder and a handful
of shot — swan-shot, two sizes of duck-shot, and sparrow-hail, mixed,
with an occasional rifle-ball dropped in to the bargain. The recoil of
the piece was tremendous, but the captain was a stout buffer — if we
may be permitted the expression — and stood the shock manfully.

Stewed squirrels formed one of their favourite dishes, it was frequently prepared by Tom Collins, whose powers in the culinary
department proved to be so great that he was unanimously voted to
the office of *chef de cuisine* — Bill Jones volunteering, (and being
accepted), to assist in doing the dirty work; for it must be borne in
mind that the old relations of master and man no longer subsisted
amongst any of the travellers now — excepting always the native
vaquero. All were equal at starting for the diggings, and the various
appointments were made by, and with the consent of the whole party.

Little Creek diggings were situated in a narrow gorge of the
mountains, through which flowed a small though turbulent stream.
The sides of the hills were in some places thickly clothed with trees, in
others they were destitute not only of vegetation but of earth, the rock
on the steeper declivities of the hills having been washed bare by the
periodical heavy rains peculiar to those regions. Although wild and
somewhat narrow, this little valley was, nevertheless, a cheerful spot,

in consequence of its facing almost in a southerly direction: while, towards the east, there were several wide and picturesque gaps in the hills which seemed to have been made for the express purpose of letting the sun shine the greater part of the day upon the diggers while they were at work — an advantage, no doubt, when the weather was cool, but rather the reverse when it was hot.

The entrance to Little Creek was about two miles wide, undulating, and beautifully diversified, resembling pleasure grounds rather than a portion of the great wilderness of the far west; but the vale narrowed abruptly, and, about three miles further into the mountains, became a mere gap or ravine through which the streamlet leaped and boiled furiously.

It was an hour before noon when our travellers came suddenly upon the wide entrance to the valley.

"How beautiful!" exclaimed Ned, as he reined up to gaze in admiration over the flowering plain, with its groups of noble trees.

"Ay," said Maxton, enthusiastically, "you may well say that. There may be, perchance, as grand, but I am certain there is not a grander country in the world than America — the land of the brave and free."

Ned did not assent at once to the latter part of this proposition.

"You forget," he said, hesitatingly, as if disinclined to hurt the feelings or prejudices of his new friend, "you forget that it is the land of *slaves!*"

"I confess that I did forget that at the moment," answered Maxton, while the blood mounted to his forehead. "It is the foulest blot upon my country's honour; but I at least am guiltless of upholding the accursed institution, as, also, are thousands of my countrymen. I feel assured, however, that the time is coming when that blot shall be wiped away."

"I am glad, my friend," said Ned, heartily, "to hear you speak thus; to be frank with you, I could not have prevailed upon myself to have held out to you the hand of intimate friendship had you proved to be a defender of slavery."

"Then you'll form few friendships in this country," said Tom Collins, "for many of the Yankees here have been slave-holders in their day, and almost all defend the custom."

The conversation was interrupted at this point by Larry O'Neil uttering a peculiarly Hibernian exclamation, (which no combination of letters will convey,) and pointing in an excited manner to an object a few hundred yards in advance of them.

"What d'ye see, lad!" inquired Bill Jones, shading his eyes with his hand.

The whole party came to a halt, and gazed earnestly before them for a few minutes in silence.

"Och!" said O'Neil, slowly, and with trembling earnestness, "av me two eyes are spakin' truth, it's — it's a *goold digger!* — the first o' the goold-diggers!" — and Larry followed up the discovery with a mingled cheer and war-whoop of delight that rang far and wide over the valley.

At such an unwonted, we might almost say, appalling, sound, the "first o' the goold-diggers," — who was up to his waist in a hole, quietly and methodically excavating the earth on the river's bank with a pick-axe — raised his head, and, leaning on the haft of his pick, scrutinised the new arrivals narrowly.

"Hooray, my hearty!" shouted Larry, as he advanced at a gallop, followed by his laughing comrades. "The top o' the mornin' to ye — it's good luck I'm wishin' ye, avic. How are ye gittin' on in the goold way, honey?"

The rough-looking, dusty, and bearded miner, smiled good-humouredly, as he replied, in a gentle tone of voice that belied his looks — "Pretty well, friend; though not quite so well as some of my neighbours. I presume that you and your friends have just arrived at the mines?"

"Tear an' ages! it's a gintleman, I do belave," cried Larry, turning to his companions with a look of surprise.

The miner laughed at the remark, and, leaping out of the hole, did his best to answer the many questions that were put to him in a somewhat excited tone by the party.

"Where's the gold?" inquired Jones, gravely, going down on his knees at the side of the excavation, and peering into it. "I don't see none, wotsomediver."

"The dust is very fine here," answered the miner, "and not easily detected until washed. Occasionally we come upon nuggets and pockets in the dry parts of the river's bed, and the *cañons* of the hills, but I find it most profitable to work steadily down here where the whole earth, below the surface, is impregnated with fine particles of gold. Many of the diggers waste their time in *prospecting*, which word, I suppose you know, means looking out for new diggings; but, according to the proverb of my country, I prefer to remain 'contented wi' little, and cantie wi' mair.'"

"Are we far-distant from the other miners in this creek?" inquired Ned.

"No; you are quite close. You will come upon the colony after passing that bluff of trees ahead of you," answered the Scotchman; "but come, I will shew you the way; it is not far from nooning-time, when I usually cease work for a couple of hours."

So saying, the miner threw his pick-axe and shovel into the hole, and led the way towards the colony of Little Creek.

"Ain't you afraid some of the bad-looking scoundrels in these parts may take a fancy to your pick and shovel?" inquired the captain, as they rode along at a foot pace.

"Not in the least. Time was when I would have feared to leave them; for at one time neither life nor property was safe here, where so many ruffians congregated from all parts of the world; but the evil wrought its own cure at last. Murders and robberies became so numerous, that the miners took to Lynch law for mutual protection. Murderers and thieves were hanged, or whipped almost to death, with such promptitude, that it struck terror into the hearts of evil-doers; and the consequence is, that we of this valley are now living in a state of perfect peace and security, while in other districts, where the laws of Judge Lynch are not so well administered, murders and thefts are occasionally heard of. Here, if a man takes a fancy to go prospecting for a time, he has only to throw his pick and shovel into his claim, or upon his heap of dirt,[1] and he will be sure to find them there untouched on his return, even though he should be absent several weeks. Our tents, too, are left unwatched, and our doors unfastened, with perfect safety, though it is well-known that hundreds and thousands of dollars in gold-dust lie within. I do not mean to assert that we have attained to absolute perfection — a murder and a theft do occasionally occur, but such are the exceptions, security is the rule."

"Truly," said Ned Sinton, "you seem to live in a golden age in all respects."

"Not in all," answered the Scot; "the terrors of the law deter from open violence, but they do not enforce morality, as the language and deportment of miners generally too plainly shew. But here we are at the colony of Little Creek."

They rounded the projecting spur of one of the hills as he spoke, and the whole extent of the little valley opened up to view. It was indeed a romantic and curious sight. The vale, as we have said, was narrow, but by no means gloomy. The noontide sun shed a flood of light over the glistening rocks and verdant foliage of the hills on the left, and cast the short, rounded shadows of those on the right upon the plain. Through the centre of this the Little Creek warbled on its course; now circling round some wooded knoll, until it almost formed an island; anon dropping, in a quiet cascade, over the edge of a flat rock; in some places sweeping close under the base of a perpendicular cliff; in others shooting out into a lake-like expanse of shallow water across a bright-green meadow, as it murmured on over its golden bed towards the Sacramento.

Higher up the valley the cliffs were more abrupt. Dark pines and cedars, in groups or singly, hung on their sides, and gave point to the landscape, in the background of which the rivulet glittered like a silver thread where the mountains rose in peaks towards the sky.

Along the whole course of this rivulet, as far as the eye could trace it, searchers for gold were at work on both banks, while their white

---

1   "Dirt" is the name given among miners to the soil in which gold is found.

tents, and rude wooden shanties, were scattered, singly or in clusters of various extent, upon the wooded slopes, in every pleasant and suitable position. From the distance at which our party first beheld the scene, it appeared as if the miners were not men, but little animals grubbing in the earth. Little or no sound reached their ears; there was no bustle, no walking to and fro, as if the hundreds there assembled had various and diverse occupations. All were intently engaged in one and the same work. Pick-axe and shovel rose and fell with steady regularity as each individual wrought with ceaseless activity within the narrow limits of his own particular claim, or rocked his cradle beside it. Dig, dig, dig; rock, rock, rock; shovel, shovel, shovel, was the order of the day, as long as day lasted; and then the gold-hunters rested until recruited strength and dawning light enabled them again to go down into the mud and dig, and rock, and shovel as before.

Many, alas! rocked themselves into a fatal sleep, and dug and shovelled their own graves among these golden hills. Many, too, who, although they dug and toiled for the precious metal, had neither made it their god nor their chief good, were struck down in the midst of their heavy toils, and retired staggering to their tents, and there, still clad in their damp garments, laid their fevered heads on their saddles — not unfrequently on their bags of gold-dust — to dream of the distant homes and the loved faces they were doomed to see no more; and thus, dreaming in solitude, or watched, mayhap, by a rough though warm-hearted mate, breathed out their spirits to Him who gave them, and were laid in their last resting-place with wealth untold beneath them, and earth impregnated with gold-dust for their winding-sheet. Happy, thrice happy, the few who in that hour could truly say to Jesus, "Whom have I in heaven but Thee? and there is *none upon earth* that I desire beside Thee."

Just as our travellers approached the nearest and largest cluster of huts and tents, a sudden change came over the scene. The hour of noon had arrived, and, as if with one consent, the miners threw down their tools, and swarmed, like the skirmishers of an invading host, up from the stream towards the huts — a few of the more jovial among them singing at the full pitch of their lungs, but most of them too wearied to care for aught save food and repose.

Noon is the universal dinner-hour throughout the gold-mines, an hour which might be adopted with profit in every way, we venture to suggest, by those who dig for gold in commercial and legal ledgers and cash-books in more civilised lands. When the new-comers reached a moderately-sized log-cabin, which was the chief hotel of the colony, they found it in all the bustle of preparation for an immediate and simple, though substantial, meal.

"Can we have dinner!" inquired Ned, entering this house of entertainment, while his companions were unsaddling and picketing their horses and mules.

"To be sure ye can, my hearty," answered the smiling landlord, "if ye pay for it."

"That's just the reason I asked the question," answered Ned, seating himself on a cask — all available chairs, stool; and benches having been already appropriated by mud-bespattered miners, "because, you must know, I *can't* pay for it."

"Ho!" ejaculated mine host, with a grin, "hard-up, eh! got cleaned out with the trip up, an' trust to diggin' for the future? Well, I'll give ye credit; come on, and stick in. It's every man for himself here, an' no favour."

Thus invited, Ned and his friends squeezed themselves into seats beside the long *table d'hôte* — which boasted a canvas table-cloth, and had casks for legs — and made a hearty meal, in the course of which they obtained a great deal of useful information from their friend McLeod the Scotchman.

After dinner, which was eaten hurriedly, most of the miners returned to their work, and Ned with his friend; under the guidance of McLeod, went down to the river to be initiated into the mysteries of gold-digging and washing. As they approached several of the claims which their owners were busy working, a Yankee swaggered up to them with a cigar in his mouth, an impudent expression on his face, and a pick-axe on his shoulder.

"Guess you've just come to locate in them diggin's, strangers," he said, addressing the party at large, but looking at Ned, whose superior height and commanding cast of countenance proved him unmistakeably to be a leader.

"We have," replied Ned, who disliked the look of the man.

"Thought so. I'm jest goin' to quit an' make tracks for the coast. 'Bliged to cut stick on business that won't wait, I calc'late. It's plaguey unlucky, too, for my claim's turnin' out no end o' dollars, but I must sell it slick off so I don't mind to let ye have it cheap."

"Is your claim better than the others in the neighbourhood?" inquired Ned.

"Wall, I jest opine it is. Look here," cried the Yankee, jumping into his claim, which was a pit of about eight feet square and three deep, and delving the shovel into the earth, while Ned and his friends, besides several of the other miners, drew near to witness the result. Maxton and Tom Collins, however, winked knowingly at each other, and, with the Scotchman, drew back to the rear of the group.

The first shovelful of earth thrown up was absolutely full of glittering particles of gold, and the second was even more richly impregnated with the precious metal.

Ned and the captain stood aghast with amazement, and Bill Jones opened mouth and eyes to their utmost extent.

"Hooroo! och! goold galore! there it is at last!" shouted Larry O'Neil, tossing up his arms with delight. "Do buy it, Mr. Ned, darlint."

"I needn't turn up more, I guess," said the Yankee, carelessly throwing down his shovel, and filling the earth into a tin bowl or pan;

"I'll jest wash it out an' shew ye what it's like."

So saying he dipped the pan into the stream gently, and proceeded to wash out the gold. As this was done in the way usually practised by diggers, we shall describe it.

Setting down the tin pan of earth and water, the Yankee dipped both hands into it and stirred its contents about until it became liquid mud, removing the stones in the operation. It was then moved round quickly with a peculiar motion which caused some off the top to escape over the edge of the pan with each revolution; more water was added from time to time, and the process continued until all the earthy matter was washed away, and nothing but a kind of black sand, in which the gold is usually contained, remained at the bottom.

"There you are," cried the man, exultingly, lifting up a handful of the heavy and shining mixture; "fifteen dollars at least in two shovel-fuls. I'll sell ye the claim, if ye like, for two hundred dollars."

"I would give it at once," said Ned, feeling at the moment deeply troubled on account of his poverty; "but, to say truth, I have not a far-thing in the world."

A peculiar grin rested on the faces of the miners who looked on as he spoke, but before he could inquire the cause, Tom Collins stepped forward, and said:

"That's a first-rate claim of yours. What did ye say was your charge for it?"

"Three hundred dollars down."

"I'll tell ye what," rejoined Tom, "I'll give you *six* hundred dollars for it, if you take out another shovelful of dirt like *that!*"

This remark was greeted by a general laugh from, the bystanders, which was joined in by the Yankee himself as he leaped out of the hole, and, shouldering his shovel, went off with his friends, leaving Ned and some others of his party staring at each other in astonishment.

"What *does* it all mean?" he inquired, turning to Tom Coffins, whose laughing countenance shewed that he at least was not involved in mystery.

"It means simply that we were all taken for green-horns, which was quite a mistake, and that we were to have been thoroughly cheated — a catastrophe which has happily been prevented. Maxton and I determined to let the rascally fellow go as far as he could, and then step in and turn the laugh against him, as we have done."

"But explain yourself. I do not yet understand," repeated Ned, with a puzzled look.

"Why, the fact is, that when strangers arrive at the diggings, full of excitement and expectation, there are always a set of sharpers on the look-out, who offer to sell their claims, as they often say, 'for a mere song,' and in order to prove their worth, dig out a little dirt, and wash it, as you have just seen done; taking care beforehand, however, to mingle with it a large quantity of gold-dust, which, of course, comes to light, and a bargain is generally struck on the spot, when the sharper goes off with the price, and boasts of having 'done' a green-horn, for which he is applauded by his comrades. Should the fraud be detected before the completion of the bargain, as in our case, he laughs with the rest, and says, probably, he 'warn't so 'cute as usual.'"

"Och, the scoundrels!" cried Larry; "an' is there no law for sich doin's?"

"None; at least in most diggings men are left to sharpen their own wits by experience. Sometimes, however, the biter is pretty well bitten. There was a poor Chilian once who was deceived in this way, and paid four hundred dollars for a claim that was scarcely worth working. He looked rather put out on discovering the imposture, but was only laughed at by most of those who saw the transaction for his softness. Some there were who frowned on the sharper, and even spoke of lynching him, but they were a small minority, and had to hold their peace. However, the Chilian plucked up heart, and, leaping into his claim, worked away like a Trojan. After a day or two he hit upon a good layer of blue clay, and from that time he turned out forty dollars a day for two months."

"Ah! good luck to him," cried Larry.

"And did the sharper hear of it?" inquired the captain.

"That he did, and tried to bully the poor fellow, and get his claim back again; but there was a strong enough sense of justice among the miners to cause such an outcry that the scoundrel was fain to seek other diggings."

CHAPTER XI.

*Gold-Washing — Our Adventurers count their Gains,
and are Satisfied — The "R'yal Bank o' Calyforny"
begins to Prosper — Frying Gold — Night Visit to the
Grave of a Murdered Man — A Murderer Caught —
The Escape and Pursuit.*

Having escaped from the Yankee land-shark, as has been related, our adventurers spent the remainder of the day in watching the various processes of digging and washing out gold, in imbibing valuable lessons, and in selecting a spot for their future residence.

The two processes in vogue at Little Creek at that time were the *pan* and the *cradle* washing. The former has been already adverted to, and was much practised because the ground at that time was rich in the precious metal and easily wrought; the extreme simplicity, too, of the operation, which only required that the miner should possess a pick, a shovel, and a tin pan, commended it to men who were anxious to begin at once. An expert man, in favourable ground, could gather and wash a panful of "dirt," as it is called, every ten minutes; and there were few places in Little Creek that did not yield half-a-dollar or more to the panful, thus enabling the digger to work out gold-dust to the value of about twenty-five dollars, (five pounds sterling), every day, while occasionally he came upon a lump or nugget, equal, perhaps, to what he could produce by the steady labour of a week or more.

Many of the more energetic miners, however, worked in companies and used cradles, by means of which they washed out a much larger quantity of gold in shorter time; and in places which did not yield a sufficient return by the pan process to render it worth while working, the cradle-owners obtained ample remuneration for their toil.

The cradle is a very simple machine, being a semicircular trough, hollowed out of a log, from five to six feet long by sixteen inches in diameter. At one end of this is a perforated copper or iron plate, with a rim of wood round it, on which the "dirt" is thrown, and water poured thereon by one man, while the cradle is rocked by another. The gold and gravel are thus separated from the larger stones, and washed down the trough, in which, at intervals, two transverse bars, half-an-inch high, are placed; the first of these arrests the gold, which, from its great weight, sinks to the bottom, while the gravel and lighter substances are swept away by the current. The lower bar catches any particles of gold that, by awkward management, may have passed the upper one. Three men usually worked together at a rocker, one digging, one carrying the "dirt" in a bucket, and one rocking the cradle.

The black sand, which, along with the gold, is usually left after all the washing and rocking processes are completed, is too heavy to be separated by means of washing. It has therefore to be blown away from the gold after the mass has been dried over a fire, and in this operation great care is requisite lest the finer particles of gold should be blown off along with it.

The spot fixed on as the future residence of our friends was a level patch of greensward about a stone-cast from the banks of the stream, and twice that distance from the lowest cabin of the colony, which was separated and concealed from them by a group of wide-spreading oaks and other trees. A short distance behind the spot the mountains ascended in steep wooded slopes, and, just in front, the cliffs of the opposite hills rose abruptly from the edge of the stream, but a narrow ravine, that split them in a transverse manner, afforded a peep into the hills beyond. At evening, when the rest of the vale of Little Creek was shrouded in gloom, this ravine permitted the last beams of the setting sun to stream through and flood their encampment with rosy light.

Here the tent was pitched, and a fire kindled by Tom Collins, he being intrusted with the command of the party, whose duty it was to prepare the camp. This party included Bill Jones, Maxton, and the vaquero. Ned, the captain, and Larry O'Neil went, under the guidance of McLeod, to select a claim, and take lessons in washing.

"This seems a likely spot," said the Scotchman, as he led his new acquaintances down to the stream, a few yards below their encampment. "You may claim as much ground as you please, for there is room enough and to spare for all at the Creek yet. I would recommend a piece of ground of ten or twelve feet square for each to begin with."

"Here is a level patch that I shall appropriate, then," said Ned, smiling at the idea of becoming so suddenly and easily a landed proprietor — and to such an extent.

"I suppose we don't require to make out title-deeds!" remarked the captain.

"There's *my* title dade," cried Larry, driving his pick into the earth.

"You are right, Larry," said McLeod, laughing, "no other deed is required in this delightfully-free country."

"Ah! thin, it's quite to my taste; sure I niver thought to see the swate spot where I could pick out me property an' pick up me fortin' so aisy."

"Don't count your chickens quite so fast," said Ned, "may be it won't be so easy as you think. But let us begin and ascertain the value of our claims; I vote that Larry shall have the honour of washing out the first panful of gold, as a reward for his enthusiasm."

"A very proper obsarvation," remarked the Irishman, as he commenced work without further delay.

In the course of ten minutes part of the layer of surface-earth was removed, revealing the bluish-clay soil in which gold was usually found; the pan was filled with this "pay-dirt," as it was called, in contradistinction to the "surface-dirt," which didn't "pay," and was taken down to the stream, where Larry washed it out under the eye of McLeod; but he did it clumsily, as might be expected, and lost a considerable amount of valuable material. Still, for a first attempt, it was pretty well done, and his companions watched the result with feelings of excited earnestness, that they felt half-ashamed to admit even to themselves. There was mingled with this feeling a sort of vague incredulity, and a disposition to ridicule the idea that they were actually endeavouring to wash gold out of the ground; but when Larry's panful began to diminish, and the black sand appeared, sparkling with unmistakeably-brilliant particles of reddish-yellow metal, they felt that the golden dream was in truth becoming a sober reality.

As the process proceeded, and the precious metal began to appear, Larry's feelings found vent in abrupt remarks.

"Och! av me tshoo eyes — musha! there it is — goold intirely — av it isn't brass. Ah ye purty little stars! — O Larry, it's yerself as'll buy yer owld mother a pig, an' a coach to boot. Hooroo! Mr. Scotchman, I misremimber yer name, wot's that?"

Larry started up in excitement, and held up between his forefinger and thumb what appeared to be a small stone.

"Ha! friend, you're in luck. That's a small nugget," replied McLeod, examining the lump of gold. "It's worth ten dollars at least. I have worked often two or three weeks at a time without coming on such a chunk as that."

"Ye don't mane it! eh! Och! give it me. Hooray!" and the Irishman, seizing the little lump with trembling eagerness, rushed off, shouting and yelling, towards the camp to make his good fortune known to Bill Jones, leaving the pan of black sand unheeded. This Ned took up, and tried his hand at the work of washing. When done, the residue was found to be exceedingly rich, so he and the captain proceeded without loss of time to test their separate claims. Soon after, their obliging friend, the miner, returned to his own claim further down the valley, leaving them hard at work.

That night, when the bright stars twinkled down upon the camp at Little Creek, our gold-hunters, wet and tired, but hearty and hopeful, assembled round the fire in front of their little tent among the oak-trees.

The entire party was assembled there, and they were gazing earnestly, as might be expected of hungry men, into the frying-pan. But they did not gaze at *supper*. No, that night the first thing they fried was a mixture of black sand and gold. In fact, they were drying and blowing the result of their first day's work at the diggings, and their friend the Scotch miner was there to instruct them in the various processes of their new profession, and to weigh the gold for them, in his little pair of scales, when it should be finally cleared of all grosser substances.

As each panful was dried and blown, the gold was weighed, and put into a large white breakfast cup, the bottom of which was soon heaped up with shining particles, varying in size from the smallest visible speck, to little lumps like grains of corn.

"Bravo!" exclaimed McLeod, as he weighed the last pan, and added the gold to that already in the cup. "I congratulate you, gentlemen, on your success. The day's work is equal to one hundred and eighty dollars — about thirty dollars per man. Few men are so lucky their first day, I assure you, unless, as has been the case once or twice they should hit upon a nugget or two."

"That being the case, we shall have supper," cried Ned Sinton; "and while we are about it, do you go, Larry, to mine host of the hotel, and pay for the dinner for which he gave us credit. I don't wish to remain an hour in debt, if I can avoid it."

"Mister McLeod," slowly said Bill Jones — who, during the whole operation of drying and weighing the gold, had remained seated on a log, looking on with an expression of imbecile astonishment, and without uttering a word — "Mister McLeod, if I may make bold to ax, how much is one hundred and eighty dollars?"

Bill's calculating powers were of the weakest possible character.

"About thirty-six pounds sterling," replied McLeod. Bill's eyes were wide open before, but the extent to which he opened them on hearing this was quite alarming, and suggested the idea that they would never close again. The same incapacity to calculate figures rendered him unable to grasp correlative facts. He knew that thirty-six pounds in one day was a more enormous and sudden accumulation of wealth than had ever entered into his nautical mind to conceive of. But to connect this with the fact that a voyage and journey of many months had brought him there; that a similar journey and voyage would be required to reconduct him home; and that in the meantime he would have to pay perhaps five pounds sterling for a flannel shirt, and probably four pounds or more for a pair of boots, and everything else in proportion, was to his limited intellectual capacity a simple impossibility. He contented himself with remarking, in reference to these things, that "w'en things in gin'ral wos more nor ord'nar'ly oncommon, an' w'en incomprehensibles was blowin' a reg'lar hurricane astarn, so that a man couldn't hold on to the belayin'-pins he'd bin used to, without their breakin' short off an' lettin' him go spin into the lee-scuppers, — why wot then? a wise man's course wos to take in all sail, an' scud before it under bare poles."

Next day all the miners in the colony were up and at work by dawn. Ned and his friends, you may be sure, were not last to leave their beds and commence digging in their separate claims, which they resolved to work out by means of pan-washing, until they made a little ready cash, after which they purposed constructing two rockers, and washing out the gold more systematically and profitably.

They commenced by removing the surface-soil to the depth of about three feet, a work of no small labour, until the subsoil, or "pay-dirt," was reached. Of this they dug out a small quantity, and washed it; put the produce of black sand and gold into leathern bags, and then, digging out another panful, washed it as before. Thus they laboured till noon, when they rested for an hour and dined. Then they worked on again until night and exhaustion compelled them to desist; when they returned to camp, dried and blew away the sand, weighed the gold, which was put carefully into a general purse — named by Larry the "R'yal Bank o' Calyforny" — after which they supped, and retired to rest.

The gold was found at various depths, the "dirt" on the bed-rock being the richest, as gold naturally, in consequence of its weight, sinks through all other substances, until arrested in its downward career by the solid rock.

Of course, the labour was severe to men unaccustomed to the peculiar and constant stooping posture they were compelled to adopt, and on the second morning more than one of the party felt as if he had been seized with lumbago, but this wore off in the course of a day or two.

The result of the second day was about equal to that of the first; the result of the third a good deal better, and Bill, who was fortunate enough to discover a small nugget, returned to camp with a self-satis-fied swagger that indicated elation, though his visage expressed nothing but stolidity, slightly tinged with surprise. On the fourth day the cradles were made, and a very large portion of their gains thereby swept away in consequence of the unconscionable prices charged for every article used in their construction. However, this mattered little, Maxton said, as the increased profits of their labour would soon repay the outlay. And he was right. On the fifth day their returns were more than trebled, and that evening the directors of the "R'yal Bank o' Calyforny" found themselves in possession of capital amounting to one thousand one hundred and fifty dollars, or, as Tom Collins care-fully explained to Bill, about £230.

On the sixth day, however, which was Saturday, Larry O'Neil, who was permitted to work with the pan in the meantime, instead of assisting with the cradles, came up to dinner with a less hearty aspect than usual, and at suppertime he returned with a terribly lugubrious visage and a totally empty bag. In fact his claim had become suddenly unproductive.

"Look at that," he cried, swaggering recklessly into camp, and throwing down his bag; "I haven't got a rap; faix the bag's as empty as my intarior."

"What! have you worked out your claim already!" inquired Max-ton.

"Troth have I, and almost worked out me own body too."

"Well, Larry, don't lose heart," said Ned, as he dried the last panful of sand over the fire, "there are plenty more claims beside your present one. We, too, have not been as successful as before. I find the result is only fifty dollars amongst us all."

"That's a sudden falling off," remarked Tom Collins; "I fear the 'pay-dirt' is not deep near us, nevertheless it pays well enough to keep us going for some time to come. I shall mark off a new space on Monday."

"By the way, Maxton," asked Ned, handing over the frying-pan to Collins, who soon filled it with a less valuable, but at that time not less needful commodity than gold-dust — namely, pork and beef — "how do the miners spend the Sabbath here? I suppose not much better than in the cities."

"Here comes McLeod, who will be better able to answer than I am," replied Maxton.

The Scot strode into the camp as he spoke, and, saluting the party, seated himself beside the fire.

"I've come to tell you a piece of news, and to ask advice," he said; "but before doing so, I may tell you, in answer to your question, that the Sabbath here is devoted to drinking, gambling, and loafing about."

"I am not surprised to hear it," said Captain Bunting; "but pray what's i' the wind? Any new diggin's discovered?"

"A new digging certainly has been discovered," replied McLeod, with a peculiar smile, "but not precisely such a digging as one is wont to search for. The fact is, that in prospecting along the edge of the woods about a mile from this today, I came upon the body of a mur-dered man. It was covered with stones and branches of trees, which I removed, and I immediately recognised it to be that of a poor man who used to work not far from my own claim. I had missed him for more than a week past, but supposed that he had either gone to other dig-gings, or was away prospecting."

"Poor fellow!" said Ned; "but how, in such a matter, can *we* help you with advice?"

"Well, you see I'm in difficult circumstances," rejoined the Scot, "for I feel certain that I could point out the murderer, yet I cannot *prove* him to be such, and I want your advice as to what I should do."

"Let it be known at once that you have discovered the murdered man at any rate," said Maxton.

"That I have done already."

"Who do you think was the murderer?" inquired Ned.

"A man who used to live in the same tent with him at one time, but who quarrelled with him frequently, and at last went off in a rage. I know not what was the cause, but I heard him vow that he would be revenged. He was a great coarse fellow, more like a brute than a man, with a black beard, and the most forbidding aspect I think I ever saw."

"Wot wos his name?" inquired Bill Jones, while the party looked at each other as if they knew of such a character.

"Smith was the name he went by oftenest, but the diggers called him Black Jim sometimes."

"Ha! Smith — black beard — forbidding aspect! It strikes me that I too have seen the man," said Ned Sinton, who related to McLeod the visit paid to them in their camp by the surly stranger. While he was speaking, Larry O'Neil sat pondering something in his mind.

"Mister McLeod," said he, when Ned concluded, "will ye shew me the body o' this man? faix, I'm of opinion I can prove the murder; but, first of all, how is the black villain to be diskivered?"

"No difficulty about that. He is even now in the colony. I saw him in a gambling-house half-an-hour since. My fear is that, now the murder's out, he'll bolt before we can secure him."

"It's little trouble we'd have in preventin' that," suggested Larry.

"The consequences might be more serious, however, than you imagine. Suppose you were to seize and accuse him, and fail to prove the murder, the jury would acquit him, and the first thing he would do, on being set free, would be to shoot you, for which act the morality of the miners would rather applaud him than otherwise. It is only on cold-blooded, unprovoked murder and theft that Judge Lynch is severe. It is a recognised rule here, that if a man, in a row, should merely make a *motion* with his hand towards his pistol, his opponent is entitled to shoot him first if he can. The consequence is, that *bloody* quarrels are very rare."

"Niver a taste do I care," cried Larry; "they may hang me tshoo times over, but I'll prove the murder, an' nab the murderin' blackguard too."

"Have a care," said Ned; "you'll get yourself into a scrape."

"Make sure you are right before you act," added Maxton. Larry O'Neil paid no attention to these warnings. "Are ye ready to go, Mister McLeod?" said he, impatiently.

"Quite," replied the other.

"Then come along." And the two left the camp together, armed with their rifles, knives, revolvers, and a shovel.

It was a dark night. Heavy clouds obscured the face of the sky, through which only one or two stars struggled faintly, and rendered darkness visible. The two men passed rapidly along the little footpath that led from the colony to the more open country beyond. This gained, they turned abruptly to the right, and, entering a narrow defile, proceeded at a more cautious pace into the gloomy recesses of the mountains.

"Have a care, Larry O'Neil," whispered the Scotchman, as they advanced; "the road is not so safe here, owing to a number of pits which have been made by diggers after gold — they lie close to the edge of the path, and are pretty deep."

"All right; I'm lookin' out," replied Larry, groping his way after his comrade, at the base of a steep precipice.

"Here is the place," said McLeod, stopping and pushing aside the bushes which lined the path. "Keep close to me — there is no road."

"Are ye sure o' the spot?" inquired Larry, in an undertone, while a feeling of awe crept over him at the thought of being within a few yards of a murdered man in such a dark, wild place.

"Quite sure. I have marked the trees. See there!" He pointed to a white spot on the stem of a tree, where a chip had been cut off, and close to which was a mound of earth and stones. This mound the two men proceeded to break up, and in less than ten minutes they disentombed the body from its shallow grave, and commenced to examine the fatal wound. It was in an advanced state of decomposition, and they hurried the process by the light of a bright solitary star, whose flickering rays pierced through the overspreading branches and fell upon the ghastly countenance of the murdered man.

While thus occupied, they were startled by the sound of breaking twigs, as if some one were slowly approaching; whispering voices were also heard.

"It must be hereabouts," said a voice in a low tone; "he pointed out the place."

"Ho!" cried McLeod, who, with Larry, had seized and cocked his rifle, "is that you, Webster?"

"Halloo! McLeod, where are you?"

In another moment a party of miners broke through the underwood, talking loudly, but they dropped their voices to a whisper on beholding the dead body.

"Whist, boys," said Larry, holding up his hand. "We've jist got hold o' the bullet. It's flattened the least thing, but the size is easy to see. There's a wound over the heart, too, made with a knife; now that's wot I want to get at the bottom of, but I don't like to use me own knife to cut down."

As none of the others felt disposed to lend their knives for such a purpose, they looked at each other in silence.

"Mayhap," said the rough-looking miner who had been hailed by McLeod as Webster — "mayhap the knife o' the corpse is lyin' about."

The suggestion was a happy one. After a few minutes' search the rusty knife of the murdered man was discovered, and with this Larry succeeded in extracting from the wound over the heart of the body a piece of steel, which had evidently been broken off the point of the knife with which the poor wretch had been slain. Larry held it up with a look of triumph.

"I'll soon shew ye who's the murderer now, boys, av ye'll help me to fill up the grave."

This was speedily accomplished; then the miners, hurrying in silence from the spot, proceeded to the chief hotel of the place, in the gambling-saloon of which they found the man Smith, *alias* Black Jim, surrounded by gamblers, and sitting on a corner of the monte table watching the game. Larry went up to him at once, and, seizing him by the collar, exclaimed — "I've got ye, have I, ye murderer, ye black villain! Come along wid ye, and git yer desarts — call a coort, boys, an' sot up Judge Lynch."

Instantly the saloon was in an uproar. Smith turned pale as death for a moment, but the blood returned with violence to his brazen forehead; he seized Larry by the throat, and a deadly struggle would speedily have taken place between the two powerful men had not Ned Sinton entered at the moment, and, grasping Smith's arms in his Herculean gripe, rendered him helpless.

"What, comrades," cried Black Jim, with an oath, and looking fiercely round, "will ye see a messmate treated like this? I'm no murderer, an' I defy any one to prove it."

There was a move among the miners, and a voice was heard to speak of rescuing the prisoner.

"Men," cried Ned, still holding Smith, and looking round upon the crowd, "men —"

"I guess there are no men here," interrupted a Yankee; "we're all *gentlemen*."

"Being a man does not incapacitate one from being a gentleman," said Ned, sharply, with a look of scorn at the speaker, who deemed it advisable to keep silence.

After a moment's pause, he continued — "If this *gentleman* has done no evil, I and my friends will be answerable to him for what we have done; but my comrade, Larry O'Neil, denounces him as a murderer; and says he can prove it. Surely the law of the mines and fair play demand that he should be tried!"

"Hear! hear! well said. Git up a bonfire, and let's have it out," cried several voices, approvingly.

The miners rushed out, dragging Black Jim along with them to an open level space in front of the hotel, where stood a solitary oak-tree, from one of whose sturdy arms several offenders against the laws of the gold-mines had, at various times, swung in expiation of their crimes. Here an immense fire was kindled, and hither nearly all the miners of the neighbourhood assembled.

Black Jim was placed under the branch, from which depended part of the rope that had hanged the last criminal. His rifle, pistols, and knife, were taken from him, amid protestations of innocence, and imprecations on the heads of his accusers. Then a speech was made by an orator who was much admired at the place, but whose coarse language would scarcely have claimed admiration in any civilised community. After this Larry O'Neil stepped forward with McLeod, and the latter described all he knew of the former life of the culprit, and his conduct towards the murdered man. When he had finished, Larry produced the bullet, which was compared with the rifle and the bullets in Smith's pouch, and pronounced similar to the latter. At this, several of the miners cried out, "Guilty, guilty; string him up at once!"

"There are other rifles with the same bore," said Smith. "I used to think Judge Lynch was just, but he's no better I find than the land-sharks elsewhere. Hang me if you like, but if ye do, instead o' gittin' rid o' one murderer, ye'll fill the Little Creek with murderers from end to end. My blood will be on *your* heads."

"Save yer breath," said Larry, drawing Smith's knife from its scabbard. "See here, boys, sure two dovetails niver fitted closer than this bit o' steel fits the pint o' Black Jim's knife. Them men standin' beside me can swear they saw me take it out o' the breast o' the morthered man, an' yerselves know that this is the murderer's knife."

Almost before Larry had concluded, Smith, who felt that his doom was sealed, exerted all his strength, burst from the men who held him, and darted like an arrow towards that part of the living circle which seemed weakest. Most of the miners shrank back — only one man ventured to oppose the fugitive; but he was driven down with such violence, that he lay stunned on the sward, while Smith sprang like a goat up the steep face of the adjacent precipice. A dozen rifles instantly poured forth their contents, and the rocks rang with the leaden hail; but the aim had been hurried, and the light shed by the fire at that distance was uncertain.

The murderer, next moment, stood on the verge of the precipice, from which he wrenched a mass of rock, and, shouting defiance, hurled it back, with a fearful imprecation, at his enemies. The rock fell into the midst of them, and fractured the skull of a young man, who fell with a groan to the earth. Smith, who paused a moment to witness the result of his throw, uttered a yell of exultation, and darted into the mountains, whither, for hours after, he was hotly pursued by the enraged miners. But one by one they returned to the Creek exhausted, and telling the same tale — "Black Jim had made his escape."

CHAPTER XI.

Gold-Washing — Our Adventurers count their Gains,
and are Satisfied — The "R'yal Bank o' Calyforny"
begins to Prosper — Frying Gold — Night Visit to
the Grave of a Murdered Man — A Murderer
Caught — The Escape and Pursuit.

Having escaped from the Yankee land-shark, as has been related, our adventurers spent the remainder of the day in watching the various processes of digging and washing out gold, in imbibing valuable lessons, and in selecting a spot for their future residence.

The two processes in vogue at Little Creek at that time were the *pan* and the *cradle* washing. The former has been already adverted to, and was much practised because the ground at that time was rich in the precious metal and easily wrought; the extreme simplicity, too, of the operation, which only required that the miner should possess a pick, a shovel, and a tin pan, commended it to men who were anxious to begin at once. An expert man, in favourable ground, could gather and wash a panful of "dirt," as it is called, every ten minutes; and there were few places in Little Creek that did not yield half-a-dollar or more to the panful, thus enabling the digger to work out gold-dust to the value of about twenty-five dollars, (five pounds sterling), every day, while occasionally he came upon a lump or nugget, equal, perhaps, to what he could produce by the steady labour of a week or more.

Many of the more energetic miners, however, worked in companies and used cradles, by means of which they washed out a much larger quantity of gold in shorter time; and in places which did not yield a sufficient return by the pan process to render it worth while working, the cradle-owners obtained ample remuneration for their toil.

The cradle is a very simple machine, being a semicircular trough, hollowed out of a log, from five to six feet long by sixteen inches in diameter. At one end of this is a perforated copper or iron plate, with a rim of wood round it, on which the "dirt" is thrown, and water poured thereon by one man, while the cradle is rocked by another. The gold and gravel are thus separated from the larger stones, and washed down the trough, in which, at intervals, two transverse bars, half-an-inch high, are placed; the first of these arrests the gold, which, from its great weight, sinks to the bottom, while the gravel and lighter substances are swept away by the current. The lower bar catches any particles of gold that, by awkward management, may have passed the upper one. Three men usually worked together at a rocker, one digging, one carrying the "dirt" in a bucket, and one rocking the cradle.

The black sand, which, along with the gold, is usually left after all the washing and rocking processes are completed, is too heavy to be separated by means of washing. It has therefore to be blown away from the gold after the mass has been dried over a fire, and in this operation great care is requisite lest the finer particles of gold should be blown off along with it.

The spot fixed on as the future residence of our friends was a level patch of greensward about a stone-cast from the banks of the stream, and twice that distance from the lowest cabin of the colony, which was separated and concealed from them by a group of wide-spreading oaks and other trees. A short distance behind the spot the mountains ascended in steep wooded slopes, and, just in front, the cliffs of the opposite hills rose abruptly from the edge of the stream, but a narrow ravine, that split them in a transverse manner, afforded a peep into the hills beyond. At evening, when the rest of the vale of Little Creek was shrouded in gloom, this ravine permitted the last beams of the setting sun to stream through and flood their encampment with rosy light.

Here the tent was pitched, and a fire kindled by Tom Collins, he being intrusted with the command of the party, whose duty it was to prepare the camp. This party included Bill Jones, Maxton, and the vaquero. Ned, the captain, and Larry O'Neil went, under the guidance of McLeod, to select a claim, and take lessons in washing.

"This seems a likely spot," said the Scotchman, as he led his new acquaintances down to the stream, a few yards below their encampment. "You may claim as much ground as you please, for there is room enough and to spare for all at the Creek yet. I would recommend a piece of ground of ten or twelve feet square for each to begin with."

"Here is a level patch that I shall appropriate, then," said Ned, smiling at the idea of becoming so suddenly and easily a landed proprietor — and to such an extent.

"I suppose we don't require to make out title-deeds!" remarked the captain.

"There's *my* title dade," cried Larry, driving his pick into the earth.

"You are right, Larry," said McLeod, laughing, "no other deed is required in this delightfully-free country."

"Ah! thin, it's quite to my taste; sure I niver thought to see the swate spot where I could pick out me property an' pick up me fortin' so aisy."

"Don't count your chickens quite so fast," said Ned, "may be it won't be so easy as you think. But let us begin and ascertain the value of our claims; I vote that Larry shall have the honour of washing out the first panful of gold, as a reward for his enthusiasm."

"A very proper obsarvation," remarked the Irishman, as he commenced work without further delay.

In the course of ten minutes part of the layer of surface-earth was removed, revealing the bluish-clay soil in which gold was usually found; the pan was filled with this "pay-dirt," as it was called, in contradistinction to the "surface-dirt," which didn't "pay," and was taken down to the stream, where Larry washed it out under the eye of McLeod; but he did it clumsily, as might be expected, and lost a considerable amount of valuable material. Still, for a first attempt, it was pretty well done, and his companions watched the result with feelings of excited earnestness, that they felt half-ashamed to admit even to themselves. There was mingled with this feeling a sort of vague incredulity, and a disposition to ridicule the idea that they were actually endeavouring to wash gold out of the ground; but when Larry's panful began to diminish, and the black sand appeared, sparkling with unmistakeably-brilliant particles of reddish-yellow metal, they felt that the golden dream was in truth becoming a sober reality.

As the process proceeded, and the precious metal began to appear, Larry's feelings found vent in abrupt remarks.

"Och! av me tshoo eyes — musha! there it is — goold intirely — av it isn't brass. Ah ye purty little stars! — O Larry, it's yerself as'll buy yer owld mother a pig, an' a coach to boot. Hooroo! Mr. Scotchman, I misremimber yer name, wot's that?"

Larry started up in excitement, and held up between his forefinger and thumb what appeared to be a small stone.

"Ha! friend, you're in luck. That's a small nugget," replied McLeod, examining the lump of gold. "It's worth ten dollars at least. I have worked often two or three weeks at a time without coming on such a chunk as that."

"Ye don't mane it! eh! Och! give it me. Hooray!" and the Irishman, seizing the little lump with trembling eagerness, rushed off, shouting and yelling, towards the camp to make his good fortune known to Bill Jones, leaving the pan of black sand unheeded. This Ned took up, and tried his hand at the work of washing. When done, the residue was found to be exceedingly rich, so he and the captain proceeded without loss of time to test their separate claims. Soon after, their obliging friend, the miner, returned to his own claim further down the valley, leaving them hard at work.

That night, when the bright stars twinkled down upon the camp at Little Creek, our gold-hunters, wet and tired, but hearty and hopeful, assembled round the fire in front of their little tent among the oak-trees.

The entire party was assembled there, and they were gazing earnestly, as might be expected of hungry men, into the frying-pan. But they did not gaze at *supper*. No, that night the first thing they fried was a mixture of black sand and gold. In fact, they were drying and blowing the result of their first day's work at the diggings, and their friend the Scotch miner was there to instruct them in the various processes of their new profession, and to weigh the gold for them, in his little pair of scales, when it should be finally cleared of all grosser substances.

As each panful was dried and blown, the gold was weighed, and put into a large white breakfast cup, the bottom of which was soon heaped up with shining particles, varying in size from the smallest visible speck, to little lumps like grains of corn.

"Bravo!" exclaimed McLeod, as he weighed the last pan, and added the gold to that already in the cup. "I congratulate you, gentlemen, on your success. The day's work is equal to one hundred and eighty dollars — about thirty dollars per man. Few men are so lucky their first day, I assure you, unless, as has been the case once or twice they should hit upon a nugget or two."

"That being the case, we shall have supper," cried Ned Sinton; "and while we are about it, do you go, Larry, to mine host of the hotel, and pay for the dinner for which he gave us credit. I don't wish to remain an hour in debt, if I can avoid it."

"Mister McLeod," slowly said Bill Jones — who, during the whole operation of drying and weighing the gold, had remained seated on a log, looking on with an expression of imbecile astonishment, and without uttering a word — "Mister McLeod, if I may make bold to ax, how much is one hundred and eighty dollars?"

Bill's calculating powers were of the weakest possible character.

"About thirty-six pounds sterling," replied McLeod. Bill's eyes were wide open before, but the extent to which he opened them on hearing this was quite alarming, and suggested the idea that they would never close again. The same incapacity to calculate figures rendered him unable to grasp correlative facts. He knew that thirty-six pounds in one day was a more enormous and sudden accumulation of wealth than had ever entered into his nautical mind to conceive of. But to connect this with the fact that a voyage and journey of many months had brought him there; that a similar journey and voyage would be required to reconduct him home; and that in the meantime he would have to pay perhaps five pounds sterling for a flannel shirt, and probably four pounds or more for a pair of boots, and everything else in proportion, was to his limited intellectual capacity a simple impossibility. He contented himself with remarking, in reference to these things, that "w'en things in gin'ral wos more nor ord'nar'ly oncommon, an' w'en incomprehensibles was blowin' a reg'lar hurricane astarn, so that a man couldn't hold on to the belayin'-pins he'd bin used to, without their breakin' short off an' lettin' him go spin into the lee-scuppers, — why wot then? a wise man's course wos to take in all sail, an' scud before it under bare poles."

Next day all the miners in the colony were up and at work by dawn. Ned and his friends, you may be sure, were not last to leave their beds and commence digging in their separate claims, which they resolved to work out by means of pan-washing, until they made a little ready cash, after which they purposed constructing two rockers, and washing out the gold more systematically and profitably.

They commenced by removing the surface-soil to the depth of about three feet, a work of no small labour, until the subsoil, or "pay-dirt," was reached. Of this they dug out a small quantity, and washed it; put the produce of black sand and gold into leathern bags, and then, digging out another panful, washed it as before. Thus they laboured till noon, when they rested for an hour and dined. Then they worked on again until night and exhaustion compelled them to desist; when they returned to camp, dried and blew away the sand, weighed the gold, which was put carefully into a general purse — named by Larry the "R'yal Bank o' Calyforny" — after which they supped, and retired to rest.

The gold was found at various depths, the "dirt" on the bed-rock being the richest, as gold naturally, in consequence of its weight, sinks through all other substances, until arrested in its downward career by the solid rock.

Of course, the labour was severe to men unaccustomed to the peculiar and constant stooping posture they were compelled to adopt, and on the second morning more than one of the party felt as if he had been seized with lumbago, but this wore off in the course of a day or two.

The result of the second day was about equal to that of the first; the result of the third a good deal better, and Bill, who was fortunate enough to discover a small nugget, returned to camp with a self-satis-fied swagger that indicated elation, though his visage expressed nothing but stolidity, slightly tinged with surprise. On the fourth day the cradles were made, and a very large portion of their gains thereby swept away in consequence of the unconscionable prices charged for every article used in their construction. However, this mattered little, Maxton said, as the increased profits of their labour would soon repay the outlay. And he was right. On the fifth day their returns were more than trebled, and that evening the directors of the "R'yal Bank o' Calyforny" found themselves in possession of capital amounting to one thousand one hundred and fifty dollars, or, as Tom Collins care-fully explained to Bill, about £230.

On the sixth day, however, which was Saturday, Larry O'Neil, who was permitted to work with the pan in the meantime, instead of assisting with the cradles, came up to dinner with a less hearty aspect than usual, and at suppertime he returned with a terribly lugubrious visage and a totally empty bag. In fact his claim had become suddenly unproductive.

"Look at that," he cried, swaggering recklessly into camp, and throwing down his bag; "I haven't got a rap; faix the bag's as empty as my intarior."

"What! have you worked out your claim already!" inquired Max-ton.

"Troth have I, and almost worked out me own body too."

"Well, Larry, don't lose heart," said Ned, as he dried the last panful of sand over the fire, "there are plenty more claims beside your present one. We, too, have not been as successful as before. I find the result is only fifty dollars amongst us all."

"That's a sudden falling off," remarked Tom Collins; "I fear the 'pay-dirt' is not deep near us, nevertheless it pays well enough to keep us going for some time to come. I shall mark off a new space on Monday."

"By the way, Maxton," asked Ned, handing over the frying-pan to Collins, who soon filled it with a less valuable, but at that time not less needful commodity than gold-dust — namely, pork and beef — "how do the miners spend the Sabbath here? I suppose not much better than in the cities."

"Here comes McLeod, who will be better able to answer than I am," replied Maxton.

The Scot strode into the camp as he spoke, and, saluting the party, seated himself beside the fire.

"I've come to tell you a piece of news, and to ask advice," he said; "but before doing so, I may tell you, in answer to your question, that the Sabbath here is devoted to drinking, gambling, and loafing about."

"I am not surprised to hear it," said Captain Bunting; "but pray what's i' the wind? Any new diggin's discovered?"

"A new digging certainly has been discovered," replied McLeod, with a peculiar smile, "but not precisely such a digging as one is wont to search for. The fact is, that in prospecting along the edge of the woods about a mile from this today, I came upon the body of a murdered man. It was covered with stones and branches of trees, which I removed, and I immediately recognised it to be that of a poor man who used to work not far from my own claim. I had missed him for more than a week past, but supposed that he had either gone to other diggings, or was away prospecting."

"Poor fellow!" said Ned; "but how, in such a matter, can *we* help you with advice?"

"Well, you see I'm in difficult circumstances," rejoined the Scot, "for I feel certain that I could point out the murderer, yet I cannot *prove* him to be such, and I want your advice as to what I should do."

"Let it be known at once that you have discovered the murdered man at any rate," said Maxton.

"That I have done already."

"Who do you think was the murderer?" inquired Ned.

"A man who used to live in the same tent with him at one time, but who quarrelled with him frequently, and at last went off in a rage. I know not what was the cause, but I heard him vow that he would be revenged. He was a great coarse fellow, more like a brute than a man, with a black beard, and the most forbidding aspect I think I ever saw."

"Wot wos his name?" inquired Bill Jones, while the party looked at each other as if they knew of such a character.

"Smith was the name he went by oftenest, but the diggers called him Black Jim sometimes."

"Ha! Smith — black beard — forbidding aspect! It strikes me that I too have seen the man," said Ned Sinton, who related to McLeod the visit paid to them in their camp by the surly stranger. While he was speaking, Larry O'Neil sat pondering something in his mind.

"Mister McLeod," said he, when Ned concluded, "will ye shew me the body o' this man? faix, I'm of opinion I can prove the murder; but, first of all, how is the black villain to be diskivered?"

"No difficulty about that. He is even now in the colony. I saw him in a gambling-house half-an-hour since. My fear is that, now the murder's out, he'll bolt before we can secure him."

"It's little trouble we'd have in preventin' that," suggested Larry.

"The consequences might be more serious, however, than you imagine. Suppose you were to seize and accuse him, and fail to prove the murder, the jury would acquit him, and the first thing he would do, on being set free, would be to shoot you, for which act the morality of the miners would rather applaud him than otherwise. It is only on cold-blooded, unprovoked murder and theft that Judge Lynch is severe. It is a recognised rule here, that if a man, in a row, should merely make a *motion* with his hand towards his pistol, his opponent is entitled to shoot him first if he can. The consequence is, that *bloody* quarrels are very rare."

"Niver a taste do I care," cried Larry; "they may hang me tshoo times over, but I'll prove the murder, an' nab the murderin' black-guard too."

"Have a care," said Ned; "you'll get yourself into a scrape."

"Make sure you are right before you act," added Maxton. Larry O'Neil paid no attention to these warnings. "Are ye ready to go, Mister McLeod?" said he, impatiently.

"Quite," replied the other.

"Then come along." And the two left the camp together, armed with their rifles, knives, revolvers, and a shovel.

It was a dark night. Heavy clouds obscured the face of the sky, through which only one or two stars struggled faintly, and rendered darkness visible. The two men passed rapidly along the little footpath that led from the colony to the more open country beyond. This gained, they turned abruptly to the right, and, entering a narrow defile, proceeded at a more cautious pace into the gloomy recesses of the mountains.

"Have a care, Larry O'Neil," whispered the Scotchman, as they advanced; "the road is not so safe here, owing to a number of pits which have been made by diggers after gold — they lie close to the edge of the path, and are pretty deep."

"All right; I'm lookin' out," replied Larry, groping his way after his comrade, at the base of a steep precipice.

"Here is the place," said McLeod, stopping and pushing aside the bushes which lined the path. "Keep close to me — there is no road."

"Are ye sure o' the spot?" inquired Larry, in an undertone, while a feeling of awe crept over him at the thought of being within a few yards of a murdered man in such a dark, wild place.

"Quite sure. I have marked the trees. See there!" He pointed to a white spot on the stem of a tree, where a chip had been cut off, and close to which was a mound of earth and stones. This mound the two men proceeded to break up, and in less than ten minutes they disentombed the body from its shallow grave, and commenced to examine the fatal wound. It was in an advanced state of decomposition, and they hurried the process by the light of a bright solitary star, whose flickering rays pierced through the overspreading branches and fell upon the ghastly countenance of the murdered man.

While thus occupied, they were startled by the sound of breaking twigs, as if some one were slowly approaching; whispering voices were also heard.

"It must be hereabouts," said a voice in a low tone; "he pointed out the place."

"Ho!" cried McLeod, who, with Larry, had seized and cocked his rifle, "is that you, Webster?"

"Halloo! McLeod, where are you?"

In another moment a party of miners broke through the underwood, talking loudly, but they dropped their voices to a whisper on beholding the dead body.

"Whist, boys," said Larry, holding up his hand. "We've jist got hold o' the bullet. It's flattened the least thing, but the size is easy to see. There's a wound over the heart, too, made with a knife; now that's wot I want to get at the bottom of, but I don't like to use me own knife to cut down."

As none of the others felt disposed to lend their knives for such a purpose, they looked at each other in silence.

"Mayhap," said the rough-looking miner who had been hailed by McLeod as Webster — "mayhap the knife o' the corpse is lyin' about."

The suggestion was a happy one. After a few minutes' search the rusty knife of the murdered man was discovered, and with this Larry succeeded in extracting from the wound over the heart of the body a piece of steel, which had evidently been broken off the point of the knife with which the poor wretch had been slain. Larry held it up with a look of triumph.

"I'll soon shew ye who's the murderer now, boys, av ye'll help me to fill up the grave."

This was speedily accomplished; then the miners, hurrying in silence from the spot, proceeded to the chief hotel of the place, in the gambling-saloon of which they found the man Smith, *alias* Black Jim, surrounded by gamblers, and sitting on a corner of the monte table watching the game. Larry went up to him at once, and, seizing him by the collar, exclaimed — "I've got ye, have I, ye murderer, ye black villain! Come along wid ye, and git yer desarts — call a coort, boys, an' sot up Judge Lynch."

Instantly the saloon was in an uproar. Smith turned pale as death for a moment, but the blood returned with violence to his brazen forehead; he seized Larry by the throat, and a deadly struggle would speedily have taken place between the two powerful men had not Ned Sinton entered at the moment, and, grasping Smith's arms in his Herculean gripe, rendered him helpless.

"What, comrades," cried Black Jim, with an oath, and looking fiercely round, "will ye see a messmate treated like this? I'm no murderer, an' I defy any one to prove it."

There was a move among the miners, and a voice was heard to speak of rescuing the prisoner.

"Men," cried Ned, still holding Smith, and looking round upon the crowd, "men —"

"I guess there are no men here," interrupted a Yankee; "we're all *gentlemen.*"

"Being a man does not incapacitate one from being a gentleman," said Ned, sharply, with a look of scorn at the speaker, who deemed it advisable to keep silence.

After a moment's pause, he continued — "If this *gentleman* has done no evil, I and my friends will be answerable to him for what we have done; but my comrade, Larry O'Neil, denounces him as a murderer; and says he can prove it. Surely the law of the mines and fair play demand that he should be tried!"

"Hear! hear! well said. Git up a bonfire, and let's have it out," cried several voices, approvingly.

The miners rushed out, dragging Black Jim along with them to an open level space in front of the hotel, where stood a solitary oak-tree, from one of whose sturdy arms several offenders against the laws of the gold-mines had, at various times, swung in expiation of their crimes. Here an immense fire was kindled, and hither nearly all the miners of the neighbourhood assembled.

Black Jim was placed under the branch, from which depended part of the rope that had hanged the last criminal. His rifle, pistols, and knife, were taken from him, amid protestations of innocence, and imprecations on the heads of his accusers. Then a speech was made by an orator who was much admired at the place, but whose coarse language would scarcely have claimed admiration in any civilised community. After this Larry O'Neil stepped forward with McLeod, and the latter described all he knew of the former life of the culprit, and his conduct towards the murdered man. When he had finished, Larry produced the bullet, which was compared with the rifle and the bullets in Smith's pouch, and pronounced similar to the latter. At this, several of the miners cried out, "Guilty, guilty; string him up at once!"

"There are other rifles with the same bore," said Smith. "I used to think Judge Lynch was just, but he's no better I find than the landsharks elsewhere. Hang me if you like, but if ye do, instead o' gittin' rid o' one murderer, ye'll fill the Little Creek with murderers from end to end. My blood will be on *your* heads."

"Save yer breath," said Larry, drawing Smith's knife from its scabbard. "See here, boys, sure two dovetails niver fitted closer than this bit o' steel fits the pint o' Black Jim's knife. Them men standin' beside me can swear they saw me take it out o' the breast o' the morthered man, an' yerselves know that this is the murderer's knife."

Almost before Larry had concluded, Smith, who felt that his doom was sealed, exerted all his strength, burst from the men who held him, and darted like an arrow towards that part of the living circle which seemed weakest. Most of the miners shrank back — only one man ventured to oppose the fugitive; but he was driven down with such violence, that he lay stunned on the sward, while Smith sprang like a goat up the steep face of the adjacent precipice. A dozen rifles instantly poured forth their contents, and the rocks rang with the leaden hail; but the aim had been hurried, and the light shed by the fire at that distance was uncertain.

The murderer, next moment, stood on the verge of the precipice, from which he wrenched a mass of rock, and, shouting defiance, hurled it back, with a fearful imprecation, at his enemies. The rock fell into the midst of them, and fractured the skull of a young man, who fell with a groan to the earth. Smith, who paused a moment to witness the result of his throw, uttered a yell of exultation, and darted into the mountains, whither, for hours after, he was hotly pursued by the enraged miners. But one by one they returned to the Creek exhausted, and telling the same tale — "Black Jim had made his escape."

CHAPTER XII.

Sabbath at the Diggings — Larry O'Neil takes to Wandering, and meets with Adventures — An Irish Yankee discovered — Terrible Calamities befall Travellers on the Overland Route.

There is no country in our fallen world, however debased and morally barren, in which there does not exist a few green spots where human tenderness and sympathy are found to grow. The atmosphere of the gold-regions of California was, indeed, clouded to a fearful extent with the soul-destroying vapours of worldliness, selfishness, and ungodliness, which the terrors of Lynch law alone restrained from breaking forth in all their devastating strength.

And this is not to be wondered at, for Europe and America naturally poured the flood of their worst inhabitants over the land, in eager search for that gold, the *love of which*, we are told in Sacred Writ, "is the root of all evil." True, there were many hundreds of estimable men who, failing, from adverse circumstances, to make a livelihood in their native lands, sought to better their fortunes in the far west; but, in too many cases, the gold-fever which raged there soon smote them down; and men who once regarded gold as the means to an end, came at last to esteem gold to be the end, and used every means, fair and foul, to obtain it. Others there were, whose constitutions were proof against the national disease; whose hearts deemed *love* to be the highest bliss of man, and doing good his greatest happiness.

But stilling and destructive though the air of the gold-mines was, there were a few hardy plants of moral goodness which defied it — and some of these bloomed in the colony of Little Creek.

The Sabbath morning dawned on Ned Sinton and his friends — the first Sabbath since they had begun to dig for gold. On that day the miners rested from their work. Shovel and pick lay quiet in the innumerable pits that had been dug throughout the valley; no cradle was rocked, no pan of golden earth was washed. Even reckless men had come to know from experience, that the Almighty in His goodness had created the Sabbath for the special benefit of man's *body* as well as his soul, and that they wrought better during the six days of the week when they rested on the seventh.

Unfortunately they believed only what *experience* taught them; they kept the Sabbath according to the letter, not according to the spirit; and although they did not work, they did not refrain from "thinking their own thoughts and finding their own pleasure," on God's holy day. Early in the morning they began to wander idly about from hut to hut, visited frequently the grog-shops, and devoted themselves to gambling, which occupation materially marred even the physical rest they might otherwise have enjoyed.

"Comrades," said Ned Sinton, as the party sat inside their tent, round the napkin on which breakfast was spread, "it is long since we have made any difference between Saturday and Sunday, and I think it would be good for us all if we were to begin now. Since quitting San Francisco, the necessity of pushing forward on our journey has prevented our doing so hitherto. How far we were right in regarding rapid travelling as being *necessary*, I won't stop to inquire; but I think it would be well if we should do a little more than merely rest from work on the Sabbath. I propose that, besides doing this, we should read a chapter of the Bible together as a family, morning and evening on Sundays. What say you?"

There was a pause. It was evident that conflicting feelings were at work among the party.

"Perhaps you're right," said Maxton; "I confess that I have troubled myself very little about religion since I came out here, but my conscience has often reproached me for it."

"Don't you think, messmates," said Captain Bunting, lighting his pipe, "that if it gets wind the whole colony will be laughin' at us?"

"Sure they may laugh," said Larry O'Neil, "an' after that they may cry, av it'll do them good. Wot's the differ to us?"

"I don't agree with you, Ned," said Tom Collins, somewhat testily; "for my part I like to see men straightforward, all fair and aboveboard, as the captain would say. Hypocrisy is an abominable vice, whether it is well meaning or ill meaning, and I don't see the use of pretending to be religious when we are not."

"Tom," replied Ned, in an earnest voice, "don't talk lightly of serious things. I don't *pretend* to be religious, but I do *desire* to be so: and I think it would be good for all of us to read a portion of God's Word on His own day, both for the purpose of obeying and honouring Him, and of getting our minds filled, for a short time at least, with other thoughts than those of gold-hunting. In doing this there is no hypocrisy."

"Well, well," rejoined Tom, "I'll not object if the rest are agreed."

"Agreed," was the unanimous reply. So Ned rose, and, opening his portmanteau, drew forth the little Bible that had been presented to him by old Mr. Shirley on the day of his departure from home.

From that day forward, every Sabbath morning and evening, Ned Sinton read a portion of the Word of God to his companions, as long as they were together; and each of the party afterwards, at different times, confessed that, from the time the reading of the Bible was begun, he felt happier than he did before.

After breakfast they broke up, and went out to stroll for an hour or two upon the wooded slopes of the mountains. Ned and Tom Collins went off by themselves, the others, with the exception of Larry, walked out together.

That morning Larry O'Neil felt less sociable than was his wont, so he sallied forth alone. For some time he sauntered about with his hands in his pockets, his black pipe in his mouth, a thick oak cudgel, of his own making, under his arm, and his hat set jauntily on one side of his head. He went along with an easy swagger, and looked particularly reckless, but no man ever belied his looks more thoroughly. The swagger was unintentional, and the recklessness did not exist. On the contrary, the reading of the Bible had brought back to his mind a flood of home memories, which forced more than one tear from his susceptible heart into his light-blue eye, as he wandered in memory over the green hills of Erin.

But the scenes that passed before him as he roamed about among the huts and tents of the miners soon drew his thoughts to subjects less agreeable to contemplate. On week-days the village, if we may thus designate the scattered groups of huts and tents, was comparatively quiet, but on Sundays it became a scene of riot and confusion. Not only was it filled with its own idle population of diggers, but miners from all the country round, within a circuit of eight or ten miles, flocked into it for the purpose of buying provisions for the week, as well as for the purpose of gambling and drinking, this being the only day in all the week in which they indulged in what they termed "a spree."

Consequently the gamblers and store-keepers did more business on Sunday than on any other day. The place was crowded with men in their rough, though picturesque, bandit-like costumes, rambling about from store to store, drinking and inviting friends to drink, or losing in the gaming-saloons all the earnings of a week of hard, steady toil — toil more severe than is that of navvies or coal-heavers. There seemed to be an irresistible attraction in these gambling-houses. Some men seemed unable to withstand the temptation, and they seldom escaped being fleeced. Yet they returned, week after week, to waste in these dens of iniquity the golden treasure gathered with so much labour during their six working days.

Larry O'Neil looked through the doorway of one of the gambling-houses as he passed, and saw men standing and sitting round the tables, watching with eager faces the progress of the play, while ever and anon one of them would reel out, more than half-drunk with excitement and brandy. Passing on through the crowded part of the village, which looked as if a fair were being held there, he entered the narrow footpath that led towards the deeper recesses at the head of the valley. O'Neil had not yet, since his arrival, found time to wander far from his own tent. It was therefore with a feeling of great delight that he left the scene of riot behind him, and, turning into a bypath that led up one of the narrow ravines, opening into the larger valley, strolled several miles into deep solitudes that were in harmony with his feelings.

The sun streamed through the entrance to this ravine, bathing with a flood of light crags and caves and bush-encompassed hollows, that at other times were shrouded in gloom. As the Irishman stood gazing in awe and admiration at the wild, beautiful scene, beyond which were seen the snowy peaks of the Sierra Nevada, he observed a small solitary tent pitched on a level patch of earth at the brow of a low cliff. Curiosity prompted him to advance and ascertain what unsociable creature dwelt in it. A few minutes sufficed to bring him close upon it, and he was about to step forward, when the sound of a female voice arrested him. It was soft and low, and the accents fell upon his ear with the power of an old familiar song. Being at the back of the tent, he could not see who spoke, but, from the monotonous regularity of the tone, he knew that the woman was reading. He passed noiselessly round to the front, and peeping over the tops of bushes, obtained a view of the interior.

The reader was a young woman, whose face, which was partially concealed by a mass of light-brown hair as she bent over her book, seemed emaciated and pale. Looking up just as Larry's eye fell upon her, she turned towards a man whose gaunt, attenuated form lay motionless on a pile of brushwood beside her, and said, tenderly:

"Are ye tired, Patrick, dear, or would you like me to go on?"

Larry's heart gave his ribs such a thump at that moment that he felt surprised the girl did not hear it. But he could not approach; he was rooted to the earth as firmly, though not as permanently, as the bush behind which he stood. An Irish voice, and an Irish girl, heard and seen so unexpectedly, quite took away his breath.

The sick man made some reply which was not audible, and the girl, shutting the book, looked up for a few moments, as if in silent prayer, then she clasped her hands upon her knees, and laying her head upon them, remained for some time motionless. The hands were painfully thin, as was her whole frame. The face was what might have been pretty at one time, although it was haggard enough now, but the expression was peculiarly sorrowful.

In a few minutes she looked up again, and spread the ragged blanket more carefully over the shoulders of the sick man, and Larry, feeling that he was at that time in the questionable position of an eavesdropper, left his place of concealment, and stood before the tent.

The sick man saw him instantly, and, raising himself slightly, exclaimed, "Who goes there? Sure I can't git lave to die in pace!"

The familiar tones of a countryman's voice fell pleasantly on Larry's ear as he sprang into the tent, and, seizing the sick man's hand, cried, "A blissin' on the mouth that said that same. O Pat, darlint! I'm glad to mate with ye. What's the matter with ye? Tell me now, an' don't be lookin' as if ye'd seen a ghost."

"Kape back," said the girl, pushing Larry aside, with a half-pleased, half-angry expression. "Don't ye see that ye've a'most made him faint? He's too wake intirely to be —"

"Ah! then, cushla, forgive me; I wint and forgot meself. Blissin's on yer pale face! sure yer Irish too."

Before the girl could reply to this speech, which was uttered in a tone of the deepest sympathy, the sick man recovered sufficiently to say —

"Sit down, friend. How comed ye to larn me name? I guess I never saw ye before."

"Sure, didn't I hear yer wife say it as I come for'ard to the tint," answered Larry, somewhat staggered at the un-Irish word "guess."

"He is my brother," remarked the girl.

"Troth, ye've got a dash o' the Yankee brogue," said Larry, with a puzzled look; "did ye not come from the owld country?"

The sick man seemed too much exhausted to reply, so the girl said, —

"Our father and mother were Irish, and left their own country to sittle in America. We have never seen Ireland, my brother nor I, but we think of it as almost our own land. Havin' been brought up in the woods, and seein' a'most no one but father and mother for days an' weeks at a time, we've got a good deal o' the Irish tone."

"Ah! thin, ye have reason to be thankful for that same," remarked Larry, who was a little disappointed that his new friends were not altogether Irish; but, after a few minutes' consideration, he came to the conclusion, that people whose father and mother were natives of the Emerald Isle could no more be Americans, simply because they happened to be born in America, than they could be fish if they chanced to be born at sea. Having settled this point to his satisfaction, he proceeded to question the girl as to their past history and the cause of their present sad condition, and gradually obtained from her the information that their father and mother were dead, and that, having heard of the mines of California, her brother had sold off his farm in the backwoods, and proceeded by the overland route to the new land of gold, in company with many other western hunters and farmers. They reached it, after the most inconceivable sufferings, in the beginning of winter, and took up their abode at Little Creek.

The rush of emigration from the western states to California, by the overland route, that took place at this time, was attended with the most appalling sufferings and loss of life. Men sold off their snug farms, packed their heavy waggons with the necessaries for a journey, with their wives and little ones, over a wilderness more than two thousand miles in extent, and set off by scores over the prairies towards the Ultima Thule of the far west. The first part of their journey was prosperous enough, but the weight of their waggons rendered the pace slow, and it was late in the season ere they reached the great barrier of the Rocky Mountains. But severe although the sufferings of those first emigrants were, they were as nothing compared with the dire calamities that befell those who started from home later in the season. All along the route the herbage was cropped bare by those who had gone before; their oxen broke down; burning sandy deserts presented themselves when the wretched travellers were well-nigh exhausted; and when at length they succeeded in reaching the great mountain-chain, its dark passes were filled with the ice and snow of early winter.

Hundreds of men, women, and children, fell down and died on the burning plain, or clambered up the rugged heights to pillow their dying heads at last on wreaths of snow. To add to the unheard-of miseries of these poor people, scurvy in its worst forms attacked them; and the air of many of their camping places was heavy with the stench arising from the dead bodies of men and animals that had perished by the way.

"It was late in the season," said Kate Morgan, as Larry's new friend was named, "when me brother Patrick an' I set off with our waggon and oxen, an' my little sister Nelly, who was just able to run about, with her curly yellow hair streamin' over her purty shoulders, an' her laughin' blue eyes, almost spakin' when they looked at ye."

The poor girl spoke with deep pathos as she mentioned Nelly's name, while Larry O'Neil sat with his hands clasped, gazing at her with an expression of the deepest commiseration.

"We got pretty well on at first," she continued, after a pause, "because our waggon was lighter than most o' the others; but it was near winter before we got to the mountains, an' then our troubles begood. First of all, one o' the oxen fell, and broke its leg. Then darlin' Nelly fell sick, and Patrick had to carry her on his back up the mountains, for I had got so weak meself that I wasn't fit to take her up. All the way over I was troubled with one o' the emigrants that kep' us company — there was thirty o' us altogether — he was a very bad man, and none o' us liked him. He took a fancy to me, an' asked me to be his wife so often that I had to make Patrick order him to kape away from us altogether. He wint off in a black rage, swearin' he'd be revenged, — an' oh!" continued Kate, wringing her hands, "he kept his word. One day there was a dispute between our leaders which way we should go, for we had got to two passes in the mountains; so one party went one way, and we went another. Through the night, my — my lover came into our camp to wish me good-bye, he said, for the last time, as he was goin' with the other party. After he was gone, I missed Nelly, and went out to seek for her among the tents o' my neighbours, but she was nowhere to be found. At once I guessed he had taken her away, for well did he know I would sooner have lost my life than my own darlin' Nell."

Again the girl paused a few moments; then she resumed, in a low voice —

"We never saw him or Nelly again. It is said the whole party perished, an' I believe it, for they were far spent, and the road they took, I've been towld, is worse than the one we took. It was dead winter when we arrived, and Patrick and me came to live here. We made a good deal at first by diggin', but we both fell sick o' the ague, and we've been scarce able to kape us alive till now. But it won't last long. Dear

Patrick is broken down entirely, as ye see, and I haven't strength a'most to go down to the diggin's for food. I haven't been there for a month, for it's four miles away, as I dare say ye know. We'll both be at rest soon."

"Ah! now, don't say that again, avic," cried Larry, smiting his thigh with energy; "ye'll be nothin' o' the sort, that ye won't; sure yer brother Pat is slaipin' now like an infant, he is, an' I'll go down meself to the stores and git ye medicines an' a doctor, an' what not. Cheer up, now —"

Larry's enthusiastic efforts to console his new friend were interrupted by the sick man, who awoke at the moment, and whispered the word "food."

His sister rose, and taking up a small tin pan that simmered on the fire in front of the tent, poured some of its contents into a dish.

"What is it ye give him?" inquired Larry, taking the dish from the girl's hands and putting it to his lips. He instantly spat out the mouthful, for it was soup made of rancid pork, without vegetables of any kind.

"'Tis all I've got left," said the girl. "Even if I was able to go down for more, he wouldn't let me; but I couldn't, for I've tried more than once, and near died on the road. Besides, I haven't a grain o' goold in the tent."

"O morther! Tare an' ages!" cried Larry, staring first at the girl and then at her brother, while he slapped his thighs and twisted his fingers together as if he wished to wrench them out of joint.

"Howld on, faix I'll do it. Don't give it him, plaze; howld on, *do!*"

Larry O'Neil turned round as he spoke, seized his cudgel, sprang right over the bushes in front of the tent, and in two minutes more was seen far down the ravine, spurning the ground beneath him as if life and death depended on the race.

CHAPTER XIII.

*Kindness to Strangers in Distress — Remarks in
Reference to Early Rising — Diggings wax
Unproductive — Ned takes a Ramble, and has a
Small Adventure — Plans Formed and Partly
Developed — Remarkable Human Creatures
Discovered, and still more Remarkable
Converse held with them.*

"I'll throuble ye for two pounds of flour," cried Larry O'Neil, dashing into one of the stores, which was thronged with purchasers, whom he thrust aside rather unceremoniously.

"You'll have to take your turn, stranger, I calculate," answered the store-keeper, somewhat sharply.

"Ah thin, avic, plaze do attind to me at wance; for sure I've run four miles to git stuff for a dyin' family — won't ye now?"

The earnest manner in which Larry made this appeal was received with a laugh by the bystanders, and a recommendation to the store-keeper to give him what he wanted.

"What's the price?" inquired Larry, as the man measured it out.

"Two dollars a pound," answered the man.

"Musha! I've seed it chaiper."

"I guess so have I; but provisions are gittin' up, for nothin' has come from Sacramento for a fortnight."

"Tay an' sugar'll be as bad, no doubt!"

"Wuss, they are; for there's next to none at all, I opine, in this here location."

"Faix, I'll have a pound o' both, av they wos two dollars the half-ounce. Have ye got raisins an' sago?"

"Yes."

"Give me a pound o' that, aich."

These articles having been delivered and paid for, Larry continued —

"Ye'll have brandy, av coorse?"

"I guess I have; plenty at twenty dollars a bottle."

"Och, morther, it'll brake the bank intirely; but it's little I care. Hand me wan bottle, plaze."

The bottle of brandy was added to his store, and then the Irishman, shouldering his bundle of good things, left the shop, and directed his steps once more towards the ravine in which dwelt Kate Morgan and her brother Pat.

It was late when the Irishman returned from his mission of kindness, and he found the fire nearly out, the tent closed, and all his comrades sound asleep, so, gently lifting the curtain that covered the entrance, he crept quietly in, lay down beside Bill Jones, whose nasal organ was performing a trombone solo, and in five minutes was sound asleep.

It seemed to him as if he had barely closed his eyes, when he was roused by his comrades making preparations to resume work; nevertheless, he had rested several hours, and the grey hue of early day that streamed in through the opening of the tent warned him that he must recommence the effort to realise his golden dreams. The pursuit of gold, however engrossing it may be, does not prevent men from desiring to lie still in the morning, or abate one jot of the misery of their condition when they are rudely roused by *early* comrades, and told that "it's time to get up." Larry O'Neil, Tom Collins, and Maxton groaned, on receiving this information from Ned, turned, and made as if they meant to go to sleep. But they meant nothing of the sort; it was merely a silent testimony to the fact of their thorough independence — an expressive way of shewing that they scorned to rise at the bidding of any man, and that they would not get up till it pleased themselves to do so. That this was the case became evident from their groaning again, two minutes afterwards, and turning round on their backs. Then they stretched themselves, and, sitting up, stared at each other like owls. A moment after, Maxton yawned vociferously, and fell back again quite flat, an act which was instantly imitated by the other two. Such is the force of bad example.

By this time the captain and Jones had left the tent, and Ned Sinton was buckling on his belt.

"Now, then, get up, and don't be lazy," cried the latter, as he stepped out, dragging all the blankets off the trio as he took his departure, an act which disclosed the fact that trousers and flannel shirts were the sleeping garments of Maxton and Tom, and that Larry had gone to bed in his boots.

The three sprang up immediately, and, after performing their toilets, sallied forth to the banks of the stream, where the whole population of the place was already hard at work.

Having worked out their claims, which proved to be pretty good, they commenced new diggings close beside the old ones, but these turned out complete failures, excepting that selected by Captain Bunting, which was as rich as the first. The gold deposits were in many places very irregular in their distribution, and it frequently happened that one man took out thirty or forty dollars a day from his claim, while another man, working within a few yards of him, was, to use a mining phrase, unable "to raise the colour;" that is, to find gold enough to repay his labour.

This uncertainty disgusted many of the impatient gold-hunters, and not a few returned home, saying that the finding of gold in California was a mere lottery, who, if they had exercised a little patience and observation, would soon have come to know the localities in which gold was most likely to be found. There is no doubt whatever, that the whole country is impregnated more or less with the precious material.

The quartz veins in the mountains are full of it; and although the largest quantities are usually obtained in the beds of streams and on their banks, gold is to be found, in smaller quantities, even on the tops of the hills.

Hitherto the miners at Little Creek had found the diggings on the banks of the stream sufficiently remunerative; but the discovery of several lumps of gold in its bed, induced many of them to search for it in the shallow water, and they were successful. One old sea-captain was met by Bill Jones with a nugget the size of a goose-egg in each hand, and another man found a single lump of almost pure gold that weighed fourteen pounds. These discoveries induced Ned Sinton to think of adopting a plan which had been in his thoughts for some time past; so one day he took up his rifle, intending to wander up the valley, for the double purpose of thinking out his ideas, and seeing how the diggers higher up got on.

As he sauntered slowly along, he came to a solitary place where no miners were at work, in consequence of the rugged nature of the banks of the stream rendering the labour severe. Here, on a projecting cliff; which overhung a deep, dark pool or eddy, he observed the tall form of a naked man, whose brown skin bespoke him the native of a southern clime. While Ned looked at him, wondering what he could be about, the man suddenly bent forward, clasped his hands above his head, and dived into the pool. Ned ran to the margin immediately, and stood for nearly a minute observing the dark indistinct form of the savage as he groped along the bottom. Suddenly he rose, and made for the shore with a nugget of gold in his hand.

He seemed a little disconcerted on observing Ned, who addressed him in English, French, and Spanish, but without eliciting any reply, save a grunt. This, however, did not surprise our hero, who recognised the man to be a Sandwich Islander whom he had met before in the village, and whose powers of diving were well-known to the miners. He ascertained by signs, however, that there was much gold at the bottom of the stream, which, doubtless, the diver could not detach from the rocks during the short period of his immersion, so he hastened back to the tent, determined to promulgate his plan to his comrades. It was noon when he arrived, and the miners were straggling from all parts of the diggings to the huts, tents, and restaurants.

"Ha! Maxton, glad I've found you alone," cried Ned, seating himself on an empty box before the fire, over which the former was engaged in culinary operations. "I have been thinking over a plan for turning the course of the stream, and so getting at a portion of its bed."

"Now that's odd," observed Maxton, "I have been thinking of the very same thing all morning."

"Indeed! wits jump, they say. I fancied that I had the honour of first hitting on the plan."

"*First* hitting on it!" rejoined Maxton, smiling. "My dear fellow, it has not only been hit upon, but hit off, many months ago, with considerable success in some parts of the diggings. The only thing that prevents it being generally practised is, that men require to work in companies, for the preliminary labour is severe, and miners seem to prefer working singly, or in twos and threes, as long as there is good 'pay-dirt' on the banks."

"Well, then, the difficulty does not affect us, because we are already a pretty strong company, although our vaquero has left us, and I have seen a place this morning which, I think, will do admirably to begin upon; it is a deep pool, a few miles up the stream, under —"

"I know it," interrupted Maxton, putting a large slice of pork into the frying-pan, which hissed delightfully in the ears of hungry men. "I know the place well, but there is a much better spot not a quarter of a mile higher up, where a Chinaman, named Ah-wow, lives; it will be more suitable, you'll find, when I shew it you."

"We'll go and have a look at it after dinner," observed Ned; "meanwhile, here are our comrades, let us hear what they have to say about the proposal."

As he spoke, Collins, Jones, Larry, and the captain advanced in single file, and with disconsolate looks, that told of hard toil and little reward.

"Well, what have you got, comrades?"

"Nothin'," answered Bill Jones, drawing forth his comforter. Bill's comforter was black and short, and had a bowl, and was at all times redolent of tobacco.

"Niver a speck," cried Larry O'Neil, setting to with energy to assist in preparing dinner.

"Well, friends, I've a plan to propose to you, so let us take the edge off our appetites, and I'll explain."

Ned sat down tailor-fashion on the ground with his companions round him, and, while they devoted themselves ravenously and silently to tea, flour-cake, salt-pork, and beans, he explained to them the details of his plan, which explanation, (if it was not the dinner), had the effect of raising their spirits greatly. Instead, therefore, of repairing to their profitless claims after dinner, they went in a body up the stream to visit the Chinaman's diggings. Captain Bunting alone remained behind, as his claim was turning out a first-rate one.

"Sure, there's a human!" cried Larry, as they turned a projecting point, about an hour and a half later, and came in sight of Ah-wow's "lo-cation," as the Yankees termed it.

"It may be a human," remarked Ned, laughing, "but it's the most inhuman one I ever saw. I think yonder fellow must be performing a surgical operation on the Chinaman's head."

Ah-wow was seated on a stone in front of his own log-hut, with his arms resting on his knees, and an expression of supreme felicity on his yellow face, while a countryman, in what appeared a night-gown, and an immense straw hat, dressed his tail for him.

Lest uninformed readers should suppose that Ah-wow belonged to the monkey-tribe, we may mention that the Chinaman's head was shaved quite bald all round, with the exception of a *tail* of hair, about two feet long, and upwards of an inch thick, which jutted from the top of his *caput*, and hung down his back. This tail he was in the act of getting dressed when our party of miners broke in upon the privacy of his dressing-room.

Ah-wow had a nose which was very flat and remarkably broad, with the nostrils pointing straight to the front. He also had a mouth which was extremely large, frightfully thick-lipped, and quite the reverse of pretty. He had two eyes, also, not placed, like the eyes of ordinary men, *across* his face, on either side of his nose, but set in an angular manner on his visage, so that the outer corners pointed a good deal upwards, and the inner corners pointed a good deal downwards — towards the point of his nose, or, rather, towards that vacant space in front of his nostrils which would have been the point of his nose if that member had had a point at all. Ah-wow also had cheek bones which were uncommonly high, and a forehead which was preposterously low, and a body which was rather squat, and a *tout ensemble* which was desperately ugly. Like his hairdresser, he wore a coat somewhat resembling a night-shirt, with a belt round it, and his feet were thrust into yellow slippers. These last, when he went to dig for gold, he exchanged for heavy boots.

When Ned and his friends walked up and stood in a grinning row before him, Ah-wow opened his little eyes to the uttermost, (which wasn't much), and said, "How!"

If he had affixed "d'ye do" to it, the sentence would have been complete and intelligible. His companion attempted to vary the style of address by exclaiming, "Ho!"

"Can you speak English?" inquired Ned, advancing.

A shake of the head, and a consequent waggle of the tail was the reply.

"Or French?"

(Shake and waggle.)

"Maybe ye can do Irish?" suggested Larry.

The shake and waggle were more vigorous than before but Ah-wow rose, and, drawing on his boots, made signs to his visitors to follow him, which they did, through the bushes, round the base of a steep precipice. A short walk brought them to an open space quite close to the banks of the stream, which at that place was broken by sundry miniature waterfalls and cascades, whose puny turmoil fell like woodland music on the ear. Here was another log-hut of minute dimensions and ruinous aspect, in front of which sat another Chinaman, eating his dinner. Him Ah-wow addressed as Ko-sing. After a brief conversation, Ko-sing turned to the strangers, and said —

"Ho! Kin speek English, me can. What you want?"

"We want to look at your diggings," answered Ned.

"We are going to turn the river here, if we can; and if you and your companions choose to join us, we will give you good wages."

"Kin speek, but not fery well kin on'erstan'. Work, work you say, an' pay we?"

"Yes, that's it; you work for us, and we'll pay you."

"How moche?" inquired the cautious Celestial.

"Five dollars a day," replied Ned.

The Chinaman put on a broad grin, and offered to shake hands, which offer was accepted, not only by Ned, but by the whole party; and the contract was thus settled on the spot, to the satisfaction of all parties.

After this they spent some time in examining the bed of the stream, and having fixed upon a spot on which to commence operations, they prepared, about sunset, to return for their tent and mining tools, intending to make a moonlight flitting in order to avoid being questioned by over-curious neighbours. All their horses and mules, except Ned's charger, having been sold a few days before to a Yankee who was returning to Sacramento, they expected to get off without much noise, with their goods and chattels on their backs.

Before starting on their return, while the rest of the party were crowding round and questioning Ko-sing, Bill Jones — whose mind since he arrived in California seemed to be capable of only one sensation, that of surprise — went up to Ah-wow, and glancing round, in order to make sure that he was not observed, laid his hand on his shoulder, and looked inquiringly into the Chinaman's face. The Chinaman returned the compliment with interest, throwing into his sallow countenance an expression of, if possible, blanker astonishment.

"O-wow!" said Bill, with solemn gravity, and pausing, as if to give him time to prepare for what was coming. "O-wow! wot do you dress your pig-tail with?"

"Ho!" replied the Chinaman.

"Ho!" echoed Bill; "now, that's curious. I thought as how you did it with grease, for it looks like it. Tell me now, how long did it take afore it growed that long?" He lifted the end of the tail as he spoke.

"How!" ejaculated the Chinaman.

"Ay, *how* long?" repeated Bill.

We regret that we cannot give Ah-wow's answer to this question, seeing that it was never given, in consequence of Bill being suddenly called away by Ned Sinton, as he and his friends turned to go.

"Come, Bill, let's be off."

"Ay, ay, sir," answered Bill, turning from the Chinaman and following his comrades with solemn stolidity, or, if you prefer the expression, with stolid solemnity.

"Don't linger, Larry," shouted Tom Collins.

"Ah! thin, it's cruel to tear me away. Good-night to ye, Bow-wow, we'll be back before mornin', ye purty creature." With this affectionate farewell, Larry ran after his friends and followed them down the banks of the tumbling stream towards the 'R'yal Bank o' Calyforny,' which was destined that night, for a time at least, to close its doors.

CHAPTER XIV.

*The New Diggings — Bright Prospects —
Great Results spring from Great Exertions, even in
California — Captain Bunting is seized with a
Great Passion for Solitary Rambling, and has two
Desperate Encounters; one with a Man,
the other with a Bear.*

The part of the Little Creek diggings to which the gold-hunters transported their camp, was a wild, secluded spot, not much visited by the miners, partly on account of its gloomy appearance, and partly in consequence of a belief that the Celestials located there were getting little or no gold. In this supposition they were correct. Ah-wow and Ko-sing being inveterately lazy, contented themselves with digging just enough gold to enable them to purchase a sufficiency of the necessaries of life. But the region was extremely rich, as our adventurers found out very soon after their arrival. One of the ravines, in particular, gave indications of being full of gold, and several panfuls of earth that were washed out shewed so promising a return, that the captain and Larry were anxious to begin at once. They were overruled, however, by the others, who wished to make trial of the bed of the stream.

Six days of severe labour were undergone by the whole party ere their task was accomplished, during which period they did not make an ounce of gold, while, at the same time, their little store was rapidly melting away. Nevertheless, they worked heartily, knowing that a few days of successful digging would amply replenish their coffers. At grey dawn they set to work; some, with trousers tucked up, paddling about in the water all day, carrying mud and stones, while others felled trees and cut them into logs wherewith to form the dam required to turn the stream from its course. This was a matter of no small difficulty. A new bed had to be cut to the extent of eight or ten yards, but for a long time the free and jovial little mountain stream scorned to make such a pitiful twist in its course, preferring to burst its way headlong through the almost completed barricade by which it was pent-up.

Twice did it accomplish this feat, and twice, in so doing, did it sweep Captain Bunting off his legs and roll him along bodily, in a turmoil of mud and stones and dirty water, roaring, as it gushed forth, as if in savage triumph. On the second occasion, Bill Jones shared the captain's ducking, and all who chanced to be working about the dam at the time were completely drenched. But, however much their bodies might be moistened, no untoward accident could damp the ardour of their spirits. They resumed work again; repaired the breach, and, finally, turned the obstinate stream out of the course which, probably, it had occupied since creation. It rushed hissing, as if spitefully, along its new bed for a few yards, and then darted, at a right angle, back into its former channel, along which it leaped exultingly as before.

But the object for which all this trouble had been undertaken was attained. About eight yards of the old bed of the torrent were laid bare, and the water was drained away, whereat each of the party exhibited his satisfaction after his own peculiar manner — Larry O'Neil, as usual, giving vent to his joy in a hearty cheer.

The result was even more successful than had been anticipated. During the next few days the party conversed little; their whole energies being devoted to eating, sleeping, and digging. The bed of the stream was filled with stones, among which they picked up numerous nuggets of various sizes — from a pea to a walnut — some being almost pure gold, while others were, more or less, mixed with quartz. A large quantity of the heavy black sand was also found at the bottom of a hole, which once had been an eddy — it literally sparkled with gold-dust, and afforded a rich return for the labour previously expended in order to bring it to light. The produce of the first two days' work was no less than fourteen pounds weight of gold!

The third day was the Sabbath, and they rested from their work. It is, however, impossible for those who have never been in similar circumstances to conceive how difficult it was for our party of gold-hunters to refrain from resuming work as usual on that morning. Some of them had never been trained to love or keep the Sabbath, and would have certainly gone to work had not Ned and the captain remonstrated. All were under great excitement in consequence of their valuable discovery, and anxious to know whether the run of luck was likely to continue, and not one of the party escaped the strong temptation to break the Sabbath-day, except, indeed, the Chinamen, who were too easy-going and lazy to care whether they worked or rested. But the inestimable advantage of good early training told at this time on Ned Sinton. It is questionable whether his principles were strong enough to have carried him through the temptation, but Ned had been *trained* to reverence the Lord's-day from his earliest years, and he looked upon working on the Sabbath with a feeling of dread which he could not have easily shaken off, even had he tried. The promise, in his case, was fulfilled — "Train up a child in the way he should go, and he will not depart from it when he is old;" and though no mother's voice of warning was heard in that wild region of the earth, and no guardian's hand was there to beckon back the straggler from the paths of rectitude, yet he was not "let alone;" the arm of the Lord was around him, and His voice whispered, in tones that could not be misunderstood, "Remember the Sabbath-day, to keep it holy."

We have already said, that the Sabbath at the mines was a day of rest as far as mere digging went, but this was simply for the sake of resting the wearied frame, not from a desire to glorify God. Had any of the reckless miners who filled the gambling-houses been anxious to work during Sunday on a prolific claim, he would not have hesitated because of God's command.

The repose to their overworked muscles, and the feeling that they had been preserved from committing a great sin, enabled the party to commence work on Monday with a degree of cheerfulness and vigour that told favourably on their profits that night, and in the course of a few days they dug out gold to the extent of nearly two thousand pounds sterling.

"We're goin' to get rich, no doubt of it," said the captain one morning to Ned, as the latter was preparing to resume work in the creek; "but I'll tell you what it is, I'm tired o' salt beef and pork, and my old hull is gettin' rheumatic with paddling about barefoot in the water, so I mean to go off for a day's shootin' in the mountains."

"Very good, captain," replied Ned; "but I fear you'll have to go by yourself, for we must work out this claim as fast as we can, seeing that the miners further down won't be long of scenting out our discovery."

Ned's words were prophetic. In less than half-an-hour after they were uttered a long-visaged Yankee, in a straw hat, nankeen trousers, and fisherman's boots, came to the spot where they were at work, and seated himself on the trunk of a tree hard by to watch their proceedings.

"Guess you've got som'thin'," he said, as Larry, after groping in the mud for a little, picked up a lump of white quartz with a piece of gold the size of a marble embedded in the side of it.

"Ah! but ye're good for sore eyes," cried Larry, examining the nugget carefully.

"I say, stranger," inquired the Yankee, "d'ye git many bits like that in this location?"

The Irishman regarded his question with an expressive leer. "Arrah! now, ye won't tell?" he said, in a hoarse whisper; "sure it'll be the death o' me av ye do. There's *no end* o' them things here — as many as ye like to pick; it's only the day before tomorrow that I turned up a nugget of pure goold the size of me head; and the capting got hold o' wan that's only half dug out yet, an' wot's seen o' 't is as big as the head o' a five-gallon cask — all pure goold."

The Yankee was not to be put off the scent by such a facetious piece of information. He continued to smoke in silence, sauntered about with his hands in his nankeen pockets, watched the proceedings of the party, inspected the dirt cast ashore, and, finally, dug out and washed a panful of earth from the banks of the stream, after which he threw away the stump of his cigar, and went off whistling. Three hours later he returned with a party of friends, laden with tents, provisions, and mining tools, and they all took up their residence within twenty yards of our adventurers, and commenced to turn the course of the river just below them.

Larry and Jones were at first so angry that they seriously meditated committing an assault upon the intruders, despite the remonstrances of Tom Collins and Maxton, who assured them that the new-comers had a perfect right to the ground they occupied, and that any attempt to interrupt them by violence would certainly be brought under the notice of Judge Lynch, whose favourite punishments, they well knew, were whipping and hanging.

Meanwhile Captain Bunting had proceeded a considerable way on his solitary hunting expedition into the mountains, bent upon replenishing the larder with fresh provisions. He was armed with his favourite blunderbuss, a pocket-compass, and a couple of ship-biscuits. As he advanced towards the head of the valley, the scenery became more and more gloomy and rugged, but the captain liked this. Having spent the greater part of his life at sea, he experienced new and delightful sensations in viewing the mountain-peaks and ravines by which he was now surrounded; and, although of a sociable turn of mind, he had no objection for once to be left to ramble alone, and give full vent to the feelings of romance and enthusiastic admiration with which his nautical bosom had been filled since landing in California.

Towards noon, the captain reached the entrance to a ravine, or gorge, which opened upon the larger valley, into which it discharged a little stream from its dark bosom. There was an air of deep solitude and rugged majesty about this ravine that induced the wanderer to pause before entering it. Just then, certain sensations reminded him of the two biscuits in his pocket, so he sat down on a rock and prepared to dine. We say prepared to dine, advisedly, for Captain Bunting had a pretty correct notion of what comfort meant, and how it was to be attained. He had come out for the day to enjoy himself and although his meal was frugal, he did not, on that account, eat it in an off-hand easy way, while sauntering along, as many would have done. By no means. He brushed the surface of the rock on which he sat quite clean, and, laying the two biscuits on it, looked first at one and then at the other complacently, while he slowly, and with great care, cut his tobacco into delicate shreds, and filled his pipe. Then he rose, and taking the tin prospecting-pan from his belt, went and filled it at the clear rivulet which murmured at his feet, and placed it beside the biscuits on the rock. This done, he completed the filling of his pipe, and cast a look of benignity at the sun, which at that moment happened in his course to pass an opening between two lofty peaks, which permitted him to throw a cloth of gold over the captain's table.

Captain Bunting's mind now became imbued with those aspirations after knowledge, which would have induced him, bad he been at sea, to inquire, "How's her head?" so he pulled out his pocket-compass, and having ascertained that his nose, when turned towards the sun, pointed exactly "south-south-west, and by south," he began dinner. Thereafter he lit his pipe, and, reclining on the green turf beside the rock, with his head resting on his left hand, and wreaths of smoke encircling his visage, he — he enjoyed himself. To elaborate a description, reader, often weakens it — we cannot say more than that he enjoyed himself — emphatically.

Had Captain Bunting known who was looking at him in that solitary place, he would not have enjoyed himself quite so much, nor would he have smoked his pipe so comfortably.

On the summit of the precipice at his back stood, or rather sat, one of the natives of the country, in the shape of a grizzly-bear. Bruin had observed the captain from the time he appeared at the entrance of the ravine, and had watched him with a curious expression of stupid interest during all his subsequent movements. He did not attempt to interrupt him in his meal, however, on two grounds — first, because the nature of the grizzly-bear, if not molested, induces him to let others alone; and secondly, because the precipice, on the top of which he sat, although conveniently close for the purposes of observation, was too high for a safe jump.

Thus it happened that Captain Bunting finished his meal in peace, and went on his way up the wild ravine, without being aware of the presence of so dangerous a spectator. He had not proceeded far, when his attention was arrested by the figure of a man seated on a ledge of rock that over hung a yawning gulf into which the little stream plunged.

So still did the figure remain, with the head drooping on the chest, as if in deep contemplation, that it might have been mistaken for a statue cut out of the rock on which it sat. A deep shadow was cast over it by the neighbouring mountain-peaks, yet, as the white sheet of a waterfall formed the background, it was distinctly visible.

The captain advanced towards it with some curiosity, and it was not until he was within a hundred yards that a movement at length proved it to be a living human being.

The stranger rose hastily, and advanced to meet a woman, who at the same moment issued from an opening in the brushwood near him. The meeting was evidently disagreeable to the woman, although, from the manner of it, and the place, it did not seem to be accidental; she pushed the man away several times, but their words were inaudible to the captain, who began to feel all the discomfort of being an unintentional observer. Uncertainty as to what he should do induced him to remain for a few moments inactive, and he had half made up his mind to endeavour to retreat unobserved, when the man suddenly struck down the female, who fell with a faint cry to the earth.

In another minute the captain was at the side of the dastardly fellow, whom he seized by the neck with the left hand, while with the right he administered a hearty blow to his ribs. The man turned round fiercely, and grappled with his assailant; and then Captain Bunting became aware that his antagonist was no other than Smith, *alias* Black Jim, the murderer.

Smith, although a strong man, was no match for the captain, who soon overpowered him.

"Ha! you villain, have I got you?" cried he, as he almost throttled the man. "Get up now, an' come along peaceably. If you don't, I'll knock your brains out with the butt of my gun."

He permitted Black Jim to rise as he spoke, but held him fast by the collar, having previously taken from him his knife and rifle.

Black Jim did not open his lips, but the scowl on his visage shewed that feelings of deadly hatred burned in his bosom.

Meanwhile, the girl had recovered, and now approached.

"Ah! plase, sir," she said, "let him off. Shure I don't mind the blow; it's done me no harm — won't ye, now?"

"Let him off!" exclaimed the captain, violently; "no, my good girl; if he has not murdered you, he has at any rate murdered one human being that I know of, and if I can, I'll bring him to justice."

Kate, (for it was she), started at this reply, and looked earnestly at the man, who hung his head, and, for the first time, shewed symptoms of a softer feeling.

"Ah! it's true, I see, an' all hope is gone. If he'd commit a murder, he'd tell a lie too. I thought he spoke truth when he said Nelly was alive, but —"

The girl turned as she spoke, and left the spot hurriedly, while the captain took out his pocket-handkerchief, and began to fasten the arms of his prisoner behind him. But Black Jim was not to be secured without a struggle. Despair lent him energy and power. Darting forward, he endeavoured to throw his captor down, and partially succeeded; but Captain Bunting's spirit was fully roused, and, like most powerful men whose dispositions are habitually mild and peaceful, he was in a blaze of uncontrollable passion. For some time Black Jim writhed like a serpent in the strong grasp of his antagonist, and once or twice it seemed as if he would succeed in freeing himself, but the captain's hands had been trained for years to grasp and hold on with vice-like tenacity, and no efforts could disengage them. The two men swayed to and fro in their efforts, no sound escaping them, save an occasional gasp for breath as they put forth renewed energy in the deadly struggle. At last Black Jim began to give way. He was forced down on one knee, then he fell heavily on his side, and the captain placed his knee on his chest.

Just then a peculiar hiss was heard behind them, and the captain, looking back, observed that a third party had come upon the scene. The grizzly-bear, which has been described as watching Captain Bunting at dinner, had left its former position on the brow of the precipice, and, whether from motives of curiosity, or by accident, we will not presume to say, had followed the captain's track. It now stood regarding the two men with an uncommonly ferocious aspect. Its indignation may, perhaps, be accounted for by the fact that they stood in the only path by which it could advance — a precipice on one side and a thicket on the other rendering the passage difficult or impossible. Grizzlies are noted for their objection to turn out of their way for man or beast, so the combatants no sooner beheld the ferocious-looking animal than they sprang up, seized their weapons, and fired together at their common enemy. Bruin shook his head, uttered a savage growl, and charged. It seemed as if Black Jim had missed altogether — not to be wondered at considering the circumstances — and the mixture of shot and slugs from the blunderbuss was little more hurtful than a shower of hail to the thick-skinned monarch of these western hills. Be this as it may, the two men were compelled to turn and flee for their lives. Black Jim, being the nimbler of the two, was soon out of sight among the rocks of the precipices, and, we may remark in passing, he did not again make his appearance. Inwardly thanking the bear for its timely appearance, he ran at top speed into the mountains, and hid himself among those wild lonely recesses that are visited but rarely by man or beast.

Captain Bunting endeavoured to save himself by darting up the face of the precipice on his left, but the foot-hold was bad, and the bear proved about as nimble as himself, compelling him to leap down again and make for the nearest tree. In doing so, he tripped over a fallen branch, and fell with stunning violence to the ground. He rose, however, instantly, and grasping the lower limb of a small oak, drew himself with some difficulty up among the branches.

The bear came thundering on, and reached the tree a few seconds later. It made several abortive efforts to ascend, and then, sitting down at the foot, it looked up, grinning and growling horribly in disappointed rage.

The captain had dropped the blunderbuss in his fall, and now, with deep regret, and not a little anxiety, found himself unarmed and a prisoner. True, his long knife was still in its place, but he was too well aware of the strength and ferocity of the grizzly-bear — from hearsay, and now from ocular demonstration — to entertain the idea of acting on the offensive with such a weapon.

The sun sank behind the mountain-peaks, and the shades of night began to fall upon the landscape, and still did Captain Bunting and the bear sit — the one at the top, and the other at the foot of the oak-tree — looking at each other. As darkness came on, the form of the bear became indistinct and shadowy; and the captain's eyes waxed heavy, from constant staring and fatigue, so that at length bruin seemed, to the alarmed fancy of the tree'd mariner, to be twice the size of an elephant. At last the darkness became so deep that its form mingled with the shadows on the ground, and for some time the uncertainty as to its actual presence kept the prisoner wakeful; but soon his eyes began to close, despite his utmost efforts to keep them open; and for two hours he endured an agonising struggle with sleep, compared to which his previous struggle with Black Jim was mere child's-play. He tried every possible position among the branches, in the hope of finding one in which he might indulge in sleep without the risk of falling, but no such position was to be found; the limbs of the tree were too small and too far apart.

At last, however, he did find a spot to lie down on, and, with a sigh of relief, lay back to indulge in repose. Alas! the spot was a myth — he merely dreamed it; the next moment he dropt, like a huge over-ripe pear, to the ground. Fortunately a bush broke the violence of his fall, and, springing up with a cry of consternation, he rushed towards the tree, expecting each instant to feel the terrible hug of his ursine enemy. The very marrow in his back-bone seemed to shrink, for he fancied that he actually felt the dreaded claws sinking into his flesh. In his haste he missed the branch, and fell violently forward, scratching himself terribly among the bushes. Again he rose, and a cold perspiration broke out upon him as he uttered an involuntary howl of terror, and once more leaped up at the limb of the oak, which he could just barely see. He caught it; despair nerved him, and in another moment he was safe, and panting violently among the branches.

We need scarcely say that this little episode gave his feelings such a tremendous shock that his tendency to sleep was thoroughly banished; but another and a better result flowed from it, — the involuntary hubbub created by his yells and crashing falls reached listening and not far-distant ears.

During their evening meal that day, Ned Sinton and his comrades had speculated pretty freely, and somewhat jocularly, on the probable result of the captain's hunting expedition — expressing opinions regarding the powers of the blunderbuss, which it was a shame, Larry O'Neil said, "to spake behind its back;" but as night drew on, they conversed more seriously, and when darkness had fairly set in they became anxious.

"It's quite clear that something's wrong," cried Ned Sinton, entering the tent hastily, "we must up and search for him. The captain's not the man to lose his way with a compass in his pocket and so many landmarks round him."

All the party rose at once, and began to buckle on belts and arm, while eagerly suggesting plans of search.

"Who can make a torch?" inquired Ned.

"Here's one ready made to hand," cried Maxton, seizing a huge pine-knot and lighting it.

"Some one must stay behind to look after our things. The new-comers who camped beside us today are not used to mining life, and don't sufficiently know the terrors of Lynch law. Do you stop, Maxton. Now then, the rest of you, come along."

Ned issued from the tent as he spoke, and walked at a rapid pace along the track leading up the valley, followed closely by Tom Collins, Larry O'Neil, and Bill Jones — all of whom were armed with rifles, revolvers, and bowie-knives. For a long time they walked on in silence, guided by the faint light of the stars, until they came to the flat rock which had formed the captain's dinner-table. Here they called a halt, in order to discuss the probability of their lost comrade having gone up the ravine. The question was soon settled by Larry, who discovered a few crumbs of the biscuit lying on the rock, and footprints leading up the ravine; for the captain, worthy man, had stepped recklessly into the little stream when he went to fill his pannikin, and his wet feet left a distinct track behind him for some distance.

"He can't have gone far up such a wild place as this," said Tom Collins, while they moved cautiously along. "Kindle the torch, Ned, it will light us on our way, and be a guide to the captain if he's within sight."

"It will enlighten enemies, too, if any are within range," replied Ned, hesitating.

"Oh, no fear," rejoined Tom, "our greatest enemy is darkness; here, Jones, hand me your match-box."

In a few seconds the torch flared forth, casting a broad glare of light on their path, as they advanced, examining the foot of precipices.

"Give a shout, Larry," said Ned.

Larry obeyed, and all listened intently, but, save the echo from the wild cliffs, no reply was heard.

Had the captain been wide-awake at the time, he would, doubtless, have heard the friendly shout, but his ears were dull from prolonged watching. It was thought needless to repeat the cry, so the party resumed their search with anxious forebodings in their hearts, though their lips were silent.

They had not proceeded far, however, when the noise occasioned by the captain's fall from the tree, as already described, struck upon their ears.

"Och! what's that?" exclaimed Larry, with a look of mingled surprise and superstitious fear.

For a minute the party seemed transformed into statues, as each listened intently to the mysterious sounds.

"They come from the other side of the point ahead," remarked Ned, in a whisper. "Light another torch, Larry, and come on — quick!"

Ned led the way at a run, holding one of the torches high above his head, and in a few minutes passed round the point above referred to. The glare of his torch immediately swept far ahead, and struck with gladsome beam on the now wakeful eye of the captain, who instantly greeted it with one of his own peculiarly powerful and eminently nautical roars.

"Hooroo!" yelled Larry, in reply, dashing forward at full speed. "Here we are all right, capting, comin' to the rescue; don't give in, capting; pitch into the blackguards —"

"Look out for the grizzly-bear," roared the captain, as his friends advanced at a run, waving their torches encouragingly.

The whole party came to a dead halt on this unexpected caution, and each cocked his piece as they looked, first into the gloom beyond, and then at each other, in surprise and perplexity.

"Halloo! captain, where are you?" shouted Ned.

"And where's the bear!" added Tom Collins.

"Right in front o' you," replied the captain, "about fifty yards on. The bear's at the bottom o' the tree, and I'm a-top of it. Come on, and fire together; but aim *low*, d'ye hear?"

"Ay, ay, sir," replied Bill Jones, as if he were answering a command on shipboard, while he advanced boldly in the direction indicated.

The others were abreast of him instantly, Ned and Larry holding the torches high in their left hands as they approached, step by step, with rifles ready for instant use.

"Have a care," cried the captain; "I see him. He seems to be crouchin' to make a rush."

This caused another halt; but as no rush was made, the party continued to advance very slowly.

"Oh! av ye would only shew yerself," said Larry, in a suppressed tone of exasperation at being kept so long in nervous expectation.

"I see him," cried Ned, taking aim.

The rest of the party cried "Where!" aimed in the same direction, and the whole fired a volley, the result of which was, that Captain Bunting fell a second time to the ground, crashing through the branches with a terrible noise, and alighting heavily at the foot of the tree. To the surprise of all, he instantly jumped up, and seizing Ned and Tom as they came up, shook them warmly by the hand.

"Och! are ye not shot, capting?" exclaimed Larry.

"Not a bit; not even hurt," answered the captain, laughing.

The fact was, that Captain Bunting, in his anxiety to escape being accidentally shot by his comrades, had climbed to the utmost possible height among the tender top branches of the oak. When the volley was fired, he lost his balance, fell through the tree, the under branches of which happily broke his fall, and finally alighted on the back of the grizzly-bear itself, which lay extended, and quite dead, on the ground.

"Faix we've polished him off for wance," cried Larry, in the excess of his triumph, as he stood looking at the fallen bear.

"Faix we've done nothing of the sort," retorted Tom Collins, who was examining the carcase. "It's been dead for hours, and is quite cold. Every bullet has missed, too, for the shot that settled him is on the side next the ground. So much for hasty shooting. Had bruin been alive when we fired, I'm inclined to think that some of us would not be alive now."

"Now, that's wot I wos sure of," remarked Bill Jones. "Wot I says is this — w'en yer goin' aloft to reef to'sails, don't be in a hurry. It's o' no manner o' use tryin' to shove on the wind. If ye've got a thing to do, do it slow — slow an' sure. If ye haven't got a thing to do, in coorse ye can't do it, but if ye have, don't be in a hurry — I says."

Bill Jones's maxim is undoubtedly a good one. Not a scratch had the bear received from any one of the party. The bullet of Black Jim had laid him low. Although hurriedly aimed, it had reached the animal's heart, and all the time that Captain Bunting was struggling to overcome his irresistible tendency to sleep, poor bruin was lying a helpless and lifeless body at the foot of the oak-tree.

CHAPTER XV.

Ah-wow saved from an Untimely Fate — Lynch Law
Enforced — Ned Sinton resolves to renounce Gold-
Digging for a Time, and Tom Collins seconds him.

Ah-wow sat on the stump of an oak-tree, looking, to use a familiar, though incorrect expression, very blue indeed. And no wonder, for Ah-wow was going to be hanged. Perhaps, courteous reader, you think we are joking, but we assure you we are not. Ah-wow had just been found guilty, or pronounced guilty — which, at the diggings, meant the same thing — of stealing two thousand dollars' worth of gold-dust, and was about to expiate his crime on the branch of a tree.

There could be no doubt of his guilt; so said the enlightened jury who tried him; so said the half-tipsy judge who condemned him; and so said the amiable populace which had assembled to witness his execution. It cannot be denied that appearances went very much against Ah-wow — so much so, that Maxton, and even Captain Bunting, entertained suspicions as to his innocence, though they pleaded hard for his pardon. The gold had been discovered hid near the Chinaman's tent, and the bag containing it was recognised and sworn to by at least a dozen of the diggers as that belonging to the man from whom the gold had been stolen. The only point that puzzled the jury was the strong assertions of Captain Bunting, Maxton, and Collins, that, to their certain belief, the poor Celestial had dug beside them each day, and slept beside them each night for three weeks past, at a distance of three miles from the spot where the robbery took place. But the jury were determined to hang somebody, so they shut their ears to all and sundry, save and except to those who cried out, "String the riptile up — sarves him right!"

Ko-sing also sat on the tree-stump, endeavouring to comfort Ah-wow by stroking his pig-tail and howling occasionally in an undertone. It seemed indeed that the poor man's career was drawing to a close, for two men advanced, and, seizing his pinioned arms, led him under the fatal limb; but a short respite occurred in consequence of a commotion in the outskirts of the crowd, where two men were seen forcing a passage towards the centre. Ned Sinton and Larry O'Neil had been away in the mountains prospecting at the time when Ah-wow was captured and led to the settlement, near the first residence of our adventurers, to stand his trial. The others accompanied the condemned man, in order, if possible, to save him, leaving Jones behind to guard their property, and acquaint Ned with the state of affairs on his return. Our hero knew too well the rapid course of Lynch law to hesitate. He started at once with Larry down the stream, to save, if possible, the life of his servant, for whom he felt a curious sort of patronising affection, and who he was sure must be innocent. He arrived just in time.

"Howld on, boys," cried Larry, flourishing his felt hat as they pushed through the crowd.

"Stay, friends," cried Ned, gaining the centre of the circle at last; "don't act hastily. This man is my servant."

"*That* don't make him an honest man, I guess," said a cynical bystander.

"Perhaps not," retorted Ned; "but it binds me in honour to clear him, if I can."

"Hear, hear," said several voices; "get up on the stump an' fire away, stranger."

Ned obeyed.

"Gentlemen," he began, "I can swear, in the first place, that the Chinaman has not been a quarter of a mile from my tent for three weeks past, so that he could not have stolen the gold —"

"How then came it beside his tent?" inquired a voice.

"I'll tell you, if you will listen. This morning early I started on a prospecting ramble up the stream, and not long after I set out I caught a glance of that villain Black Jim, who, you know, has been supposed for some time back to have been lurking in the neighbourhood. He ran off the moment he caught sight of me, and although I followed him at full speed for a considerable distance, he succeeded in escaping. However, I noticed the print of his footsteps in a muddy place over which he passed, and observed that his right boot had no heel. On returning home this afternoon, and hearing what had happened, I went to the spot where the bag of gold had been discovered, and there, sure enough, I found footprints, one of which shewed that the wearer's right boot had *no heel*. Now, gentlemen, it don't need much speaking to make so clear a matter clearer, I leave you to judge whether this robbery has been committed by the Chinaman or not."

Ned's speech was received with various cries; some of which shewed that the diggers were not satisfied with his explanation, and Ah-wow's fate still trembled in the balance, when the owner of the bag of gold stepped forward and admitted that he had observed similar foot-marks in the neighbourhood of his tent just after the robbery was committed, and said that he believed the Chinaman was innocent. This set the matter at rest. Ah-wow was cast loose and congratulated by several of the bystanders on his escape, but there seemed a pretty general feeling amongst many of the others that they had been unjustly deprived of their prey, and there is no saying what might have happened had not another culprit appeared on the scene to divert their attention.

The man who was led forward had all the marks of a thorough desperado about him. From his language it was impossible to judge what country had the honour of giving him birth, but it was suspected that his last residence had been Botany Bay. Had this man's innocence been ever so clearly proved he could not have escaped from such judges in their then disappointed state of mind; but his guilt was unquestionable. He had been caught in the act of stealing from a monté table. The sum was not very large, however, so it was thought a little too severe to hang him; but he was condemned to have his head shaved, his ears cut off, and to receive a hundred lashes.

The sentence was executed promptly, notwithstanding the earnest remonstrances of a few of the better-disposed among the crowd: and Ned, seeing that he could do nothing to mitigate the punishment of the poor wretch, left the spot with his comrades and the rescued Chinaman.

That night, as they all sat round their camp-fire, eating supper with a degree of zest known only to those who labour at severe and out-of-door occupation all day, Ned Sinton astonished his companions not a little, by stating his intention to leave them for the purpose of making a tour through the country.

"Make a tour!" exclaimed Maxton, in surprise.

"An' lave all the goold!" cried Larry O'Neil, pausing in his mastication of a tough lump of bear-steak.

"Why, boy," said Captain Bunting, laying down his knife, and looking at Ned in amazement, "what's put that in your head, eh?"

"Being somewhat tired of grubbing in the mud has put it into my head," replied Ned, smiling. "The fact is, comrades, that I feel disposed for a ramble, and I *don't* feel bent on making a fortune. You may, perhaps, be surprised to hear such a statement, but —"

"Not at all — by no means," interrupted Bill Jones; "I'm surprised at nothin' in this here country. If I seed a first-rate man-o'-war comin' up the valley at fifteen knots, with stun'-sails alow and aloft, stem on, against the wind, an' carryin' all before it, like nothin', I wouldn't be surprised, not a bit, so I wouldn't!"

"Well, perhaps not," resumed Ned; "but, surprised or not, my statement is true. I don't care about making my 'pile' in a hurry. Life was not given to us to spend it in making or digging gold; and, being quite satisfied, in the meantime, with the five or six hundred pounds of profits that fall to my share, I am resolved to make over my unfinished claim to the firm, and set out on my travels through the country. I shall buckle on my bowie-knife and revolver, and go where fancy leads me, as long as my funds last; when they are exhausted, I will return, and set to work again. Now, who will go with me?"

"Are you in earnest?" asked Tom Collins.

"In earnest! ay, that am I; never was more so in my life. Why, I feel quite ashamed of myself. Here have I been living for weeks in one of the most romantic and beautiful parts of this world, without taking more notice of it, almost, than if it did not exist. Do you think that with youth and health, and a desire to see everything that is beautiful in creation, I'm going to stand all day and every day up to the knees in dirty water, scraping up little particles of gold? Not I! I mean to travel as long as I have a dollar in my pocket; when that is empty, I'll work."

Ned spoke in a half-jesting tone, but there is no doubt that he gave utterance to the real feelings of his heart. He felt none of that eager thirst for gold which burned, like a fever, in the souls of hundreds and thousands of the men who poured at that time in a continuous and ever-increasing stream into California. Gold he valued merely as a means of accomplishing present ends; he had no idea of laying it up for the future; married men, he thought, might, perhaps, with propriety, amass money for the benefit of their families, but *he* wasn't a married man, and didn't mean to be one, so he felt in duty bound to spend all the gold he dug out of the earth.

We do not pretend to enter into a disquisition as to the correctness or incorrectness of Ned's opinions; we merely state them, leaving our reader to exercise his own reasoning powers on the subject, if so disposed.

For a few seconds after Ned's last speech, no sound escaped the lips of his comrades, save those resulting from the process of mastication. At last, Tom Collins threw down his knife, and slapped his thigh energetically, as he exclaimed, "I'll go with you, Ned! I've made up my mind. I'm tired of digging, too; and I'm game for a ramble into the heart of the Rocky Mountains, if you like."

"Bravo! Tom," cried Captain Bunting, slapping his companion on the shoulder — "well and bravely spoken; but you're a goose for all that, and so, saving his presence, is Commodore Ned Sinton. Why, you'll just waste two months or so in profitless wandering, and return beggars to the Little Creek to begin the work all over again. Take my advice, lads — the advice of an old salt, who knows a thing or two — and remain where you are till we have worked out all the gold hereabouts. After that you may talk of shifting."

"You're a very sour old salt to endeavour to damp our spirits in that way at the outset, but it won't do; my mind is made up, and I'm glad to find that there is at least one of the party who is strong enough to break these golden chains."

"Faix I comed here for goold, an' I stop here for the same raison," remarked Larry, scraping the last morsels from the bottom of the kettle with an iron spoon; "I've thravelled more nor enough in me day, so I can affoord to stop at home now."

"Get out, you renegade! do you call this home?" cried Ned.

"'Tis all that's of it at present, anyhow."

"When shall we start?" inquired Tom Collins.

"Tomorrow. We have few preparations to make, and the sooner we go the better; for when the rainy season sets in, our journeying will be stopped perforce. I have a plan in my mind which I shall detail to you after we retire to rest. Meanwhile I'll go and improve my bed, which has been so uncomfortable for some nights past that my very bones are aching."

Ned rose, took up an axe, and, going into the bush in rear of the tent, cut down a young pine-tree, the tender shoots and branches of which he stripped off and strewed thickly on the ground on which he was wont to sleep; over these he spread two thick blankets, and on this simple but springy and comfortable couch he and Tom Coffins lay down side by side to talk over their future plans, while their comrades snored around them.

Daylight found them still talking; so, pausing by mutual consent, they snatched an hour's repose before commencing the needful preparations for their contemplated journey.

CHAPTER XVI.

Ned and Tom take to Wandering —
Philosophical Speculations — A Startling
Apparition — The Digger Indians —
Water boiled in a Basket — The Gloomy Pass —
The Attack by Robbers — The Fight —
A Surprise — The Encampment.

Change is one of the laws of nature. We refer not to small-change, reader, but to physical, material change. Everything is given to change; men, and things, and place, and circumstances, all change, more or less, as time rolls on in its endless course. Following, then, this inevitable law of nature, we, too, will change the scene, and convey our reader deeper in among the plains and mountains of the far, "far west."

It is a beautiful evening in July. The hot season has not yet succeeded in burning up all nature into a dry russet-brown. The whole face of the country is green and fresh after a recent shower, which has left myriads of diamond-drops trembling from the point of every leaf and blade. A wide valley, of a noble park-like appearance, is spread out before us, with scattered groups of trees all over it, blue mountain-ranges in the far distance circling round it, and a bright stream winding down its emerald breast. On the hill-sides the wild-flowers grow so thickly that they form a soft, thick couch to lie upon, immense trees, chiefly pines and cedars, rise here and there like giants above their fellows. Oaks, too, are numerous, and the scene in many places is covered with mansanita underwood, a graceful and beautiful shrub. The trees and shrubbery, however, are not so thickly planted as to intercept the view, and the ground undulates so much that occasionally we overtop them, and obtain a glimpse of the wide vale before us. Over the whole landscape there is a golden sunny haze, that enriches while it softens every object, and the balmy atmosphere is laden with the sweet perfume called forth by the passing shower.

One might fancy Eden to have been somewhat similar to this, and here, as there, the presence of the Lord might be recognised in a higher degree than in most other parts of this earth, for, in this almost untrodden wilderness, His pre-eminently beautiful works have not yet to any great extent been marred by the hand of man.

Far away towards the north, two horsemen may be seen wending their way through the country at a slow, ambling pace, as if they would fain prolong their ride in such a lovely vale. The one is Ned Sinton, the other Tom Collins.

It had cost these worthies a week of steady riding to reach the spot on which we now find them, during which time they had passed through great varieties of scenery, had seen many specimens of digging-life, and had experienced not a few vicissitudes; but their griefs were few and slight compared with their enjoyments, and, at the moment we overtake them, they were riding they knew not and they cared not whither! Sufficient for them to know that the wilds before them were illimitable; that their steeds were of the best and fleetest Mexican breed; that their purses were well-lined with dollars and gold-dust; that they were armed with rifles, pistols, knives, and ammunition, to the teeth; and that the land was swarming with game.

"'Tis a perfect paradise!" exclaimed Tom Collins, as they reined up on the brow of a hill to gaze at the magnificent prospect before them.

"Strange," murmured Ned, half soliloquising, "that, although so wild and uncultivated, it should remind me so forcibly of home. Yonder bend in the stream, and the scenery round it, is so like to the spot where I was born, and where I spent my earliest years, that I can almost fancy the old house will come into view at the next turn."

"It does indeed remind one of the cultivated parks of England," replied Tom; "but almost all my early associations are connected with cities. I have seen little of uncontaminated nature all my life, except the blue sky through chimney tops, and even that was seen through a medium of smoke."

"Do you know," remarked Ned, as they resumed their journey at a slow pace, "it has always seemed to me that cities are unnatural monstrosities, and that there should be no such things!"

"Indeed," replied Tom, laughing; "how, then, would you have men to live?"

"In the country, of course, in cottages and detached houses. I would sow London, Liverpool, Manchester, etcetera, broadcast over the land, so that there would be no spot in Britain in which there were not clusters of human dwellings, each with its little garden around it, and yet no spot on which a *city* could be found."

"Hum, rather awkward for the transaction of business, I fear," suggested Tom.

"Not a bit; our distances would be greater, but we could overcome that difficulty by using horses more than we do — and railroads."

"And how would you manage with huge manufactories?" inquired Tom.

"I've not been able to solve that difficulty yet," replied Ned, smiling; "but my not being able to point out how things may be put right, does not, in the least degree, alter the fact that, as they are at present, they are wrong."

"Most true, my sagacious friend," said Tom; "but, pray, how do you prove the fact that things *are* wrong?"

"I prove it thus: You admit, I suppose, that the air of all large cities is unhealthy, as compared with that of the country, and that men and women who dwell in cities are neither so robust nor so healthy as those who dwell in country places?"

"I'm not sure that I do admit it," answered Tom.

"Surely you don't deny that people of the cities deem it a necessary of life to get off to the country at least once a year, in order to recruit, and that they invariably return better in health than when they left?"

"True; but that is the result of change."

"Ay," added Ned, "the result of change from worse to better."

"Well, I admit it for the sake of argument."

"Well, then, if the building of cities necessarily and inevitably creates a condition of atmosphere which is, to some extent, no matter how slight, prejudicial to health, those who build them and dwell in them are knowingly damaging the life which has been given them to be cherished and taken care of."

"Ned," said Tom, quietly, "you're a goose!"

"Tom," retorted Ned, "I know it; but, in the sense in which you apply the term, all men are geese. They are divided into two classes — namely, geese who are such because they can't and won't listen to reason, and geese who are such because they take the trouble to talk philosophically to the former; but to return from this digression, what think you of the argument?"

Tom replied by reining up his steed, pointing to an object in front, and inquiring, "What think you of *that?*"

The object referred to was a man, but, in appearance at least, he was not many degrees removed from the monkey. He was a black, squat, hideous-looking native, and his whole costume, besides the little strip of cloth usually worn by natives round the loins, consisted of a black silk hat and a pair of Wellington boots!

Dear reader, do not suppose that I am trying to impose upon your good-natured credulity. What I state is a *fact*, however unlikely it may appear in your eyes.

The natives of this part of the country are called digger Indians, not with reference to gold-digging, but from the fact of their digging subterranean dwellings, in which they pass the winter, and also from the fact that they grub in the earth a good deal for roots, on which they partly subsist. They are degraded, miserable creatures, and altogether uncivilised, besides being diminutive in stature.

Soon after the first flood of gold-hunters swept over their lands these poor creatures learned the value of gold, but they were too lazy to work diligently for it. They contented themselves with washing out enough to purchase a few articles of luxury, in the shape of cast-off apparel, from the white men. When stores began to be erected here and there throughout the country, they visited them to purchase fresh provisions and articles of dress, of which latter they soon became passionately fond.

But the digger Indians were not particular as to style or fashion — glitter and gay colour were the chief elements of attraction. Sometimes a naked savage might be seen going about with a second-hand dress-coat put on the wrong way, and buttoned up the back. Another would content himself with a red silk handkerchief tied round his head or shoulders. A third would thrust his spindle-shanks through the arms of a sleeved vest, and button the body round his loins; while a fourth, like the one now under consideration, would parade about in a hat and boots.

The poor digger had drawn the right boot on the left foot, and the left boot on the right — a matter of little moment, however, as they were immensely too large for him, as was also the hat, which only remained on his brows by being placed very much back on the head. He was a most singular being, and Ned and Tom, after the first glance of astonishment, were so un-mannered as to laugh at him until they almost fell off their horses. The digger was by no means disconcerted. He evidently was accustomed to the free and easy manners of white men, and while they rolled in their saddles, he stood quietly beside them, grinning hideously from ear to ear.

"Truly, a rare specimen of humanity," cried Ned, when he recovered his composure. "Where did *you* come from, old boy?"

The digger shook his head, and uttered some unintelligible words.

"It's of no use speaking to him; he don't understand English," said Tom Collins, with a somewhat puzzled expression.

The two friends made several attempts to ask him, by signs, where he lived, but they utterly failed. Their first efforts had the effect of making the man laugh, but their second attempts, being more energetic and extravagant, frightened him so that he manifested a disposition to run away. This disposition they purposely encouraged until he fairly took to his heels, and, by following him, they at last came upon the village in which his tribe resided.

Here they found an immense assemblage of men, and women, and children, whose appearance denoted dirtiness, laziness, and poverty. They were almost all in a state bordering on nudity, but a few of them wore miscellaneous portions of European apparel. The hair of the men was long, except on the forehead, where it was cut square, just above the eyebrows. The children wore no clothes at all. The infants were carried on stiff cradles, similar to those used by North American Indians. They all resided in tents, made of brushwood and sticks, and hundreds of mangy, half-starved curs dwelt along with them.

The hero of the hat and boots was soon propitiated by the gift of a few inches of tobacco, and Ned Sinton and Tom Collins were quickly on intimate terms with the whole tribe.

It is difficult to resist the tendency to laugh when a human being stands before you in a ludicrously-meagre costume, making hideous grimaces with his features, and remarkable contortions with his limbs, in the vain efforts to make himself understood by one who does not speak his language! Ned's powers of endurance were tested in this way by the chief of the tribe, an elderly man with a beard so sparse that each stumpy hair might have been easily counted.

This individual was clad in the rough, ragged blue coat usually worn by Irish labourers of the poorest class. It was donned with the tails in front; and two brass buttons, the last survivors of a once glittering double row, fastened it across the back of its savage owner.

"What *can* he mean?" said Ned, at the close of a series of pantomimic speeches, in which the Indian vainly endeavoured to get him to understand something having reference to the mountains beyond, for he pointed repeatedly towards them.

"It seems to me that he would have us understand," said Tom, "that the road lies before us, and the sooner we take ourselves off the better."

Ned shook his head. "I don't think that likely; he seems rather to wish us to remain; more than once he has pointed to his tent, and beckoned us to enter."

"Perhaps the old fellow wants us to become members of his tribe," suggested Tom. "Evidently he cannot lead his braves on the war-path as he was wont to do, and he wishes to make you chief in his room. What think you? Shall we remain? The blue coat would suit you admirably."

During this colloquy the old savage looked from one speaker to another with great eagerness, as if trying to comprehend what they said, then, renewing his gesticulations, he succeeded at last in convincing the travellers that he wished them not to pursue their journey any further in the direction in which they were going. This was a request with which they did not, however, feel disposed to comply; but seeing that he was particularly anxious that they should accept of his hospitality, they dismounted, and, fastening their horses to a tree close beside the opening of the chief's hut, they entered.

The inside of this curious bee-hive of a dwelling was dirty and dark, besides being half-full of smoke, created by the pipe of a squaw — the old man's wife — who regaled herself there with the soothing weed. There were several dogs there also, and two particularly small infants in wooden cradles, who were tied up like mummies, and did nothing but stare right before them into space.

"What's that?" inquired Tom, pointing to a basketful of smoking water.

"It looks like a basket," replied Ned.

"It *is* a basket," remarked Tom, examining the article in question, "and, as I live, superb soup in it."

"Tom," said Ned Sinton, solemnly, "have a care; if it is soup, depend upon it, dogs or rats form the basis of its composition."

"Ned," said Tom, with equal solemnity, "eat, and ask no questions."

Tom followed his own advice by accepting a dish of soup, with a large lump of meat in it, which was at that moment offered to him by the old chief who also urged Ned Sinton to partake; but he declined, and, lighting his pipe, proceeded to enjoy a smoke, at the same time handing the old man a plug of tobacco, which he accepted promptly, and began to use forthwith.

While thus engaged, they had an opportunity of observing how the squaw boiled water in a basket. Laying aside her pipe, she hauled out a goody-sized and very neatly-made basket of wicker-work, so closely woven by her own ingenious hands, that it was perfectly water-tight; this she three-quarters filled, and then put into it red-hot stones, which she brought in from a fire kindled outside. The stones were thrown in in succession, till the temperature was raised to the boiling point, and afterwards a little dead animal was put into the basket.

The sight of this caused Tom Collins to terminate his meal somewhat abruptly, and induced Ned to advise him to try a little more.

"No, thank you," replied Tom, lighting his pipe hastily, and taking up a bow and several arrows, which he appeared to regard with more than usual interest. The bow was beautifully made; — rather short, and tipped with horn.

The arrows were formed of two distinct pieces of wood spliced together, and were shod with flint; they were feathered in the usual way. All the articles manufactured by these natives were neatly done, and evinced considerable skill in the use of their few and simple tools.

After resting half-an-hour, the two friends rose to depart, and again the old Indian manifested much anxiety to prevail on them to remain; but resisting all his entreaties, they mounted their horses and rode away, carrying with them the good wishes of the community, by the courtesy of their manners, and a somewhat liberal distribution of tobacco at parting.

The country through which they passed became wilder at every step, for each hour brought them visibly nearer the mountain-range, and towards night-fall they entered one of the smaller passes or ravines that divided the lower range of hills at which they first arrived. Here a rugged precipice, from which projected pendent rocks and scrubby trees, rose abruptly on the right of the road, and a dense thicket of underwood, mingled with huge masses of fallen rock, lay on their left. We use the word road advisedly, for the broad highway of the flowering plains, over which the horsemen had just passed, narrowed at this spot as it entered the ravine, and was a pretty-well-defined path, over which parties of diggers and wandering Indians occasionally passed.

"Does not this wild spot remind you of the nursery tales we used to read?" said Ned, as they entered the somewhat gloomy defile, "which used to begin, 'Once upon a time — '"

"Hist, Ned, is that a grizzly?"

Both riders drew up abruptly, and grasped their rifles.

"I hear nothing," whispered Ned.

"It must have been imagination," said Tom, throwing his rifle carelessly over his left arm, as they again advanced. The gloom of the locality, which was deepened by the rapidly-gathering shades of night, quieted their spirits, and induced them to ride on in silence.

About fifty yards further on, the rustling in the bushes was again heard, and both travellers pulled up and listened intently.

"Pshaw!" cried Ned, at last, urging his horse forward, and throwing his piece on his shoulder, "we are starting at the rustling of the night wind; come, come, Tom, don't let us indulge superstitious feelings —"

At that moment there was a crash in the bushes on both sides of them, and their horses reared wildly, as four men rushed upon them. Before their steeds became manageable, they were each seized by a leg, and hurled from their saddles. In the fall, their rifles were thrown out of their grasp into the bushes; but this mattered little, for in a close struggle pistols are better weapons. Seizing their revolvers, Ned and Tom instantly sprang up, and fired at their assailants, but without effect, both being so much shaken by their fall. The robbers returned the fire, also without effect. In the scuffle, Ned was separated from his friend, and only knew that he maintained the fight manfully, from the occasional shots that were fired near him. His whole attention, however, had to be concentrated on the two stalwart ruffians with whom he was engaged.

Five or six shots were fired at a few yards' distance, quick as lightning, yet, strange to say, all missed. Then the taller of the two opposed to Ned, hurled his revolver full in his face, and rushed at him. The pistol struck Ned on the chest, and almost felled him, but he retained his position, and met the highwayman with a well-directed blow of his fist right between the eyes. Both went down, under the impetus of the rush, and the second robber immediately sprang upon Ned, and seized him by the throat. But he little knew the strength of the man with whom he had to deal. Our hero caught him in the iron grasp of his right hand, while, with his left, he hurled aside the almost inanimate form of his first assailant; then, throwing the other on his back, he placed his knee on his chest, and drew his bowie-knife.

Even in the terrible passion of mortal combat, Ned shuddered at the thought of slaying a helpless opponent. He threw the knife aside, and struck the man violently with his fist on the forehead, and then sprang up to rescue Tom who, although he had succeeded at the outset in felling one of the robbers with the butt of his pistol, was still engaged in doubtful strife with a man of great size and power. When Ned came up, the two were down on their knees, each grasping the other's wrist in order to prevent their bowie-knives from being used. Their struggles were terrible; for each knew that the first who freed his right hand would instantly take the other's life. Ned settled the matter, however, by again using his fist, which he applied so promptly to the back of the robber's neck, that he dropped as if he had been shot.

"Thank you — God bless you, Ned," gasped Tom, as soon as he recovered breath; "you have saved my life, for certainly I could not have held out a minute longer. The villain has all but broken my right arm."

"Never mind," cried Ned, stooping down, and turning the stunned robber over on his face, "give me a hand, boy; we must not let the fellows recover and find themselves free to begin the work over again. Take that fellow's neckcloth and tie his hands behind his back."

Tom obeyed at once, and in a few minutes the four highwaymen were bound hand and foot, and laid at the side of the road.

"Now," said Ned, "we must push on to the nearest settlement hot-haste, and bring a party out to escort — Halloo! Tom, are you wounded?"

"Not badly — a mere cut on the head."

"Why, your face is all covered with blood!"

"It's only in consequence of my wiping it with a bloody handkerchief, then; but you can examine, and satisfy yourself."

"The wound is but slight, I see," rejoined Ned, after a brief manipulation of Tom's skull; "now, then, let us away."

"We'll have to catch our horses first, and that won't be an easy matter."

Tom was right. It cost them half-an-hour to secure them and recover their rifles and other arms, which had been scattered over the field of battle. On returning to the spot where the robbers lay, they found them all partially recovered, and struggling violently to free themselves. Three of them failed even to slacken their bonds, but the fourth, the powerful man who had nearly overcome Tom Collins, had well-nigh freed his hands when his captors came up.

"Lie quiet," said Ned, in a low tone, "if you don't want the butt of my rifle on your skull."

The man lay down instantly.

"Tom, go and cut a stake six feet long, and I'll watch these fellows till you come back."

The stake was soon brought and lashed to the robber's back in such a manner that he was rendered utterly powerless. The others were secured in a similar manner, and then the two travellers rode forward at a gallop.

For nearly an hour they continued to advance without speaking or drawing rein. At the end of that time, while sweeping round the jutting base of a precipitous rock, they almost ran into a band of horsemen who were trotting briskly towards them. Both parties halted, and threw forward their rifles, or drew their revolvers for instant use, gazing at each other the while in silent surprise at the suddenness of their meeting.

"Give in, ye villains," at last shouted a stern voice, "or we'll blow ye out o' the saddle. You've no chance; down your arms, I say."

"Not until I know what right *you* have to command us," replied Ned, somewhat nettled at the overbearing tone of his opponent. "We are peaceable travellers, desiring to hurt no one; but if we were not, surely so large a party need not be afraid. We don't intend to run away, still less do we intend to dispute your passage."

The strangers lowered their fire-arms, as if half-ashamed at being surprised into a state of alarm by two men.

"Who said we were 'afraid,' young man?" continued the first speaker, riding up with his comrades, and eyeing the travellers narrowly. "Where have you come from, and how comes it that your clothes are torn, and your faces covered with blood?"

The party of horsemen edged forward, as he spoke, in such a manner as to surround the two friends, but Ned, although he observed the movement, was unconcerned, as, from the looks of the party, he felt certain they were good men and true.

"You are a close interrogator for a stranger," he replied. "Perhaps you will inform me where *you* have come from, and what is your errand in these lonesome places at this hour of the night?"

"I'll tell ye wot it is, stranger," answered another of the party — a big, insolent sort of fellow — "we're out after a band o' scoundrels that have infested them parts for a long time, an' it strikes me you know more about them than we do."

"Perhaps you are right," answered Ned.

"Mayhap they're not *very*, far off from where we're standin'," continued the man, laying his hand on Tom Collins's shoulder. Tom gave him a look that induced him to remove the hand.

"Right again," rejoined Ned, with a smile. "I know where the villains are, and I'll lead you to them in an hour, if you choose to follow me."

The men looked at each other in surprise.

"You'll not object to some o' us ridin' before, an' some behind ye!" said the second speaker, "jist by way o' preventin' yer hosses from runnin' away; they looks a little skeary."

"By no means," answered Ned, "lead on; but keep off the edge of the track till I call a halt."

"Why so, stranger?"

"Never mind, but do as I bid you."

The tone in which this was said effectually silenced the man, and during the ride no further questions were asked. About a quarter-of-an-hour afterwards the moon rose, and they advanced at such a rapid pace that in a short time they were close upon the spot where the battle had taken place. Just before reaching it Ned called a halt, and directed the party to dismount and follow him on foot. Although a good deal surprised, they obeyed without question; for our hero possessed, in an eminent degree, the power of constituting himself a leader among those with whom he chanced to come into contact.

Fastening his horse to a tree, Ned led the men forward a hundred yards.

"Are these the men you search for!" he inquired.

"They are, sir," exclaimed one of the party, in surprise, as he stooped to examine the features of the robbers, who lay where they had been left.

"Halloo!" exclaimed Tom Collins, "I say, the biggest fellow's gone! Didn't we lay him hereabouts?"

"Eh! dear me, yes; why, this is the very spot, I do believe —"

All further remarks were checked at that moment by the sound of horses' hoofs approaching, and, almost before any one could turn round, a horseman came thundering down the pass at full gallop. Uttering a savage laugh of derision, he discharged his pistol full into the centre of the knot of men as he passed, and, in another moment, was out of sight. Several of the onlookers had presence of mind enough to draw their pistols and fire at the retreating figure, but apparently without effect.

"It's him!" cried Tom Collins; "and he's mounted on your horse, Ned."

"After him, lads!" shouted Ned, as he ran back towards the place where the horses were fastened. "Whose is the best horse?"

"Hold on, stranger," said one of the men, as he ran up to Ned, "ye may save yer wind. None o' the horses can overtake your one, I guess. I was lookin' at him as we came along. It would only be losin' time for nothin', an' he's miles ahead by this time."

Ned Sinton felt that the man's remarks were too true, so he returned to the spot where the remaining robbers lay, and found that the miners had cut their fastenings, and were busily engaged in rebinding their hands behind them, preparatory to carrying them back to their settlement. It was discovered that the lashings of one of the men had been partly severed with a knife, and, as he could not have done it himself, it was plain that the robber who had escaped must have done it, and that the opportune arrival of the party had prevented him from accomplishing his purpose. How the man had broken his own bonds was a mystery that could not now be solved, but it was conjectured they must have been too weak, and that he had burst them by main strength.

Another discovery was now made, namely, that one of the three robbers secured was no other than Black Jim himself; the darkness of the night had prevented Ned and Tom from making this discovery during the fight.

In less time than we have taken to describe it, the robbers were secured, and each was mounted behind one of his captors.

"Ain't you goin' with us?" inquired one of the men, observing that Ned Sinton stood leaning on his rifle, as if he meant to remain behind.

"No," answered Ned; "my companion and I have travelled far today, besides fighting a somewhat tough battle; we mean to camp here for the night, and shall proceed to your settlement tomorrow."

The men endeavoured to dissuade them from their purpose, but they were both fatigued, and persisted in their determination. The impression they had made, however, on their new friends was so favourable, that one of their number, a Yankee, offered the loan of his horse to Ned, an offer which the latter accepted thankfully, promising to return it safe and sound early on the following day. Five minutes later the sound of the retreating hoofs died away, and the travellers stood silently side by side in the gloomy ravine.

For a few minutes neither spoke; then Ned heaved a sigh, and, looking in his companion's face with a serio-comically-sad expression, said:

"It may not, perhaps, have occurred to you, Tom, but are you aware that we are a couple of beggars?"

"If you use the term in its slang sense, and mean to insinuate that we are a couple of unfortunate beggars, I agree with you."

"Well, I've no objection," rejoined Ned, "to your taking my words in that sense; but I mean to say that, over and above that, we are real, veritable, *bona fide* beggars, inasmuch as we have not a sixpence in the world."

Tom Collins's visage grew exceedingly long.

"Our united purse," pursued Ned, "hung, as you are aware, at my saddle-bow, and yon unmitigated villain who appropriated my good steed, is now in possession of all our hard-earned gold!"

Tom's countenance became preternaturally grave, but he did not venture to speak.

"Now," continued Ned, forcing a smile, "there is nothing for it but to make for the nearest diggings, commence work again, and postpone our travels to a future and more convenient season. We may laugh at it as we please, my dear fellow, but there's no denying that we are in what the Yankees would call an 'oncommon fix.'"

Ned's remark as to "laughing at it," was altogether uncalled for and inappropriate, for his own smile might have been more correctly termed a grin, and nothing was further from Tom Collins's thoughts at that moment than laughing.

"Are the victuals gone too?" inquired Ned, hastily.

Both turned their eyes towards Tom Collins's horse, which grazed hard by, and both heaved a sigh of relief on observing that the saddle-bags were safe. This was a small drop of comfort in their otherwise bitter cup, and they made the most of it. Each, as if by a common impulse, pretending that he cared very little about the matter, and assuming that the other stood in need of being cheered and comforted, went about the preparations for encamping with a degree of reckless joviality that insensibly raised their spirits, not only up to but considerably above the natural level; and when at last they had spread out their viands, and lighted their fire and their pipes, they were, according to Tom's assertion, "happy as kings."

The choosing of a spot to encamp on formed the subject of an amicable dispute.

"I recommend the level turf under this oak," said Ned, pointing to a huge old tree, whose gnarled limbs covered a wide space of level sward.

"It's too low," objected Tom, (Tom could always object — a quality which, while it acted like an agreeable dash of cayenne thrown into the conversation of some of his friends, proved to be sparks applied to gunpowder in that of others;) "it's too low, and, doubtless, moist. I think that yonder pine, with its spreading branches and sweet-smelling cones, and carpet of moss below, is a much more fitting spot."

"Now, who is to decide the question if I don't give in, Tom? For I assume, of course, that you will never give in."

At that moment an accident occurred which decided the question for them. It frequently happens that some of the huge, heavy branches of the oaks in America become so thoroughly dried and brittle by the intense heat of summer, that they snap off without a moment's warning, often when there is not a breath of air sufficient to stir a leaf. This propensity is so well-known to Californian travellers that they are somewhat careful in selecting their camping ground, yet, despite all their care, an occasional life is lost by the falling of such branches.

An event of this kind occurred at the present time. The words had barely passed Ned's lips, when a large limb of the oak beside which they stood snapt off with a loud report, and fell with a crash to the ground.

"That settles it," said Tom, somewhat seriously, as he led his horse towards the pine-tree, and proceeded to spread his blanket beneath its branches.

In a few minutes the bright flame of their camp-fire threw a lurid glare on the trees and projecting cliffs of the wild pass, while they cooked and ate their frugal meal of jerked beef and biscuit. They conversed little during the repast or after it, for drowsiness began to steal over them, and it was not long before they laid their heads, side by side, on their saddles, and murmuring "Good-night," forgot their troubles in the embrace of deep, refreshing slumber.

CHAPTER XVII.

A Curious and Valuable Draught — Lynch Law applied — Black Jim's Confession — Ned becomes a Painter, and finds the Profession Profitable as well as Amusing — The First Portrait.

Next morning the travellers were up and away by daybreak, and in the afternoon they came upon a solitary miner who was prospecting in a gulch near the road-side.

This word gulch is applied to the peculiarly abrupt, short ravines, which are a characteristic feature in Californian more than in any other mountains. The weather was exceedingly hot, and the man took off his cap and wiped his streaming brow as he looked at the travellers who approached him.

"Ha! you've got water there, I see," cried Tom Collins, leaping off his horse, seizing a cup which stood on the ground full of clear water, and draining it eagerly.

"Stop!" cried the man, quickly.

"Why!" inquired Tom, smacking his lips.

The miner took the empty cup and gazed inquiringly into it.

"Humph! you've drunk it, every grain."

"Drop, you mean," suggested Tom, laughing at the man's expression; "of course I have, and why not? There's plenty more of the same tap here."

"Oh, I wouldn't mind the water," replied the man, "if ye had only left the gold-dust behind, but you've finished that too."

"You *don't* mean it!" gasped Tom, while the questions flashed across his mind — Is gold-dust poison? And if not, is it digestible? "How — how much have I swallowed?"

"Only about two dollars — it don't signify," answered the man, joining in the burst of laughter to which Ned and Tom gave way on this announcement.

"I'm afraid we must owe you the sum, then," said Ned, recovering his composure, "for we have only one dollar left, having been robbed last night; but as we mean to work in this neighbourhood, I dare say you will trust us."

The man agreed to this, and having directed the travellers to the settlement of Weaver Creek, resumed his work, while they proceeded on their way. Tom's digestion did not suffer in consequence of his golden draught, and we may here remark, for the benefit of the curious, that he never afterwards experienced any evil effects from it. We may further add, that he did not forget to discharge the debt.

After half-an-hour's ride they came in sight of a few straggling diggers, from whom they learned that the settlement, or village, or town of Weaver Creek was about two miles further on, and in a quarter of an hour they reached it.

The spot on which it stood was wild and romantic, embosomed among lofty wooded hills, whose sides were indented by many a rich ravine, and seamed by many a brawling water-course. Here digging was, as the miners have it, in full blast. Pick, and shovel, and cradle, and long-tom, and prospecting-pan — all were being plied with the utmost energy and with unwearied perseverance. The whole valley was cut up and converted into a net-work of holes and mud-heaps, and the mountain slopes were covered with the cabins, huts, and canvas tents of the miners.

About the centre of the settlement, which was a very scattered one, stood a log-house or cabin, of somewhat larger dimensions than the generality of those around it. This was the grand hotel, restaurant, and gambling-house of the place, besides being the scene of the trials and executions that occasionally took place. Some such work was going forward when our travellers rode up, for the area in front of the hotel was covered with a large concourse of miners.

"I suspect they are about to try the poor wretches who attacked us last night," said Ned, dismounting at the door of the house.

He had scarcely spoken, when a couple of men ran towards them.

"Here you are, strangers," they cried, "come along and bear witness agin' them blackguards; they're just about to be strung up. We'll look after your horses."

The duty was a disagreeable one, but it could not be avoided, so Ned and Tom suffered themselves to be led into the centre of the ring where the three culprits were standing already pinioned, and with the ropes round their necks. For a short time silence was obtained while Ned stated the circumstances of the robbery, and also the facts regarding the murder of which Black Jim had been previously found guilty. Then there was a general shout of "String 'em up!" "Up wi' the varmints!" and such phrases; but a short respite was granted in consequence of Black Jim expressing a desire to speak with Ned Sinton.

"What have you to say to me?" inquired Ned, in a low tone, as he walked close up to the wretched man, who, although his minutes on earth were numbered, looked as if he were absolutely indifferent to his fate.

"I've only to say," answered the culprit, sternly, "that of all the people I leaves behind me in this world there's but one I wish I hadn't bin bad to, and that's Kate Morgan. You know something of her, though you've never seen her — I know that. Tell her I — no, tell her she'll find the gold I robbed her of at the foot o' the pine-tree behind the tent she's livin' in jist now. An' tell her that her little sister's not dead, though she don't believe me. I took the child to —"

"Come, come, ha' done wi' yer whisperin'," cried several of the bystanders, who were becoming impatient of delay.

"Have patience," said Ned, raising his hand. "The man is telling me something of importance."

"I've done," growled Black Jim, scowling on the crowd with a look of hate; "I wish I hadn't said so much."

The rope was tightened as he spoke, and Ned, turning abruptly on his heel, hurried away with his friend from the spot just as the three robbers were run up and suspended from the branch of the tree, beneath and around which the crowd stood.

Entering the inn, and seating themselves in a retired corner of the crowded gambling-room, Ned and Tom proceeded to discuss their present prospects and future plans in a frame of mind that was by no means enviable. They were several hundreds of miles distant from the scene of their first home at the diggings, without a dollar in their pockets, and only a horse between them. With the exception of the clothes on their backs, and Ned's portfolio of drawing materials, which he always carried slung across his shoulder, they had nothing else in the world. Their first and most urgent necessity was supper, in order to procure which it behoved them to sell Tom's horse. This was easily done, as, on application to the landlord, they were directed to a trader who was on the point of setting out on an expedition to Sacramento city, and who readily purchased the horse for less than half its value.

Being thus put in possession of funds sufficient at least for a few days, they sat down to supper with relieved minds, and afterwards went out to stroll about the settlement, and take a look at the various diggings. The miners here worked chiefly at the bars or sand-banks thrown up in various places by the river which coursed through their valley; but the labour was severe, and the return not sufficient to attract impatient and sanguine miners, although quite remunerative enough to those who wrought with steady perseverance. The district had been well worked, and many of the miners were out prospecting for new fields of labour. A few companies had been formed, and these, by united action and with the aid of long-toms, were well rewarded, but single diggers and pan-washers were beginning to become disheartened.

"Our prospects are not bright," observed Tom, sitting down on a rock close to the hut of a Yankee who was delving busily in a hole hard by.

"True," answered Ned, "in one sense they are not bright, but in another sense they are, for I never yet, in all my travels, beheld so beautiful and bright a prospect of land and water as we have from this spot. Just look at it, Tom; forget your golden dreams for a little, if you can, and look abroad upon the splendid face of nature."

Ned's eye brightened as he spoke, for his love and admiration of the beauties and charms of nature amounted almost to a passion. Tom, also, was a sincere admirer of lovely, and especially of wild, scenery, although he did not express his feelings so enthusiastically.

"Have you got your colours with you?" he inquired.

"I have; and if you have patience enough to sit here for half-an-hour I'll sketch it. If not, take a stroll, and you'll find me here when you return."

"I can admire nature for even longer than that period, but I cannot consent to watch a sketcher of nature even for five minutes, so I'll take a stroll."

In a few minutes Ned, with book on knee and pencil in hand, was busily engaged in transferring the scene to paper, oblivious of gold, and prospects, and everything else, and utterly ignorant of the fact that the Yankee digger, having become curious as to what the stranger could be about, had quitted his hole, and now stood behind him quietly looking over his shoulder.

The sketch was a very beautiful one, for, in addition to the varied character of the scenery and the noble background of the Sierra Nevada, which here presented some of its wildest and most fantastic outlines, the half-ruined hut of the Yankee, with the tools and other articles scattered around it, formed a picturesque foreground. We have elsewhere remarked that our hero was a good draughtsman. In particular, he had a fine eye for colour, and always, when possible, made coloured sketches during his travels in California. On the present occasion, the rich warm glow of sunset was admirably given, and the Yankee stood gazing at the work, transfixed with amazement and delight. Ned first became aware of his proximity by the somewhat startling exclamation, uttered close to his ear, —

"Wall, stranger, you *air* a screamer, that's a fact!"

"I presume you mean that for a compliment," said Ned, looking up with a smile at the tall, wiry, sun-burnt, red-flannel-shirted, straw-hatted creature that leaned on his pick-axe beside him.

"No, I don't; I ain't used to butter nobody. I guess you've bin raised to that sort o' thing?"

"No, I merely practise it as an amateur," answered Ned, resuming his work.

"Now, that is cur'ous," continued the Yankee; "an' I'm kinder sorry to hear't, for if ye was purfessional I'd give ye an order."

Ned almost laughed outright at this remark, but he checked himself as the idea flashed across him that he might perhaps make his pencil useful in present circumstances.

"I'm not professional as yet," he said, gravely; "but I have no objection to become so if art is encouraged in these diggings."

"I guess it will be, if you shew yer work. Now, what'll ye ax for that bit!"

This was a home question, and a poser, for Ned had not the least idea of what sum he ought to ask for his work, and at the same time he had a strong antipathy to that species of haggling, which is usually prefaced by the seller, with the reply, "What'll ye give?" There was no other means, however, of ascertaining the market-value of his sketch, so he put the objectionable question.

"I'll give ye twenty dollars, slick off."

"Very good," replied Ned, "it shall be yours in ten minutes."

"An' I say, stranger," continued the Yankee, while Ned put the finishing touches to his work, "will ye do the inside o' my hut for the same money?"

"I will," replied Ned.

The Yankee paused for a few seconds, and then added, —

"I'd like to git myself throwd into the bargain, but I guess ye'll ask more for that."

"No, I wont; I'll do it for the same sum."

"Thank'ee; that's all square. Ye see, I've got a mother in Ohio State, an' she'd give her ears for any scrap of a thing o' me or my new home; an' if ye'll git 'em both fixed off by the day arter tomorrow, I'll send 'em down to Sacramento by Sam Scott, the trader. I'll rig out and fix up the hut tomorrow mornin', so if ye come by breakfast-time I'll be ready."

Ned promised to be there at the appointed hour, as he rose and handed him the sketch, which the man, having paid the stipulated sum, carried away to his hut with evident delight.

"Halloo, I say," cried Ned.

"Wall?" answered the Yankee, stopping with a look of concern, as if he feared the artist had repented of his bargain.

"Mind you tell no one my prices, for, you see, I've not had time to consider about them yet."

"All right; mum's the word," replied the man, vanishing into his little cabin just as Tom Collins returned from his ramble.

"Halloo, Ned, what's that I hear about prices? I hope you're not offering to speculate in half-finished holes, or anything of that sort, eh?"

"Sit down here, my boy, and I'll tell you all about it."

Tom obeyed, and, with a half-surprised and more than half-amused expression, listened to his companion's narration of the scene that had just taken place, and of the plan which he had formed in his mind. This plan was carried out the following day.

By daybreak Ned was up preparing his drawing materials; then he and Tom breakfasted at the *table d'hôte*, after which the latter went to hunt for a suitable log-hut in which to carry on their joint labours, while the former proceeded to fulfil his engagement. Their night's lodging and breakfast made a terribly large gap in their slender fortune, for prices at the time happened to be enormously high, in consequence of expected supplies failing to arrive at the usual time. The bill at the hotel was ten dollars a day per man; and provisions of all kinds were so dear, that the daily earnings of the miners barely sufficed to find them in the necessaries of life. It therefore behoved our friends to obtain a private dwelling and remunerative work as fast as possible.

On reaching the little log-hut, Ned found the Yankee ready to receive him. He wore a clean new red-flannel shirt, with a blue silk kerchief round the throat; a broad-brimmed straw hat, corduroys, and fisherman's long boots. To judge from his gait, and the self-satisfied expression of his bronzed countenance, he was not a little proud of his personal appearance.

While Ned arranged his paper and colours, and sharpened the point of his pencil, the Yankee kept up a running commentary on men and things in general, rocking himself on a rudely-constructed chair the while, and smoking his pipe.

The hut was very small — not more than twelve feet by eight, and just high enough inside to permit of a six-foot man grazing the beams when he walked erect. But, although small, it was exceedingly comfortable. Its owner was his own architect and builder, being a jack-of-all-trades, and everything about the wooden edifice betokened the hand of a thorough workman, who cared not for appearance, but was sensitively alive to comfort. Comfort was stamped in unmistakeable characters on every article of furniture, and on every atom that entered into the composition of the Yankee's hut. The logs of which it was built were undressed; they were not even barked, but those edges of them that lay together were fitted and bevelled with such nicety that the keenest and most searching blast of north wind failed to discover an entrance, and was driven baffled and shrieking from the walls. The small fire-place and chimney, composed of mud and dry grass, were rude in appearance; but they were substantial, and well calculated for the work they had to perform. The seats, of which there were four — two chairs, a bench, and a stool — were of the plainest wood, and the simplest form; but they were solid as rocks, and no complaining creak, when heavy men sat down on them, betokened bad or broken constitutions. The little table — two feet by sixteen inches — was in all respects worthy of the chairs. At one end of the hut there was a bed-place, big enough for two; it was variously termed a crib, a shelf, a tumble-in, and a bunk. Its owner called it a "snoosery." This was a model of plainness and comfort. It was a mere shell about two and a half feet broad, projecting from the wall, to which it was attached on one side, the other side being supported by two wooden legs a foot high. A plank at the side, and another at the foot, in conjunction with the walls of the cottage, converted the shelf into an oblong box. But the mattress of this rude couch was formed of buffalo-skins, covered with thick, long luxurious hair; above which were spread two large green mackinaw blankets of the thickest description; and the canvas pillow-case was stuffed with the softest down, purchased from the wild-fowl of California with leaden coin, transmitted through the Yankee's unerring rifle.

There was a fishing-rod in one corner, a rifle in another, a cupboard in a third; poles and spears, several unfinished axe-handles, and a small fishing-net lay upon the rafters overhead; while various miscellaneous articles of clothing, and implements for mining hung on pegs from the walls, or lay scattered about everywhere; but in the midst of apparent confusion comfort reigned supreme, for nothing was placed so as to come in one's way; everything was cleverly arranged, so as to *lie close* and *fit in*; no article or implement was superfluous; no necessary of a miner's life was wanting; an air of thorough completeness invested the hut and everything about it; and in the midst of all sat the presiding genius of the place, with his long legs comfortably crossed, the tobacco wreaths circling round his lantern jaws, the broad-brimmed straw hat cocked jauntily on one side, his arms akimbo, and his rather languid black eyes gazing at Ned Sinton with an expression of comfortable self-satisfaction and assurance that was quite comforting to behold.

"Wall, mister, if you're ready, I guess ye'd better fire away."

"One second more and I shall commence," replied Ned; "I beg pardon, may I ask your name?"

"Jefferson — Abel Jefferson to command," answered the Yankee, relighting the large clay pipe which he had just filled, and stuffing down the glowing tobacco with the end of his little finger as slowly and deliberately as though that member were a salamander. "What's yourn!"

"Edward Sinton. Now, Mr. Jefferson, in what position do you intend to sit?"

"Jest as I'm settin' now."

"Then you must sit still, at least for a few minutes at a time, because I cannot sketch you while you keep rocking so."

"No! now that's a pity, for I never sits no other way when I'm to home; an' it would look more nat'ral an' raal like to the old 'ooman if I was drawd rockin'. However, fire away, and sing out when ye want me to stop. Mind ye, put in the whole o' me. None o' yer half-lengths. I never goes in for half-lengths. I always goes the whole length, an' a leetle shave more. See that ye don't forget the mole on the side o' my nose. My poor dear old mother wouldn't believe it was me if the mole warn't there as big as life, with the two hairs in the middle of it. An' I say, mister, mind that I hate flatterers, so don't flatter me no how."

"It wouldn't be easy to do so," thought Ned, as he plied his pencil, but he did not deem it advisable to give expression to his thoughts.

"Now, then, sit still for a moment," said Ned.

The Yankee instantly let the front legs of his chair come to the ground with a bang, and gazed right before him with that intensely-grave, cataleptic stare that is wont to overspread the countenances of men when they are being photographed.

Ned laughed inwardly, and proceeded with his work in silence.

"I guess there's Sam at the door," said Abel Jefferson, blowing a cloud of smoke from his mouth that might have made a small cannon envious.

The door flew open as he spoke, and Sam Scott, the trader, strode into the hut. He was a tall, raw-boned man, with a good-humoured but intensely impudent expression of countenance, and tanned to a rich dark brown by constant exposure to the weather in the prosecution of his arduous calling.

"Halloo! stranger, what air *you* up to!" inquired Sam, sitting down on the bench behind Ned, and looking over his shoulder.

Ned might perhaps have replied to this question despite its unceremoniousness, had not the Yankee followed it up by spitting over his shoulder into the fire-place. As it was, he kept silence, and went on with his work.

"Why I *do* declare," continued Sam, "if you ain't *photogged* here as small as life, mole an' all, like nothin'. I say, stranger, ain't you a Britisher?"

Sam again followed up his question with a shot at the fire-place.

"Yes," answered Ned, somewhat angrily, "and I am so much of a Britisher, that I positively object to your spitting past my ear."

"No, you don't, do you? Now, that is cur'ous. I do believe if you Britishers had your own way, you'd not let us spit at all. What air you better than we, that you hold your heads so high, and give yourselves sich airs! that's what *I* want to know."

Ned's disgust having subsided, he replied —

"If we do hold our heads high, it is because we are straightforward, and not afraid to look any man in the face. As to giving ourselves airs, you mistake our natural reserve and dislike to obtrude ourselves upon strangers for pride; and in this respect, at least, if in no other, we are better than you — we don't spit all over each other's floors and close past each other's noses."

"Wall, now, stranger, if you choose to be resarved, and we choose to be free-an'-easy, where's the differ? We've a right to have our own customs, and do as we please as well as you, I guess."

"Hear, hear!" cried Abel Jefferson, commencing to rock himself again, and to smoke more violently than ever. "What say ye to that, mister?"

"Only this," answered Ned, as he put the finishing touches to his sketch, "that whereas we claim only the right to do to and with ourselves what we please, you Yankees claim the right to do to and with *everybody, else* what you please. I have no objection whatever to your spitting, but I do object to your spitting over my shoulder."

"Do you?" said Sam Scott, in a slightly sarcastic tone, "an' suppose I don't stop firin' over your shoulder, what then?"

"I'll make you," replied Ned, waxing indignant at the man's cool impudence.

"How?" inquired Sam.

Ned rose and shook back the flaxen curls from his flushed face, as he replied, "By opening the door and kicking you out of the hut."

He repented of the hasty expression the moment it passed his lips, so he turned to Jefferson and handed him the drawing for inspection. Sam Scott remained seated. Whether he felt that Ned was thoroughly capable of putting his threat in execution or not we cannot tell, but he evinced no feeling of anger as he continued the conversation.

"I guess if you did that, you'd have to fight me, and you'd find me pretty smart with the bowie-knife an' the revolver, either in the dark or in daylight."

Sam here referred to the custom prevalent among the Yankees in some parts of the United States of duelling with bowie-knives or with pistols in a darkened room.

"And suppose," answered Ned, with a smile — "suppose that I refused to fight, what then?"

"Why, then, you'd be called a coward all over the diggin's, and you'd have to fight to clear your character."

"And suppose I didn't care a straw for being called a coward, and wouldn't attempt to clear my character?"

"Why, then, I guess, I'd have to kick you in public till you were obligated to fight."

"But suppose still further," continued Ned, assuming the air of a philosopher discussing a profoundly-abstruse point in science — "suppose that, being the stronger man, I should prevent you from kicking me by knocking you down, what then?"

"Why, then, I'd be compelled to snuff you out slick off?"

Sam Scott smiled as he spoke, and touched the handle of his revolver.

"Which means," said Ned, "that you would become a cold-blooded murderer."

"So you Britishers call it."

"And so Judge Lynch would call it, if I am not mistaken, which would insure your being snuffed out too, pretty effectually."

"Wrong, you air, stranger," replied the trader; "Judge Lynch regards affairs of honour in a very different light, I guess. I don't think he'd scrag me for that."

Further investigation of this interesting topic was interrupted by Abel Jefferson, who had been gazing in wrapt admiration at the picture for at least five minutes, pronouncing the work "fuss rate," emphatically.

"It's jest what'll warm up the old 'ooman's heart, like a big fire in a winter day. Won't she screech when she claps her peepers on't, an' go yellin' round among the neighbours, shewin' the pictur' o' 'her boy Abel,' an' his house at the gold diggin's?"

The two friends commented pretty freely on the merits of the work, without the smallest consideration for the feelings of the artist. Fortunately they had nothing but good to say about it. Sam Scott, indeed, objected a little to the sketchy manner in which some of the subordinate accessories were touched in, and remarked that the two large hairs on the mole were almost invisible; but Jefferson persisted in maintaining that the work was "fuss rate," and faultless.

The stipulated sum was paid; and Ned, bidding his new friends good-morning, returned to the inn, for the purpose of discussing dinner and plans with Tom Collins.

CHAPTER XVIII.

*Ned's New Profession pays admirably — He and Tom
Wax Philosophical — "Pat" comes for a "Landscape"
of himself — Lynch Law and the Doctors — Ned's
Sitters — A Yankee Swell receives a Gentle Rebuff.*

The ups and downs, and the outs and ins of life are, as every one is
aware, exceedingly curious, — sometimes pleasant, often the reverse,
and not infrequently abrupt.

On the day of their arrival at the settlement, Ned and Tom were
almost beggars; a dollar or two being all the cash they possessed,
besides the gold-dust swallowed by the latter, which being, as Tom
remarked, sunk money, was not available for present purposes.

One week later, they were, as Abel Jefferson expressed it, "driving
a roaring trade in pictur's," and in the receipt of fifty dollars, or £10 a
day! Goods and provisions of all kinds had been suddenly thrown into
the settlement by speculators, so that living became comparatively
cheap; several new and profitable diggings had been discovered, in
consequence of which gold became plentiful; and the result of all was
that Edward Sinton, esquire, portrait and landscape painter, had
more orders than he could accept, at almost any price he chose to
name. Men who every Saturday came into the settlement to throw
away their hard-earned gains in the gambling-houses, or to purchase
provisions for the campaign of the following week, were delighted to
have an opportunity of procuring their portraits, and were willing to
pay any sum for them, so that, had our hero been so disposed, he could
have fleeced the miners to a considerable extent. But Ned was not so
disposed, either by nature or necessity. He fixed what he considered
fair remunerative prices for his work, according to the tariff of the diggings, and so arranged it that he made as much per day as he would
have realised had he been the fortunate possessor of one of the best
"claims" in the neighbourhood.

Tom Collins, meanwhile, went out prospecting, and speedily discovered a spot of ground which, when wrought with the pan, turned
him in twenty dollars a day. So that, in the course of a fortnight, our
adventurers found themselves comparatively rich men. This was satisfactory, and Ned admitted as much one morning to Tom, as he sat on
a three-legged stool in his studio — i.e., a dilapidated log-hut — preparing for a sitter, while the latter was busily engaged in concluding
his morning repast of damper, pork, and beans.

"There's no doubt about it, Tom," said he, pegging a sheet of
drawing-paper to a flat board, "we are rapidly making our fortunes,
my boy; but d'you know, I'm determined to postpone that desirable
event, and take to rambling again."

"There you go," said Tom, somewhat testily, as he lit a cigar, and lay down on his bed to enjoy it; "you are never content; I knew it wouldn't last; you're a rolling stone, and will end in being a beggar. Do you really mean to say that you intend to give up a lucrative profession and become a vagrant? — for such you will be, if you take to wandering about the country without any object in view."

"Indeed, I do," answered Ned. "How often am I to tell you that I don't and *won't* consider the making of money the chief good of this world? Doubtless, it is an uncommonly necessary thing, especially to those who have families to support; but I am firmly convinced that this life was meant to be enjoyed, and I mean to enjoy it accordingly."

"I agree with you, Ned, heartily; but if every one enjoyed life as you propose to do, and took to rambling over the face of the earth, there would be no work done, and nothing could be had for love or money — except what grew spontaneously; and that would be a joyful state of things, wouldn't it?"

Tom Collins, indulging the belief that he had taken up an unassailable position, propelled from his lips a long thin cloud of smoke, and smiled through it at his friend.

"Your style of reasoning is rather wild, to say the least of it," answered Ned, as he rubbed down his colours on the bottom of a broken plate. "In the first place, you assume that I propose to spend *all* my life in rambling; and, in the second place, you found your argument on the absurd supposition that everybody else must find their sole enjoyment in the same occupation."

"How I wish," sighed Tom Collins, smoking languidly, "that there was no such thing as reasoning. You would be a much more agreeable fellow, Ned, if you didn't argue."

"It takes two to make an argument," remarked Ned. "Well, but couldn't you *converse* without arguing?"

"Certainly, if you would never contradict what I say, nor make an incorrect statement, nor draw a wrong conclusion, nor object to being contradicted when I think you are in the wrong."

Tom sighed deeply, and drew comfort from his cigar. In a few minutes he resumed, — "Well, but what do you mean by enjoying life?"

Ned Sinton pondered the question a few seconds, and then replied, —

"I mean this: the way to enjoy life is to do all the good you can, by working just enough to support yourself and your family, if you have one; to assist in spreading the gospel, and to enable you to help a friend in need; and to alleviate the condition of the poor, the sick, and the destitute. To work for more than this is to be greedy; to work for less is to be reprehensibly lazy. This amount of work being done, men ought to mingle with their fellow-creatures, and wander abroad as much as may be among the beautiful works of their Creator."

"A very pretty theory, doubtless," replied Tom; "but, pray, in what manner will your proposed ramble advance the interests of religion, or enable you to do the extra ordinary amount of good you speak of?"

"There you go again, Tom; you ask me the abstract question, 'What do you mean by enjoying life?' and when I reply, you object to the answer as not being applicable to the present case. Of course, it is not. I did not intend it to be. The good I mean to do in my present ramble is chiefly, if not solely, to my own body and mind —"

"Stop, my dear fellow," interrupted Tom, "don't become energetic! I accept your answer to the general question; but how many people, think you, can afford to put your theory in practice?"

"Very, very few," replied Ned, earnestly; "but that does not affect the truth of my theory. Men *will* toil night and day to accumulate gold, until their bodies and souls are incapable of enjoying the good things which gold can purchase, and they are infatuated enough to plume themselves on this account, as being diligent men of business; while others, alas! are compelled thus to toil in order to procure the bare necessaries of life; but these melancholy facts do not prove the principle of 'grind-and-toil' to be a right one; much less do they constitute a reason for my refusing to enjoy life in the right way when I have the power."

Tom made no reply, but the vigorous puffs from his cigar seemed to indicate that he pondered these things deeply. A few minutes afterwards, Ned's expected sitter entered. He was a tall burly Irishman, with a red-flannel shirt, open at the neck, a pair of huge long boots, and a wide-awake.

"The top o' the mornin' to yees," said the man, pulling off his hat as he entered.

"Good-morning, friend," said Ned, as Tom Collins rose, shouldered his pick and shovel, and left the hut. "You are punctual, and deserve credit for so good a quality. Pray, sit down."

"Faix, then, I don't know what a 'quality' is, but av it's a good thing I've no objection," replied the man, taking a seat on the edge of the bed which Tom had just vacated. "I wos wantin' to ax ye, sir, av ye could put in me pick and shovel in the lan'scape."

"In the landscape, Pat!" exclaimed Ned, addressing his visitor by the generic name of the species; "I thought you wanted a portrait."

"Troth, then, I don't know which it is ye call it; but I wants a pictur' o' meself all over, from the top o' me hat to the sole o' me boots. Isn't that a lan'scape?"

"No, it's a portrait."

"Then it's a porthraite I wants; an' if ye'll put in the pick and shovel, I'll give ye two dollars a pace for them."

"I'll put them in, Pat, for nothing," replied Ned, smiling, as he commenced his sketch. "I suppose you intend to send this to some fair one in old Ireland?"

Pat did not reply at once. "Sure," said he, slowly, "I niver thought of her in that way before, but maybe she was fair wance, though she's been a'most as black as bog-oak for half-a-cintury. It's for me grandmother I want it."

"Your grandmother! that's curious, now; the last man I painted meant to send the likeness to his mother."

"Not so cur'ous neither," replied the man, with some feeling; "it's my opinion, the further a man goes from the owld country, and the rougher he becomes wi' scrapin' up and down through the world, the more tinder his heart gits when he thinks o' his mother. Me own mother died whin I wos a bit spalpeen, an' I lived wi' me grandmother, bliss her heart, ever since, — at laste till I took to wanderin', which was tin years past."

"So long! Pat, you must have wandered far in that time. Have you ever been away far into the interior of this country, among the mountains, in the course of your wanderings!"

"Among the mountains, is it? Indeed I have, just; an' a most tree-mendous beautiful sight it is. Wos ye goin' there?"

"I've been thinking about it. Is the shooting good?"

"Shootin', ah! av ye'd bin wi' me an' Bill Simmons, two summers ago, ye'd have had more nor enough o' shootin'. The grizzlies are thick as paes, and the buffaloes swarm in the valleys like muskaitoes, not to mintion wolves, and beavers, and badgers, and deer, an' sich like — forby the red Injuns; we shot six o' them critters about the legs an' arms in self defence, an' they shot us too — they put an arrow dane through the pint o' Bill's nose, an' wan ripped up me left arm, it did." (Pat bared the brawny limb, and exhibited the wound as he spoke.) "Shootin', is it? faix there's the hoith o' shootin' there, an' no end o' sainery."

The conversation was interrupted at this point by the door being burst violently open, and several men rushing into the hut. They grasped the Irishman by the arms, and attempted to drag him out, but Pat seized hold of the plank on the edge of which he sat, and refused to move at first.

"Come along, boy," cried one, boisterously; "we're goin' to lynch a doctor, an' we want you to swear to him."

"Ay, an' to swear *at* him too, if ye like; he's a rig'lar cheat; bin killin' us off by the dozen, as cool as ye like, and pretendin' to be an M.D. all the time."

"There's more than wan," cried another man, seizing Pat again by the arm; "won't ye come, man?"

"Och! av coorse I will; av it's to do any good to the public, I'm yer man. Hooray! for the people, an' down wi' the aristock-racy."

This sentiment was received with a shout of delight, and several exclamations of "Bah!" as the party hurried in a body from the studio. Ned, having thus nothing to do, rose, and followed them towards the centre of the settlement, where a large crowd was collecting to try the unhappy doctors above referred to.

There were six of them, all disreputable-looking rascals, who had set up for doctors, and had carried on a thriving business among the sick miners, — of whom there were many at that time, — until a genuine doctor arrived at the place, and discovered and exposed them. The miners were fortunately not bloodthirsty at this time, so the six self-dubbed M.D.s, instead of being hanged, were banished for ever from the settlement. Half-an-hour later the miners were busy in their respective claims, and Ned Sinton was again seated before his "lan'scape" of the Irishman.

Just as he was completing the sketch, the door opened slowly, and a very remarkable man swaggered into the room, and spat on the centre of the floor. He was dressed in the extreme of the fashion then prevalent in the Eastern States. A superfine black coat, silk vest, superfine black trousers, patent-leather boots, kid gloves, and a black silk hat! A more unnatural apparition at the diggings could not well be imagined. Ned Sinton could hardly credit his eyes, but no rubbing of them would dispel the vision. There he stood, a regular Broadway swell, whose love of change had induced him to seek his fortune in the gold-regions of California, and whose vanity had induced him to retain his drawing-room costume.

This man, besides being possessed of a superabundance of super-cilious impudence, also possessed a set of digging tools, the handles of which were made of polished oak and walnut, with bright brass ferrules. With these he proposed to dig his fortune in a leisurely way; meanwhile, finding the weather rather hot, he had made up his mind to have his portrait done.

Thrusting his hands into his pockets, this gentleman shut the door with his heel, turned his back to the fire-place — from the mere force of habit, for there was no fire — and again spat upon the floor, after which he said:

"I say, stranger, what's your charge for a likeness?"

"You will excuse me, sir," answered Ned, "if, before replying to that question, I beg of you not to spit on my floor."

The Yankee uttered an exclamation of surprise, and asked, "Why not, stranger?"

"Because I don't like it."

"You wouldn't have me spit in my hat, would you?" inquired the dandy.

"Certainly not."

"Where then?"

Ned pointed to a large wooden box which stood close to the fire-place, and said, "There — I have provided a box for the accommodation of those sitters who indulge in that disagreeable practice. If you can't avoid spitting, do it there."

"Wall, now, you Britishers are strange critters. But you haven't told me your price for a portrait."

"I fear that I cannot paint you at any price," replied Ned, without looking up from his paper, while Pat listened to the conversation with a comical leer on his broad countenance.

"Why not, stranger?" asked the dandy, in surprise.

"Because I'm giving up business, and don't wish to take any more orders."

"Then I'll set here, I guess, an' look at ye while ye knock off that one," said the man, sitting down close to Ned's elbow, and again spitting on the floor. Whether he did so intentionally or not we cannot tell, probably not, but the effect upon Ned was so strong that he rose deliberately, opened the door, and pointed to the passage thus set free, without uttering a word. His look, however, was quite sufficient. The dandy rose abruptly, and walked out in silence, leaving Ned to shut the door quietly behind him and return to his work, while the Irishman rolled in convulsions of laughter on Tom Collins's bed.

Ned's sitters, as we have hinted, were numerous and extremely various. Sometimes he was visited by sentimental and home-sick miners, and occasionally by dandy miners, such as we have described, but his chief customers were the rough, hearty men from "old England," "owld Ireland," and from the Western States; with all of whom he had many a pleasant and profitable hour's conversation, and from many of whom, especially the latter, he obtained valuable and interesting information in reference to the wild regions of the interior which he longed so much to see.

CHAPTER XIX.

*The Wilderness again — A Splendid Valley —
Gigantic Trees and Waterfalls — Tom meets with an
Accident — Both meet with many Surprises —
Mysteries, Caverns, Doleful Sounds,
and Grizzly-Bear-Catchers.*

Mounted on gallant steeds, Ned and his friend again appear in the
wilderness in the afternoon of a beautiful autumn day. They had
ridden far that day. Dust covered their garments, and foam bespat-
tered the chests of their horses, but the spirits of men and beasts were
not yet subdued, for their muscles, by long practice, were inured to
hardship. Many days had passed since they left the scene of their
recent successful labours, and many a weary league had been tra-
versed over the unknown regions of the interior. They were lost, in
one sense of that term — charmingly, romantically lost — that is to
say, neither Ned nor Tom had the most distant idea of where they
were, or what they were coming to, but both of them carried pocket-
compasses, and they knew that by appealing to these, and to the daily
jotting of the route they had travelled, they could ascertain pretty
closely the direction that was necessary to be pursued in order to
strike the great San Joaquin river.

Very different was the scenery through which they now rode from
that of the northern diggings. The most stupendous and magnificent
mountains in the world surrounded, on all sides, the valley through
which they passed, giving to it an air of peaceful seclusion; yet it was
not gloomy, for the level land was broad and fertile, and so varied in
aspect that it seemed as though a beautiful world were enclosed by
those mighty hills.

Large tracts of the valley were covered with wild oats and rich
grass, affording excellent pasturage for the deer that roamed about in
large herds. Lakes of various sizes sustained thousands of wild-fowl
on their calm breasts, and a noble river coursed down its entire
length. Oaks, chestnuts, and cypresses grew in groups all over the
landscape, and up on the hill-sides firs of gigantic size reared their
straight stems high above the surrounding trees.

But the point in the scenery which struck the travellers as being
most peculiar was the precipitous character of the sides of many of the
vast mountains and the flatness of their summits. Tom Collins, who
was a good judge of heights, having travelled in several mountainous
regions of the world, estimated the nearest precipices to be upwards of
three thousand feet, without a break from top to bottom, but the
ranges in the background towered far above these, and must have
been at least double.

"I never saw anything like this before, Tom," said Ned, in a suppressed voice.

"I did not believe such sublime scenery existed," replied his companion. "I have travelled in Switzerland and Norway, but this surpasses both. Truly it was worth while to give up our gold-digging in order to see this."

"Yet there are many," rejoined Ned, "who travel just far enough into California to reach the diggings, where they remain till their fortunes are made, or till their hopes are disappointed, and then return to England and write a book, perchance, in which they speak as authoritatively as if they had swept the whole region, north and south, east and west. Little wonder that we find such travellers contradicting each other flatly. One speaks of 'California' as being the most splendid agricultural country in the world, and advises every one to emigrate at once; while another condemns it as an arid, unproductive region, fit only for the support of Indians and grizzly-bears; — the fact being, that both speak, (correctly enough, it may be), of the very small portion of California they have respectively visited. Why, the more I travel in this wonderful land the more I feel how very little I know about it; and had I returned to England without having seen this valley, I should have missed one of the most remarkable sights, not only in the country, but, I verily believe, in the world. If you ever return home, Tom, and are persuaded, 'at the earnest request of numerous friends,' to write a book, *don't* dogmatise as to *facts*; remember how limited your experience has been, and don't forget that *facts* in one valley are not facts at all in another valley eight or ten miles off."

"Perhaps," suggested Tom Collins, patting the arched neck of his steed — "perhaps the advice with which you have just favoured me might, with greater propriety, have proceeded from me to you; for, considering the copious variety of your sentiments on this and other subjects, and the fluency with which you utter them, it is likely that you will rush into print long before I timidly venture, with characteristic modesty, even to grasp the pen!"

As Tom ceased speaking they came upon a forest of pine, or fir trees, in the midst of which towered a tree of such gigantic height, that its appearance caused them simultaneously to draw up, and gaze at it in silent wonder.

"Can it be possible," said Ned, "that our eyes don't deceive us! Surely some peculiarity in the atmosphere gives that tree false proportions?"

Without answering, Tom galloped towards the tree in question, closely followed by his friend.

Instead of any delusive haze being cleared away, however, the tree grew larger as they approached, and when they halted about twenty yards from it, they felt that they were indeed in the presence of the monarch of the forest. The tree, which they measured, after viewing it in wondering admiration from all points of view, was ninety-three feet in circumference, and it could not have been less than three hundred and sixty feet high. They little knew that, many years afterwards, the bark of this giant tree, to the height of a hundred and sixteen feet, was to be removed to England, built up in its original form, and exhibited in the great Crystal Palace of Sydenham; yet so it was, and part of the "mother of the forest" may be seen there at this day.

Towards evening the travellers drew near to the head of the valley.

"We must be approaching a waterfall of no ordinary size," remarked Tom, as they rode through the dark shades of the forest, which were pretty extensive there.

"I have heard its roar for some time," answered Ned, "but until we clear this belt of trees we shan't see it."

Just then the roar of the fall burst upon them with such deafening violence, that they involuntarily started. It seemed as if a mighty torrent had burst its bounds and was about to sweep them away, along with the forest through which they rode. Pressing forward in eager haste, they soon found that their having doubled round a huge mountain barrier, which the trees had hitherto concealed from them, was the cause of the sudden increase in the roar of the fall, but they were still unable to see it, owing to the dense foliage that overshadowed them. As they galloped on, the thunder of falling waters became more deep and intense, until they reached an elevated spot, comparatively free from trees, which overlooked the valley, and revealed a sight such as is not equalled even by Niagara itself.

A succession of wall-like mountains rose in two tiers before them literally into the clouds, for several of the lower clouds floated far below the highest peaks, and from the summit of the highest range a river, equal to the Thames at Richmond, dropt sheer down a fall of above two thousand feet. Here it met the summit of the lower mountain-range, on which it burst with a deep-toned, sullen, never-ceasing roar, comparable only to eternal thunder. A white cloud of spray received the falling river in its soft embrace, and sent it forth again — turbulent and foam bespeckled — towards its second leap, another thousand feet, into the plain below. The entire height of the fall was above three thousand feet. Its sublimity no language can convey. Its irresistible effect on the minds of the wanderers was to turn their thoughts to the almighty Creator of so awe-inspiring and wonderful a scene.

Here they discovered another tree, which was so large that their thoughts were diverted even from the extraordinary cataract for a short time. Unlike the previous one, this monarch of the woods lay prostrate on the ground, but its diameter near the root was so great that they could not see over it though seated on horseback. It measured a hundred and twenty feet in circumference, and, when standing, must have been little, if at all, short of five hundred feet in height.

Surrounded as they were by such noble and stupendous works of God, the travellers could not find words to express their feelings. Deep emotion has no articulate language. The heaving breast and the glowing eye alone indicate the fervour of the thoughts within. For a long time they sat gazing round them in silent wonder and admiration, then they dismounted to measure the great tree, and after that Ned sat down to sketch the fall, while his companion rode forward to select a spot for camping on.

Tom had not proceeded far when he came upon the track of wheels in the grass, a sight which surprised him much, for into that remote region he had supposed few travellers ventured, even on horseback. The depth and breadth of the tracks, too, surprised him not a little. They were much deeper and broader than those caused by any species of cart he had yet seen or heard of in the country, and the width apart was so great, that he began to suspect he must have mistaken a curious freak of nature for the tracks of a gigantic vehicle. Following the track for some distance, he came to a muddy spot, where the footprints of men and horses became distinctly visible. A little further on he passed the mouth of what appeared to be a cavern, and, being of an inquisitive disposition, he dismounted and tied his horse to a tree, intending to examine the entrance.

To enter a dark cave, in a wild, unknown region, with the din of a thundering cataract filling the ears, just after having discovered tracks of a mysterious nature in the neighbourhood, was so trying to Tom's nervous system, that he half resolved to give it up; but the exploration of a cavern has a fascination to some dispositions which every one cannot understand. Tom said "Pshaw!" to himself in an undertone, and boldly stepping into the dark portals of the cave, he disappeared.

Meanwhile, Edward Sinton finished his sketch, and, supposing that Tom was waiting for him in advance, he mounted and galloped forward as fast as the nature of the ground would allow.

Soon he came to the tracks before mentioned, and shortly after to the muddy spot with the footprints. Here he drew rein, and dismounted to examine the marks more closely. Our hero was as much perplexed as his friend had been at the unusually broad tracks of the vehicle which had passed that way. Leading his horse by the bridle, he advanced slowly until he came to the spot where Tom's horse stood fastened to a tree, — a sight which alarmed him greatly, for the place was not such as any one would have selected for an encampment, yet had any foul play befallen his friend, he knew well that the horse would not have been left quietly there.

Sorely puzzled, and filled with anxious fears, he examined the spot carefully, and at last came upon the entrance to the cavern, before which he paused, uncertain what to do. The shadows of evening were fast falling on the scene, and he experienced a feeling of dread as he gazed into the profound gloom. He was convinced that Tom must be there; but the silence, and the length of time he had been absent, led him to fear that some accident had befallen his friend.

"Ho! Tom!" he shouted, on entering, "are you there?" There was a rolling echo within, but no voice replied to the question.

Again Ned shouted at the full pitch of his lungs, and this time he thought he heard a faint reply. Hurrying forward eagerly, as quickly as he dared, he repeated his shout, but the declivity of the entrance became so great that he lost his footing and well-nigh fell headlong down a steep incline. He succeeded, however, in regaining his hold, and clambered back to the entrance as quickly as possible.

Here he caught up a pine-knot, struck a light and kindled it, and, with this torch held high above his head, advanced once more into the cavern.

The voice of Tom Collins at this moment came loud and full from the interior, — "Take care, Ned, there's a sharp descent; I've tumbled down it, but I don't think I'm much hurt."

"Cheer up, my boy," cried Ned, heartily; "I'll get you out in a minute."

The next moment he stood beside his friend, who had risen from the rugged floor of the cave, and sat on a piece of rock, resting his head on his hand.

"Are you badly hurt, my poor fellow?" said Ned, anxiously, going down on one knee and endeavouring to raise his friend's head. "I fear you are. Here, try a drop of this brandy. That's it. Why, you look better already. Come, now, let me examine you."

The spirit revived Tom at once, and he replied cheerfully, as he submitted to inspection, — "All right, I was only stunned a little by the fall. Catch me exploring again without a light!"

On examination, Ned found, to his great relief; that his friend's hurts were slight. He had been stunned by the severity of his fall, but no bones were broken, and only a few scratches received, so that, after another sip of brandy, he felt almost as well as ever. But he firmly resisted his companion's entreaty to leave the cavern.

"No, my boy," said he, "after paying such a price as entrance fee, I'm not going to quit until I have explored the whole of this cave, so please go out for another pine-knot or two, and I'll wait for you."

Seeing that he was determined, Ned obeyed, and soon returned with several fresh torches, two of which were ignited, and a bright light sent far and wide into the roof of the cave, which was at a great height above them.

The walls were of curious, and in some places grotesque, forms. Immense stalactites hung from the roof, and these were of varied colours, — pale green, pink, and white, — while some of them looked like cascades, which sprang from the walls, and had been petrified ere they quite reached the ground. The roof was supported by natural pillars, and various arched openings led into similar chambers, some of which were larger and more curious than the outer one.

"Do you know," said Ned Sinton, as they sat down on a rock in one of the inner chambers to rest, "this place recalls vividly to my remembrance a strange dream which I had just before leaving England."

"Indeed!" said Tom; "I hope you're not a believer in dreams. Don't, I beseech you, take it into your head that it's going to be realised at this particular moment, whatever it was."

"It would take a very strong amount of belief indeed to induce me to expect the realisation of *that* dream. Shall I tell it you?"

"Is it a very ghostly one?" inquired Tom.

"No; not at all."

"Then out with it."

Ned immediately began the narration of the remarkable dream with which this story opens, and as he went on to tell of how the stout old gentleman snuffed gold-dust, and ultimately shot up to the roof of the cave, and became a golden stalactite, Tom Collins, whose risible tendencies were easily roused, roared with laughter, until the vaulted caverns echoed again. At the end of one of these explosions, the two friends were struck dumb by certain doleful and mysterious sounds which proceeded from the further end of the inmost chamber. In starting to his feet, Tom Collins let fall his torch, and in the convulsive clutch which he made to catch it, he struck the other torch out of Ned's hand, so that instantly both were left in the profoundest darkness, with their hearts beating like sledge-hammers against their ribs.

To flee was their first and natural impulse; but to flee in the dark, over rough ground, and with very imperfect ideas as to the position of the cave's outlet, was dangerous.

"What *is* to be done?" ejaculated Tom Collins in a tone that indicated the perturbation of his heart too clearly.

At that moment Ned remembered that he had a box of matches in the pocket of his hunting-coat; so, without answering, he drew it forth, struck a light, and re-ignited the torches.

"Now, Tom," he said, "don't let us give way to unmanly fears. I have no belief whatever in ghosts or spirits, good or evil, being permitted to come in visible or audible form to frighten poor mortals. Every effect has a cause, and I'm determined to find out the cause of these strange sounds. They certainly proceed from animal lungs, whether from man or beast remains to be seen."

"Go ahead, then, I'll follow," said Tom, whose courage had returned with the light, "I'm game for anything that I can see; but I confess to you that I can *not* stand howls, and groans and darkness."

Notwithstanding their utmost efforts they failed to discover the cause of the mysterious sounds, which seemed at times to be voices muttering, while at other times they swelled out into a loud cry. All that could be certainly ascertained was, that they proceeded from the roof of the innermost cavern, and that the centre of that roof was too high to be discerned by torch-light.

"What shall we do now?" inquired Tom.

"We shall go to the summit of the hill above this cave, and see what is to be seen there. Always look at both sides of a mystery if you would fathom it; come along."

In a few minutes they stood in open air, and once more breathed freely. Mounting their horses, they ascended the steep slope of the hill above the cave, and, after some trouble, reached the summit. Here the first thing that met their gaze was a camp-fire, and near to it several men engaged in harnessing their horses to a large waggon or van. The frantic haste with which they performed the operation convinced Ned that he had discovered the cause of the mysterious voices, and that he and Tom had been the innocent cause of frightening the strangers nearly out of their wits. So engrossed were they with their work, that our travellers advanced within the circle of light of their fire before they were discovered. The man who first saw them uttered a yell, and the whole party turned round, seized their rifles, and, with terror depicted on their countenances, faced the intruders.

"Who comes here?" shouted one.

"Friends," answered Ned, laying down his rifle and advancing.

Instantly the men threw down their arms and resumed the work of harnessing their horses.

"If ye be friends," cried the one who spoke first, "give us a hand. I guess all the fiends in the bottomless pit are lo-cated jist below our feet."

"Listen to me for one moment, gentlemen," cried Ned Sinton. "I think I can relieve your minds. What have you heard or seen?"

At these words the men stopped, and looked inquiringly at their questioner.

"Seen! stranger, we've seed nothin', but we've *hear'd* a sight, we have, I calc'late. We hear'd the imps o' darkness talkin' as plain as I hear you. At first I thought it was somebody at the foot o' the hill, but all of a suddent the imps took to larfin' as if they'd split, jist under my feet, so I yelled out to my mate here to come an' yoke the beasts and git away as slick as we could. We wos jist about ready to slope when you appeared."

Ned now explained to them the cause of their alarms, and on search being made, a hole was found, as he had anticipated, close at hand among the bushes, which communicated with the cavern below, and formed a channel for the conveyance of the so-called mysterious sounds.

"And now," said Ned, "may I ask permission to pass the night with you?"

"You're welcome, stranger," replied he who seemed to be the chief of the band — a tall, bearded American, named Croft, who seemed more like a bandit than an honest man. His comrades, too, six in number, appeared a wild and reckless set of fellows, with whom one would naturally desire to hold as little intercourse as possible; but most men at the Californian diggings had more or less the aspect of brigands, so Ned Sinton and his companion felt little concern as to their characters, although they did feel a little curious as to what had brought them to such a wild region.

"If it is not taking too great a liberty," said Ned, after answering the thousand questions put to him in rapid succession by his Yankee host, "may I ask what has brought you to this out-of-the-way valley?"

"Bear-catchin'," answered the man, shortly, as he addressed himself to a large venison steak, which a comrade had just cooked for him.

"Bear-catching?" ejaculated Ned.

"Ay, an' screamin' hard work it is too, I guess; but it pays well."

"What do you do with them when caught?" inquired Tom Collins, in a somewhat sceptical tone.

"Take 'em down to the cities, an' sells 'em to fight with wild bulls."

At this answer our travellers stared at the man incredulously.

"You're strangers here, I see," he resumed, "else you'd know that we have bull and bear fights. The grizzlies are chained by one leg and the bulls let loose at 'em. The bulls charge like all possessed, but they find it hard to do much damage to Caleb, whose hide is like a double-extra rhinoceros. The grizzlies ginerally git the best of it; an' if they was let loose, they'd chaw up the bulls in no time, they would. There's a great demand for 'em jist now, an' my trade is catchin' 'em alive here in the mountains."

The big Yankee stretched out his long limbs and smoked his pipe with the complacent aspect of a man who felt proud of his profession.

"Do you mean that you seven men catch fall-grown grizzly-bears alive and take them down to the settlements?" inquired Ned in amazement.

"Sartinly I do," replied the bear-catcher; "an' why not, stranger?"

"Because I should have thought it impossible."

"Nothin"s impossible," replied the man, quietly.

"But how do you manage it?"

Instead of replying, the Yankee inquired if "the strangers" would stay over next forenoon with them.

"With much pleasure," answered Ned, not a little amused at the invitation, as well as the man's *brusque* manner.

"Well, then," continued the bear-catcher, shaking the ashes out of his pipe, and putting it into his hat, "I'll let ye see how we do it in the mornin'. Good-night."

So saying, he drew his blanket over his head and resigned himself to sleep, an example which was speedily followed by the whole party.

CHAPTER XX.

Grizzly-Bear-Catching in the Mountains — Ned and Tom dine in the midst of Romantic Scenery, and hold Sagacious Converse — The Strange Devices of Woodpeckers.

Just as day began to peep on the following morning, the camp was roused by one of the bear-catchers, a Mexican, who had been away to visit the bear-trap during the night, and now came rushing in among the sleepers, shouting —

"Hoor-roo! boy, him cotch, him cotch! big as twinty mans! fact!"

At first Ned thought the camp was attacked by savages, and he and Tom sprang to their feet and grasped their rifles, while they sought to rub their eyes open hastily. A glance at the other members of the camp, however, shewed that they were unnecessarily alarmed. Croft leisurely stretched his limbs, and then gathered himself slowly into a sitting posture, while the others arose with various degrees of reluctance.

"Bin long in?" inquired Croft.

"No, jist cotched," answered the Mexican, who sat down, lit his pipe, and smoked violently, to relieve his impatient feelings.

"Big 'un?" inquired Croft, again.

To this the Mexican answered by rolling his eyes and exclaiming "Hoh!" with a degree of vigour that left his hearers to imagine anything they pleased, and then settle it in their minds that the thing so imagined was out of all sight short of the mark.

The excitement of the man at last fully roused the sleepy crew, and Croft sprang up with the agility of a cat.

"Ho! boys," he cried, proceeding to buckle his garments round him, "up with you. Ketch the hosses, an' put to. Look alive, will you? grease your jints, *do*. Now, strangers, I'll shew you how we ketch a bar in this lo-cation; bring yer rules, for sometimes he breaks his trap, an' isn't there a spree jist!"

We need scarcely remark, that the latter part of this speech was made to Sinton and his comrade, who were drawing the charges of their revolvers and reloading.

"Is the trap far off?" inquired Ned.

"Quarter of an hour, or so. Look sharp, lads."

This exhortation was unnecessary, for the men had already caught three stout horses, all of which were attached to an enormous waggon or van, whose broad wheels accounted for the tracks discovered in the valley on the previous evening.

"That's his cage," said the bear-catcher, replying to Ned's look of inquiry. "It's all lined with sheet-iron, and would hold an ontamed streak o' lightnin', it would. Now, then, drive ahead."

The lumbering machine jolted slowly down the hill as he spoke, and while several of the party remained with the horses, Croft and our travellers, with the remainder, pushed on ahead. In less than twenty minutes, they came to a ravine filled with thick underwood, from the recesses of which came forth sounds of fierce ursine wrath that would have deterred most men from entering; but Croft knew his game was secure, and led the way confidently through the bushes, until he reached a spot on which stood what appeared to be a small log-cabin without door or window. Inside of this cabin an enormous grizzly-bear raged about furiously, thrusting his snout and claws through the interstices of the logs, and causing splinters to fly all round him, while he growled in tones of the deepest indignation.

"Oh! ain't he a bit o' thunder?" cried Croft, as he walked round the trap, gazing in with glittering eyes at every opening between the logs.

"How in the world did you get him in there?" asked Ned Sinton, as soon as his astonishment had abated sufficiently to loosen his tongue.

"Easy enough," replied Croft. "If ye observe the top o' the trap, ye'll see the rope that suspended it from the limb o' that oak. Inside there was a bit o' beef, so fixed up, that when Mister Caleb laid hold of it, he pulled a sort o' trigger, an' down came the trap, shuttin' him in slick, as ye see."

At this moment the powerful animal struggled so violently that he tilted his prison on one side, and well-nigh overturned it.

"Look out, lads," shouted Croft, darting towards a tree, and cocking his rifle, — actions in which he was imitated by all the rest of the party, with surprising agility.

"Don't fire till it turns over," he cried, sternly, on observing that two of the more timid members of his band were about to fire at the animal's legs, which appeared below the edge of the trap. Fortunately, the bear ceased its efforts just at that critical moment, and the trap fell heavily back to its original position.

"By good luck!" shouted Croft; "an' here comes the cage. Range up on the left, boys, and out with the hosses, they won't stand this."

The terrified animals were removed from the scene, trembling violently from head to foot, and the whole band, applying their shoulders to the wheels, slowly pushed the vehicle alongside of the trap until the sides of the two met.

There was a strong door in the side of the trap, which was now removed by being pulled inwards, revealing to bruin an aperture which corresponded to another door opening into the iron-lined cage. There were stout iron bars ready to be shot home the instant he condescended to pass through this entrance; but Caleb, as Croft called him, shewed himself sadly destitute of an inquiring disposition. He knew that there was now a hole in his prison-wall, for he looked at it; he knew that a hole either conducted into a place or out of it, for life-long experience had taught him that; yet he refused to avail himself of the opportunity, and continued to rage round the trap, glaring between the logs at his foes outside. It is unreasonable to suppose that he was afraid to go into the hole because it was a *dark* one, for he was well accustomed to such dark dens; besides, no one who looked at him could for a moment suppose that he was, or could be, afraid of anything at all. We must, therefore, put his conduct down to sheer obstinacy.

The men poked him with sticks; shouted at him; roared in his face; threw water over him; and even tried the effect of a shot of powder at his flank; but all to no purpose, although their efforts were continued vigorously for full two hours. The bear would *not* enter that hole on any account whatever.

"Try another shot of powder at him," cried Croft, whose patience was now almost exhausted.

The shot was fired at his flank, and was received with a ferocious growl, while the strong wood-work of the trap trembled under his efforts to escape.

"Ain't it vexin'?" said Croft, sitting down on the stump of a tree and wiping the perspiration from his forehead. Ned Sinton and Tom, who had done their utmost to assist their new acquaintance, sat down beside him and admitted that it *was* vexing. As if by one impulse, the whole party then sat down to rest, and at that moment, having, as it were, valiantly asserted his right of independent action, the bear turned slowly round and quietly scrambled through the hole. The men sprang up; the massive iron bars were shot into their sockets with a clang; and bruin was a prisoner for life.

As neither Edward Sinton nor Tom Collins had any particular desire to become bear-catchers, they bade their new friends adieu that afternoon, and continued their journey. The road, as they advanced, became more and more steep and rugged, so that they could only proceed at a walk, and in many places experienced considerable difficulty, and ran no little risk, in passing along the faces of cliffs, where the precipices ascended hundreds of feet upwards like walls, on the one hand, and descended sheer down into an unfathomable abyss, on the other. But the exceeding grandeur of the scenery amply repaid their toils, and the deep roar of that mighty cataract ever sounded in their ears. At length they reached the head of the valley, and stood under the spray of the fall, which, expanding far above and around the seething caldron whence it sprang, drenched the surrounding country with perpetual showers.

Here a gap or pass in the mountains was discovered, ascending on the left, and affording, apparently, an exit from the valley. Up this the travellers toiled until they cleared the spray of the falls, and then sat down beside a clump of trees to dry their garments in the sunshine and to cook their mid-day meal.

"What a glorious thing it is, Tom, to wander thus unrestrained amid such scenes!" said Ned Sinton, as he busied himself roasting a piece of venison, which his rifle had procured but half-an-hour before.

"How infinitely more delightful than travelling in the civilised world, where one is cheated at every turn, and watched and guarded as if robbery, or murder, or high treason were the only probable objects a traveller could have in view."

"'Comparisons,' my dear fellow — you know the proverb," replied Tom Collins; "don't uphold California at the expense of the continent. Besides, there are many in this world who would rather a thousand times wander by the classic lake of Como, with its theatrical villas and its enchanting sunshine and perfume, or paddle up the castellated Rhine, than scramble here among wild rocks, and woods, and cataracts, with the chance of meeting an occasional savage or a grizzly-bear."

"Go on, my boy," said Ned, with a touch of sarcasm in his tone, "you haven't read me half a lesson yet. Besides, the 'many' you refer to, are there not hundreds, ay, thousands, whose chief enjoyment in travelling is derived from the historical associations called up by the sight of the ruined castles and temples of classic ground — whose delight it is to think that here Napoleon crossed the Alps, as Hannibal did before him, (and many a nobody has done after him), that there, within these mouldering ruins, the oracles of old gave forth their voice — forgetting, perhaps, too easily, while they indulge in these reminiscences of the past, that the warrior's end was wholesale murder, and that the oracle spoke only to deceive poor ignorant human nature. Ha! I would not give one hearty dash into pure, uncontaminated nature for all the famous 'tours' put together."

Ned looked round him as he spoke, with a glow of enthusiasm that neither badinage nor philosophy could check.

"Just look around thee," he continued; "open thine ears, Tom, to the music of yon cataract, and expand thy nostrils to the wild perfume of these pines."

"I wouldn't, at this moment," quietly remarked Tom, "exchange for it the perfume of that venison steak, of which I pray thee to be more regardful, else thou'lt upset it into the fire."

"Oh! Tom — incorrigible!"

"Not at all, Ned. While you flatter yourself that you have all the enthusiastic study of nature to yourself, here have I succeeded, within the last few minutes, in solving a problem in natural history which has puzzled my brains for weeks past."

"And, pray thee, what may that be, most sapient philosopher?"

"Do you see yonder bird clinging to the stem of that tree, and pitching into it as if it were its most deadly foe?"

"I do — a woodpecker it is."

"Well," continued Tom, sitting down before his portion of the venison steak, "that bird has cleared up two points in natural history, which have, up till this time, been a mystery to me. The one was, why woodpeckers should spend their time in pecking the trees so incessantly; the other was, how it happened that several trees I have cut down could have had so many little holes bored in their trunks, and an acorn neatly inserted into each. Now that little bird has settled the question for me. I caught him in the act not ten minutes ago. He flew to that tree with an acorn in his beak, tried to insert it into a hole, which didn't fit, being too small; so he tried another, which did fit, poked the nut in, small end first, and tapped it scientifically home. Now, why did he do it? That's the question."

"Because he wanted to, probably," remarked Ned; "and very likely he lays up a store of food for winter in this manner."

"Very possibly. I shall make a note of this, for I'm determined to have it sifted to the bottom. Meanwhile, I'll trouble you for another junk of venison."

It was many weeks afterwards ere Tom Collins succeeded in sifting this interesting point to the bottom; but perhaps the reader may not object to have the result of his inquiries noted at this point in our story.

Many of the trees in California, on being stripped of their bark, are found to be perforated all over with holes about the size of a musket-ball. These are pierced by the woodpecker with such precision and regularity that one might believe they had been cut out by a ship-carpenter. The summer is spent by this busy little bird in making these holes and in filling them with acorns. One acorn goes to one hole, and the bird will not try to force the nut into a hole that is too small for it, but flutters round the tree until it finds one which fits it exactly. Thus one by one the holes are filled, and a store of food is laid up for winter use in a larder which secures it from the elements, and places it within reach of the depositor when the winter snows have buried all the acorns that lie upon the ground, and put them beyond the reach of woodpeckers. The birds never encroach on their store until the snow has covered the ground, then they begin to draw upon their bank; and it is a curious fact that the bills of these birds are always honoured, for their instinct enables them to detect the bad nuts with unerring certainty, so that their bank is always filled with good ones. This matter of selecting the good nuts is a mere chance with men, for often those shells which seem the soundest, are found to contain a grub instead of a nut. Even the sagacious Indian is an uncertain judge in this respect, but the woodpecker, provided by an all-wise Creator with an unerring instinct, never makes a mistake in selecting its store of food for winter.

CHAPTER XXI.

Curious Trees, and still more Curious Plains — An Interesting Discovery, followed by a Sad one — Fate of Travellers in the Mountains — A Sudden Illness — Ned proves himself to be a friend in Need and in Deed, as well as an Excellent Doctor, Hunter, Cook, and Nurse — Deer-Shooting by Firelight.

During the course of their wanderings among the mountains our hero and his companion met with many strange adventures and saw many strange sights, which, however, we cannot afford space to dwell upon here. Their knowledge in natural history, too, was wonderfully increased, for they were both observant men, and the school of nature is the best in which any one can study. Audubon, the hunter-naturalist of America, knew this well! and few men have added so much as he to the sum of human knowledge in his peculiar department, while fewer still have so wonderfully enriched the pages of romantic adventure in wild, unknown regions.

In these wanderings, too, Ned and Tom learned to know experimentally that truth is indeed stranger than fiction, and that if the writers of fairy-tales had travelled more they would have saved their imaginations a deal of trouble, and produced more extraordinary works.

The size of the trees they encountered was almost beyond belief, though none of them surpassed the giant of which an account has been already given. Among other curious trees they found *sugar-pines* growing in abundance in one part of the country. This is, perhaps, the most graceful of all the pines. With a perfectly straight and cylindrical stem and smooth bark, it rears its proud crest high above other trees, and flings its giant limbs abroad, like a sentinel guarding the forest. The stem rises to about four-fifths of its height perfectly free of branches; above this point the branches spread out almost horizontally, drooping a little at the ends from the weight of the huge cones which they bear. These cones are about a foot-and-a-half long, and under each leaf lies a seed the size of a pea, which has an agreeably sweet taste, and is much esteemed by the Indians, who use it as an article of food.

Another remarkable sight they saw was a plain, of some miles in extent, completely covered with shattered pieces of quartz, which shone with specks and veins of pure gold. Of course they had neither time nor inclination to attempt the laborious task of pulverising this quartz in order to obtain the precious metal; but Ned moralised a little as they galloped over the plain, spurning the gold beneath their horses' hoofs, as if it had been of no value whatever! They both puzzled themselves also to account for so strange an appearance; but the only solution that seemed to them at all admissible was, that a quartz vein had, at some early period of the world's history, been shattered by a volcanic eruption, and the plain thus strewn with gold.

But from the contemplation of these and many other interesting sights and phenomena we must pass to an event which seriously affected the future plans of the travellers.

One beautiful evening — such an evening as, from its deep quiet and unusual softness, leaves a lasting impression on the memory — the two horsemen found themselves slowly toiling up the steep acclivity of a mountain-ridge. Their advance was toilsome, for the way was rugged, and no track of any kind assisted them in their ascent.

"I fear the poor horses will give in," said Ned, dismounting and looking back at his companion, who slowly followed him.

"We are near the summit," answered Tom, "and they shall have a long rest there."

As he spoke, they both dismounted and advanced on foot, leading their fatigued horses by the bridles.

"Do you know," said Tom, with a sigh, "I feel more used up today than I have been since we started on this journey. I think we had better encamp and have a cup of tea; there is a little left yet, if I mistake not."

"With all my heart, Tom; I, too, feel inclined to rest, and —"

Ned paused, for at that moment they overtopped the highest edge of the ridge, and the view that burst upon them was well fitted to put to flight every previous train of thought.

The ridge on which they stood rose several hundred feet above the level of the plain beyond, and commanded a view of unknown extent towards the far west.

The richest possible sweep of country was spread out at their feet like a huge map, bathed in a glow of yellow sunshine. Lakes and streams, crags and rocks, sward, and swamp, and plain — undulating and abrupt, barren and verdant — all were there, and could be embraced in a single wide-sweeping glance. It seemed, to the entranced travellers, like the very garden of Eden. Water-fowl flew about in all directions, the whistling of their wings and their wild cries being mellowed by distance into pleasant music; and, far away on the right, where a clear lake mirrored each tree on its banks, as if the image were reality, a herd of deer were seen cooling their sides and limbs in the water, while, on the extreme horizon, a line of light indicated the shores of the vast Pacific Ocean.

Ere the travellers could find words to express their feelings, a rock, with a piece of stick and a small rag attached to it, attracted their attention.

"We are not the first who have set their feet here, it seems," said Ned, pointing to the signal.

"Strange!" muttered Tom Collins, as they turned towards the rock; "that does not look like an Indian mark; yet I would have thought that white men had never stood here before, for the spot is far removed from any known diggings, and, as we know fail well, is not easily reached."

On gaining the rock, they found that the rag was a shred of linen, without mark of any kind to tell who had placed it there.

"It must have been the freak of some Indian hunter," said Ned, examining the rock on which the little flag-staff was raised. "Stay — no — here are some marks cut in the stone! Look here, Tom, can you decipher this? It looks like the letter D. — D.B."

"D.B.?" cried Tom Collins, with a degree of energy that surprised his friend. "Let me see!"

Tom carefully removed the moss, and cleared out the letters, which were unmistakeable.

"Who can D.B. have been?" said Ned.

Tom looked up with a flushed countenance and a glittering eye, as he exclaimed —

"Who? Who but Daniel Boone, Cooper's great hero — Hawk-eye, of the 'Last of the Mohicans' — Deer-slayer — Leather-stocking! *He* has been here before us — ay, brave spirit! Long before other hunters had dared to venture far into the territory of the scalping, torturing, yelling red-skin, this bold heart had pushed westward, fearless and alone, until his eagle eye rested on the great Pacific. It *must* have been he. I have followed him, Ned, in spirit, throughout all his wild career, for I knew him to be a *real* man, and no fiction; but little did I think that I should see a spot where his manly foot had rested, or live to discover his *farthest step* in the 'far west!'"

Ned Sinton listened with interest to the words of his friend, but he did not interrupt him, for he respected the deep emotions that swelled his heart and beamed from his flashing eye.

"We spoke, Ned, sometime ago, of historical associations," continued Tom, — "here are historical associations worth coming all this way to call up. Here are associations that touch *my* heart more than all the deeds of ancient chivalry. Ah! Daniel Boone, little didst thou think when thy hawk's eye rested here, that in a few short years the land would be overrun by gold-diggers from all ends of the earth!"

"But this flag," said Ned; "*he* could never have placed that here. It would have been swept away by storms years ago."

"You are right," said Tom, turning over the stones that supported the staff — "halloo! what have we here?"

He pulled out a roll of oiled cloth as he spoke, and, on opening it, discovered a scrap of paper, on which were written, in pencil, the words, "*Help us! — for God's sake help us! We are perishing at the foot of the hill to the southward of this.*"

No name or date was attached to this strange paper, but the purport of it was sufficiently clear so, without wasting time in fruitless conjecture, the young men immediately sprang on their horses, and rode down the hill in the direction indicated.

The route proved more rugged and steep than that by which they had ascended, and, for a considerable distance, they wound their way between the trunks of a closely-planted cypress grove; after passing which they emerged upon a rocky plain of small extent, at the further extremity of which a green oasis indicated the presence of a spring.

Towards this they rode in silence.

"Ah!" exclaimed Ned, in a tone of deep pity, as he reined up at the foot of an oak-tree, "too late!"

They were indeed too late to succour the poor creatures who had placed the scrap of paper on the summit of that mountain-ridge, in the faint hope that friendly hands might discover it in time.

Six dead forms lay at the foot of the oak, side by side, with their pale faces turned upwards, and the expression of extreme suffering still lingering on their shrunken features. It needed no living witness to tell their sad history. The skeletons of oxen, the broken cart, the scattered mining tools, and the empty provision casks, shewed clearly enough that they were emigrants who had left their homesteads in the States, and tried to reach the gold-regions of California by the terrible overland journey. They had lost their way among the dreary fastnesses of the mountains, travelled far from the right road to the mines, and perished at last of exhaustion and hunger on the very borders of the golden land. The grey-haired father of the family lay beside a young girl, with his arm clasped round her neck. Two younger men also lay near them, one lying as if, in dying, he had sought to afford support to the other. The bodies were still fresh, and a glance shewed that nearly all of them were of one family.

"Alas! Ned, had we arrived a few days sooner we might have saved them," said Tom.

"I think they must have been freed from their pains and sorrows here more than a week since," replied the other, fastening his horse to a tree, and proceeding to search the clothes of the unfortunates for letters or anything that might afford a clue to their identity. "We must stay here an hour or two, Tom, and bury them."

No scrap of writing, however, was found — not even a book with a name on it — to tell who the strangers were. With hundreds of others, no doubt, they had left their homes, full of life and hope, to seek their fortunes in the land of gold; but the Director of man's steps had ordered it otherwise, and their golden dreams had ended with their lives in the unknown wilderness.

The two friends covered the bodies with sand and stones, and, leaving them in their shallow grave, pursued their way; but they had not gone far when a few large drops of rain fell, and the sky became overcast with dark leaden clouds.

"Ned," said Tom, anxiously, "I fear we shall be caught by the rainy season. It's awkward being so far from the settlements at such a time."

"Oh, nonsense! surely you don't mind a wetting?" cried Ned; "we can push on in spite of rain."

"Can we?" retorted Tom, with unwonted gravity. "It's clear that you've never seen the rainy season, else you would not speak of it so lightly."

"Why, man, you seem to have lost pluck all of a sudden; come, cheer up; rain or no rain, I mean to have a good supper, and a good night's rest; and here is just the spot that will suit us."

Ned Sinton leaped off his horse as he spoke, and, fastening him to a tree, loosened the saddle-girths, and set about preparing the encampment. Tom Collins assisted him; but neither the rallying of his comrade, nor his own efforts could enable the latter to shake off the depression of spirits with which he was overpowered. That night the rain came down in torrents, and drenched the travellers to the skin, despite their most ingenious contrivances to keep it out. They spent the night in misery, and when morning broke Ned found that his companion was smitten down with ague.

Even Ned's buoyant spirits were swamped for a time at this unlooked-for catastrophe; for the dangers of their position were not slight. It was clear that Tom would not be able to travel for many days, for his whole frame trembled, when the fits came on, with a violence that seemed to threaten dislocation to all his joints. Ned felt that both their lives, under God, depended on his keeping well, and being able to procure food for, and nurse, his friend. At the same time, he knew that the rainy season, if indeed it had not already begun, would soon set in, and perhaps render the country impassable. There was no use, however, in giving way to morbid fears, so Ned faced his difficulties manfully, and, remembering the promise which he had given his old uncle at parting from him in England, he began by offering up a short but earnest prayer at the side of his friend's couch.

"Ned," said Tom, sadly, as his companion ceased, "I fear that you'll have to return alone."

"Come, come, don't speak that way, Tom; it isn't right. God is able to help us here as well as in cities. I don't think you are so ill as you fancy — the sight of these poor emigrants has depressed you. Cheer up, my boy, and I'll let you see that you were right when you said I could turn my hand to anything. I'll be hunter, woodcutter, cook, and nurse all at once, and see if I don't make you all right in a day or two. You merely want rest, so keep quiet for a little till I make a sort of sheltered place to put you in."

The sun broke through the clouds as he spoke and shed a warm beam down on poor Tom, who was more revived by the sight of the cheering orb of day than by the words of his companion.

In half-an-hour Tom was wrapped in the driest portion of the driest blanket; his wet habiliments were hung up before a roaring fire to dry, and a rude bower of willows, covered with turf, was erected over his head to guard him from another attack of rain, should it come; but it didn't come. The sun shone cheerily all day, and Ned's preparations were completed before the next deluge came, so that when it descended on the following morning, comparatively little found its way to Tom's resting-place.

It was scarcely a *resting-place*, however. Tom turned and groaned on his uneasy couch, and proved to be an uncommonly restive patient. He complained particularly when Ned left him for a few hours each day to procure fresh provisions; but he smiled and confessed himself unreasonable when Ned returned, as he always did, with a dozen wild ducks, or several geese or hares attached to his belt, or a fat deer on his shoulders. Game of all kinds was plentiful, the weather improved, the young hunter's rifle was good, and his aim was true, so that, but for the sickness of his friend, he would have considered the life he led a remarkably pleasant one.

As day after day passed by, however, and Tom Collins grew no better, but rather worse, he began to be seriously alarmed about him. Tom himself took the gloomiest view of his case, and at last said plainly he believed he was dying. At first Ned sought to effect a cure by the simple force of kind treatment and care; but finding that this would not do, he bethought him of trying some experiments in the medicinal way. He chanced to have a box of pills with him, and tried one, although with much hesitation and fear, for he had got them from a miner who could not tell what they were composed of, but who assured him they were a sovereign remedy for the blues! Ned, it must be confessed, was rather a reckless doctor. He was anxious, at the time he procured the pills, to relieve a poor miner who seemed to be knocked up with hard work, but who insisted that he had a complication of ailments; so Ned bought the pills for twenty times their value, and gave a few to the man, advising him, at the same time, to rest and feed well, which he did, and the result was a complete cure.

Our hero did not feel so certain, however, that they would succeed as well in the present case; but he resolved to try their virtues, for Tom was so prostrate that he could scarcely be induced to whisper a word. When the cold fit seized him he trembled so violently that his teeth rattled in his head; and when that passed off it was followed by a burning fever, which was even worse to bear.

At first he was restive, and inclined to be peevish under his illness, the result, no doubt, of a naturally-robust constitution struggling unsuccessfully against the attacks of disease, but when he was completely overcome, his irascibility passed away, and he became patient, sweet-tempered, and gentle as a child.

"Come, Tom, my boy," said Ned, one evening, advancing to the side of his companion's couch and sitting down beside him, while he held up the pill — "Open your mouth, and shut your eyes, as we used to say at school."

"What is it?" asked the sick man, faintly.

"Never you mind; patients have no business to know what their doctors prescribe. It's intended to cure ague, and that's enough for you to know. If it doesn't cure you it's not my fault, anyhow — open your mouth, sir!"

Tom smiled sadly and obeyed; the pill was dropt in, a spoonful of water added to float it down, and it disappeared.

But the pill had no effect whatever. Another was tried with like result — or rather with like absence of all result, and at last the box was finished without the sick man being a whit the better or the worse for them. This was disheartening; but Ned, having begun to dabble in medicines, felt an irresistible tendency to go on. Like the tiger who has once tasted blood, he could not now restrain himself.

"I think you're a little better tonight, Tom," he said on the third evening after the administration of the first pill; "I'm making you a decoction of bark here that will certainly do you good."

Tom shook his head, but said nothing. He evidently felt that a negative sign was an appropriate reply to the notion of his being better, or of any decoction whatever doing him good. However, Ned stirred the panful of bark and water vigorously, chatting all the while in a cheering tone, in order to keep up his friend's spirits, while the blaze of the camp-fire lit up his handsome face and bathed his broad chest and shoulders with a ruddy glow that rendered still more pallid the lustre of the pale stars overhead.

"It's lucky the rain has kept off so long," he said, without looking up from the mysterious decoction over which he bent with the earnest gaze of an alchymist. "I do believe that has something to do with your being better, my boy — either that or the pills, or both."

Ned totally ignored the fact that his friend did not admit that he was better.

"And this stuff," he continued, "will set you up in a day or two. It's as good as quinine, any day; and you've no notion what wonderful cures that medicine effects. It took me a long time, too, to find the right tree. I wandered over two or three leagues of country before I came upon one. Luckily it was a fine sunny day, and I enjoyed it much. I wish you had been with me, Tom; but you'll be all right soon. I lay down, too, once or twice in the sunshine, and put my head in the long grass, and tried to fancy myself in a miniature forest. Did you ever try that, Tom!"

Ned looked round as he spoke, but the sick man gave a languid smile, and shut his eyes, so he resumed his stirring of the pot and his rambling talk.

"You've no idea, if you never tried it, how one can deceive one's-self in that way. I often did it at home, when I was a little boy. I used to go away with a companion into a grass-field, and, selecting a spot where the grass was long and tangled, and mixed with various kinds of weeds, we used to lie flat down with our faces as near to the ground as possible, and gaze through the grass-stems until we fancied the blades were trees, and the pebbles were large rocks, and the clods were mountains. Sometimes a huge beetle would crawl past, and we instantly thought of Saint George and the dragon, and, as the unwieldy monster came stumbling on through the forest, we actually became quite excited, and could scarcely believe that what we tried to imagine was not real.

"We seldom spoke on these occasions, my companion and I," continued Ned, suspending the stirring of the decoction and filling his pipe, as he sat down close to the blazing logs; "speaking, we found, always broke the spell, so we agreed to keep perfect silence for as long a time as possible. You must try it, Tom, some day, for although it may seem to you a childish thing to do, there are many childish things which, when done in a philosophical spirit, are deeply interesting and profitable to men."

Ned ceased talking for a few minutes while he ignited his pipe; when he spoke again his thoughts had wandered into a new channel.

"I'm sorry we have no fresh meat today," he said, looking earnestly at his friend. "The remainder of that hare is not very savoury, but we must be content; I walked all the country round today, without getting within range of any living thing. There were plenty both of deer and birds, but they were so wild I could not get near them. It would matter little if you were well, Tom, but you require good food just now, my poor fellow. Do you feel better tonight?"

Tom groaned, and said that he "felt easier," in a very uneasy voice, after which they both relapsed into silence, and no sound was heard save the crackling of the logs and the bubbling of the mysterious decoction in the pot. Suddenly Tom uttered a slight hiss, — that peculiar sound so familiar to backwoods ears, by which hunters indicate to each other that something unusual has been observed, and that they had better be on the alert.

Ned Sinton's nerves were of that firm kind which can never be startled or taken by surprise. He did not spring to his feet, but, quick as thought, he stretched forth his long arm, and, seizing his rifle, cocked it, while he glanced at his friend's eye to see in what direction he was looking. Tom pointed eagerly with his thin hand straight across the fire. Ned turned in that direction, and at once saw the objects which had attracted his attention. Two bright gleaming balls shone in the dark background of the forest, like two lustrous Irish diamonds in a black field of bog-oak. He knew at once that they were the eyes of a deer, which, with a curiosity well-known as peculiar to many wild animals, had approached the fire to stare at it.

Ned instantly threw forward his rifle; the light of the fire enabled him easily to align the sights on the glittering eyes; the deadly contents belched forth, and a heavy crash told that his aim had been true.

"Bravo!" shouted Tom Collins, forgetting his ailments in the excitement of the moment, while Ned threw down his rifle, drew his hunting-knife, sprang over the fire, and disappeared in the surrounding gloom. In a few minutes he returned with a fine deer on his shoulders.

"So ho! my boy," he cried, flinging the carcase down; "that was a lucky shot. We shall sup well tonight, thanks to curiosity, which is a most useful quality in beast as well as man. But what's wrong; you look pale, and, eh? you don't mean to say you're — laughing?"

Tom was indeed pale, for the sudden excitement, in his exhausted condition had been too much for him; yet there did seem a peculiar expression about the corners of his mouth that might have been the remains of a laugh.

"Ned," he said, faintly, "the — the decoction's all gone." Ned sprang up and ran to the fire, where, sure enough, he found the pan, over which he had bent so long with necromantic gaze, upset, and most of the precious liquid gone.

"Ha!" he cried, catching up the pot, "not *all* gone, lad, so your rejoicing was premature. There's quite enough left yet to physic you well; and it's in fit state to be taken, so open your mouth at once, and be a good boy."

A little of the medicine, mixed in water, was administered, and Tom, making a wry face, fell back on his couch with a sigh. Immediately after he was seized with, perhaps, the severest shaking fit he had yet experienced, so that Ned could not help recalling the well-known caution, so frequently met with on medicine vials, "When taken, to be well shaken," despite the anxiety he felt for his friend. But soon after, the trembling fit passed away, and Tom sank into a quiet slumber, — the first real rest he had enjoyed for several days.

Ned felt his pulse and his brow, looked long and earnestly into his face, nodded approvingly once or twice, and, having tucked the blankets gently in round the sick man, he proceeded to prepare supper. He removed just enough of the deer's skin to permit of a choice morsel being cut out; this he put into the pot, and made thereof a rich and savoury soup, which he tasted; and, if smacking one's lips and tasting it again twice, indicated anything, the soup was good. But Ned Sinton did not eat it. That was Tom's supper, and was put just near enough the fire to keep it warm.

This being done, Ned cut out another choice morsel of deer's-meat, which he roasted and ate, as only those can eat who are well, and young, and robust, and in the heart of the wilderness. Then he filled his pipe, sat down close to Tom's couch, placed his back against a tree, crossed his arms on his breast, and smoked and watched the whole night long.

He rose gently several times during the night, however, partly for the purpose of battling off his tendency to sleep, and partly for the purpose of replenishing the fire and keeping the soup warm.

But Tom Collins took no supper that night. Ned longed very much to see him awake, but he didn't. Towards morning, Ned managed for some time to fight against sleep, by entering into a close and philosophical speculation as to what was the precise hour at which that pot of soup could not properly be called supper, but would merge into breakfast. This question still remained unsettled in his mind when grey dawn lit up the peaks of the eastern hills, and he was still debating it, and nodding like a Chinese mandarin, and staring at intervals like a confused owl, when the sun shot over the tree-tops, and, alighting softly on the sleeper's face, aroused him.

Tom awoke refreshed, ate his breakfast with relish, took his medicine without grumbling, smiled on his comrade, and squeezed his hand as he went to sleep again with a heavy sigh of comfort. From that hour he mended rapidly, and in a week after he was well enough to resume his journey.

CHAPTER XXII.

*Powerful Effects of Gold on the Aspect of Things in
General — The Doings at Little Creek Diggings —
Larry becomes Speculative, and digs a Hole which
nearly proves the Grave of many Miners —
Captain Bunting takes a Fearful Dive —
Ah-wow is smitten to the Earth —
A Mysterious Letter, and a Splendid Dish.*

We must now beg our reader to turn with us to another scene.

The appearance of Little Creek diggings altered considerably, and
for the worse, after Ned Sinton and Tom Collins left. A rush of miners
had taken place in consequence of the reports of the successful adventurers who returned to Sacramento for supplies, and, in the course of
a few weeks, the whole valley was swarming with eager gold-hunters.
The consequence of this was that laws of a somewhat stringent nature
had to be made. The ground was measured off into lots of about ten
feet square, and apportioned to the miners. Of course, in so large and
rough a community, there was a good deal of crime, so that Judge
Lynch's services were frequently called in; but upon the whole, considering the circumstances of the colony, there was much less than might
have been expected.

At the time of which we write, namely, several weeks after the
events narrated in our last chapter, the whole colony was thrown into
a state of excitement, in consequence of large quantities of gold
having been discovered on the banks of the stream, in the ground on
which the log-huts and tents were erected. The result of this discovery
was, that the whole place was speedily riddled with pits and their con-
comitant mud-heaps, and, to walk about after night-fall, was a difficult as well as a dangerous amusement. Many of the miners pulled
down their tents, and began to work upon the spots on which they previously stood. Others began to dig all round their wooden huts, until
these rude domiciles threatened to become insular, and a few pulled
their dwellings down in order to get at the gold beneath them.

One man, as he sat on his door-step smoking his pipe after dinner,
amused himself by poking the handle of an axe into the ground, and,
unexpectedly, turned up a small nugget of gold worth several dollars.
In ten minutes there was a pit before his door big enough to hold a
sheep, and, before night, he realised about fifty dollars. Another, in
the course of two days, dug out one hundred dollars behind his tent,
and all were more or less fortunate.

At this particular time, it happened that Captain Bunting had
been seized with one of his irresistible and romantic wandering fits,
and had gone off with the blunderbuss, to hunt in the mountains.
Maxton, having heard of better diggings elsewhere, and not caring for

the society of our adventurers when Ned and Tom were absent, had bid them good-bye, and gone off with his pick and shovel on his shoulder, and his prospecting-pan in his hand, no one knew whither. Bill Jones was down at Sacramento purchasing provisions, as the prices at the diggings were ruinous; and Ko-sing had removed with one of the other Chinamen to another part of the Creek.

Thus it came to pass that Larry O'Neil and Ah-wow, the Chinaman, were left alone to work out the claims of the party.

One fine day, Larry and his comrade were seated in the sunshine, concluding their mid-day meal, when a Yankee passed, and told them of the discoveries that had been made further down the settlement.

"Good luck to ye!" said Larry, nodding facetiously to the man, as he put a tin mug to his lips, and drained its contents to the bottom. "Ha! it's the potheen I'm fond of; not but that I've seen better; faix I've seldom tasted worse, but there's a vartue in goold-diggin' that would make akifortis go down like milk — it would. Will ye try a drop?"

Larry filled the pannikin as he spoke, and handed it to the Yankee, who, nothing loth, drained it, and returned it empty, with thanks.

"They're diggin' goold out o' the cabin floors, are they?" said Larry, wiping his mouth with the sleeve of his shirt.

"They air," answered the man. "One feller dug up three hundred dollars yesterday, from the very spot where he's bin snorin' on the last six months."

"Ah! thin that's a purty little sum," said Larry, with a leer that shewed he didn't believe a word of it. "Does he expect more tomorrow, think ye?"

"Don't know," said the man, half offended at the doubt thus cast on his veracity; "ye better go an' ax him. Good day, stranger;" and the Yankee strode away rapidly.

Larry scratched his head; then he rubbed his nose, and then his chin, without, apparently, deriving any particular benefit from these actions. After that, he looked up at Ah-wow, who was seated cross-legged on the ground opposite to him, smoking, and asked him what was *his* opinion.

"Dun no," said the Chinaman, without moving a muscle of his stolid countenance.

"Oh! ye're an entertainin' cratur, ye are; I'll just make a hole here where I sit, an' see what comes of it. Sure it's better nor doin' nothin'."

Saying this, Larry refilled his empty pipe, stretched himself at full length on his side, rested his head on his left hand, and smoked complacently for three minutes; after which he took up the long sheath-knife, with which he had just cut up his supper, and began carelessly to turn over the sod.

"Sure, there *is* goold," he said, on observing several specks of the shining metal. As he dug deeper down, he struck upon a hard substance, which, on being turned up, proved to be a piece of quartz, the size of a hen's egg, in which rich lumps and veins of gold were embedded.

"May I niver!" shouted the Irishman, starting up, and throwing away his pipe in his excitement, "av it isn't a nugget. Hooray! where's the pick!"

Larry overturned the Chinaman, who sat in his way, darted into the tent for his pick and shovel, and in five minutes was a foot down into the earth.

He came upon a solid rock, however, much to his chagrin, a few inches further down.

"Faix I'll tell ye what I'll do," he said, as a new idea struck him, "I'll dig inside o' the tint. It 'll kape the sun an' the rain off."

This remark was made half to himself and half to Ah-wow, who, having gathered himself up, and resumed his pipe, was regarding him with as much interest as he ever regarded anything. As Ah-wow made no objection, and did not appear inclined to volunteer an opinion, Larry entered the tent, cleared all the things away into one corner, and began to dig in the centre of it.

It was fortunate that he adopted this plan: first, because the rainy season having now set in, the tent afforded him shelter; and secondly, because the soil under the tent turned out to be exceedingly rich — so much so, that in the course of the next few days he and the Chinaman dug out upwards of a thousand dollars.

But the rains, which for some time past had given indubitable hints that they meant to pay a long visit to the settlement, at last came down like a waterspout, and flooded Larry and his comrade out of the hole. They cut a deep trench round the tent, however, to carry off the water, and continued their profitable labour unremittingly.

The inside of the once comfortable tent now presented a very remarkable appearance. All the property of the party was thrust into the smallest possible corner, and Larry's bed was spread out above it; the remainder of the space was a yawning hole six feet deep, and a mound of earth about four feet high. This earth formed a sort of breast-work, over which Larry had to clamber night and morning in leaving and returning to his couch. The Chinaman slept in his own little tent hard by.

There was another inconvenience attending this style of mining which Larry had not foreseen when he adopted it, and which caused the tent of our adventurers to become a sort of public nuisance. Larry had frequently to go down the stream for provisions, and Ah-wow being given to sleep when no one watched him, took advantage of those opportunities to retire to his own tent; the consequence was, that strangers who chanced to look in, in passing, frequently fell headlong into the hole ere they were aware of its existence, and on more than one occasion Larry returned and found a miner in the bottom of it with his neck well-nigh broken.

To guard against this he hit upon the plan of putting up a cautionary ticket. He purchased a flat board and a pot of black paint with which he wrote the words:

"*Mind Yer Feet Thars A Big Hol*," and fixed it up over the entrance. The device answered very well in as far as those who could read were concerned, but as there were many who could not read at all, and who mistook the ticket for the sign of a shop or store, the accidents became rather more frequent than before.

The Irishman at last grew desperate, and, taking Ah-wow by the pig-tail, vowed that if he deserted his post again, "he'd blow out all the brains he had — if he had any at all — an' if that wouldn't do, he'd cut him up into mince-meat, so he would."

The Chinaman evidently thought him in earnest, for he fell on his knees, and promised, with tears in his eyes, that he would never do it again — or words to that effect.

One day Larry and Ah-wow were down in the hole labouring for gold as if it were life. It was a terribly rainy day — so bad, that it was almost impossible to keep the water out. Larry had clambered out of the hole, and was seated on the top of the mud-heap, resting himself and gazing down upon his companion, who slowly, but with the steady regularity of machinery, dug out the clay, and threw it on the heap, when a voice called from without —

"Is this Mr. Edward Sinton's tent?"

"It is that same," cried Larry, rising; "don't come in, or it'll be worse for ye."

"Here's a letter for him, then, and twenty dollars to pay."

"Musha! but it's chape postage," said Larry, lifting the curtain, and stepping out; "couldn't ye say thirty, now?"

"Come, down with the cash, and none o' yer jaw," said the man, who was a surly fellow, and did not seem disposed to stand joking.

"Oh! be all manes, yer honour," retorted Larry, with mock servility, as he counted out the money. "Av it wouldn't displase yer lordship, may I take the presumption to ax how the seal come to be broken?"

"I know nothin' about it," answered the man, as he pocketed the money; "I found it on the road between this an' Sacramento, and, as I was passin' this way anyhow, I brought it on."

"Ah, thin, it was a great kindness, intirely, to go so far out o' yer way, an' that for a stranger, too, an' for nothin' — or nixt thing to it!" said Larry, looking after the man as he walked away.

"Well, now," he continued, re-entering the tent, and seating himself again on the top of the mud-heap, while he held the letter in his hand at arm's length, "this bates all! An' whot am I to do with it? Sure it's not right to break the seal o' another man's letter; but then it's broke a'ready, an' there can be no sin in raidin' it. Maybe," he continued, with a look of anxiety, "the poor lad's ill, or dead, an' he's wrote to say so. Sure, I would like to raid it — av I only know'd how; but me edication's bin forgot, bad luck to the schoolmasters; I can only make out big print — wan letter at a time."

The poor man looked wistfully at the letter, feeling that it might possibly contain information of importance to all of them, and that delay in taking action might cause irreparable misfortune. While he meditated what had best be done, and scanned the letter in all directions, a footstep was heard outside, and the hearty voice of Captain Bunting shouted:

"Ship ahoy! who's within, boys!"

"Hooroo! capting," shouted Larry, jumping up with delight; "mind yer fut, capting, dear; don't come in."

"Why not?" inquired the captain, as he lifted the curtain.

"Sure, it's no use tellin' ye *now!*" said Larry, as Captain Bunting fell head-foremost into Ah-wow's arms, and drove that worthy creature — as he himself would have said — "stern-foremost" into the mud and water at the bottom. The captain happened to have a haunch of venison on his shoulder, and the blunderbuss under his arm, so that the crash and the splash, as they all floundered in the mud, were too much for Larry, who sat down again on the mud-heap and roared with laughter.

It is needless to go further into the details of this misadventure. Captain Bunting and the Chinaman were soon restored to the upper world, happily, unhurt; so, having changed their garments, they went into Ah-wow's tent to discuss the letter.

"Let me see it, Larry," said the captain, sitting down on an empty pork cask.

Larry handed him the missive, and he read as follows: —

"San Francisco.
"Edward Sinton, Esquire, Little Creek Diggings.

"My Dear Sir, — I have just time before the post closes, to say that I only learned a few days ago that you were at Little Creek, otherwise I should have written sooner, to say that —"

Here the captain seemed puzzled. "Now, ain't that aggravatin'?" he said; "the seal has torn away the most important bit o' the letter. I wish I had the villains by the nose that opened it! Look here, Larry, can you guess what it was?"

Larry took the letter, and, after scrutinising it with intense gravity and earnestness, returned it, with the remark, that it was "beyant him entirely."

"That — that —" said the captain, again attempting to read, "that — somethin' — great success; so you and Captain Bunting had better come down at once.

"Believe me, my dear Sir, Yours faithfully, John Thomson."

"Now," remarked the captain, with a look of chagrin, as he laid down the letter, folded his hands together, and gazed into Larry's grave visage, "nothin' half so tantalisin' as that has happened to me since the time when my good ship, the *Roving Bess*, was cast ashore at San Francisco."

"It's purvokin'," replied Larry, "an' preplexin'."

"It's most unfortunate, too," continued the captain, knitting up his visage, "that Sinton should be away just at this time, without rudder, chart, or compass, an' bound for no port that any one knows of. Why, the fellow may be deep in the heart o' the Rocky Mountains, for all I can tell. I might start off at once without him, but maybe that would be of no use. What can it be that old Thompson's so anxious about? Why didn't the old figur'-head use his pen more freely — his tongue goes fast enough to drive the engines of a seventy-four. What *is* to be done?"

Although Captain Bunting asked the question with thorough earnestness and much energy, looking first at Larry and then at Ah-wow, he received no reply. The former shook his head, and the latter stared at him with a steady, dead intensity, as if he wished to stare him through.

After a few minutes' pause, Larry suddenly asked the captain if he was hungry, to which the latter replied that he was; whereupon the former suggested that it was worth while "cookin' the haunch o' ven'son," and offered to do it in a peculiar manner, that had been taught to him not long ago by a hunter, who had passed that way, and fallen into the hole in the tent and sprained his ankle, so that he, (Larry), was obliged to "kape him for a week, an' trate him to the best all the time." The proposal was agreed to, and Larry, seizing the haunch, which was still covered with the mud contracted in "the hole," proceeded to exhibit his powers as a cook.

The rain, which had been coming down as if a second flood were about to deluge the earth, had ceased at this time, and the sun succeeded, for a few hours, in struggling through the murky clouds and pouring a flood of light and heat over hill and plain; the result of which was, that, along the whole length of Little Creek, there was an eruption of blankets, and shirts, and inexpressibles, and other garments, which stood much in need of being dried, and which, as they fluttered and flapped their many-coloured folds in the light breeze, gave the settlement the appearance — as Captain Bunting expressed it — of being "dressed from stem to stern." The steam that arose from these habiliments, and from the soaking earth, and from the drenched forest, covered the face of nature with a sort of luminous mist that was quite cheering, by contrast with the leaden gloom that had preceded it, and filled with a romantic glow the bosoms of such miners as had any romance left in their natures.

Larry O'Neil was one of these, and he went about his work whistling violently. We will not take upon us to say how much of his romance was due to the haunch of venison. We would not, if called on to do it, undertake to say how much of the romance and enjoyment of a pic-nic party would evaporate, if it were suddenly announced that "the hamper" had been forgotten, or that it had fallen and the contents been smashed and mixed. We turn from such ungenerous and gross contemplations to the cooking of that haunch of venison, which, as it was done after a fashion never known to Soyer, and may be useful in after-years to readers of this chronicle, whose lot it may be, perchance, to stand in need of such knowledge, we shall carefully describe.

It is not necessary to enlarge upon the preliminaries. We need hardly say that Larry washed off the mud, and that he passed flattering remarks upon his own abilities and prowess, and, in very irreverent tones and terms, addressed Ah-wow, who smoked his pipe and looked at him. All that, and a great deal more, we leave to our reader's well-known and vivid imagination. Suffice it that the venison was duly washed, and a huge fire, with much difficulty, kindled, and a number of large stones put into it to heat. This done, Larry cut off a lump of meat from the haunch — a good deal larger than his own head, which wasn't small — the skin with the hair on being cut off along with the meat. A considerable margin of flesh was then pared off from the lump, so as to leave an edging of hide all round, which might overlap the remainder, and enclose it, as it were, in a natural bag.

At this stage of the process Larry paused, looked admiringly at his work, winked over the edge of it at Ah-wow, and went hastily into the tent, whence he issued with two little tin canisters, — one containing pepper, the other salt.

"Why, you beat the French all to nothing!" remarked the captain, who sat on an upturned tea-box, smoking and watching the proceedings.

"An! thin, don't spake, capting; it'll spile yer appetite," said Larry, sprinkling the seasoning into the bag and closing it up by means of a piece of cord. He then drew the red-hot stones and ashes from the fire, and, making a hot-bed thereof, placed the venison-dumpling — if we may be allowed the term — on the centre of it. Before the green hide was quite burned through, the dish was "cooked," as Yankees express it, "to a curiosity," and the tasting thereof would have evoked from an alderman a look, (he would have been past speaking!) of ecstasy, while a lady might have exclaimed, "Delicious!" or a schoolboy have said, "Hlpluhplp,"[2] or some such term which ought only to be used in

2   Note 1. Hlpluhplp. As the reader may have some difficulty in pronouncing the above word, we beg to inform him, (or her), that it is easily done, by simply drawing in the breath, and, at the same time,

reference to intellectual treats, and should never be applied to such low matters as meat and drink.

waggling the tongue between the lips.

CHAPTER XXIII.

*The Rainy Season, and its Effects — Disease and
Misery at Little Creek — Reappearance of Old
Friends — An Emigrant's Death —
An Unexpected Arrival.*

Captain Bunting, after two days' serious consideration, made up his mind to go down alone to San Francisco, in order to clear up the mystery of the letter, and do all that he could personally in the absence of his friend. To resolve, however, was easy; to carry his resolution into effect was almost impracticable, in consequence of the inundated state of the country.

It was now the middle of November, and the rainy season, which extends over six months of the year, was in full play. Language is scarcely capable of conveying, to those who have not seen it, an adequate idea of how it rained at this period of the year. It did not pour — there were no drops — it roared a cataract of never-ending ramrods, as thick as your finger, straight down from the black sky right through to the very vitals of the earth. It struck the tents like shot, and spirted through the tightest canvas in the form of Scotch-mist. It swept down cabin chimneys, and put out the fires; it roared through every crevice, and rent and seam of the hills in mad cataracts, and swelled up the Little Creek into a mighty surging river.

All work was arrested; men sat in their tents on mud-heaps that melted from below them, or lay on logs that well-nigh floated away with them; but there was not so much grumbling as one might have expected. It was too tremendous to be merely annoying. It was sublimely ridiculous, — so men grinned, and bore it.

But there were many poor miners there, alas! who could not regard that season in a light manner. There were dozens of young and middle-aged men whose constitutions, although good, perhaps, were not robust, and who ought never to have ventured to seek their fortunes in the gold-regions. Men who might have lived their full time, and have served their day and generation usefully in the civilised regions of the world, but who, despite the advice of friends, probably, and certainly despite the warnings of experienced travellers and authors, rushed eagerly to California to find, not a fortune, but a grave. Dysentery, scurvy in its worst and most loathsome type, ague, rheumatism, sciatica, consumption, and other diseases, were now rife at the diggings, cutting down many a youthful plant, and blasting many a golden dream.

Doctors, too, became surprisingly numerous, but these disciples of Esculapius failed to effect cures, and as their diplomas, when sought for, were not forthcoming, they were ultimately banished *en masse* by the indignant miners. One or two old hunters and trappers turned out in the end to be the most useful doctors, and effected a good many cures with the simple remedies they had become acquainted with among the red-men.

What rendered things worse was that provisions became scarce, and, therefore, enormously dear. No fresh vegetables of any kind were to be had. Salt, greasy and rancid pork, bear's-meat, and venison, were all the poor people could procure, although many a man there would have given a thousand dollars — ay, all he possessed — for a single meal of fresh potatoes. The men smitten with scurvy had, therefore, no chance of recovering. The valley became a huge hospital, and the banks of the stream a cemetery.

There were occasional lulls, however, in this dismal state of affairs. Sometimes the rain ceased; the sun burst forth in irresistible splendour, and the whole country began to steam like a caldron. A cart, too, succeeded now and then in struggling up with a load of fresh provisions; reviving a few sinking spirits for a time, and almost making the owner's fortune; but, at the best, it was a drearily calamitous season, — one which caused many a sick heart to hate the sight and name of gold, and many a digger to resolve to quit the land, and all its treasures, at the first opportunity.

Doubtless, too, many deep and earnest thoughts of life, and its aims and ends, filled the minds of some men at that time. It is often in seasons of adversity that God shews to men how mistaken their views of happiness are, and how mad, as well as sinful, it is in them to search for joy and peace apart from, and without the slightest regard for, the Author of all felicity. Yes, there is reason to hope and believe that many seeds of eternal life were sown by the Saviour, and watered by the Holy Spirit, in that disastrous time of disease and death, — seed which, perhaps, is now blessing and fertilising many distant regions of the world.

In one of the smallest and most wretched of the huts, at the entrance of the valley of Little Creek, lay a man, whose days on earth were evidently few. The hut stood apart from the others, in a lonely spot, as if it shrank from observation, and was seldom visited by the miners, who were too much concerned about their own misfortunes to care much for those of others. Here Kate Morgan sat by the couch of her dying brother, endeavouring to soothe his last hours by speaking to him in the most endearing terms, and reading passages from the Word of God, which lay open on her knee. But the dying man seemed to derive little comfort from what she said or read. His restless eye roamed anxiously round the wretched hut, while his breath came short and thick from between his pale lips.

"Shall I read to ye, darlin'?" said the woman, bending over the couch to catch the faint whisper, which was all the poor man had strength to utter.

Just then, ere he could reply, the clatter of hoofs was heard, and a bronzed, stalwart horseman was seen through the doorless entrance of the hut, approaching at a brisk trot. Both horse and man were of immense size, and they came on with that swinging, heavy tread, which gives the impression of irresistible weight and power. The rider drew up suddenly, and, leaping off his horse, cried, "Can I have a draught of water, my good woman?" as he fastened the bridle to a tree, and strode into the hut.

Kate rose hurriedly, and held up her finger to impose silence, as she handed the stranger a can of water. But he had scarcely swallowed a mouthful when his eye fell on the sick man. Going gently forward to the couch, he sat down beside it, and, taking the invalid's wrist, felt his pulse.

"Is he your husband?" inquired the stranger, in a subdued voice.

"No, sir, — my brother."

"Does he like to have the Bible read to him?"

"Sometimes; but before his voice failed he was always cryin' out for the priest. He's a Catholic, sir, though I'm not wan meself and thinks he can't be saved unless he sees the priest."

The stranger took up the Bible, and, turning towards the man, whose bright eyes were fixed earnestly upon him, read, in a low impressive voice, several of those passages in which a free salvation to the chief of sinners is offered through Jesus Christ. He did not utter a word of comment; but he read with deep solemnity, and paused ever and anon to look in the face of the sick man as he read the blessed words of comfort. The man was not in a state either to listen to arguments or to answer questions, so the stranger wisely avoided both, and gently quitted the hut after offering up a brief prayer, and repeating twice the words —

"Jesus says, 'Him that cometh to *Me*, I will in no wise cast out.'"

Kate followed him out, and thanked him earnestly for his kindness, while tears stood in her eyes.

"Have you no friends or relations here but him!" he inquired.

"Not wan. There was wan man as came to see us often when we stayed in a lonesome glen further up the Creek, but we've not seen him since we came here. More be token he didn't know we were goin' to leave, and we wint off in a hurry, for my poor brother was impatient, and thought the change would do him good."

"Take this, you will be the better of it."

The stranger thrust a quantity of silver into Kate's hand, and sprang upon his horse.

"I don't need it, thank 'ee," said Kate, hurriedly.

"But you *may* need it; at any rate, *he* does. Stay, what was the name of the man who used to visit you?"

"O'Neil, sir — Larry O'Neil."

"Indeed! he is one of my mates. My name is Sinton — Edward Sinton; you shall hear from me again ere long."

Ned put spurs to his horse as he spoke, and in another moment was out of sight.

CHAPTER XXIV.

Ned decides on visiting San Francisco —
Larry pays a Visit, and receives a Severe
Disappointment — The Road and the City —
Unexpected News.

Few joys in this life are altogether without alloy. The delight experienced by Larry O'Neil and Captain Bunting, when they heard the hearty tones of Ned Sinton's voice, and the satisfaction with which they beheld his face, when, in their anxiety to prevent his falling headlong into "the hole," they both sprang out of the tent and rushed into his arms, were somewhat damped on their observing that Tom Collins was not with him. But their anxieties were speedily relieved on learning that Tom was at Sacramento City, and, it was to be hoped, doing well.

As Ned had eaten nothing on the day of his arrival since early morning, the first care of his friends was to cook some food for him; and Larry took special care to brew for him, as soon as possible, a stiff tumbler of hot brandy and water, which, as he was wet and weary, was particularly acceptable.

While enjoying this over the fire in front of the tent, Ned related the adventures of himself and Tom Collins circumstantially; in the course of which narration he explained, what the reader does not yet know, how that, after Tom had recovered from his illness sufficiently to ride, he had conducted him by easy stages to the banks of the great San Joaquin river, down which they had proceeded by boat until they reached Sacramento.

Here Ned saw him comfortably settled in the best room of the best hotel in the town, and then, purchasing the largest and strongest horse he could find, he set off, in spite of the rains, to let his comrades know that they were both safe, and, in Ned's case at least, sound.

"And, now, with reference to that letter."

"Ay, that letter," echoed the captain; "that's what I've bin wantin' you to come to. What can it mean?"

"I am as ignorant of that as yourself," answered Ned; "if it had only been you who were mentioned in the letter, I could have supposed that your old ship had been relaunched and refitted, and had made a successful voyage to China during your absence; but, as I left no property of any kind in San Francisco, and had no speculations afloat, I cannot conceive what it can be."

"Maybe," suggested Larry, "they've heard o' our remarkable talents up here in the diggin's, and they've been successful in gittin' us app'inted to respansible sitivations in the new government I've heared they're sottin' up down there. I wouldn't object to be prime minister meself av they'd only allow me enough clarks to do the work."

"And did you say you were all ready for a start tomorrow, captain?" inquired Ned.

"Quite. We've disposed of the claims and tools for fifteen hundred dollars, an' we sold Ah-wow along with the lot; that's to say, he remains a fixture at the same wage; and the little we meant to take with us is stowed away in our saddle-bags. Ye see, I couldn't foresee that you'd plump down on us in this fashion, and I felt that the letter was urgent, and ought to be acted on at once."

"You did quite right," returned Ned. "What a pity I missed seeing Bill Jones at Sacramento; but the city has grown so much, and become so populous, in a few months, that two friends might spend a week in it, unknown to each other, without chancing to meet. And now as to the gold. Have you been successful since I left?"

"Ay," broke in Larry, "that have we. It's a great country intirely for men whose bones and muscles are made o' iron. We've dug forty thousand dollars — eight thousand pounds — out o' that same hole in the tint; forby sprainin' the ankles, and well-nigh breakin' the legs, o' eight or tin miners. It's sorry I'll be to lave it. But, afther all, it's a sickly place, so I'm contint to go."

"By the way, Larry, that reminds me I met a friend o' yours at the other end of the settlement."

"I belave ye," answered Larry; "ivery man in the Creek's my fri'nd. They'd die for me, they would, av I only axed them."

"Ay, but a particular friend, named Kate, who —"

"Och! ye don't mane it!" cried the Irishman, starting up with an anxious look. "Sure they lived up in the dark glen there; and they wint off wan fine day, an' I've niver been able to hear o' them since."

"They are not very far off," continued Ned, detailing his interview with the brother and sister, and expressing a conviction that the former could not now be in life.

"I'll go down tonight," said Larry, drawing on his heavy boots.

"You'd better wait till tomorrow," suggested the captain. "The poor thing will be in no humour to see any one tonight, and we can make a halt near the hut for an hour or so."

Larry, with some reluctance, agreed to this delay, and the rest of the evening was spent by the little party in making preparations for a start on the following day; but difficulties arose in the way of settling with the purchasers of their claims, so that another day passed ere they got fairly off on their journey towards Sacramento.

On reaching the mouth of the Little Creek, Larry O'Neil galloped ahead of his companions, and turned aside at the little hut, the locality of which Sinton had described to him minutely. Springing off his horse, he threw the reins over a bush and crossed the threshold. It is easier to conceive than to describe his amazement and consternation on finding the place empty. Dashing out, he vaulted into the saddle, and almost galloped through the doorway of the nearest hut in his anxiety to learn what had become of his friends.

"Halloo! stranger," shouted a voice from within, "no thoroughfare this way; an' I wouldn't advise ye for to go an' try for to make one."

"Ho! countryman, where's the sick Irishman and his sister gone, that lived close to ye here?"

"Wall, I ain't a countryman o' yourn, I guess; but I can answer a civil question. They're gone. The man's dead, an' the gal took him away in a cart day b'fore yisterday."

"Gone! took him away in a cart!" echoed Larry, while he looked aghast at the man. "Are ye sure?"

"Wall, I couldn't be surer. I made the coffin for 'em, and helped to lift it into the cart."

"But where have they gone to?"

"To Sacramento, I guess. I advised her not to go, but she mumbled something about not havin' him buried in sich a wild place, an' layin' him in a churchyard; so I gave her the loan o' fifty dollars — it was all I could spare — for she hadn't a rap. She borrowed the horse and cart from a countryman, who was goin' to Sacramento at any rate."

"You're a trump, you are!" cried Larry, with energy; "give us your hand, me boy! Ah! thin yer parents were Irish, I'll be bound; now, here's your fifty dollars back again, with compound interest to boot — though I don't know exactly what that is —"

"I didn't ax ye for the fifty dollars," said the man, somewhat angrily. "Who are you that offers 'em!"

"I'm her — her — friend," answered Larry, in some confusion; "her intimate friend; I might almost say a sort o' distant relation — only not quite that."

"Wall, if that's all, I guess I'm as much a friend as you," said the man, re-entering his cabin, and shutting the door with a bang.

Larry sighed, dropped the fifty dollars into his leather purse, and galloped away.

The journey down to Sacramento, owing to the flooded state of the country, was not an easy one. It took the party several days' hard riding to accomplish it, and during all that time Larry kept a vigilant look-out for Kate Morgan and the cart, but neither of them did he see. Each day he felt certain he would overtake them, but each evening found him trying to console himself with the reflection that a "stern chase" is proverbially a long one, and that *next* day would do it. Thus they struggled on, and finally arrived at the city of Sacramento, without having set eyes on the wanderer. Poor Larry little knew that, having gone with a man who knew the road thoroughly, Kate, although she travelled slowly, had arrived there the day before him; while Ned had lengthened the road by unwittingly making a considerable and unnecessary detour. Still less did he know that, at the very hour he arrived in the city, Kate, with her sad charge, embarked on board a small river steamer, and was now on her way to San Francisco.

As it was, Larry proposed to start back again, supposing they must have passed them; but, on second thoughts, he decided to remain where he was and make inquiries. So the three friends pushed forward to the City Hotel to make inquiries after Tom Collins.

"Mr. Collins?" said the waiter, bowing to Sinton — "he's gone, sir, about a week ago."

"*Gone!*" exclaimed Ned, turning pale.

"Yes, sir; gone down to San Francisco. He saw some advertisement or other in the newspaper, and started off by the next steamer."

Ned's heart beat freely again. "Was he well when he left?"

"Yes, sir, pretty well. He would have been the better of a longer rest, but he was quite fit to travel, sir."

Captain Bunting, who, during this colloquy, had been standing with his legs apart, and his eyes glaring at the waiter, as if he had been mad, gave a prolonged whistle, but made no further remark. At this moment Larry, who had been conversing with one of the under-waiters, came rushing in with a look of desperation on his countenance.

"Would ye belave it," he cried, throwing himself down on a splendid crimson sofa, that seemed very much out of keeping with the dress of the rough miners whom it was meant to accommodate — "would ye belave it, they're gone!"

"Who are gone, and where to!" inquired Ned.

"Kate an' — an' the caffin. Off to San Francisco, be all that's onlucky; an' only wint little more nor an hour ago."

The three friends looked at each other.

"Waiter," said Captain Bunting, in a solemn voice, "bear-chops for three, pipes and baccy for six, an' a brandy-smash for one; an', d'ye hear, let it be stiff!"

"Yes, sir."

A loud laugh from Ned and Larry relieved their over-excited and pent-up feelings; and both agreed that, under the circumstances, the captain's order was the best that could be given at that stage of their perplexities. Having ascertained that there was not another steamer to San Francisco for a week, they resolved to forget their anxieties as much as possible, and enjoy themselves in the great city of Sacramento during the next few days; while they instituted inquiries as to what had become of their comrade, Bill Jones, who, they concluded, must still be in the city, as they had not met him on the way down.

CHAPTER XXV.

Gold not All-Powerful — Remarkable Growth of Sacramento — New Style of bringing a Hotel into Notice — A Surprising Discovery — Death of a Mexican Horse-Tamer — The Concert, and another Discovery — Mademoiselle Nelina creates a Sensation.

It is said that gold can accomplish anything; and, in some respects, the saying is full of truth; in some points of view, however, the saying is altogether wrong. Gold can, indeed, accomplish almost anything in the material world — it can purchase stone, and metal, and timber; and muscles, bones, thews, and sinews, with life in them, to any extent. It can go a step further — it can purchase brains, intellect, genius; and, throwing the whole together, material and immaterial, it can cut, and carve, and mould the world to such an extent that its occupants of fifty years ago, were they permitted to return to earth, would find it hard to recognise the scene of their brief existence. But there are things and powers which gold cannot purchase. That worn-out old *millionnaire* would give tons of it for a mere tithe of the health that yonder ploughman enjoys. Youth cannot be bought with gold. Time cannot be purchased with gold. The prompt obedience of thousands of men and women may be bought with that precious metal, but one powerful throb of a loving heart could not be procured by all the yellow gold that ever did or ever will enrich the human family.

But we are verging towards digression. Let us return to the simple idea with which we intended to begin this chapter — the wonder-working power of gold. In no country in the wide world, we venture to affirm, has this power been exemplified so strikingly as in California. The knowledge of the discovery of gold was so suddenly and widely disseminated over the earth, that human beings flowed into the formerly-uninhabited wilderness like a mighty torrent, while thousands of ships flooded the markets with the necessaries of life. Then gold was found to be so abundant, and, *at first*, so easily procured, that the fever was kept up at white-heat for several years. The result of this was, as we have remarked elsewhere, that changes, worthy of Aladdin's lamp or Harlequin's wand, were wrought in the course of a few weeks, sometimes in a few days.

The city of Sacramento was one of the most remarkable of the many strange and sudden growths in the country. The river on which it stands is a beautiful stream, from two to three hundred yards wide, and navigable by large craft to a few miles above the city. The banks, when our friends were there, were fringed with rich foliage, and the wild trees of the forest itself stood growing in the streets. The city was laid out in the form of a square, with streets crossing each other at right angles; a forest of masts along the *embarcadero* attested the growing importance and wealth of the place; and nearly ten thousand inhabitants swarmed in its streets. Many of those streets were composed of canvas tents, or erections scarcely more durable. Yet here, little more than a year before, there were only *four thousand* in the place!

Those who chanced to be in possession of the land here were making fortunes. Lots, twenty feet by seventy, in the best situations, brought upwards of 3500 dollars. Rents, too, were enormous. One hotel paid 30,000 dollars (£6000) per annum; another, 35,000 dollars. Small stores fetched ten and twelve thousand dollars a year; while board at the best hotels was five dollars a day. Truly, if gold was plentiful, it was needed; for the common necessaries of life, though plentiful, were bought and sold at fabulous prices. The circulation of gold was enormous, and the growth of the city did not suffer a check even for a day, although the cost of building was unprecedented. And this commercial prosperity continued in spite of the fact that the place was unhealthy — being a furnace in summer, and in winter little better than a swamp.

"It's a capital hotel," remarked Captain Bunting to his companions, as they sat round their little table, enjoying their pipes after dinner; "I wonder if they make a good thing out of it?"

"Sure, if they don't," said Larry, tilting his chair on its hind legs, and calmly blowing a cloud of smoke towards the roof, "it's a losin' game they're playin', for they sarve out the grub at a tearin' pace."

"They are doing well, I doubt not," said Ned Sinton; "and they deserve to, for the owner — or owners, I don't know how many or few there are — made a remarkable and enterprising start."

"How was that?" asked the captain.

"I heard of it when I was down here with Tom," continued Sinton. "You must know that this was the first regular hotel opened in the city, and it was considered so great an event that it was celebrated by salvos of artillery, and, on the part of the proprietors, by a great unlimited feast to all who chose to come."

"What!" cried Larry, "free, gratis, for nothin'?"

"Ay, for nothing. It was done in magnificent style, I assure you. Any one who chose came and called for what he wanted, and got it at once. The attendance was prompt, and as cheerfully given as though it had been paid for. Gin-slings, cocktails, mint-juleps, and brandy-smashes went round like a circular storm, even champagne flowed like water; and venison, wild-fowl, salmon, grizzly-bear-steaks, and pastry — all the delicacies of the season, in short — were literally to be had for the asking. What it cost the spirited proprietors I know not, but certainly it was a daring stroke of genius that deserved patronage."

"Faix it did," said Larry, emphatically; "and they shall have it, too; — here, waiter, a brandy-smash and a cheroot, and be aisy as to the cost; I think me bank'll stand it."

"What say you to a stroll!" said Ned, rising.

"By all means," replied Captain Bunting, jumping up, and laying down his pipe. Larry preferred to remain where he was; so the two friends left him to enjoy his cheroot, and wandered away, where fancy led, to see the town. There was much to be seen. It required no theatrical representation of life to amuse one in Sacramento at that time. The whole city was a vast series of plays in earnest.

Every conceivable species of comedy and farce met the eye at every turn. Costumes the most remarkable, men the most varied and peculiar, and things the most incomprehensible and unexpected, presented themselves in endless succession. Here a canvas restaurant stood, or, rather leaned against a log-store. There a tent spread its folds in juxtaposition to a deck-cabin, which seemed to have walked ashore from a neighbouring brig, without leave, and had been let out as a grog-shop by way of punishment. Chinamen in calico jostled sailors in canvas, or diggers in scarlet flannel shirts, or dandies in broad-cloth and patent-leather, or red Indians in nothing! Bustle, and hurry, and uproar, and joviality prevailed. A good deal of drinking, too, unfortunately, went on, and the results were occasional melodramas, and sometimes serious rows.

Tragedies, too, were enacted, but these seldom met the eye; as is usually the case, they were done in the dark.

"What have we here?" cried Captain Bunting, stopping before a large placard, and reading. "'Grand concert, this evening — wonderful singer — Mademoiselle Nelina, first appearance — Ethiopian serenaders.' I say, Ned, we must go to this; I've not heard a song for ages that was worth listening to."

"At what hour?" inquired Ned — "oh! seven o'clock; well, we can stroll back to the hotel, have a cup of coffee, and bring Larry O'Neil with us. Come along."

That evening our three adventurers occupied the back seat of a large concert-room in one of the most crowded thoroughfares of the town, patiently awaiting the advent of the performers. The room was filled to overflowing, long before the hour for the commencement of the performances, with every species of mortal, except woman. Women were exceedingly rare creatures at that time — the meetings of all sorts were composed almost entirely of men, in their varied and motley garbs.

Considering the circumstances in which it was got up, the room was a very creditable one, destitute, indeed, of ornament, but well lighted by an enormous wooden chandelier, full of wax candles, which depended from the centre of the ceiling. At the further end of the room was a raised stage, with foot-lights in front, and three chairs in the middle of it. There was a small orchestra in front, consisting of two fiddles, a cornopian, a trombone, a clarionet, and a flute; but at first the owners of these instruments kept out of sight, wisely reserving themselves until that precise moment when the impatient audience would — as all audiences do on similar occasions — threaten to bring down the building with stamping of feet, accompanied with steam-engine-like whistles, and savage cries of "Music!"

While Ned Sinton and his friends were quietly looking round upon the crowd, Larry O'Neil's attention was arrested by the conversation of two men who sat just in front of him. One was a rough-looking miner, in a wide-awake and red-flannel shirt; the other was a negro, in a shirt of blue-striped calico.

"Who be this Missey Nelina?" inquired the negro, turning to his companion.

"I dun know; but I was here last night, an' I'd take my davy, I saw the little gal in the ranche of a feller away in the plains, five hundred miles to the east'ard, two months ago. Her father, poor chap, was killed by a wild horse."

"How was dat?" inquired the negro, with an expression of great interest.

"Well, it was this way it happened," replied the other, putting a quid of tobacco into his cheek, such as only a sailor would venture to masticate. "I was up at the diggin's about six months, without gittin' more gold than jist kep' me in life — for, ye see, I was always an unlucky dog — when one day I goes down to my claim, and, at the very first lick, dug up two chunks o' gold as big as yer fists; so I sold my claim and shovel, and came down here for a spree. Well, as I was sayin', I come to the ranche o' a feller called Bangi, or Bongi, or Bungi, or some sort o' bang, with a gi at the end o' 't. He was clappin' his little gal on the head, when I comed up, and said good-bye to her. I didn't rightly hear what she said; but I was so taken with her pretty face that I couldn't help axin' if the little thing was his'n. 'Yees,' says he — for he was a Mexican, and couldn't come round the English lingo — 'she me darter.' I found the man was goin' to catch a wild horse, so, says I, 'I'll go with ye,' an', says he, 'come 'long,' so away we went, slappin' over the plains at a great rate, him and me, and a Yankee, a friend o' his and three or four servants, after a drove o' wild horses that had been seen that mornin' near the house. Well, away we went after the wild horses. Oh! it was grand sport! The man had lent me one of his beasts, an' it went at such a spankin' pace, I could scarce keep my seat, and had to hold on by the saddle — not bein' used to ridin' much, d'ye see. We soon picked out a horse — a splendid-lookin' feller, with curved neck, and free gallop, and wide nostrils. My eye! how he did snort and plunge, when the Mexican threw the lasso, it went right over his head the first cast, but the wild horse pulled the rope out o' his grip. 'It's all up,' thought I; but never a bit. The Mexican put spurs to his horse, an' while at full gallop, made a dive with his body, and actually caught the end o' the line, as it trailed over the ground, and recovered his seat again. It was done in a crack; an', I believe, he held on by means of his spurs, which were big enough, I think, to make wheels for a small carronade. Takin' a turn o' the line round the horn of his saddle, he reined in a bit, and then gave the spurs for another spurt, and soon after reined in again — in fact, he jist played the wild horse like a trout, until he well-nigh choked him; an', in an hour, or less, he was led steamin', and startin', and jumpin', into the corral, where the man kept his other horses."

At this point in the narrative, the cries for music became so deafening, that the sailor was obliged to pause, to the evident annoyance of the negro, who seemed intensely interested in what he had heard; and, also, to the regret of Larry, who had listened eagerly the whole time. In a few minutes the "music" came in, in the shape of two bald-headed Frenchmen, a wild-looking bearded German, and several lean men, who might, as far as appearance went, have belonged to almost any nation; and who would have, as far as musical ability went, been repudiated by every nation, except, perhaps, the Chinese. During the quarter of an hour in which these performers quieted the impatient audience with sweet sounds, the sailor continued his anecdote.

"Well, you see," said he to the negro, while Larry bent forward to listen, "the Mexican mounted, and raced and spurred him for about an hour; but, just at the last, the wild horse gave a tremendous leap and a plunge, and we noticed the rider fall forward, as if he'd got a sprain. The Yankee an' one o' the servants ran up, and caught the horse by the head, but its rider didn't move — he was stone dead, and was held in his seat by the spurs sticking in the saddle-cloth. The last bound must have ruptured some blood-vessel inside, for there was no sign of hurt upon him anywhere."

"You don' say dat?" said the negro, with a look of horror.

"'Deed do I; an' we took the poor feller home, where his little daughter cried for him as if she'd break her heart. I asked the Yankee what we should do, but he looked at me somewhat offended like, an' said he was a relation o' the dead man's wife, and could manage the affairs o' the family without help; so I bid him good mornin', and went my way. But I believe in my heart he was tellin' a lie, and that he's no right to go hawkin' the poor gal about the country in this fashion."

Larry was deeply interested in this narrative, and felt so strong a disposition to make further inquiries, that he made up his mind to question the sailor, and was about to address him when a small bell tinkled, the music ceased, and three Ethiopian minstrels, banjo in hand, advanced to the foot-lights, made their bow, and then seated themselves on the three chairs, with that intensity of consummate, impudent, easy familiarity peculiar to the ebony sons of song.

"Go it, darkies!" shouted an enthusiastic individual in the middle of the room.

"Three cheers for the niggers!" roared a sailor, who had just returned from a twelvemonth's cruise at the mines, and whose delight at the prospect of once more hearing a good song was quite irrepressible.

The audience responded to the call with shouts of laughter, and a cheer that would have done your heart good to listen to, while the niggers shewed their teeth in acknowledgment of the compliment.

The first song was "Lilly Dale," and the men, who, we need scarcely say, were fictitious negroes, sang it so well that the audience listened with breathless attention and evident delight, and encored it vociferously. The next song was "Oh! Massa, how he wopped me," a ditty of quite a different stamp, but equally popular. It also was encored, as indeed was every song sting that evening; but the performers had counted on this. After the third song there was a hornpipe, in the performance of which the dancer's chief aim seemed to be to shew in what a variety of complex ways he could shake himself to pieces if he chose. Then there was another trio, and then a short pause, in order duly to prepare the public mind for the reception of the great *cantatrice* Mademoiselle Nelina. When she was led to the footlights by the tallest of the three negroes, there was a momentary pause, as if men caught their breath; then there was a prolonged cheer of enthusiastic admiration. And little wonder, for the creature that appeared before these rough miners seemed more like an angelic visitant than a mortal.

There was nothing strikingly beautiful about the child, but she possessed that inexpressibly *sweet* character of face that takes the human heart by storm at first sight; and this, added to the fact that she was almost the only one of her sex who had been seen for many months by any of those present, — that she was fair, blue-eyed, delicate, modestly dressed, and innocent, filled them with an amount of enthusiasm that would have predisposed them to call a scream melodious, had it been uttered by Mademoiselle Nelina.

But the voice which came timidly from her lips was in harmony with her appearance. There was no attempt at execution, and the poor child was too frightened to succeed in imparting much expression to the simple ballad which she warbled; but there was an inherent richness in the tones of her voice that entranced the ear, and dwelt for weeks and months afterwards on the memory of those who heard it that night.

It is needless to add, that all her songs were encored with rapturous applause. The second song she sang was the popular one, "Erin, my country!" and it created quite a *furore* among the audience, many of whom were natives of the Green Isle.

"Oh! ye purty creature! sing it again, do!" yelled an Irishman in the front seats, while he waved his hat, and cheered in mad enthusiasm. The multitude shouted, "Encore!" and the song was sung for the third time.

While it was singing, Larry O'Neil sat with his hands clasped before him, his bosom heaving, and his eyes riveted on the child's face.

"Mr. Sinton," he said, in a deep, earnest tone, touching Ned on the shoulder, as the last sweet notes of the air were drowned in the thunder of applause that followed Mademoiselle Nelina off the stage; "Mr. Sinton, I'd lay me life that it's *her!*"

"Who?" inquired Ned, smiling at the serious expression of his comrade's face.

"Who but Nelly Morgan, av course. She's the born image o' Kate. They're as like as two paise. Sure av it's her, I'll know it, I will; an' I'll make that black thief of a Yankee explain how he comed to possess stolen goods."

Ned and the captain at first expressed doubts as to Larry's being able to swear to the identity of one whom he had never seen before; but the earnest assurances of the Irishman convinced them that he must be right, and they at once entered into his feelings, and planned, in an eager undertone, how the child was to be communicated with.

"It won't do," said Ned, "to tax the man right out with his villainy. The miners would say we wanted to get possession of the child to make money by her."

"But if the child herself admitted that the man was not her relative!" suggested Captain Bunting.

"Perhaps," returned Ned, "she might at the same time admit that she didn't like the appearance of the strangers who made such earnest inquiries about her, and prefer to remain with her present guardian."

"Niver fear," said Larry, in a hoarse whisper; "she'll not say that if I tell her I know her sister Kate, and can take her to her. Besides, hasn't she got an Irish heart? an' don't I know the way to touch it? Jist stay where ye are, both o' ye, an' I'll go behind the scenes. The niggers are comin' on again, so I'll try; maybe there's nobody there but herself."

Before they could reply, Larry was gone. In a few minutes he reached the front seats, and, leaning his back against the wall, as if he were watching the performers, he gradually edged himself into the dark corner where the side curtain shut off the orchestra from the public. To his great satisfaction he found that this was only secured to the wall by one or two nails, which he easily removed, and then, in the midst of an uproarious laugh, caused by a joke of the serenaders, he pushed the curtain aside, and stood before the astonished gaze of Mademoiselle Nelina, who sat on a chair, with her hands clasped and resting on her knee. Unfortunately for the success of Larry's enterprise, he also stood before the curtain-raiser — a broad, sturdy man, in rough miner's costume — whose back was turned towards him, but whose surprised visage instantly faced him on hearing the muffled noise caused by his entry. There was a burly negro also in the place, seated on a small stool, who looked at him with unqualified astonishment.

"Halloo! wot do *you* want?" exclaimed the curtain-raiser.

"Eh! tare an' ages!" cried Larry, in amazement. "May I niver! Sure it's draimin' I am; an' the ghost o' Bill Jones is comed to see me!"

It was, indeed, no other than Bill Jones who stood revealed before him; but no friendly glance of recognition did his old comrade vouch-safe him. He continued, after the first look of surprise, to frown steadily on the intruder.

"You've the advantage o' me, young man," said Bill, in a stern, though subdued tone, for he feared to disturb the men on the stage; "moreover, you've comed in where ye've got no right to be. When a man goes where he shouldn't ought to, an' things looks as if they wasn't all square, in them circumstances, blow high or blow low, I always goes straight for'ard an' shoves him out. If he don't shove easy, why, put on more steam — that's wot *I* say."

"But sure ye don't forgit me, Bill!" pleaded Larry, in amazement.

"Well, p'r'aps I don't, an' p'r'aps I do. W'en I last enjoyed the dis-honour o' yer acquaintance, ye wos a blackguard. It ain't likely yer improved, so be good enough to back yer top-sails, and clear out."

Bill Jones pointed, as he spoke, to the opening through which Larry had entered, but, suddenly changing his mind, he said, "Hold on; there's a back door, an' it'll be easier to kick you through that than through the consart-room."

So saying, Bill seized Larry O'Neil by the collar, and led that indi-vidual, in a state of helpless and wondering consternation, through a back door, where, however, instead of kicking him out, he released him, and suddenly changed his tone to an eager whisper.

"Oh! Larry, lad, I'm glad to see ye. Wherever did ye come from? I've no time to speak. Uncle Ned's jist buried, and Jim Crow comes on in three minutes. I had to pretend, ye know, 'cause it wouldn't do to let Jim see I know'd ye — that wos him on the stool — I know wot brought ye here — an' I've fund out who *she* is. Where d'ye stop?"

Larry's surprise just permitted him to gasp out the words "City Hotel," when a roar of laughter and applause met their ears, followed by the tinkle of a small bell. Bill sprang through the doorway, and slammed the door in his old comrade's face.

It would be difficult to say, looking at that face at that particular time, whether the owner thereof was mad or drunk — or both — so strangely did it wrinkle and contort as it gradually dawned upon its owner that Bill Jones, true to his present profession, was acting a part; that he knew about the mystery of Mademoiselle Nelina; was now acquainted with his, (Larry's), place of abode; and would infal-libly find him out after the concert was over. As these things crossed his mind, Larry smote his thigh so often and so vigorously, that he ran the risk of being taken up for unwarrantably discharging his revolver in the streets, and he whistled once or twice so significantly, that at least five stray dogs answered to the call. At last he hitched up the band of his trousers, and, hastening round to the front door, essayed to re-enter the concert-room.

"Pay here, please," cried the money-taker, in an extremely nasal tone, as he passed the little hole in the wall.

"I've paid already," answered Larry.

"Shew your check, then."

"Sure I don't know what that is."

The doorkeeper smiled contemptuously, and shut down with a bang the bar that kept off the public. Larry doubled his fist, and flushed crimson; then he remembered the importance of the business he had on hand, and quietly drew the requisite sum from his leather purse.

"Come along," said he to Ned Sinton, on re-entering the room. "I've see'd her; an' Bill Jones, too!"

"Bill Jones!" cried Ned and the captain simultaneously.

"Whist!" said Larry; "don't be makin' people obsarve us. Come along home; it's all right — I'll tell ye all about it when we're out."

In another minute the three friends were in the street, conversing eagerly and earnestly as they hastened to their quarters through the thronged and noisy streets of Sacramento.

CHAPTER XXVI.

Deep Plots and Plans — Bill Jones relates his Misadventures — Mademoiselle Nelina consents to run off with Larry O'Neil — A Yankee Musician outwitted — The Escape.

As Larry had rightly anticipated, Bill Jones made his appearance at the City Hotel the moment the concert was over, and found his old comrades waiting anxiously for him.

It did not take long to tell him how they had discovered the existence of Nelly Morgan, as we shall now call her, but it took much longer to drag from Bill the account of his career since they last met, and the explanation of how he came to be placed in his present circumstances.

"Ye see, friends," said he, puffing at a pipe, from which, to look at him, one would suppose he derived most of his information, "this is how it happened. When I set sail from the diggin's to come here for grub, I had a pleasant trip at first. But after a little things began to look bad; the feller that steered us lost his reckoning, an' so we took two or three wrong turns by way o' makin' short cuts. That's always how it Is. There's a proverb somewhere —"

"In Milton, maybe, or Napier's book o' logarithms," suggested Captain Bunting.

"P'r'aps it wos, and p'r'aps it wosn't," retorted Bill, stuffing the end of his little finger, (if such a diminutive may be used in reference to any of his fingers), into the bowl of his pipe. "I rather think myself it wos in *Bell's Life* or the *Royal Almanac*; hows'ever, that's wot it is. When ye've got a short road to go, don't try to make it shorter, say I —"

"An' when ye've got a long story to tell, don't try to make it longer," interrupted Larry, winking at his comrade through the smoke of his pipe.

"Well, as I wos sayin'," continued Bill, doggedly, "we didn't git on so well after a bit; but somehow or other we got here at last, and cast anchor in this very hotel. Off I goes at once an' buys a cart an' a mule, an' then I sets to work to lay in provisions. Now, d'ye see, lads, 'twould ha' bin better if I had bought the provisions first an' the mule and the cart after, for I had to pay ever so many dollars a day for their keep. At last I got it all square; packed tight and tied up in the cart — barrels o' flour, and kegs o' pork, an' beans, an' brandy, an' what not; an' away I went alone; for, d'ye see, I carry a compass, an' when I've once made a voyage, I never need to be told how to steer.

"But my troubles began soon. There's a ford across the river here, which I was told I'd ha' to cross; and sure enough, so I did — but it's as bad as Niagara, if not worse — an' when I gits half way over, we wos capsized, and went down the river keel up. I dun know yet very well how I got ashore, but I did somehow —"

"And did the cart go for it?" inquired Captain Bunting, aghast.

"No, the cart didn't. She stranded half-a-mile further down, on a rock, where she lies to this hour, with a wheel smashed and the bottom out, and about three thousand tons o' water swashin' right through her every hour; but all the provisions and the mule went slap down the Sacramento; an', if they haven't bin' picked up on the way, they're cruisin' off the port o' San Francisco by this time."

The unfortunate seaman stopped at this point to relight his pipe, while his comrades laughingly commented on his misadventure.

"Ah! ye may laugh; but I can tell ye it warn't a thing to be laughed at; an' at this hour I've scarce one dollar to rub 'gainst another."

"Never mind, my boy," said Ned, as he and the others laughed loud and long at the lugubrious visage of their comrade; "we've got well-lined pockets, I assure you; and, of course, we have *your* share of the profits of our joint concern to hand over whenever you wish it."

The expression of Bill Jones's face was visibly improved by this piece of news, and he went on with much greater animation.

"Well, my story's short now. I comed back here, an' by chance fell in with this feller — this Yankee-nigger — who offered me five dollars a day to haul up the curtain, an' do a lot o' dirty work, sich as bill stickin', an' lightin' the candles, an' sweepin' the floor; but it's hard work, I tell ye, to live on so little in sich a place as this, where everything's so dear."

"You're not good at a bargain, I fear," remarked Sinton; "but what of the little girl?"

"Well, I wos comin' to that. Ye see, I felt sure, from some things I overheerd, that she wasn't the man's daughter, so one day I axed her who she wos, an' she said she didn't know, except that her name was Nelly Morgan; so it comed across me that Morgan wos the name o' the Irish family you wos so thick with up at the diggin's, Larry; an' I wos goin' to ask if she know'd them, when Jolly — that's the name o' the gitter up o' the concerts — catched me talkin', an' he took her away sharp, and said he'd thank me to leave the girl alone. I've been watchin' to have another talk with her, but Jolly's too sharp for me, an' I haven't spoke to her yet."

Larry manifested much disappointment at this termination, for he had been fully prepared to hear that the girl had made Bill her confidant, and would be ready to run away with him at a moment's notice. However, he consoled himself by saying that he would do the thing himself; and, after arranging that Bill was to tell Nelly that a friend of his knew where her sister was, and would like to speak with her, they all retired to rest, at least to rest as well as they could in a house which, like all the houses in California, swarmed with rats.

Next night Bill Jones made a bold effort, and succeeded in conveying Larry's message to Nelly, very adroitly, as he thought, while she was standing close to him waiting for Mr. Jolly to lead her to the foot-lights. The consequence was that the poor child trembled like a leaf when she attempted to sing, and, finally, fainted on the stage, to the consternation of a crowded house.

The point was gained, however; Nelly soon found an opportunity of talking in private with Bill Jones, and appointed to meet Larry in the street next morning early, near the City Hotel.

It was with trembling eagerness, mixed with timidity, that she took the Irishman's arm when they met, and asked if he really knew where her sister was.

"Oh, how I've longed for her! But are you *sure* you know her?"

"Know her!" said Larry, with a smile. "Do I know meself?"

This argument was unanswerable, so Nelly made no reply, and Larry went on. "Yes, avic, I know'd her, an' faix I hope to know her better. But here's her picture for ye."

Larry then gave the earnest listener at his side a graphic description of her sister Kate's personal appearance, and described her brother also, but he did not, at that time, acquaint her with the death of the latter. He also spoke of Black Jim, and described the circumstances of her being carried off. "So ye see, darlin'," said he, "I know all about ye; an' now I want ye to tell me what happened to ye after that."

"It's a sad story," said the child, in a low tone, as if her mind were recalling melancholy incidents in her career. Then she told rapidly, how she had been forsaken by those to whom she had been intrusted, and left to perish in the mountain snow; and how, in her extremity, God had sent help; how another party of emigrants found her and carried her on; how, one by one, they all died, till she was left alone a second time; and how a Mexican horseman found her, and carried her to his home, and kept her there as his adopted daughter, till he was killed while taming a wild horse. After that, Nelly's story was a repetition of what Larry had already overheard accidentally in the concert-room.

"Now, dear," said Larry, "we haven't time to waste, will ye go with me to San Francisco?"

The tones of the rough man's voice, rather than his words, had completely won the confidence of the poor child, so she said, "Yes," without hesitation. "But how am I to escape from Mr. Jolly?" she added; "he has begun to suspect Mr. Jones, I see quite well."

"Lave that to me, darlin', an' do you kape as much as ye can in the house the nixt day or two, an' be lookin' out for what may turn up. Good day to ye, mavourneen; we must part here, for fear we're seen by any lynx-eyed blackguards. Kape up yer heart."

Nelly walked quickly away, half laughing at, and half perplexed by, the ambiguity of her new friend's parting advice.

The four friends now set themselves to work to outwit Mr. Jolly, and rob him of Mademoiselle Nelina. At last they hit upon a device, which did not, indeed, say much for the ingenuity of the party, but which, like many other bold plans, succeeded admirably.

A steamer was to start in three days for San Francisco — one of

those splendid new vessels which, like floating palaces, had suddenly made their appearance on these distant waters — having
made the long and dangerous voyage from the United States round
the Horn. Before the steamer started, Larry contrived to obtain
another interview with Nelly Morgan, and explained their plan,
which was as follows: —

On the day of the steamer sailing, a few hours before the time of
starting, Mr. Jolly was to receive the following letter, dated from a
well-known ranche, thirty miles up the river: —

"Sir, — I trust that you will forgive a perfect stranger addressing you, but the
urgency of the case must be my excuse. There is a letter lying here for you,
which, I have reason to know, contains information of the utmost importance to yourself; but which — owing to circumstances that I dare not explain
in a letter that might chance to fall into wrong hands — must be opened here
by your own hands. It will explain all when you arrive; meanwhile, as I am a
perfect stranger to the state of your finances, I send you a sufficient quantity
of gold-dust by the bearer to enable you to hire a horse and come up. Pray excuse the liberty I take, and believe me to be,
    "Your obedient servant,
        "Edward Sinton."

At the appointed time Larry delivered this epistle, and the bag of
gold into Mr. Jolly's hands, and, saying that no answer was required,
hurried away.

If Mr. Jolly had been suddenly informed that he had been appointed secretary of state to the king of Ashantee, he could not have
looked more astonished than when he perused this letter, and
weighed the bag of gold in his hand. The letter itself, had it arrived
alone, might, very likely would, have raised his suspicions, but accompanied as it was by a bag of gold of considerable value, it commended
itself as a genuine document; and the worthy musician was in the
saddle half-an-hour later. Before starting, he cautioned Nelly not to
quit the house on any account whatever, a caution which she heard
but did not reply to. Three hours later Mr. Jolly reached his destina-
tion, and had the following letter put into his hands.

"Sir, — By the time you receive this, your late charge, Mademoiselle Nelina,
will be on her way to San Francisco, where you are welcome to follow her,
and claim her from her sister, if you feel so disposed.
    "I am, Sir, etcetera,
        "Edward Sinton."

We need not repeat what Mr. Jolly said, or try to imagine what he
felt, on receipt of *this* letter! About the time it was put into his hands
the magnificent steamer at the *embarcadero* gave a shrill whistle,
then it panted violently, the paddles revolved, — and our adventurers

were soon steaming swiftly down the noble river on their way to San Francisco.

CHAPTER XXVII.

San Francisco again — A Terrible Misfortune —
An Old Friend in surprisingly New Circumstances —
Several Remarkable Discoveries and New Lights.

There is no time or place, perhaps, more suitable for indulging in ruminations, cogitations, and reminiscences, than the quiet hours of a calm night out upon the sea, when the watchful stars look down upon the bosom of the deep, and twinkle at their reflections in placid brilliancy.

Late at night, when all the noisy inmates of the steamer had ceased to eat, and drink, and laugh, and had sought repose in their berths, Edward Sinton walked the deck alone, meditating on the past, the present, and the future. When he looked up at the serene heavens, and down at the tranquil sea, whose surface was unruffled, save by the long pure white track of the vessel, he could scarcely bring himself to believe that the whirl of incident and adventure in which he had been involved during the last few and short months was real. It seemed like a brilliant dream. As long as he was on shore it all appeared real enough, and the constant pressure of *something to be done*, either immediately, or in an hour, or tomorrow, kept his mind perpetually chained down to the consideration of visible, and tangible, and passing events; but now the cord of connexion with land had been suddenly and completely severed. The very land itself was out of sight. Nothing around him tended to recall recent events; and, as he had nothing in the world to do but wait until the voyage should come to an end, his mind was left free to bound over the recent-past into the region of the long-past, and revel there at pleasure.

But Ned Sinton was not altogether without anxieties. He felt a little uneasy as to the high-handed manner in which he had carried off Nelly Morgan from her late guardian; and he was a good deal perplexed as to what the important affairs could be for which he had so hastily overturned all the gold-digging plans of his whole party. With these thoughts mingled many philosophic inquiries as to the amount of advantage that lay — if, indeed, there was any advantage at all — in making one's fortune suddenly and at the imminent hazard of one's life. Overpowering sleep at last put an end to Ned's wandering thoughts, and he too bade the stars good-night, and sought his pillow. In due course the vessel cast anchor off the town of San Francisco.

"There is many a slip 'tween the cup and the lip." It is an old proverb that, but one which is proved, by frequent use, on the part of authors in all ages, to be a salutary reminder to humanity. Its truth was unpleasantly exemplified on the arrival of the steamer. As the tide was out at the time, the captain ordered the boats to be lowered, in order to land the passengers. The moment they touched the water they were filled by impatient miners, who struggled to be first ashore. The boat into which Ned and his friends got was soon overloaded with passengers, and the captain ordered her to be shoved off.

"Hold on!" shouted a big coarse-looking fellow, in a rough blue jacket and wide-awake, who was evidently drunk; "let me in first."

"There's no room!" cried several voices. "Shove off."

"There's room enough!" cried the man, with an oath; at the same time seizing the rope.

"If ye do come down," said a sailor, sternly, "I'll pitch ye overboard."

"Will ye!" growled the man; and the next instant he sprang upon the edge of the boat, which upset, and left its freight struggling in the water. The other boats immediately picked them all up; and, beyond a wetting, they were physically none the worse. But, alas! the bags of gold which our adventurers were carrying ashore with them, sank to the bottom of the sea! They were landed on the wharf at San Francisco as penniless as they were on the day of their arrival in California.

This reverse of fortune was too tremendous to be realised in a moment. As they stood on the wharf; dripping wet, and gazing at each other in dismay, they suddenly, as if by one consent, burst into a loud laugh. But the laugh had a strong dash of bitterness in its tone; and when it passed, the expression of their countenances was not cheerful.

Bill Jones was the first to speak, as they wandered, almost helplessly, through the crowded streets, while little Nelly ever and anon looked wistfully up into Larry's face, as he led her by the hand.

"It's a stunnin' smash," said Bill, fetching a deep sigh. "But w'en a thing's done, an' can't be undone, then it's unpossible, that's wot it is; and wot's unpossible there's no use o' tryin' for to do. 'Cause why? it only wastes yer time an' frets yer sperrit — that's *my* opinion."

Not one of the party ventured to smile — as was their wont in happier circumstances — at the philosophy of their comrade's remark. They wandered on in silence till they reached — they scarce knew how or why — the centre plaza of the town.

"It's of no use giving way to it," said Ned Sinton, at last, making a mighty effort to recover: "we must face our reverses like men; and, after all, it might have been worse. We might have lost our lives as well as our gold, so we ought to be thankful instead of depressed."

"What shall we do now?" inquired Captain Bunting, in a tone that proved sufficiently that he at least could not benefit by Ned's advice.

"Sure we'll have to go an' work, capting," replied Larry, in a tone of facetious desperation; "but first of all we'll have to go an' see Mr. Thompson, and git dry clo'se for Nelly, poor thing — are ye cowld, darlin'?"

"No, not in the least," answered the child, sadly. "I think my things will dry soon, if we walk in the sun."

Nelly's voice seemed to rouse the energies of the party more effectually than Ned's moralising.

"Yes," cried the latter, "let us away to old Thompson's. His daughter, Lizette, will put you all to rights, dear, in a short time. Come along."

So saying, Ned led the way, and the whole party speedily stood at the door of Mr. Thompson's cottage.

The door was merely fastened by a latch, and as no notice was taken of their first knock, Ned lifted it and entered the hall, then advancing to the parlour door, he opened it and looked in.

The sight that met his gaze was well calculated to make him open his eyes, and his mouth too, if that would in any way have relieved his feelings.

Seated in old Mr. Thompson's easy-chair, with one leg stretched upon an ottoman, and the other reposing on a stool, reclined Tom Collins, looking, perhaps, a little paler than was his wont, as if still suffering from the effects of recent illness, but evidently quite happy and comfortable.

Beside Tom, on another stool, with her arm resting on Tom's knee, and looking up in his face with a quiet smile, sat Elizabeth Thompson.

"Tom! Miss Thompson!" cried Ned Sinton, standing absolutely aghast.

Miss Thompson sprang up with a face of crimson, but Tom sat coolly still, and said, while a broad grin overspread his handsome countenance, "No, Ned, not Miss Thompson — Mrs. *Collins*, who, I know, is rejoiced to see you."

"You are jesting, Tom," said Ned, as he advanced quickly, and took the lady's hand, while Tom rose and heartily welcomed his old companions.

"Not a bit of it, my dear fellow," he repeated. "This, I assure you, is my wife. Pray, dear Lizette, corroborate my statement, else our friends won't believe me. But sit down, sit down, and let's hear all about you. Go, Lizette, get 'em something to eat. I knew you would make your appearance ere long. Old Thompson's letter — halloo! why what's this? You're wet! and *who's* this — a wet little girl?"

"Faix, ye may well be surprised, Mister Tom," said Larry, "for we're all wet *beggars*, ivery wan o' us — without a dollar to bless ourselves with."

Tom Collins looked perplexed, as he turned from one to the other. "Stay," he shouted; "wife, come here. There's a mystery going on. Take this moist little one to your room; and there," he added, throwing open a door, "you fellows will all find dry apparel to put on — though I don't say to fit. Come along with me, Ned, and while you change, give an account of yourself."

Ned did as he was desired; and, in the course of a lengthened conversation, detailed to Tom the present condition of himself and his friends.

"It's unfortunate," said Tom, after a pause; "ill-luck seems to follow us wherever we go."

"You ought to be ashamed of yourself," cried Ned, "for saying so, considering the wife you have got."

"True, my boy," replied the other, "I ought indeed to be ashamed, but I spoke in reference to money matters. What say you to the fact, that I am as much a beggar as yourself?"

"Outward appearances would seem to contradict yon."

"Nevertheless, it is true, I assure you. When you left me, Ned, in the hotel at Sacramento, I became so lonely that I grew desperate; and, feeling much stronger in body, I set off for this town in the new steamer — that in which you arrived. I came straight up here, re-introduced myself to Mr. Thompson; and, two days after — for I count it folly to waste time in such matters when one's mind is made up — I proposed to Lizette, and was accepted conditionally. Of course, the condition was that papa should be willing. But papa was *not* willing. He said that three thousand dollars, all I possessed, was a capital sum, but not sufficient to marry on, and that he could not risk his daughter's happiness, etcetera, etcetera — you know the rest. Well, the very next day news came that one of Thompson's best ships had been wrecked off Cape Horn. This was a terrible blow, for the old man's affairs were in a rickety condition at any rate, and this sank him altogether. His creditors were willing enough to wait, but one rascal refused to do so, and swore he would sequestrate him. I found that the sum due him was exactly three thousand dollars, so I paid him the amount in full, and handed Thompson the discharged account. 'Now,' said I, 'I'm off to the diggings, so good-bye!' for, you see, Ned, I felt that I could not urge my suit at that time, as it would be like putting on the screw — taking an unfair advantage of him.

"'Why, what do you mean, my lad?' said he.

"'That I'm off tomorrow,' replied I.

"'That you must not do,' said he.

"'Why not?' said I.

"'Because,' said he, 'now that things are going smooth, I must go to England by the first ship that sails, and get my affairs there put on a better footing, so you must stay here to look after my business, and to — to — take care of Lizette.'

"'Eh! what!' said I, 'what do you mean? You know *that* is impossible.'

"'Not at all, boy, if you marry her!'

"Of course I could not refuse, and so, to cut it short, we were married right off and here we are, the representatives of the great firm of Thompson and Company, of California."

"Then, do you mean to say that Thompson is gone?" Inquired Ned, with a look of horror.

"Near the Horn, I should think, by this time; but why so anxious?"

"Because," sighed Ned, sitting down on the edge of the bed, with a look of despair, "I came here by his invitation; and —"

"Oh! it's all right," interrupted Tom; "I know all about it, and am commissioned by him to settle the affair for you."

"But what *is* the affair?" inquired Ned, eagerly.

"Ah! my dear boy, do try to exercise patience. If I tell you every-thing before we go down to our comrades, I fear we shall have to send a message to say that we are not coming till tomorrow morning."

Tom rose as he spoke, and led the way to the parlour, where bread and cheese were spread out for them.

"The only drawback to my felicity," whispered Tom to Sinton, as they entered, "is that I find Thompson's affairs far worse than he him-self was aware of; and it's a fact, that at this moment I can scarcely draw enough out of the business to supply the necessaries of life."

There was a slight bitterness in Tom's tone as he said this, but the next moment he was jesting with his old companions as lightheart-edly as ever. During the meal he refused, however, to talk business, and, when it was concluded, he proposed that they should go out for a stroll through the town.

"By the way," remarked Ned, as they walked along, "what of Cap-tain Bunting's old ship?"

"Ay!" echoed the captain, "that's the uppermost thing in *my* mind; but master Tom seems determined to keep us in the dark. I do believe the *Roving Bess* has been burned, an' he's afraid to tell us."

"You're a desperately inquisitive set," cried Tom Collins, laughing. "Could you not suppose that I wanted to give you a surprise, by shewing you how curiously she has been surrounded by houses since you last saw her. You'll think nothing of it, now that I have told you."

"Why, where are ye goin'?" cried Larry, as Tom turned up a street that led a little away from the shore, towards which they had been walking!

Tom made no reply, but led on. They were now in that densely-crowded part of the town where shops were less numerous, ware-houses more plentiful, and disagreeable odours more abundant, than elsewhere. A dense mass of buildings lay between them and the sea, and in the centre of these was a square or plaza, on one side of which stood a large hotel, out of the roof of which rose a gigantic flag-staff. A broad and magnificent flight of wooden steps led up to the door of this house of entertainment, over which, on a large board, was written its name — "The Roving Bess Tavern."

"Dear me! that's a strange coincidence," exclaimed the captain, as his eye caught the name.

"Tare an' ages!" yelled Larry, "av it isn't the owld ship! Don't I know the mizzen-mast as well as I know me right leg?"

"The *Roving Bess* Tavern!" muttered Captain Bunting, while his eyes stared incredulously at the remarkable edifice before him.

Bill Jones, who, up to this point, had walked beside his comrades in silent meditation, here lost presence of mind and, putting both hands to his mouth, sang out, in true stentorian boatswain tones, "All hands ahoy! tumble up there — tumble up!"

"Ay, ay, sir!" roared half-a-dozen jack tars, who chanced to be regaling themselves within, and who rushed out, hat in hand, ready for a spree, at the unexpected but well-known summons.

"Major Whitlaw," said Tom Collins, springing up the steps, and addressing a tall, cadaverous-looking Yankee, "allow me to introduce to you your landlord, Captain Bunting — your tenant, captain. I dare say you have almost forgotten each other."

The captain held out his hand mechanically and gazed at his tenant unbelievingly, while the major said —

"Glad to see ye, cap'n, I guess. Wanted to for a long time. Couldn't come to terms with old Thompson. Won't you step in and take a cocktail or a gin-sling? I'd like to have a private talk — this way."

The landlord of the *Roving Bess* Tavern led the captain to what was once his own cabin, and begged him to be seated on his own locker at the head of his own table. He accepted these civilities, staring round him in mute wonder all the time, as if he thought it was a dream, out of which he should wake in due course, while, from all parts of the tavern, came sounds of mirth, and clatter of knives and forks and dishes, and odours of gin-slings and bear-steaks and pork-pies.

"Jist sit there a minute," said the Yankee, "till I see to your friends bein' fixed off comfortable; of course, Mr. Collins may stay, for he knows all about it."

When he was gone, the captain rose and looked into his old berth. It had been converted into a pantry, so he shut the door quickly and returned to his seat.

"Tom," said he, in a low whisper, as if he feared to break the spell, "how *did* they get her up here!"

"She's never been moved since you left her," answered Tom, laughing; "the town has gradually surrounded her, as you see, and crept out upon the shore, filling up the sea with rubbish, till it has left her nearly a quarter of a mile inland."

The captain's eyes opened wider than ever, but before he could find words again to speak, Major Whitlaw returned.

"They're all square now, gentlemen, so, if you please, we'll proceed to business. I suppose your friend has told you how the land lies?"

"He certainly has," replied the captain, who accepted the phrase literally.

"Wall, I reckon your property's riz since ye wor here; now, if you give me leave to make the alterations I want to, I'll give you 1000 dollars a month, payable in advance."

"You'd better tell Captain Bunting what the alterations you refer to are," suggested Tom Collins, who saw that the captain's state of mind rendered him totally incapable of transacting business.

"That's soon done. I'll give it ye slick off. I want to cut away the companion-hatch and run up a regular stair to the deck; then it's advisable to cut away at least half o' the main deck to heighten the gamin' saloon. But I guess the main point is to knock out half-a-dozen windows in the hold, for gas-light is plaguey dear, when it's goin' full blast day and night. Besides, I must cut the entrance-door down to the ground, for this tree-mendous flight o' stairs'll be the ruin o' the business. It's only a week since a man was shot by a comrade here in the cabin, an' as they rushed out after him, two customers fell down the stair and broke their arms. And I calc'late the gentlemen that's overtaken by liquor every night won't stand it much longer. There isn't a single man that quits this house after 12 p.m. but goes down that flight head-foremost. If you don't sanction that change, I guess I'll have to get 'em padded, and spread feather-beds at the foot. Now, cap'n, if you agrees to this right off, I'll give the sum named."

Captain Bunting's astonishment had now reached that point at which extremes are supposed to meet, and a reaction began to take place.

"How much did you propose?" he inquired, taking out a pencil and an old letter, as if he were about to make notes, at the same time knitting his brows, and endeavouring to look intensely sagacious.

"One thousand dollars a month," answered the Yankee; "I railly can't stand more."

"Let me see," muttered the captain slowly, in an under tone, while he pressed his forehead with his fore-finger; "one thousand dollars — £200 sterling — hum, equal to about £2400 a year. Well," he added, raising his voice, "I don't mind if I do. I suppose, Tom, it's not *much* below the thing, as rents go!"

"It's a fair offer," said Tom, carelessly; "we might, perhaps, get a higher, but Major Whitlaw is in possession, and is, besides, a good tenant."

"Then I'll conclude the bargain — pray get pen, ink, and paper."

While the major turned for a moment to procure writing materials, the captain looked at Tom and winked expressively. Then, a document was drawn up, signed, and witnessed, and then the captain, politely declining a brandy-smash, or any other smash whatever, left the *Roving Bess* Tavern with his friends, and with £200 — the first month's rent — in his pocket.

It is needless to remark, that his comrades congratulated him heartily, and that the worthy captain walked along the streets of San Francisco chuckling.

In a few minutes, Tom Collins stopped before a row of immense warehouses. There was one gap in the row, a space of several yards square, that might have held two good-sized houses. Four wooden posts stood at the corners of the plot, and an old boat, turned keel up, lay in the middle of it.

"I know it!" cried Ned Sinton, laughing in gleeful surprise; "it's my old boat, isn't it? Well, I can scarcely credit my eyes! I saw it last on the sea-shore, and now it's a quarter of a mile into the town!"

"More than that, Ned," said Tom Collins, "the plot of ground is worth ten thousand dollars at this moment. Had it been a little further south, it would have been worth ten times that sum. And more than that still, the Irish family you lent the boat to — you remember them — well, they dug up a bag from under the boat which contained five thousand dollars; the honest people at once gave it up, and Mr. Thompson rewarded them well; but they did not live to enjoy it long, they're all dead now. So you see, Ned, you're just £3000 richer than you thought you were this morning."

"It's a great day!" remarked Larry O'Neil, looking round upon his comrades, who received all this information with an expression of doubting surprise; "a great day intirely! Faix, I'm only hopin' we won't waken up an' find it's all a dhrame!"

Larry's companions quite agreed with him. They did not indeed say so, but, as they returned home after that stroll, talking eagerly of future plans and prospects, the ever-recurring sentiment broke from their lips, in every style of phrase, "It's a great day, intirely!"

CHAPTER XXVIII.

More Unexpected Discoveries — Captain Bunting
makes Bill Jones A First Mate — Larry O'Neil Makes
himself a First Mate — The Parting — Ned Sinton
proves himself, a Second Time, to be a Friend in Need
and in Deed.

"It never rains but it pours," saith the proverb. We are fond of prov-
erbs. We confess to a weakness that way. There is a depth of meaning
in them which courts investigation from the strongest intellects. Even
when they are nonsensical, which is not unfrequently the case, their
nonsense is unfathomable, and, therefore, invested with all the zest
which attaches, metaphysically speaking, to the incomprehensible.

Astonishing circumstances had been raining for some time past
around our bewildered adventurers, and, latterly, they had begun to
pour. On the afternoon of the day, the events of which have been
recorded in the last chapter, there was, metaphorically speaking, a
regular thunder-plump. No sooner had the party returned to old Mr.
Thompson's cottage, than down it came again, heavy as ever.

On entering the porch, Lizette ran up to Tom, in that pretty trip-
ping style peculiar to herself, and whispered in his ear.

"Well, you baggage," said he, "I'll go with you; but I don't like
secrets. Walk into the parlour, friends; I'll be with you in a minute."

"Tom," said Lizette, pursing up her little mouth and elevating her
pert nose; "you can't guess what an interesting discovery I've made."

"Of course I can't," replied Tom, with affected impatience; "now,
pray, don't ask me to try, else I shall leave you instantly."

"What an impatient creature you are!" said Lizette. "Only think! I
have discovered that my maid, whom we hired only two days ago,
has —"

"Bolted with the black cook, or somebody else, and married him,"
interrupted Tom, with a look of horror, as he threw himself into any
easy-chair.

"Not at all," rejoined Lizette, hurriedly; "nothing of the sort; she
has discovered that the little girl Mr. Sinton brought with him is her
sister."

"What! Kate Morgan's sister!" cried Tom, with a look of surprise.
"I knew it; I was sure I had heard the name before, but I couldn't
remember when or where; I see it now; she must be the girl Larry
O'Neil used to talk about up at the diggin's; but as I never saw her
there, of course I couldn't know her."

"Well, I don't know about that; I suppose you're right," replied
Lizette; "but isn't it nice? They're kissing and hugging each other, and
crying, in the kitchen at this moment. Oh! I'm *so* happy — the dear
little thing!"

If Lizette was happy she took a strange way to shew it, for she sat down beside Tom and began to sob.

While the above conversation was going on up-stairs, another conversation — interesting enough to deserve special notice — was going on in the parlour.

"Sure don't I know me own feelin's best?" remarked Larry, addressing Ned Sinton. "It's all very well at the diggin's; but when it comes to drawin'-rooms and parlours, I feels — an' so does Bill Jones here — that we're out 'o place. In the matter o' diggin' we're all equals, no doubt; but we feels that we ain't gintlemen born, and that it's a'k'ard to the lady to be havin' sich rough customers at her table, so Bill an' me has agreed to make the most o' ourselves in the kitchen."

"Larry, you're talking nonsense. We have messed together on equal terms for many months; and, whatever course we may follow after this, you *must* sup with us tonight, as usual. I know Tom will be angry if you don't."

"Ay, sir, but it ain't 'as oosual,'" suggested Bill Jones, turning the quid in his cheek; "it's quite on-oosual for the likes o' us to sup with a lady."

"That's it," chimed in Larry; "so, Mister Ned, ye'll jist plaise to make our excuges to Mrs. Tom, and tell her where we've gone to locate, as the Yankees say. Come away, Bill."

Larry took his friend by the arm, and, leading him out of the room, shut the door.

Five seconds after that there came an appalling female shriek, and a dreadful masculine yell, from the region of the kitchen, accompanied by a subdued squeak of such extreme sweetness, that it could have come only from the throat of Mademoiselle Nelina. Ned and the captain sprang to the door, and dashed violently against Tom and his wife, whom they unexpectedly met also rushing towards the kitchen. In another moment a curious and deeply interesting *tableau vivant* was revealed to their astonished gaze.

In the middle of the room was Larry O'Neil, down on one knee, while with both arms he supported the fainting form of Kate Morgan. By Kate's side knelt her sister Nelly, who bent over her pale face with anxious, tearful countenance, while, presiding over the group, like an amiable ogre, stood Bill Jones, with his hands in his breeches-pockets, his legs apart, one eye tightly screwed up, and his mouth expanded from ear to ear.

"That's yer sort!" cried Bill, in ecstatic glee. "W'en a thing comes all right, an' tight, an' ship-shape, why, wot then? In coorse it's all square — that's wot *I* say."

"She's comin' to," whispered Larry. "Ah! thin, spake, won't ye, darlin'? It'll do ye good, maybe, an' help to open yer two purty eyes."

Kate Morgan recovered — we need scarcely tell our reader that — and Nelly dried her eyes, and that evening was spent in a fashion that conduced to the well-being, and comfort, and good humour of all parties concerned. Perhaps it is also needless to inform our reader that Larry O'Neil and Bill Jones carried their point. They supped in the kitchen that night. Our informant does not say whether Kate Morgan and her sister Nelly supped with them — but we rather think they did.

A week afterwards, Captain Bunting had matured his future plans. He resolved to purchase a clipper-brig that was lying at that time useless in the harbour, and embark in the coasting trade of California. He made Bill Jones his first mate, and offered to make Larry O'Neil his second, but Larry wanted a mate himself, and declined the honour; so the captain gave him five hundred pounds to set him up in any line he chose. Ned Sinton sold his property, and also presented his old comrade with a goodly sum of money, saying, that as he, (Ned), had been the means of dragging him away from the diggings, he felt bound to assist him in the hour of need. So Kate Morgan became Mrs. O'Neil the week following; and she, with her husband and her little sister, started off for the interior of the country to look after a farm.

About the same time, Captain Bunting having completed the lading of his brig, succeeded in manning her by offering a high wage, and, bidding adieu to Ned and Tom, set sail for the Sacramento.

Two days afterwards, Ned got a letter from old Mr. Shirley — the first that he had received since leaving England. It began thus: —

"My Dearest Boy, — What has become of you? I have written six letters, at least, but have never got a single line in reply. You must come home immediately, as affairs here require your assistance, and I'm getting too old to attend to business matters. Do come at once, my dear Ned, unless you wish me to reprove you. Moxton says only a young and vigorous man of business can manage things properly; but when I mentioned you, he shook his head gravely. 'Too wild and absurd in his notions,' said he. I stopped him, however, by saying that I was fully aware of your faults —"

The letter then went rambling on in a quaint, prosy, but interesting style; and Ned sat long in his room in old Mr. Thompson's cottage poring over its contents, and gradually maturing his future plans.

"It's awkward," soliloquised he, resting his head on both hands. "I shall have to go at once, and so won't have a chance of seeing Bunting again, to tell him of poor Tom's circumstances. He would only be too glad to give him a helping hand; but I know Tom will never let him know how hard-up he is. There's nothing else for it," he added, determinedly; "my uncle will laugh at my profitless tour — but, *n'importe*, I have learned much. — Come in!"

This last remark was addressed to some one who had tapped gently at the door.

"It's only me, Ned; can I come in? I fear I interrupt you," said Tom, as he entered the room.

"Not at all; sit down, my boy. I have just been perusing a letter from my good old uncle Shirley: he writes so urgently that I fear I must return to England by the first homeward-bound ship."

"Return to England!" exclaimed Tom, in surprise. "What! leave the gold-fields just as the sun is beginning to shine on you?"

"Even so, Tom."

"My dear Ned, you are mad! This is a splendid country. Just see what fortunes we should have made, but for the unfortunate accidents that have happened!" Tom sighed as he spoke.

"I know it," replied his friend, with sadden energy. "This is a splendid country; gold exists all over it — not only in the streams, but on the hill-sides, and even on hill-tops, as you and I know from personal experience — but gold, Tom, is not *everything* in this world, and the getting of it should not be our chief aim. Moreover, I have come to the conclusion, that *digging* gold ought to be left entirely to such men as are accustomed to dig ditches and throw up railway embankments. Men whose intelligence is of a higher order ought not to ignore the faculties that have been given to them, and devote their time — too often, alas! their lives — to a species of work that the merest savage is equally capable of performing. Navvies may work at the mines with propriety; but educated men who devote themselves to such work are, I fear, among the number of those to whom Scripture specially speaks, when it says, 'Make not haste to be rich.'"

"But there are other occupations here besides digging for gold," said Tom.

"I know it; and I would be happy and proud to rank among the merchants, and engineers, and such men, of California; but duty calls me home, and, to say truth," added Ned, with a smile, "inclination points the way."

Tom Collins still for some time attempted to dissuade his friend from quitting the country, and his sweet little wife, Lizette, seconded his efforts with much earnestness; but Ned Sinton was immovable. He took passage in the first ship that sailed for England.

The night before he sailed, Ned, after retiring to his room for the last time in his friend's house, locked his door, and went through a variety of little pieces of business that would have surprised his hosts had they seen him. He placed a large strong-box on the table, and cautiously drew from under his bed a carpet-bag, which, from the effort made to lift it, seemed to be filled with some weighty substance. Unlocking the bag, he proceeded to lift out handful after handful of shining dollars and gold pieces, interspersed here and there with massive nuggets. These he transferred into the wooden box until it was full. This was nearly the whole of Ned's fortune. It amounted to a little more than £3000 sterling. Having completed the transfer, Ned counted the surplus left in the bag, and found it to be about £500. This he secured in a leather purse, and then sat down to write a letter. The letter was short when finished, but it took him long to write, for he meditated much during the writing of it, and several times laid his head on his hands. At last it was completed, put into the box, and the lid screwed down above it. Then Ned read a chapter in the Bible, as was his wont, and retired to rest.

Next day Tom and Lizette stood on the wharf to see him embark for England. Long and earnest was the converse of the two friends, as they were about to part, probably for ever, and then, for the first time, they became aware how deep was the attachment which each had formed for the other. At last the mate of the ship came up, and touched his hat.

"Now, sir, boat's ready, sir; and we don't wish to lose the first of the ebb."

"Good-bye, Lizette — good-bye, Tom! God be with and bless you, my dear fellow! Stay, I had almost forgotten. Tom, you will find a box on the table in my room; you can keep the contents — a letter in it will explain. Farewell!"

Tom's heart was too full to speak. He squeezed his friend's hand in silence, and, turning hurriedly round, walked away with Lizette the instant the boat left the shore.

Late in the evening, Tom and his wife remembered the box, and went up-stairs to open it. Their surprise at its rich contents may be imagined. Both at once understood its meaning; and Lizette sat down, and covered her face with her hands, to hide the tears that flowed, while her husband read the letter. It ran thus: —

"My Dearest Tom, — You must not be angry with me for leaving this trifle — it *is* a trifle compared with the amount of gold I would give you if I had it. But I need not apologise; the spirit of love in which it is given demands that it shall be unhesitatingly received in the same spirit. May God, who has blessed us and protected us in all our wanderings together, cause your worldly affairs to prosper, and especially may He bless your soul. Seas and continents may separate us, but I shall never forget you, Tom, or your dear wife. But I must not write as if I were saying farewell. I intend this epistle to be the opening of a correspondence that shall continue as long as we live. You shall hear from me again ere long.

"Your sincerely-attached friend,
"Edward Sinton."

At the time Tom Collins was reading the above letter to Lizette, in a broken, husky voice, our hero was seated on the taffrail of the ship that bore him swiftly over the sea, gazing wistfully at the receding shore, and bidding a final adieu to California and all his golden dreams.

CHAPTER XXIX.
Our Story comes to an End.

Home! What a host of old and deep and heart-stirring associations arise in every human breast at the sound of that old familiar word! How well we know it — how vividly it recalls certain scenes and faces — how pleasantly it falls on the ear, and slips from the tongue — yet how little do we appreciate home until we have left it, and longed for it, perhaps, for many years.

Our hero, Ned Sinton, is home at last. He sits in his old place beside the fire, with his feet on the fender. Opposite to him sits old Mr. Shirley, with a bland smile on his kind, wrinkled visage, and two pair of spectacles on his brow. Mr. Shirley, as we formerly stated, regularly loses one pair of spectacles, and always searches for them in vain, in consequence of his having pushed them too far up on his bald head; he, therefore, is frequently compelled to put on his second pair, and hence makes a spectacle, to some extent, of himself. Exactly between the uncle and the nephew, on a low stool, sits the cat — the cat, *par excellence* — Mr. Shirley's cat, a creature which he has always been passionately fond of since it was a kitten, and to which, after Ned's departure for California, he had devoted himself so tenderly, that he felt half-ashamed of himself, and would not like to have been asked how much he loved it.

Yes, the cat sits there, looking neither at old Mr. Shirley nor at young Mr. Sinton, but bestowing its undivided attentions and affections on the fire, which it enjoys extremely, if we may judge from the placid manner in which it winks and purrs.

Ned has been a week at home, and he has just reached that point of experience at which the wild life of the diggings through which he has passed begins to seem like a vivid dream rather than reality.

Breakfast had just been concluded, although the cloth had not yet been removed.

"Do you know, uncle," remarked Ned, settling his bulky frame more comfortably in the easy-chair, and twirling his watch-key, "I find it more difficult every day to believe that the events of the last few months of my life have actually occurred. When I sit here in my old seat, and look at you and the cat and the furniture — everything, in fact, just the same as when I left — I cannot realise that I have been nearly two years away."

"I understand your feelings, my dear boy," replied Mr. Shirley, taking off his spectacles, (the lower pair,) wiping them with his handkerchief putting them on again, and looking *over* them at his nephew, with an expression of unmitigated admiration. "I can sympathise with you, Ned, for I have gone through the same experience more than once in the course of my life. It's a strange life, boy, a very strange life this, as you'll come to know, if you're spared to be as old as I am."

Ned thought that his knowledge was already pretty extended in reference to life, and even flattered himself that he had had some stranger views of it than his uncle, but he prudently did not give expression to his thoughts; and, after a short pause, Mr. Shirley resumed —

"Yes, lad, it's a very strange life; and the strangest part of it is, that the longer we live the stranger it gets. I travelled once in Switzerland — ," (the old gentleman paused, as if to allow the statement to have its full weight on Ned's youthful mind,) "and it's a curious fact, that when I had been some months there, home and all connected with it became like a dream to me, and Switzerland became a reality. But after I came back to England, and had spent some time here, home again became the reality, and Switzerland appeared like a dream, so that I sometimes said to myself, 'Can it be possible that I have been there!' Very odd, isn't it?"

"It is, uncle; and I have very much the same feelings now."

"Very odd, indeed," repeated Mr. Shirley. "By the way, that reminds me that we have to talk about that farm of which I spoke to you on the day of your arrival."

We might feel surprised that the above conversation could in any way have the remotest connexion with "that farm" of which Mr. Shirley was so suddenly reminded, did we not know that the subject was, in fact, never out of his mind.

"True, uncle, I had almost forgotten about it, but you know I've been so much engaged during the last few days in visiting my old friends and college companions, that —"

"I know it, I know it, Ned, and I don't want to bother you with business matters sooner than I can help, but —"

"My dear uncle, how can you for a moment suppose that I could be 'bothered' by —"

"Of course not, boy," interrupted Mr. Shirley. "Well, now, let me ask you, Ned, how much gold have you brought back from the diggings?"

Ned fidgeted uncomfortably on his seat — the subject could no longer be avoided.

"I — I — must confess," said he, with hesitation, "that I haven't brought much."

"Of course, you couldn't be expected to have done much in so short a time; but *how* much?"

"Only £500," replied Ned, with a sigh, while a slight blush shone through the deep bronze of his countenance.

"Oh!" said Mr. Shirley, pursing up his mouth, while an arch twinkle lurked in the corners of each eye.

"Ah! but, uncle, you mustn't quiz me. I *had* more, and might have brought it home too, if I had chosen."

"Then why didn't you?"

Ned replied to this question by detailing how most of his money had been lost, and how, at the last, he gave nearly all that remained to his friend Tom Collins.

"You did quite right, Ned, *quite right*," said Mr. Shirley, when his nephew had concluded; "and now I'll tell you what I want you to do. You told me the other day, I think, that you wished to become a farmer."

"Yes, uncle. I do think that that life would suit me better than any other. I'm fond of the country and a quiet life, and I don't like cities; but, then, I know nothing about farming, and I doubt whether I should succeed without being educated to it to some extent at least."

"A very modest and proper feeling to entertain," said Mr. Shirley, with a smile; "particularly when it is considered that farming is an exceedingly difficult profession to acquire a knowledge of. But I have thought of that for you, Ned, and I think I see a way out of the difficulty."

"What way is that?"

"I won't tell you just yet, boy. But answer me this. Are you willing to take any farm I suggest to you, and henceforth to give up all notion of wandering over the face of the earth, and devote yourself steadily to your new profession?"

"I am, uncle; if you will point out to me how I am to pay the rent and stock the farm, and how I am to carry it on in the meantime without a knowledge of husbandry."

"I'll do that for you, all in good time; meanwhile, will you put on your hat, and run down to Moxton's office — you remember it?"

"That I do," replied Ned, with a smile.

"Well, go there, and ask him for the papers I wrote about to him two days ago. Bring them here as quickly as you can. We shall then take the train, and run down to Brixley, and look at the farm."

"But are you really in earnest!" asked Ned, in some surprise.

"Never more so in my life," replied the old gentleman, mildly. "Now be off; I want to read the paper."

Ned rose and left the room, scarcely believing that his uncle did not jest. As he shut the door, old Mr. Shirley took up the paper, pulled down the upper pair of spectacles — an act which knocked the lower pair off his nose, whereat he smiled more blandly than ever — and began to read.

Meanwhile, Edward Sinton put on his great-coat — the identical one he used to wear before he went away — and his hat and his gloves, and walked out into the crowded streets of London, with feelings somewhat akin, probably, to those of a somnambulist. Having been so long accustomed to the free-and-easy costume of the mines, Ned felt about as uncomfortable and stiff as a warrior of old must have felt when armed *cap-à-pie*. His stalwart frame was some what thinner and harder than when he last took the same walk; his fair moustache and whiskers were somewhat more decided, and less like wreaths of smoke, and his countenance was of a deep-brown colour; but in other respects Ned was the same dashing fellow that he used to be — dashing by *nature*, we may remark, not by *affectation*.

In half-an-hour he stood before Moxton's door. There it was, as large as life, and as green as ever. Ned really found it impossible to believe that it was so long since he last saw it. He felt as if it had been yesterday. The brass knocker and the brass plate were there too, as dirty as ever — perhaps a thought dirtier — and the dirty house still retreated a little behind its fellows, and was still as much ashamed of itself — seemingly — as ever.

Ned raised the knocker, and smote the brass knob. The result was, as formerly, a disagreeable-looking old woman, who replied to the question, "Is Mr. Moxton in?" with a sharp, short, "Yes." The dingy little office, with its insufficient allowance of daylight, and its compensating mixture of yellow gas, was inhabited by the same identical small dishevelled clerk who, nearly two years before, was busily employed in writing his name interminably on scraps of paper, and who now, as then, answered to the question, "Can I see Mr. Moxton?" by pointing to the door which opened into the inner apartment, and resuming his occupation — the same occupation — writing his name on scraps of paper.

Ned tapped — as of yore.

"Come in," cried a stern voice — as of ditto.

Ned entered; and there, sure enough, was the same tall, gaunt man, with the sour cast of countenance, standing, (as formerly,) with his back to the fire.

"Ah!" exclaimed Moxton, "you're young Sinton, I suppose?"

Ned almost started at the perfect reproduction of events, and questions, and answers. He felt a species of reckless incredulity in reference to everything steal over him, as he replied —

"Yes; I came, at my uncle's request, for some papers that —"

"Ah, yes, they're all ready," interrupted the lawyer, advancing to the table. "Tell your uncle that I shall be glad to hear from him again in reference to the subject of those papers; and take care of them — they are of value. Good-morning!"

"Good-morning!" replied our hero, retreating.

"Stay!" said Moxton.

Ned stopped, and turned round.

"You've been in California, since I last saw you, I understand?"

"I have," replied Ned.

"Umph! You haven't made your fortune, I fancy?"

"No, not quite."

"It's a wild place, if all reports are true?"

"Rather," replied Ned, smiling; "there's a want of law there."

"Ha! and lawyers," remarked Moxton, sarcastically.

"Indeed there is," replied Ned, with some enthusiasm, as he thought of the gold-hunting spirit that prevailed in the cities of California. "There is great need out there of men of learning — men who can resist the temptation to collect gold, and are capable of doing good to the colony in an intellectual and spiritual point of view. Clergymen, doctors, and lawyers are much wanted there. You'd find it worth your while to go, sir."

Had Edward Sinton advised Mr. Moxton to go and rent an office in the moon, he could scarcely have surprised that staid gentleman more than he did by this suggestion. The lawyer gazed at him for one moment in amazement. Then he said —

"These papers are of value, young man: be careful of them. Good-morning —" and sat down at his desk to write. Ned did not venture to reply, but instantly retired, and found himself in the street with — not, as formerly, an indistinct, but — a distinct impression that he had heard the dishevelled clerk chuckling vociferously as he passed through the office.

That afternoon Ned and old Mr. Shirley alighted from the train at a small village not a hundred miles out of London, and wended their way leisurely — for it was a warm sunny day for the season — towards a large, quaint, old farm-house, about two miles distant from the station.

"What a very pleasant-looking house that is on the hill-top!" remarked Ned, as he gave his arm to his uncle.

"D'you think so? Well, I'm glad of it, because that's the farm I wish you to take."

"Indeed!" exclaimed Ned, in surprise. "Surely the farm connected with such a house must be a large one?"

"So it is," replied the other.

Ned laughed. "My dear uncle," said he, "how can *I* manage such a place, without means or knowledge?"

"I said before, boy, that I would overcome both these difficulties for you."

"You did, dear uncle; and if you were a rich man, I could understand how you might overcome the first; but you have often told me you had no money in the world except the rent of a small property."

"Right, Ned; I said so; and I say it again. I shan't leave you a six-pence when I die, and I can't afford to give you one while I am alive."

"Then I must just leave the matter in your own hands," replied Ned, smiling, "for I cannot comprehend your plans."

They had now reached the gate of the park that surrounded the fine old building of Brixley Hall.

The house was one of those rambling, picturesque old mansions, which, although not very large in reality, have a certain air of magnitude, and even grandeur, about them. The windows were modern and large, so that the rooms were well lighted, and the view in all directions was magnificent. Wherever the eye turned, it met knolls, and mounds, and fields, and picturesque groves, with here and there a substantial farm-steading, or a little hamlet, with its modest church-spire pointing ever upwards to the bright sky. Cattle and sheep lowed and bleated in the meadows, while gentle murmurs told that a rivulet flowed along its placid course at no great distance.

The spot was simply enchanting — and Ned said so, in the fulness of his heart, emphatically.

"'Tis a sweet spot!" remarked his uncle, in a low, sad tone, as he entered the open door of the dwelling, and walked deliberately into the drawing-room.

"Now, Ned, sit down — here, opposite that window, where you can see the view — and I'll tell you how we shall manage. You tell me you have £500?"

"Yes, uncle."

"Well, your dear mother left you her fortune when she died — it amounts to the small sum of £200. I never told you of it before, my boy, for reasons of my own. That makes £700."

"Will that suffice to stock and carry on so large a farm," inquired Ned?

"Not quite," replied Mr. Shirley, "but the farm is partly stocked already, so it'll do. Now, I've made arrangements with the proprietor to let you have it for the first year or two rent free. His last tenant's lease happens to have expired six months ago, and he is anxious to have it let immediately."

Ned opened his eyes very wide at this.

"He says," continued the old gentleman, "that if you can't manage to make the two ends meet in the course of a year or two, he will extend the *gratis* lease."

Ned began to think his uncle had gone deranged. "Why, what *do* you mean," said he, "who is this extraordinary proprietor?"

"He's an eccentric old fellow, Ned, who lives in London — they call him Shirley, I believe."

"Yourself, uncle!" cried Ned, starting up.

Dear reader, the conversation that followed was so abrupt, exclamatory, interjectional, and occasionally ungrammatical, as well as absurd, that it could not be reduced to writing. We therefore leave it to your imagination. After a time, the uncle and nephew subsided, and again became sane.

"But," said Ned, "I shall have to get a steward — is that what you call him? or overseer, to manage affairs until I am able to do it myself."

"True, Ned; but I have provided one already."

"Indeed! — but I might have guessed that. What shall I have to pay him? a good round sum, I suppose."

"No," replied Mr. Shirley; "he is very moderate in his expectations. He only expects his food and lodging, besides a little care, and attention, and love, particularly in his old age."

"He must be a cautious fellow, to look so far forward," said Ned, laughing. "What's his name?"

"His name — is Shirley."

"What! yourself again?"

"And why not, nephew? I've as much right to count myself fit to superintend a farm, as you had, a year ago, to think yourself able to manage a gold mine. Nay, I have a better right — for I was a farmer the greater part of my life before I went to reside in London. Now, boy, as I went to live in the Great City — which I *don't* like — in order to give you a good education, I expect that you'll take me to the country — which I *do* like — to be your overseer. I was born and bred here, Ned; this was my father's property, and, when I am gone, it shall be yours. It is not much to boast of. You won't be able to spend an idle life of it here; for, although a goodly place, it must be carefully tended if you would make it pay."

"I don't need to tell *you*," replied Ned, "that I have no desire to lead an idle life. But, uncle, I think your terms are very high."

"How so, boy?"

"*Love* is a very high price to pay for service," replied Ned. "Your kindness and your generosity in this matter make me very happy and very grateful, and, perhaps, might make me very obedient and extremely attentive; but I cannot give you *love* at any price. I must refuse you *as an overseer*, but if you will come to me as old Uncle Shirley —"

"Well, well, Ned," interrupted the old gentleman, with a benign smile, "we'll not dispute about that. Let us now go and take a run round the grounds."

*   *   *

It is needless, dear reader, to prolong our story. Perchance we have taxed your patience too much already — but we cannot close without a word or two regarding the subsequent life of those whose fortunes we have followed so long.

Ned Sinton and old Mr. Shirley applied themselves with diligence and enthusiasm to the cultivation of their farm, and to the cultivation of the friendship and good-will of their neighbours all round. In both efforts they were eminently successful.

Ned made many interesting discoveries during his residence at Brixley Hall, chief among which was a certain Louisa Leslie, with whom he fell desperately in love — so desperately that his case was deemed hopeless. Louisa therefore took pity on him, and became Mrs. Sinton, to the unutterable delight of old Mr. Shirley — and the cat, both of whom benefited considerably by this addition to the household.

About the time this event occurred, Ned received a letter from Tom Collins, desiring him to purchase a farm for him as near to his own as possible. Tom had been successful as a merchant, and had made a large fortune — as was often the case in those days — in the course of a year or two. At first, indeed, he had had a hard struggle, and was more than once nearly driven, by desperation, to the gaming-table, but Ned's advice and warnings came back upon him again and again — so he fought against the temptation manfully, and came off victorious. Improved trade soon removed the temptation — perhaps we should say that his heavenly Father took that means to remove it — and at last, as we have said, he made a fortune, as many had done, in like circumstances, before him. Ned bought a farm three miles from his own, and, in the course of a few months, Tom and he were once more walking together, arm in arm, recalling other days, and — arguing.

Lizette and Louisa drew together like two magnets, the instant they met. But the best of it was, Tom had brought home Larry O'Neil as his butler, and Mrs. Kate O'Neil as his cook while Nelly became his wife's maid.

Larry, it seems, had not taken kindly to farming in California, the more so that he pitched unluckily on an unproductive piece of land, which speedily swallowed up his little fortune, and refused to yield any return. Larry, therefore, like some men who thought themselves much wiser fellows, pronounced the country a wretched one, in refer-ence to agriculture, and returned to San Francisco, where he found Tom Collins, prospering and ready to employ himself and his family.

As butler to an English squire, Larry O'Neil was, according to his own statement, "a continted man." May he long remain so!

Nelly Morgan soon became, out of sight, the sweetest girl in the countryside, and, ere long, one of the best young fellows in the district carried her off triumphantly, and placed her at the head of affairs in his own cottage. We say he was one of the best young fellows — this husband of Nelly's — but he was by no means the handsomest; many a handsome strapping youth there failed to obtain so good a wife as Nelly. Her husband was a steady, hard working, thriving, good man — and quite good-looking enough for her — so Nelly said.

As for Captain Bunting and Bill Jones, they stuck to each other to the last, like two limpets, and both of them stuck to the sea like fish. No shore-going felicities could tempt these hardy sons of Neptune to forsake their native element again. He had done it once, Bill Jones said, "in one o' the splendidest countries goin', where gold was to be had for the pickin' up, and all sorts o' agues and rheumatizes for nothin'; but w'en things didn't somehow go all square, an' the anchor got foul with a gale o' adverse circumstances springin' up astarn, why, wot then? — go to sea again, of coorse, an' stick to it; them wos *his* sentiments." As these were also Captain Bunting's sentiments, they naturally took to the same boat for life.

But, although Captain Bunting and Bill did not live on shore, they occasionally, at long intervals, condescended to revisit the terrestrial globe, and, at such seasons of weakness, made a point of running down to Brixley Hall to see Ned and Tom. Then, indeed, "the light of other days" shone again in retrospect on our adventurers with refulgent splendour; then Larry sank the butler, and came out as the miner — as one of the partners of the "R'yal Bank o' Calyforny" — then Ned and Tom related marvellous adventures, to the admiration of their respective wives, and the captain smote his thigh with frequency and emphasis, to the terror of the cat, and Bill Jones gave utterance to deeply-pregnant sentences, and told how that, on his last voyage to China, he had been up at Pekin, and had heard that Ah-wow had dug up a nugget of gold three times the size of his own head, and had returned to his native land a *millionnaire*, and been made a mandarin, and after that something else, and at last became prime minister of China — so Bill had been *told*, but he wouldn't vouch for it, no how.

All this, and a great deal more, was said and done on these great and rare occasions — and our quondam gold-hunters fought their battles o'er again, to the ineffable delight of old Mr. Shirley, who sat in his easy-chair, and gazed, and smiled, and stared, and laughed, and even wept, and chuckled — but never spoke — he was past that.

In the course of time Ned and Tom became extremely intimate with the pastor of their village, and were at last his right and left-hand men. This pastor was a man whose aim was to live as his Master had lived before him — he went about doing good — and, of all the happy years our two friends spent, the happiest were those in which they followed in the footsteps and strengthened the hands of this good man, Lizette and Louisa were helpmates to their husbands in this respect, as in all others, and a blessing to the surrounding country.

Ned Sinton's golden dream was over now, in one sense, but by no means over in another. His sleeping and his waking dreams were still, as of old, tinged with a golden hue, but they bad not a metallic ring. The *golden rule* was the foundation on which his new visions were reared, and that which we are told is *better* than gold, "yea, than much fine gold," was thenceforth eagerly sought for and coveted by him. As for other matters — he delighted chiefly in the sunshine of Louisa's smile, and in fields of golden grain.

THE END.

www.ingramcontent.com/pod-product-compliance
Lightning Source LLC
Chambersburg PA
CBHW020838260626
47169CB00003B/1043